PRAISE FOR
Recipe for a Charmed Life

"Rachel Linden beautifully shows how people—and dreams—can change, often in the very best ways, and that finding passion just might be what this journey is all about. With humor, heart, and Linden's signature pinch of magic, *Recipe for a Charmed Life* enchants. Linden has a permanent place on my list of auto-buy authors!"

—Kristy Woodson Harvey, *New York Times* bestselling author of *The Summer of Songbirds*

"The perfect mix of delicious backdrop details, family secrets, and the quest for purpose and lasting love. Enchantingly delightful from first page to last."

—Susan Meissner, *USA Today* bestselling author of *Only the Beautiful*

"A delightful tale of food, family, and sweet romance. Channeling Julia Child, Linden's main character Georgia, a sous chef at a famed Parisian restaurant, follows her own path to reclaiming her purpose and passion, one delicious bite at a time. This story is an absolute feast!"

—Lauren K. Denton, *USA Today* bestselling author of *The Hideaway* and *The Summer House*

"Completely charming! Take a spunky heroine, add a swoon-worthy, orange-rubber-overall-wearing-oyster farmer, throw in a dash of the real-life messiness we all understand, and sprinkle a dusting of Linden's signature magical realism, and you've got the recipe for a delightful story you can't put down. I giggled, I sighed, and I got swept away from the first page in Paris to the final moment in the Pacific Northwest's Friday Harbor."

—Katherine Reay, bestselling author of A *Shadow in Moscow*

"*Recipe for a Charmed Life* satisfied my voracious appetite for delectable foodie novels. Linden's writing simmers with intoxicating sensory overload: the fresh pine scent of the Pacific Northwest, the sophisticated textures of Paris, and the hot-sour-salty-sweet emotions of life. Her exploration of what we lose when we can no longer taste the flavors we love is savory food for thought. This magical story offers the perfect recipe for a gratifying read."

—Kim Fay, national bestselling author of *Love & Saffron*

"With a dash of magic, a dollop of romance, a sprinkling of family secrets, and exquisite 'places I want to visit' settings, the ingredient list of *Recipe for a Charmed Life* adds up to a deliciously satisfying read."

—Marie Bostwick, *New York Times* and *USA Today* bestselling author of *Esme Cahill Fails Spectacularly*

"Filled with suspense, magic, and mouthwatering descriptions of food, and set against a backdrop of a gorgeous island in the Pacific Northwest, *Recipe for a Charmed Life* brings us a spunky, gritty heroine who must try to reinvent herself after a devastating heartbreak. This beautiful story is a feast not to be missed!"

—Maddie Dawson, bestselling author of *Snap Out of It*

The Magic of Lemon Drop Pie

. . . .

"Heartfelt, heartwarming, joyful, and uplifting. You can't go wrong with a Rachel Linden book."
—Debbie Macomber, #1 *New York Times* bestselling author
of *Must Love Flowers*

"A magical novel about second chances! Warm, witty, and wise, I loved it! Linden is a master at creating loveable characters! *The Magic of Lemon Drop Pie* is escapist reading at its best!"
—Jill Shalvis, *New York Times* bestselling author
of *The Sweetheart List*

"An enchanting tale about the one thing we've all imagined: a magical second chance. Rachel Linden expertly mixes romance, mystery, and family-drama into a delicious recipe of a story. With her trademark warmth, Linden delivers a captivating story with a magical heartbeat at its center."
—Patti Callahan, *New York Times* bestselling author
of *The Secret Book of Flora Lea*

"Magic, sweet treats, heartfelt charm . . . this dreamy tale has it all!" —*Woman's World*

"Rachel Linden whips up an irresistible family drama oozing with charm and magic! *The Magic of Lemon Drop Pie* is a must read for anyone who longs for second chances. A gem of a novel that charmed me from [the] get-go, perfect for fans of Sarah Addison Allen and Alice Hoffman."

—Lori Nelson Spielman, *New York Times* bestselling author of *The Star-Crossed Sisters of Tuscany*

"A delicious read, down to the very last lemon drop! Rachel Linden delivers a delightful escape, wonderful characters, and a magical experience that will leave readers hungry for her next book."

—Julie Cantrell, *New York Times* and *USA Today* bestselling author of *Perennials*

"A charming, heartwarming story about 'what ifs' and second chances. Readers will fall in love with the cast of delightful characters, and I defy anyone to read this book and not want to immediately eat lemon meringue pie. A beautiful, life-affirming read."

—Freya Sampson, author of *The Lost Ticket*

"A deliciously sweet tale about refusing to give up on your dreams and finding your bliss against all odds. Linden gives readers so much to enjoy—romance, family drama, and bittersweet second chances—all served up with the perfect dash of magic."

—Kate Bromley, author of *Ciao For Now* and *Talk Bookish to Me*

Berkley titles by Rachel Linden

THE MAGIC OF LEMON DROP PIE

RECIPE FOR A CHARMED LIFE

Recipe for a Charmed Life

Rachel Linden

BERKLEY

New York

BERKLEY
An imprint of Penguin Random House LLC
penguinrandomhouse.com

Copyright © 2024 by Rachel Linden
Readers Guide copyright © 2024 by Rachel Linden

BERKLEY and the BERKLEY & B colophon are registered trademarks of Penguin Random House LLC.

Library of Congress Cataloging-in-Publication Data

Names: Linden, Rachel, author.
Title: Recipe for a charmed life / Rachel Linden.
Description: First edition. | New York: Berkley, 2024.
Identifiers: LCCN 2023031481 (print) | LCCN 2023031482 (ebook) |
ISBN 9780593440216 (trade paperback) | ISBN 9780593440223 (ebook)
Subjects: LCSH: Women cooks—Fiction. | Self-realization in women—Fiction. |
Family secrets—Fiction. | LCGFT: Novels.
Classification: LCC PS3612.I5327426 R43 2024 (print) |
LCC PS3612.I5327426 (ebook) | DDC 813/.6—dc23/eng/20230713
LC record available at https://lccn.loc.gov/2023031481
LC ebook record available at https://lccn.loc.gov/2023031482

First Edition: January 2024

Printed in the United States of America
1st Printing

Book design by Ashley Tucker
Interior art by momo sama/Shutterstock

This is a work of fiction. Names, characters, places, and incidents either are the product of the author's imagination or are used fictitiously, and any resemblance to actual persons, living or dead, business establishments, events, or locales is entirely coincidental.

PUBLISHER'S NOTE: The recipes contained in this book are to be followed exactly as written. The publisher is not responsible for your specific health or allergy needs that may require medical supervision. The publisher is not responsible for any adverse reactions to the recipes contained in this book.

For my mother, Adelle—small yet mighty.
Thank you for all the prayers and pot roasts.

Heaven smelled like melted butter, Georgia May Jackson was sure of it. And a bustling kitchen in Paris on a chilly early April evening was as close to heaven as she'd come in her thirty-three years. Glancing around at the hive of activity surrounding her in the kitchen of La Pomme d'Or, the Michelin-starred restaurant where she served as sous-chef, Georgia inhaled the satisfying aroma of garlic sizzling in melting butter and tried her best to ignore the two men observing her from the doorway. Their careful scrutiny made her queasy with nerves. So much was riding on tonight. She scrubbed her hands on her kitchen whites and tried hard to look cool, confident, and collected. She could do this, right? She'd been training for it her entire adult life.

"Come on, Georgia, you've got this," she murmured. "It's just like any other night." But that was a big fat lie. Tonight could change everything. If all went well, it could prove, once and for all, that she had the experience and skills to run her own kitchen in Paris. It had been her biggest dream since she was ten years old, and it was finally within her grasp. She simply had to prove she was ready . . .

Georgia darted a glance at the kitchen doorway where her mentor, famed Parisian chef Michel Laurent, was standing with Etienne Fontaine, the head chef of La Pomme d'Or. They were both watching her carefully, arms crossed in identical postures. Michel gave her a brief nod and a small, polite smile. Etienne, her boss for the past six years and her boyfriend for the past two, threw her a wink and a cheeky grin. She exhaled in relief. Etienne knew how important this assessment was for her. He wouldn't look so enthusiastic if it didn't seem promising.

In the blink of an eye, she caught a glimpse of herself as a young girl, avidly glued to a rerun of *The French Chef* on the old television set in the front room of her dad's dusty West Texas ranch. Ten-year-old Georgia had been all gawky elbows and bright curly ginger pigtails, filled with grand dreams and aspirations, filled with a longing to prove she was worth something. There in that faded living room, watching Julia Child, the iconic star of 1960s French cooking in America, she'd found her inspiration. Julia became her patron saint of the kitchen. Day after day, as she watched Julia craft a startlingly impressive flaming cheese soufflé or spatchcock a turkey, Georgia had imagined what it would be like to be the star of her own restaurant kitchen in Paris. She yearned to be like Julia, so cheerfully capable, in charge of her own future, filled to the brim with a zest for life. Even at that young age, she was determined to show her family and the world that she was good enough, that she could do big things. She was desperate to matter. In all the years since, she had never wavered from that desire. And now, if all went well tonight, her dream would finally come true.

Georgia drew a deep breath and tucked a loose ginger curl back into her chef's beret. No time to falter now; she had worked too long and hard for this moment. By habit, her fingers drifted to the tiny four-leaf clover charm she wore around her neck on a delicate gold chain. Made of green enamel, the charm was chipped and worn from years of rubbing. It was a cheap trinket, but the most precious thing she owned. She'd had it since she was five years old. Georgia rubbed it again now for luck, sending up a little prayer to Julia in heaven.

"Help me show them I can do this, Julia," she whispered. "Let all those years of hard work, all my sacrifices finally pay off."

It was time.

"Is everything ready?" Georgia called out in French. The kitchen staff nodded in unison.

"Oui, all is in order," Celine, one of the assistant chefs, responded crisply, not pausing as she deboned a fillet of sole.

"Bon." Georgia slowly circled the kitchen, observing each station. Every member of the kitchen staff was performing their duties with well-oiled precision, and the kitchen rang with the sound of sharp steel dicing vegetables and the hiss and bubble of delicious things cooking in pots and cast-iron pans.

It was just past six o'clock, not yet the dinner hour in Paris, but already the tables in the dining room were filling with tourists who typically ate earlier than Parisians. Tonight promised to be long and busy. Georgia gave a small nod of reassurance. So far everything was running smoothly.

"Pardon me, Georgia, could you taste this pistou?" Ismael, the newest prep cook, stood at her elbow, anxiously holding out a spoonful of bright green sauce. "Cyril says it is inedible." He looked distressed.

Georgia frowned and glanced over Cyril, a hulking, swarthy man standing at the long, gleaming gas range. A Frenchman from Lyon, he had been working in kitchens longer than she'd been alive. Although he was skilled in the kitchen, he was often cruel to the other staff, particularly the younger prep cooks. Georgia found his meanness intolerable and tried to make up for it by being extra encouraging to those he cut down.

"Inedible, hmm?" she said, reaching for the spoon. "Let me see."

She took the spoon and tasted a few drops of the pistou. For a brief moment she felt a flutter of apprehension. Would she be able to taste the ingredients this time? Recently her normally keen sense of taste had inexplicably and intermittently begun to fail her, a phenomenon that was mystifying and terrifying in equal measure.

She concentrated hard. Garlic. Basil. Pistachio. Comté cheese. She exhaled in relief. She could taste it all. It was bright and fresh, very flavorful, actually, though in truth missing . . . a little something.

"It's good," she assured Ismael, who was standing by her elbow like a puppy eager to please. "It just needs a little . . ." She tasted the pistou again, letting the ingredients speak to her. She could feel the nuttiness of the cheese at the hinge of her jaw, the raw garlic on the tip of her tongue, sharp and bright as steel hitting flint, that luxurious umami of the buttery roasted pistachios. What was it missing? She stilled herself and closed her eyes, allowing the clamor of the kitchen to die away until there were only the flavors in her mouth and the certainty that this dish was asking for something more . . .

Her eyes popped open. "Got it!"

She added two small pinches of fresh ground black pepper and a dash of lemon juice and tasted it again. Perfect.

Ismael watched her closely. "How do you do that?" he asked in wonder. "How do you know exactly what it needs?"

Georgia shrugged. "I don't know. I just feel it."

She had always cooked by instinct. Etienne joked that as a chef she was more like a mystic than a scientist, and it was true. She had graduated from culinary school in the States and endured twelve years of brutal practical apprenticeship in various kitchens of Paris. As a chef she used the techniques she'd acquired every day in the kitchen, but she relied most on her sixth sense about food, an intuition that had rarely led her astray. That is until recently . . . She pushed the thought away. For tonight, her luck seemed to be holding. Right now that was enough.

"Here, try this." She handed Ismael a tasting spoon dabbed with a few drops of the bright pistou.

He tasted it. "C'est délicieux." He nodded approvingly. It's delicious.

"Good. Tell Cyril it's ready to serve."

Ismael cast a nervous glance over to Cyril. "Could you tell him?" he asked meekly. "He won't believe me." The tips of his ears turned pink, and he looked down at his kitchen clogs, murmuring, "He called me garbage, only fit to take out the trash I cook."

"He said that?" Georgia asked indignantly. She put her hands on her hips and cast a quick glance over at Michel and Etienne. She didn't want to risk an ugly scene with Michel watching, but she was in charge of this kitchen right now and she couldn't stand by and let Cyril's bullying go unchallenged, not even on a night as crucial as this. She took a deep breath and marched over to Cyril's station. He was at the stove, searing duck liver.

"Cyril," she said calmly in French. "I need to speak with you."

"What?" He glanced up and leveled a hard stare in her direction, challenging her. Georgia knew that he resented her elevation to sous-chef over him, even though she was the better choice. She raised her chin and met his gaze, not backing down. He was muscle-bound and taller than her by a head, but she refused to be intimidated. She hated a bully. She'd learned early on in life that the only way to face one was to ball your fists and stand your ground. She was aware of Ismael hovering nervously behind her, and Michel observing the exchange with clinical interest from across the room. She leaned in close, feeling the heat from the gas stovetop, so close she could see the sweat beading on Cyril's upper lip. She swallowed hard and murmured fiercely.

"The next time you call one of your fellow cooks garbage, you will find yourself scraping dishes and hauling garbage in this kitchen until you remember how to use kinder words. Is that clear?" She met his gaze, holding it for what felt like an eternity. The smell of seared duck liver was rich and fatty in her nostrils. It was the most high-stakes game of chicken she'd ever played. What if he challenged her, right here in front of Michel? What would she do? She forced herself to not budge. She was his superior in this kitchen, and she had Etienne's backing. Surely, Cyril would not challenge the hierarchy of the kitchen. It simply wasn't done. Cyril's eyes narrowed in contempt. Georgia didn't even blink.

After a long moment, he broke the glance, shooting a narrow, spiteful glare at Ismael, then looked back down at the sizzling pan in front of him and expertly flipped the duck liver over, his lip curled in disdain. He gave the barest of nods in acknowledgment. As she turned away, she heard him mutter a string of crude insults in French, all aimed at her. She pretended not to hear. Wiping her damp palms on her kitchen whites, she stepped away and took a moment to collect herself. Her hands were shaking.

"Thank you," Ismael whispered gratefully as he passed her with the pistou.

She nodded and took a deep breath. "You're welcome."

Then she straightened her shoulders and plastered a confident smile on her lips, relieved that she'd narrowly averted disaster and restored order in the kitchen. She was also grateful that her sense of taste seemed to be functioning normally this evening. There was no guarantee these days that it would. In the past few months, her ability to taste ingredients in Technicolor, the intuition that guided her creative genius, had begun to falter. It was unpredictable. She'd go for days at a time with everything humming along like normal, then pop a whole raw clove of garlic in her mouth and strangely taste nutmeg and cinnamon, or even more alarmingly, sometimes she could taste nothing at all. She would eat a spoonful of caviar or bite into a Valencia orange, and instead of tasting the brine of the sea or the candy-sweet acidity of the citrus, it was like drinking water or crunching ice. Completely blank, devoid of flavor.

Those moments terrified her. She'd been to the doctor and even a seen a few specialists on the sly. There had been a battery of tests. No brain tumor, nothing abnormal. The results were clear. Physically, she was fine, but Georgia knew something was very wrong. Each day, her concern grew stronger, like a fist tightening itself in the hollow space inside her rib cage. She had no idea what was happening to her, but she was desperate to figure out the problem and find a way to fix it. Her lifelong dream depended on it.

2

Three hours later, the dinner rush was in full swing. Every table was filled, and the kitchen was operating with brisk efficiency and precision.

"Ismael, be careful with the amount of sauce," Georgia cautioned as she spooned a bit of browned butter sauce off the house-made bacon, ricotta, and chicken ravioli. "Let the pasta shine."

"Yes, Chef. Of course." Ismael nodded deferentially. She gave him a quick smile, taking the sting from her correction.

Michel had left some time ago. Georgia wasn't sure when. She'd glanced up and he'd been gone. Etienne had disappeared too, saying something in passing about a quick meeting with Manon, the restaurant's new pastry chef. But he hadn't returned, so Georgia was continuing to oversee the kitchen until he came back. She was, on the whole, feeling good about what Michel had witnessed. She'd handled the kitchen with poise and confidence. Even that nasty interaction with Cyril had smoothed out quickly.

Suddenly, Damien, La Pomme d'Or's head waiter, burst into the kitchen. "We have an emergency!" he cried breathlessly.

"What?" Georgia looked up, startled. "What's wrong?"

Damien wore an expression of barely controlled panic. "It's Antoine Dupont," he hissed, gesturing frantically toward the dining room. "He's here. Tonight. Amelie is seating him now!"

"Antoine Dupont? Are you sure?" Georgia froze, spoon in

hand. The entire kitchen stopped, awaiting his reply. No one breathed.

"Positive." Damien wrung his hands. "He is trying to disguise his identity with a false mustache, but he is as round as a wine barrel. And that nose. I am positive it is him. Amelie agrees with me."

"Merde," Georgia murmured softly in French, looking around for Etienne. What in the world was taking him so long? Where was he? La Pomme d'Or's star chef needed to know that at this very second, Antoine Dupont, arguably Paris's most preeminent restaurant critic, was in the dining room. A negative review from Dupont could spell trouble for any restaurant that displeased him, regardless of Michelin stars. In the Parisian restaurant scene, Dupont's word was gospel, and he was notoriously difficult to please.

Unfortunately, Etienne was nowhere to be seen.

"Okay," Georgia addressed the kitchen staff who were awaiting her instructions. She adopted a calm and capable air although her heart was pounding. "Nothing changes just because Antoine Dupont is one of our guests tonight," she assured them. "We will continue to do what we do for our guests every night— make delicious food as always. Don't worry about impressing Antoine Dupont. If we all do our jobs, everything will be okay. We've got this." She clapped her hands briskly. "Now back to work!"

The kitchen immediately sprang back into action, everything orderly but with an underlying frisson of tightly controlled panic. Satisfied that things were stable for the moment, Georgia set off hastily in search of Etienne. He needed to know Dupont was here. He needed to be in charge of his own kitchen in this pivotal moment. Etienne was a brilliant chef, but sometimes frustrating to work for. Or to be in a romantic relationship with, for that matter. Handsome as sin with a sulky mouth and dark, melt-ing eyes, he had just been voted Sexiest Chef in Paris, a title no one could really argue with, but he was prone to mercurial moods and could be intense and demanding. This was not the first time he'd disappeared during the dinner rush, but it was the first time he'd done so while a renowned restaurant critic had been seated in the dining room awaiting his dinner. The stakes were con-siderably higher.

Cyril glanced up from the stove as Georgia passed by.

"Looking for your boyfriend?" There was an ugly undercur-rent to his tone. Georgia hesitated, then nodded.

"Check the refrigerator. I hear he's been spending a lot of time there recently," Cyril suggested. His eyes were cold as he gazed at her. Georgia frowned, her confusion tinged with a hint of foreboding. What in the world would Etienne be doing there? But she headed down the short hallway that housed the restau-rant's walk-in refrigerator at the end. As she neared it, Georgia heard a peculiar rhythmic thumping noise coming from inside. Puzzled, she reached for the handle, noting with surprise that the heavy metal door was ajar just a hair. That was odd. She wrenched it open.

"What in the . . . ?"

What she saw inside left her speechless.

Amid wheels of cheese and hanging legs of cured ham, stood Manon, the restaurant's new pastry chef, pressed up against a metal shelf of chilled butter with her blouse unbut-toned down to her navel. And wedged between her creamy thighs was Etienne. His mouth was pressed again Manon's neck, his eyes closed. Manon gave a little shriek and Etienne glanced up. He met Georgia's eyes, his own widening in sud-den horror.

"Georgie . . ." His pet name for her. He stumbled back,

struggling with his fly, and put out a hand as though to stop her.

Swearing in French and laughing, Manon fumbled to button her blouse. "I told you someone would find us," she scolded him.

Georgia slammed the refrigerator door shut and pressed her back against it, standing wide-eyed and stunned for a long second. There was a buzzing in her head, loud as a swarm of bees. She could not stop picturing what she had just seen. Manon. Etienne. His lips against her neck, the silky length of her thigh wrapped around him, both of them locked in a lovers' embrace. She splayed a hand across her chest, pressing against the tightness coiling there, the pain sharp as the point of a paring knife.

"Oh, Etienne," she gasped, "what have you done?"

From inside the refrigerator came a loud hammering, fists pounding against metal, and Etienne's voice raised, pleading in heavily accented English. "Georgie, open the door. I can explain."

But Georgia did not open the door. She couldn't seem to draw a breath. She felt as though she were choking on betrayal. Six years she had worked in this restaurant. For the last two she and Etienne had been dating, sharing an apartment, a bed, a life. They had spent almost every waking moment together. This was her entire world. And in an instant, Etienne had shattered it all.

In a daze, she moved toward the bright bustle of the kitchen. She stood in the doorway, staring at the energetic scene in bewilderment. One by one, the voices fell silent as the staff noticed her peculiar stillness. Cyril's hands paused over the sizzling cast-iron skillet where he was searing a fillet of sole in butter and garlic. Celine stopped chopping fresh thyme. All eyes were trained on her. From the hallway, in the sudden silence, she could hear Etienne and Manon swearing loudly in French from the refrigerator, demanding to be let out.

"Georgie, please let me explain!" Etienne pleaded, his voice muffled. "It isn't what you think."

Georgia saw Celine dart a knowing glance at Cyril, who crossed his arms and smirked at Georgia. Ismael stood looking at the floor. They knew, she realized with a cold wash of certainty. They were not surprised about Manon and Etienne. She was the one who had been kept in the dark.

"You knew?" Her voice was little more than a whisper. She hated the smallness of it, the pitiful tone, robbed of her usual bright confidence. She cleared her throat and asked more loudly. "You all knew about this?"

Celine looked at her with sorrowful eyes and nodded once. It was enough.

Damien burst back into the kitchen, calling out in French, "Is the sole meunière done yet? We cannot keep Monsieur Dupont waiting!"

"Merde!" Cyril spit out. "I've ruined the sole. It is dry as a bone." He grabbed the hot pan where a shriveled piece of white fish lay surrounded by crusty burnt bits. An unpleasant odor of burnt butter wafted heavily up from the ruined fish. "I'll start another."

"No," Georgia cried with a sudden stab of white-hot fury. She rushed to the stove, snatched a clean plate and shoveled the badly overcooked fish onto it. "I'm serving it."

It was a decision she would bitterly regret later, but in that moment, incandescent with hurt and humiliation, she wanted nothing more than to wound Etienne as he had just wounded her.

Cyril tried to wrestle the plate from her. "You cannot," he growled, tugging at the edge of the china. "You can't serve Monsieur Dupont this food. It is inedible. He'll give us a bad review."

Georgia did not stop to consider the ramifications of her

hasty reaction. She drew herself up to her full height of five feet five inches and stared Cyril dead in the eye. "Turns out there are consequences when the head chef is so busy banging his pastry chef against the butter that he can't be bothered to oversee his own kitchen," she said sharply. "Now let go."

She snatched the plate from his grasp and marched into the dining room before anyone could stop her, head high, jaw set. She recognized Antoine Dupont easily, wedged into a corner table, lifting a glass of red wine to his lips. The false mustache looked ridiculous. She came to a halt in front of his table, breathing hard, and slid the plate of ruined sole meunière in front of him. He looked at it, then up at her in consternation.

"What is this?" he demanded in French.

"Compliments of the chef," she responded briskly, then turned on her heel and marched back into the kitchen, heart pounding wildly.

When she came through the door, the entire kitchen staff was standing motionless in shocked disbelief. Georgia looked at them, the hurt blooming hot and tight beneath her breastbone. These were her friends, her world, the nearest thing to family she had in Paris, and they had all betrayed her. She pressed her hand to her chest again, trying to ease the pressure. In the course of a few minutes, her entire world had imploded. How could she ever again work in this kitchen under Etienne's direction? How could she possibly hold her head up knowing that they had all been aware that Etienne was cheating on her and yet they had said nothing? The magnitude of Etienne's—and their—betrayal took her breath away. She could not imagine staying a moment longer.

And just like that, her future and her place here evaporated in an instant. She could feel the tears prickling behind her eyelids, but she blinked them back furiously, determined not to fall apart in front of everyone. She could crumble later, but right now she would leave with whatever small shreds of her dignity were still intact.

The thumping and yelling coming from the refrigerator was reaching a fever pitch. Georgia saw Celine glance in the direction of the hallway, her brow furrowed with concern. It was probably getting quite chilly in the refrigerator. Especially given that Manon was wearing such a short skirt.

"Someone go let them out," Georgia said in resignation. She steadied her voice, raised her chin, and looked around the kitchen. "And tell Etienne I quit." Then she grabbed her purse and knife kit and walked out the door, leaving behind the smoldering ruins of her life.

3

In shocked disbelief, Georgia wandered through the narrow cobblestone streets of Paris's famed Latin Quarter, clutching her knives to her chest.

"What did I just do?" she gasped. How could her life have imploded so completely with the opening of a refrigerator door, in the space of one breath? She passed a small café that had one empty table for two near the street. Numbly, she sank into a chair. A moment later, a waiter appeared. He took one look at her face and set down a tall glass containing a small amount of Pastis de Marseille and a carafe of water, murmuring, "For you, madame, on the house."

"Merci," Georgia said gratefully. She poured a splash of water from the carafe into the glass and took a gulp of the aperitif. The strong licorice flavor righted her a little, and she drew a shaky breath. The night was warm and slightly muggy around her, smelling of exhaust, cooking food, and the dusty pavement scent that Georgia always associated with Paris. Behind her, clusters of patrons were eating and drinking, the lively atmosphere spilling light and music into the soft evening air. She could hear the clink of glasses and muted laughter from the tables around her. She was surrounded by people enjoying the evening, enjoying the City of Light, but Georgia felt removed from it all. She shivered.

Her phone buzzed and she checked the number. Etienne. She declined the call. He called back immediately. She let it go to voice mail and dropped her phone into the generous pocket of her double-breasted chef's jacket. She couldn't face him right now. She did not want to hear his excuses or justifications, or even an apology. Nothing could erase what she'd seen in that refrigerator. Nothing could erase what he—and she—had just done. She took off her chef's beret and ruffled a hand through her damp curls with a groan. What should she do now?

Instinctively, her fingers drifted to the four-leaf clover charm on the delicate chain at her throat, and she rubbed the little leaves. Long ago, her mother had told her that the four leaflets on the clover stood for faith, hope, love, and luck.

"Those four elements are the recipe for a charmed life, Georgia May," her mother had promised her. Georgia was a little short on all four right now. She could use any of them. She swallowed hard, trying to force her mind into problem-solving mode, but all she could see was the ardor on Etienne's face, his dark hair thrown across his brow, the creamy globes of Manon's pert breasts. She shook her head, trying to clear the images. It hurt too much to dwell on his betrayal.

"Julia, what should I do?" she whispered. Georgia had gotten out of more than one scrape by asking herself the simple question: What would Julia Child do? She pictured Julia neatly hacking a large piece of beef into chunks with her sturdy cleaver, all practical optimism and American can-do attitude.

"I think it's important that every woman have her very own blowtorch," Julia said conversationally.

Georgia sighed. No help from that quarter. She took another sip of the pastis. It was growing late, but she couldn't go back to the apartment she shared with Etienne, not tonight. That was obvious. It was his apartment, passed down to him through his family, and it slowly dawned on her as she sat there that she could not live there again. For all intents and purposes, in the space of one evening, she was jobless, boyfriend-less, and also homeless.

Rattled by the realization, she reached into her pocket to pull out her phone. As she did so, a little green sprig fell onto the pavement. She picked it up, staring at it in puzzlement. It was a four-leaf clover. Where in the world had that come from? She'd been in Paris for over a decade and had never seen a four-leaf clover here. She looked at the four little rounded leaves, bewildered, then dropped it back into her pocket. How bizarre.

Taking another large, fortifying sip of the pastis, she scrolled through her phone contacts. Who could she call? Almost all of her friends were connected to Etienne or the restaurant. She could not ask any of them for help, but it was clear she needed somewhere to go at least for tonight. She thought for a moment. Phoebe. Of course. Her closest nonwork friend in Paris. She called Phoebe, but there was no answer and Phoebe's voice mail box was full as usual. Georgia called again immediately.

"Come on, Phoebs, pick up," she whispered with a touch of desperation. A click and then . . .

"Georgia May!!!" a cheerful British voice yelled loudly and tipsily. Georgia winced and held the phone away from her ear.

"Hey, Phoebe."

They'd met in French class years ago and bonded over their shared struggle to unravel the complexities of the French language. Originally from Liverpool, Phoebe now worked for a fashion branding and marketing company in Paris and lived in a gorgeous and exorbitantly expensive apartment in the chic Le Marais neighborhood in the third arrondissement. They often met up on Georgia's day off to swap work stories and drink a little too much very good wine. Phoebe had excellent taste in wine. Well, in everything, really.

"How are you, babe?" Phoebe shrieked. Georgia could barely hear her over the earsplitting thump of some truly terrible electronic dance music in the background.

"Where are you?" Georgia yelled over the din.

"I'm in Oberkampf at Panic Room with some of the girls from work," Phoebe yelled back. "The Polish models wanted to see some Paris nightlife. Lucky me, I'm playing tour guide."

Georgia's heart sank, imagining Phoebe dancing the night away in a sweaty nightclub.

"Hold on, I'm going to the loo so I can hear you," Phoebe shouted. A moment later, the music faded to a low throbbing pulse of bass through the phone. "That's better," Phoebe came back on at normal volume. "What's going on?" She sounded slightly more sober.

Georgia took a deep breath. She was not used to asking for help from anyone, preferring to rely on her own grit and determination, but tonight it was all too much. She needed a friend. "I'm in trouble," she admitted frankly. "Phoebs, I need your help."

Thirty minutes later, Phoebe met Georgia in the opulent stairwell of her apartment building. For clubbing, she was wearing a white leather miniskirt, which she actually managed to look fabulous in, and was teetering on the most outrageous pair of black leather spiked Louboutin ankle boots. Her hair fell down her back in a milky sheet of pale blond. She threw her arms around Georgia in a hug, enveloping her in a cloud of equal parts sympathy and vodka.

"I don't know what's happening, but I'm sure it will be all right," she whispered loudly in Georgia's ear. "Also, why are you holding knives?" She stepped back and peered at Georgia's knife kit, then looked up, wide-eyed. "I think we need wine."

She unlocked the door to her apartment and waved Georgia into the living room, then disappeared into the kitchen and reappeared a moment later with a pricey bottle of chilled Vouvray. She poured them both generous glasses and then collapsed on the velvet sofa next to Georgia, kicking off the spiked ankle boots and curling up like a cat.

"Okay, tell me everything," she urged.

Georgia took a large, fortifying swallow of wine and confessed the entire horrible evening including Etienne and Manon in the refrigerator, and her own retaliation with the overcooked fish and Antoine Dupont. When she was done, Phoebe shook her head slowly, her mouth a perfect O of surprise. "Oh my word, babe. I don't know what to say. Etienne is an arse, a complete arse. Sure, he's super sexy and talented in the kitchen, but he's a prick. Always has been. Good riddance to bad rubbish. I don't blame you for serving that bad fish. Etienne deserved it!"

She topped up Georgia's empty glass with a great glug of wine and then scooted closer and put her arm around her friend. Georgia laid her head on Phoebe's shoulder, miserable but grateful for the comfort. Phoebe smelled like vodka and Miss Dior perfume, a somehow reassuring combination. Maybe Etienne had deserved it, but now that her fury was waning, Georgia was beginning to regret her hasty action. She had been humiliated, but that didn't make it right. She felt sick when she thought of the events of the evening—Etienne's betrayal, the staff's complicit silence, and her own retaliation. Altogether they meant the unraveling of her entire life. And Etienne. She closed her eyes, grieved at the memory of his infidelity. She'd thought he loved her. How foolish she'd been.

"This is the worst night of my life," Georgia murmured desolately. "I've lost my job, friends, boyfriend, and apartment. I don't even have anywhere to stay tonight." She felt wrung out and completely unmoored.

"You can stay here with me for as long as you need to," Phoebe assured her, squeezing her shoulder comfortingly. "And tomorrow we'll figure out what to do. Things will look better in the morning, you'll see."

Georgia sat up and drained her glass of wine. "I hope you're right," she said grimly. "I don't see how they could get much worse."

4

Unfortunately, things did not look better in the morning. Georgia woke late, sprawled across Phoebe's guest futon, swathed in one of Phoebe's silk negligee and robe sets that no doubt cost a fortune but barely covered her bum cheeks. She had no clothes of her own other than her soiled chef's whites. High on her to-do list was getting back into the apartment she shared with Etienne to gather her belongings as soon as she could be sure Etienne would not be there. She rolled to a sitting position on the edge of the bed. Her head ached dully. Too much pastis and pricey Vouvray on an empty stomach.

She blinked and the entire catastrophic evening came back in a rush. She groaned, putting her head in her hands. It had not been a dream then. It was all terribly real.

"Okay, Georgia, pull yourself together," she whispered, forcing herself to take stock of her situation. "You have to figure out what to do now." She needed a shower, food, and coffee, probably not in that order. Her stomach was gnawing itself raw. Food first then. The shower could wait.

She tiptoed into Phoebe's gleaming and seldom-used galley kitchen and gingerly took inventory of the contents of the fridge. A wilted bunch of carrots and a half-full cup of yogurt that had spoiled. Thankfully, there was an excellent boulangerie just down the street. Quickly, she changed back into her rumpled chef's whites, pulled back her riotous hair into some semblance of respectability, and let herself out of the apartment with a few euros in hand.

Ten minutes later, she was seated at the two-person dining table in Phoebe's kitchen, looking out over the rooftops of Paris. On the table in front of her sat an espresso she'd managed to make with Phoebe's expensive and befuddling Italian espresso maker, the only well-used appliance in the kitchen, and a small grease-stained paper bag. She added a lump of sugar to the bottom of the tiny white cup and stirred, then opened the paper bag and inhaled the aroma of fresh croissant. It was still warm. If you were going to be jilted and publicly humiliated, at least there were still French pastries to comfort you, Georgia thought glumly. It was a small mercy. She closed her eyes and bit into the buttery, flaky pastry, savoring the crack of the thin layers against her teeth. But instead of luscious butter, she tasted something terribly wrong.

With a muffled cry of disgust, she spit the mouthful of croissant back into the bag. It was as bitter as the skin of an almond. So bitter it puckered her mouth. What in the world was wrong with that pastry? She peered in bewilderment at the croissant, then dropped it into the bag. She took a cleansing sip of espresso, but promptly spit it out too. It tasted exactly the same. Not pleasantly bitter like a good espresso should taste, but as bitter and inedible as an unripe grape picked too soon off the vine.

Oh no. Georgia froze, a terrible suspicion flitting through her mind. All those momentary glitches in her ability to discern flavors over the past few months. The garlic that tasted like cinnamon. The bitter rind of an orange rendered as bland as water. Was it happening again? Had it gotten worse?

"Oh, please not this," she murmured. She leaped from her chair, eager to prove herself wrong, and rummaged through Phoebe's kitchen looking for anything edible. She took a bite from one of the wilted carrots—bitter. In desperation, she snatched a sugar cube from the sugar bowl and set it on her tongue, praying fervently that all she'd taste was pure, sweet cane sugar. But a moment later, she spit it into the sink and stared at the little white lump in horror. It was true. All she could taste was bitter.

She slumped against the sink in utter defeat. How had her life spun so completely out of control in just a few short hours? Etienne, her job, the apartment she called home. And now she'd lost her sense of taste? How could she be expected to be anointed as the head chef of a much-anticipated new restaurant in Paris if she could taste nothing but the flavor of scorched coffee grounds? It felt impossible.

"Um, babe?" Phoebe tiptoed into the kitchen in a long white satin robe, her pale hair hanging loose over her shoulders. "I think there's something you need to see." She held her phone out to Georgia, her face sober. Warily, Georgia took the phone.

SABOTAGE IN THE KITCHEN read the headline of the article on Phoebe's screen. It was from a popular Parisian restaurant and nightlife gossip site called Une Pipelette, roughly translated, "A Chatterbox." And it was about last night.

Which sexiest chef in Paris was caught in an awkward position by his sous-chef girlfriend during dinner? the article teased before quoting anonymous sources who spilled all the sordid details about Georgia, Etienne, and Manon. Georgia scanned the story in growing disbelief and horror.

Sources reveal that Antoine Dupont is furious over his horrible dinner at La Pomme d'Or and that a scathing review is coming soon, the article promised, then posed the awful question: *Will this scandal in the kitchen soil the reputation of Etienne Fontaine, newly crowned sexiest chef in Paris, or will it only dampen the career aspirations of up-and-coming American chef Georgia May*

Jackson? Georgia made a strangled little sound and handed back the phone. Now all of Paris knew about Etienne's betrayal, her hot-tempered retaliation, and all the details of the worst night of her life. This was too much.

Phoebe looked at her sympathetically but said nothing. What was there to say?

Georgia massaged her temples where a stress headache was blooming. She should have expected something like this. A story as juicy as last night's was not going to stay secret for long. Especially when Cyril had seen everything. She'd bet every euro she had that he was the anonymous source. She leaned against the counter, feeling sick with regret. How could she have been so hastily vindictive last night? Spurned and humiliated, she had acted thoughtlessly, and that act of revenge could end up costing her everything. One ruined sole meunière could be her undoing in Paris. The Parisian restaurant world was small, and everyone she knew loved to read Une Pipelette. Its gossip was a frequent source of discussion in the kitchen of La Pomme d'Or. Every restaurant owner and chef in Paris would soon know about this if they didn't already. And Michel. Her stomach sank. Had he seen the article yet?

"What are you going to do?" Phoebe asked quietly.

Georgia shook her head. "I don't know."

For a self-pitying second, she was tempted to crumple onto Phoebe's inviting sofa and sob herself into a mushy puddle, to give in to the crushing series of setbacks and allow herself to wallow in despair. But if she did, she would be giving up everything she'd worked so hard for all these years. She was not a quitter. She'd faced hard things before. This was bad, very, very bad, but she had two choices. Admit defeat, or get back up and keep trying. She could not control Etienne's choices or her own errant taste buds, nor could she cook a new, perfectly flaky sole meunière and serve it to Antoine Dupont as penance. She could not reverse time two years or six and warn herself about what was to come.

She bit her lip and considered her options. *In hard times*, her father, Buck, always told her, *there is always something a body can do.* She might not see eye to eye with her dad on almost anything in life, but he was right about that. She had to do whatever she could to fix this mess. Perhaps there was still something she could salvage from this disaster.

"I need to go see Michel," Georgia said, straightening up. "Even though I made a mistake last night, maybe if he understands what happened, I can convince him that I'm still the best choice for La Lumière Dorée."

"How can I help?" Phoebe asked promptly.

Georgia considered for a moment. "Can I raid your closet? I don't have any clothes and I need to look presentable to plead my case to Michel."

Phoebe studied her critically for a moment. "Anything you want. I'll give you a makeover too. When we're done, you'll look like a million bucks," she said, then wrinkled her nose. "But first you need a shower. You smell like burnt butter."

They sprang into action. Thirty minutes later, a freshly showered Georgia stood in Phoebe's luxurious bathroom, surveying herself in the outfit Phoebe had selected from her own closet. The emerald green silk blouse paired with slim black cigarette pants looked chic and sophisticated on her. Phoebe was taller and narrower in the hips than Georgia, but Georgia could make the outfit work if she sucked in her stomach and didn't pop the buttons on the blouse that was a little snug across her breasts.

Most of the time, she wore her unflattering but comfortable chef's whites, but on the rare occasions when she was out and about in public, Georgia loved to adopt a Parisian style of understated classic elegance. She had more curves than most Parisian women, who on the whole kept themselves extremely slim. *You know you are the right weight,* Etienne's cousin Gisele had confided to her once, *when you can balance a sugar cube in the hollow of your clavicle.* Georgia had never been able to do that, but she still loved to dress like a French woman. After all, she may have been raised in Texas, but Paris was the city of her heart.

Phoebe looked her up and down in the new outfit. "That's more like it. What about jewelry?"

Georgia's hand went to the charm at her throat. "I'll just wear this."

Phoebe looked doubtful. "You sure?"

Georgia nodded. "It was the last thing my mom gave me. It's always brought me luck."

"I hope it gives you lots of luck today," Phoebe said sympathetically, riffling through a bathroom drawer filled with brushes and mascara wands and tubes of makeup. "Come on, babe. Let's fix your face."

Twenty minutes later, as Georgia slipped on a borrowed black trench coat and grabbed her purse to leave, she glanced at her reflection in the front hall mirror. Phoebe had worked a miracle with foundation, bronzer, and mascara. She looked like a confident, sophisticated Parisian. Even her usually wild-child hair had settled down into fairly tame-looking waves. No one could tell that her entire life had just melted.

Just before she walked out the door, in a final touch, Georgia slicked on her favorite lipstick, a Lancôme shade of red so rich it looked like she'd been biting into pie cherries. Even when she was cooking in the kitchen she wore it. It gave her a much-needed boost of confidence now. Georgia looked herself in the eye and squared her shoulders. "Okay, Georgia May Jackson," she said firmly. "Go see if you can save your dream in Paris."

5

"*Bonjour, Michel*." *Georgia* greeted her mentor with a cheerfulness she hoped masked her nerves when he opened the door of his seventeenth-century villa in Trocadéro in the sixteenth arrondissement.

"Bonjour, Georgia," Michel said mildly, looking surprised but ushering her in graciously. Her heart was thumping in her chest as she stepped into the foyer. She could not fix anything that had happened the night before, but she was determined to do her best to keep her mistake from derailing her dreams for the future. She was so close. She clasped her hands together to keep them from shaking. Even now she could feel it rising, the nervous excitement fizzing through her chest like Moët bubbles when she thought of the decision Michel would be making any day now. She had worked for this opportunity for fifteen long years—first culinary school in the US and then over a decade in the kitchens of Paris. Now finally, finally, she was on the cusp of success. She couldn't let the debacle with Etienne mess things up. She had to convince Michel that she was still the right choice to steer the kitchen of his much-anticipated new restaurant, La Lumière Dorée.

Michel led Georgia through a narrow hallway that opened up into a surprisingly modern and spacious industrial kitchen. When he bought the villa, Michel had transformed a section of the lower level into a beautiful, top-of-the-line test kitchen so he could experiment and create in the comfort of his own home.

The pristine, light-filled space with its gleaming stainless-steel counters was often bustling with his assistants, but this morning it was quiet and empty. He appeared to be working alone. For that, she was grateful.

"To what do I owe the pleasure of your visit this morning?" Michel asked in a slightly questioning tone, taking up a position at the kitchen island in front of a cutting board with a square of dark chocolate that he'd been cutting into tiny, even pieces. His English was delicately accented with French. Originally from Brittany, he'd spent a couple of years in New York working for a famous American chef before returning to Paris. Somehow he managed to exude the best of both worlds. His silver hair was cut short with not a strand out of place, and his only concession to being in the kitchen was to roll the sleeves of his sky blue dress shirt up to his elbows. He was wearing very expensive, spotless shoes and had a pair of small, round wire glasses perched on his nose.

Georgia glanced around, not answering his question about her unexpected appearance. "Experimenting today?" Beside her on the counter was a tray holding tiny, delicate macarons in a rainbow of colors, a tarte tatin made with pears was cooling on a rack by the large double sink, and at the far end of the counter sat a tall pile of snowy meringues.

"Playing with a few new ideas," Michel replied with a small smile. "Here." He went to the sink and cut a sliver of the tarte tatin. "Tell me what you think. A new twist on an old classic." He offered it to her. Reluctantly, Georgia took a bite. As he watched, she chewed and swallowed, careful to not grimace. It tasted, predictably, horrible.

"Interesting," Georgia hedged. "Your desserts are always so creative." It was the truth and also a statement that had nothing to do with the taste of whatever was in her mouth. She did not want to lie to Michel. She prided herself on being forthright and honest, but she also wasn't ready to tell him about losing her sense of taste. After what happened at La Pomme d'Or, it felt disastrous to also admit that she had lost her ability to taste anything but bitter. Two strikes against her was too many. She could not risk ruining any chance she had of getting La Lumière Dorée.

La Lumière Dorée, translated the Golden Light in English, was the new sister restaurant to La Pomme d'Or. It was located in Montmartre, within a stone's throw of the sublimely beautiful Sacré-Coeur Basilica. There was much speculation in the Paris restaurant scene over who Michel would name as head chef. There were a few names in the running, including Georgia's, and Etienne had hinted to her last week that Michel was favoring her for the position. But that was before the disaster of last night.

Michel raised an eyebrow at her assessment of the tarte tatin. "That's all? No critique? I've always known you to try to improve everything I've ever made."

Georgia flushed. "I must be feeling generous today," she said cheekily, teasing him a little. "That or you're getting better." She set the rest of the tarte tatin sample aside.

Michel rewarded her with a small, amused half smile. "I am not convinced it is as good as it could be." He narrowed his eyes in thought. As one of the most influential chefs in Europe, Michel had a reputation for impossibly high standards and impeccable taste. He was a businessman first, though, not just an artist, and was known for his precision and his even temper, an anomaly in the high-pressure world of professional chefs.

"A little bird told me you had an eventful evening," Michel remarked calmly, picking up the knife and resuming chopping the chocolate.

Startled, Georgia glanced at him in alarm. What did he know? "Did Etienne call you?"

That could complicate things substantially if he'd already heard about last night from Etienne. She wanted to tell him herself and explain why she'd done what she did.

Michel did not pause. "No, Antoine Dupont called me this morning."

Georgia's mouth went dry.

"Monsieur Dupont was very displeased by every aspect of his visit to the restaurant, especially his inedible meal—which he told me you served him." Michel threw her a quick glance as he scraped the chocolate into a bowl. "And he was especially non-plussed when Etienne tried to convince him to not write a review. He said Etienne cited a domestic dispute with you as the reason the food was abominable. And so far this morning I have received no fewer than half a dozen messages, all about an article on the Internet? You know I don't read such things, but many people have already contacted me to let me know. You are quite the talk of Paris today, my dear."

Georgia said nothing. Michel looked at her, his expression mild but questioning. "Is it true? Did you sabotage Monsieur Dupont's meal as Etienne claims?"

Georgia crossed her arms and hesitated, feeling like a scolded child. "Yes and no," she said. "I caught Etienne cheating on me with the new pastry chef, so I shut them in the walk-in refrigerator and then in the uproar afterward, Monsieur Dupont's sole meunière got quite overdone. I could have had the kitchen make him a new plate, but I didn't. I . . ." She paused, embarrassed. "I served it to Monsieur Dupont on purpose," she admitted regretfully.

"Ah," Michel said mildly. "You've always had a hot temper to match that glorious hair of yours." He shook his head and gave her a gently reproving glance. Going to the refrigerator, he took out a tray with little ramekins of creamy white blancmange and set it on the counter.

"I was angry and humilated," Georgia blurted out, "but I shouldn't have done it."

"You're right," Michel agreed calmly, picking up a ramekin of blancmange and examining it. He withdrew a small spoon from his pocket and tasted a bite, eyes narrowed, assessing. "It was a regrettable lapse in judgment." He set the ramekin down and looked at her reprovingly. "Of course you were angry, Georgia, but did you consider what a bad review would do to your colleagues, to everyone else who works as hard as you do in that kitchen? You have every right to be angry with Etienne. He is a brilliant chef, but when it comes to matters of the heart, he lets what is between his legs lead him, like a street dog. But I expected better of you." He sounded so sober, and her heart sank. She hated to disappoint him. "Your choice shows a lack of care for others around you," he admonished. "That is not the way to inspire and lead people, Georgia. You must always think of serving those around you, not just yourself. Only then will you be ready to lead your own restaurant."

Georgia nodded miserably. How could she have let one bad choice ruin so many years of grueling work? She was bitterly disappointed in herself.

"So now what?" Georgia asked quietly. She picked up a tiny lavender macaron, the size of an American quarter and light as a little cloud, from a tray of them on the counter by her elbow, then set it back down. She looked up to find Michel watching her carefully.

"I must be honest, Georgia. I was considering you for La Lumière Dorée," Michel admitted.

Georgia's stomach sank at his use of the past tense.

"But something gives me pause," Michel continued. "It is not just about last night, but something far more grave, I fear." Michel went to the stove and came back with a small saucepan of a clear amber liquid. It gave off the tantalizing fragrance of rosemary and caramelized sugar.

"More grave?" Georgia asked with a touch of dread. How could this get worse? Did he somehow already know about her losing her sense of taste?

"We all suffer from moments of insanity when it comes to passions of the heart." Michel spooned a few teaspoons of the liquid over the top of each blancmange. "That is regrettable but understandable. But it is more than that. I fear you are losing your spark, Georgia." He looked up at her, his expression assessing.

"My spark?" Georgia repeated blankly.

Michel gave her a small smile. "When I first met you, do you know what I saw?"

"My body flying across the hood of your car?" Georgia guessed wryly. She and Michel had met when Georgia had been thrown in his path quite literally one morning during her first few weeks in Paris. A rowdy student tour group had shouldered past her near the Eiffel Tower, bumping her into the street and straight into the path of Michel's car. In truth, the hood had barely grazed her hip, but Michel had been so appalled and so apologetic about hitting her that he had insisted his driver take her wherever she was heading. She was returning to her hotel after being rejected by another restaurant unwilling to hire a female, American-trained chef. They had actually laughed in her face. It was not the first time.

On the way back to her hotel in a dodgy arrondissement, she and Michel struck up a conversation. Intrigued by the brash redheaded American with the Texas twang, Michel asked if she would mind taking a small detour. He drove her to one of his restaurants, not open at that time of day, and invited her to prepare a simple lunch for him. After eating her food, he generously offered to have a word with a couple of restaurants about a possible position. As it turned out, his word was a golden ticket. She had started at the bottom, just above a dishwasher, but it was a start. Thanks to Michel, she had gotten the chance to prove herself at a good restaurant in Paris. And he had continued to mentor her in the twelve years since, providing invaluable advice and guidance as she'd worked her way up the ranks of several restaurant kitchens.

Michel waved away her attempt at humor. "Georgia, that day I saw the spark you carry within you. You were so new, so idealistic and unprepared, but you did extraordinary things with food, things I'd never tasted before. I ate what you cooked and it filled me with a sense of wonder, of possibility, of . . . joie de vivre, for lack of a better term. It was not because your technique was so superior. You are a talented and well-trained chef, but so are dozens of chefs in this city. No, it was something more. When I sampled what you made for me that first time, it was as though with every bite I could taste a better future, the possibilities yet to come."

Michel paused, searching for the right words. He spooned more of the rosemary caramelized sugar syrup into the ramekins of blancmange, filling the kitchen with a sugary evergreen scent. "Your food gave me hope in the strangest way. And that's why I've invested so much of my time into your career, because your potential seemed boundless, because the food you make has a touch of the . . . what is the English word? Transcendent? No. Sublime. That is it. There is something about your food that feels sublime, as though when I eat it, I see everything more clearly, I catch a glimpse of a better world. It is a beautiful thing. Almost a holy thing." He gazed at her with a look of consideration.

Georgia waited wordlessly, dumbfounded. He had never told her this.

"But now," Michel paused. "I fear you've lost your way. I've suspected it for some time. I can taste the change in your food. It's still technically excellent, but it lacks that spark. I cannot taste the life in the food you touch anymore; there is no joy. You are so focused on your goal of making head chef that I fear you have forgotten why you wanted to become a chef in the first place. And if that happens, everything suffers. Your team, your food, your inspiration." He gazed at her sternly. "You are so talented, Georgia, and so determined. You have so much potential, but if you lose your spark, you will burn out, burn up. Your life will become bitter, without true meaning. You must not let that happen." He paused a moment. "I have not yet made up my mind about La Lumière Dorée. I am considering you, but I am considering a few others as well."

"What can I do to make it right?" Georgia asked, feeling both relief and disappointment. He was strongly considering others, chefs who presumably could still taste the food they made. But at least she still had a shot. "Tell me what to do. Give me a chance," she begged softly, chastened. "I can prove to you I haven't lost my touch. I just need a little time to get my head on straight, to get over what happened with Etienne and . . . regain my spark. I can do this. You know I can. No one works harder or longer than I do. No one wants this more. You know that, Michel. Please."

Carefully Michel set the saucepan aside and wiped up a few drops of spilled sugary syrup. He gazed out the window, over the lush green lawn and budding trees, considering her words. "Perhaps it is not about working harder or longer, mon amie," he mused. "Perhaps it is simply about asking yourself why you want the things you've been striving for, the things you've wanted for so long." He glanced back at her. "I wonder if the answer might surprise you."

She said nothing, just waited. After a long pause, he nodded, seeming to come to a decision. He picked up a small bowl of pine nuts and scooped up a heaping teaspoonful, sprinkling some on each of the blancmanges. "Very well. This is my advice. Go somewhere for a few weeks. Get out of Paris. Go home to Texas, go to Antarctica, it makes no difference to me. Disappear and let this all blow over. Right now, Etienne has made it his personal mission to make sure no respectable kitchen in Paris will take you on. He wants you blackballed entirely. But his temper will cool and people will forget the gossip. When Dupont's review is published, it will make a scene for a few days before it is replaced by a new scandal. Paris will forget, as it always does, but this will take some time. You need to disappear. Go somewhere where you can rest, where you can rediscover your own inspiration, where you can be reminded of why you became a chef in the first place. Then when the time is right, come back and prove to me why I should place La Lumière Dorée in your hands. I will give you one more chance, but you will have to prove yourself— how do you Americans say it—fair and square?"

He straightened and wiped his hands on a clean white kitchen towel. Their time was over. She was dismissed. Georgia followed Michel out of the kitchen, reluctant but relieved. Even if the odds were stacked against her currently, at least she still had a chance. She was used to long odds. She'd beaten them before. Now she just had to get out of Paris and regain her spark, whatever that meant. She wondered if he could somehow sense her gradual loss of taste. Was that what he meant by her losing

her spark? Regardless, she would do as he said. She would leave
Paris and figure out how to regain her sense of taste and her
spark somehow. But where in the world could she go?

At the door, Michel cupped her shoulders, leaning in and
air-kissing her on both cheeks. "Au revoir, mon amie," he said.

He smelled delicious, like rosemary and chocolate and buttery
crumbs fresh from the oven. She sniffed him discreetly as she
returned the air-kisses. Her sense of smell was as keen as ever.
It just didn't seem to translate to her tongue.

"Merci, Michel."

He drew back, and she caught a glimmer of amusement in
his eyes. "Did you really shut Etienne and that pastry chef in
the walk-in refrigerator?" he asked, his mouth twitching up at
one corner.

She closed her eyes, feeling the humiliation afresh. "Yes, I
did. And then I left them there," she admitted.

"You are not a woman to be trifled with," Michel said, his
tone dry. "Good for you. Now go, and come back when you
have discovered afresh your special spark in the kitchen."

6

An hour later, Georgia paced the gravel walkways under the graceful chestnut trees of the Jardin du Luxembourg. A few pedestrians wandered along nearby paths, exercising dogs or talking on their phones, but thankfully, she was alone. The breeze was still quite chilly in early April, though it smelled fresh and green, like new leaves and wet earth. She shivered and pulled the trench coat she'd borrowed from Phoebe more snugly around her.

Where could she go to get out of Paris? That was the most pressing question. Phoebe was at work, so Georgia had to try to puzzle things out by herself for a few more hours. She wound her way through the garden, considering her options. They were scanty.

"What would you do if you were me, Julia?" Georgia whispered an entreaty.

She tried to envision her tall, cheerful patron saint. What would Julia advise? She could always go back to Texas. The thought felt deflating. Georgia would always have a place on the ranch. Her father and Aunt Hannah would never turn her away, she knew that. But the knowledge was cold comfort. There was nothing for her there, no inspiration, no one who understood why she'd made the choices she had.

She'd been an only child, raised on the ranch and expected to marry a fellow rancher's son and spend her life birthing and rearing a new generation of ranchers to carry on the family legacy. It was a hard life but satisfying to those who embraced it—but it was a life she had never wanted. From an early age she had longed for something else, and she'd bolted from under her family's heavy mantle of legacy and expectations the first chance she got. The week she turned eighteen, she'd left the ranch and never looked back. Her choice to veer so drastically from the path they thought best was a constant source of disappointment to her father and aunt, a sore spot that never seemed to heal between her and her family. She had not been home in years. To go back now with her tail between her legs, trying to find her way again in a place that did not embrace who she was, felt nearly impossible. No, Texas was out of the question.

Georgia imagined Julia standing in her famous television kitchen, nodding approvingly as she massaged a chicken with butter in preparation for roasting it.

"Illegitimi non carborundum" Julia trilled as she poked a slice of lemon into the bird's body cavity. "That's Latin for 'Don't let the bastards get you down.'"

"So what other choices do I have?" Georgia asked. Julia neatly trussed the chicken and offered no further advice. Georgia blew out a little puff of air in frustration and paused by an empty bench near the edge of the park. She clicked on her phone, ignoring the dozens of texts from acquaintances who had no doubt read or heard the gossip and were eager for more details. The texts had been coming in since before she woke that morning, but she was choosing not to look at them. She didn't want to add fuel to the fire of scandal. Best to let the drama die down on its own as quickly as possible. What she needed now was a way out of Paris.

Georgia briefly checked her social media accounts, hoping

for inspiration. Big mistake. Apparently, she had some haters out there, and shutting Paris's sexiest chef in a walk-in refrigerator had enraged them. She was being called any number of unflattering things in French AND English. She quickly swiped out of Instagram, cheeks flaming at the vitriol, and navigated to her email instead. It seemed like safer terrain. Maybe there would be someone in her contact list that could help?

Georgia scrolled through her unread messages, mostly advertisements and junk. She often didn't check her email more than once or twice a week as there was seldom anything pressing in her inbox. It had been almost a week this time, and now there were dozens of new emails waiting. She scrolled through hurriedly, erasing as she went. She almost deleted the email message sandwiched between an EasyJet airfare sale and a payment reminder from her cell phone provider, but then her eye caught the name of the sender and she stopped cold. For a long moment, she stared at it in disbelief. It couldn't be. It had been sent five days ago. The subject line said simply, "Please read."

Georgia's heart skipped a beat, and her hand went instinctively to her charm, fingers clenched around the smooth, worn leaves. In an instant, she was five years old, standing in the dusty driveway back at the ranch in West Texas, the August afternoon sun blazing hot on the crown of her head, feeling the slip of the chain as it was clasped around her neck, the coolness of her mother's guitar string—calloused fingers caressing her cheek briefly. Her mother's voice, warm and rough as the gravel beneath her bare feet.

"You hold on to this necklace, Georgia May. Keep it till you see me coming for you. This is the recipe for a charmed life right here in these four leaves, see? Faith, hope, love, and luck. I wish all of those for you, sweet girl." And then her mother had left. She had never come back.

Heart pounding, Georgia clicked on the message.

Dear Georgia May,

*My name is Star Stevens and I am your mama. I'm sorry
to be writing like this out of the blue, but there is something
I need to tell you, something that could change your life. I
don't know what you've been told about me since you were
little, but please know I never stopped loving you.*

*If you want to know the truth about yourself and our
family, then come to San Juan Island. I hope you'll give me
a chance to explain.*

Love,
Star

Dumbfounded, Georgia stared at the message, rereading it
over and over. Star Stevens, the woman who had walked out
the door twenty-eight years ago and disappeared from her life
forever. Why in the world was she contacting Georgia now?
How had Star even found her?

"*If you want to know the truth about yourself and our family,
then come to San Juan Island . . .*" Georgia read the words aloud
slowly, as though trying to decipher their true meaning. In a
flash, she saw her mother, slender and wiry, wearing a flowing
orange batik dress as she threw her guitar case in the back of a
beat-up brown Eldorado and drove away. Georgia couldn't
quite recall her mother's face, but she remembered her hair—
untamed, spilling down her back in a mass of unruly red-gold
spirals. Over the years, Star had become an almost mythic figure in her mind. The woman who had left her daddy, a dusty

ranch in Texas, and a heartbroken five-year-old with her mama's red curls. The woman she'd always longed for, always wondered about, always secretly wished would come back one day. The woman she'd been waiting on for almost thirty years.

"Star Stevens," Georgia murmured. "I always hoped you'd find me." And then without warning, she burst into tears.

"*Well of course* you have to go!" Phoebe exclaimed. "How could you not?"

It was late afternoon, and Georgia had just told Phoebe about her visit to Michel and the email from her mother. She'd reread it at least a dozen times since that moment on the bench in the Luxembourg Gardens, but it still felt as mysterious and astonishing as ever.

Phoebe leaned over the tiny table in her kitchen and considered the assortment of macarons nestled in a narrow pistachio green box in front of her, running her fingers lightly over the brilliant rainbow colors, each a delicate, delicious flavor. "Orange blossom, my favorite. You remembered!" she exclaimed, plucking a pale peach–hued one from the box.

Undisputedly the best macarons in Paris, Ladurée's had always been Georgia's go-to treat for every birthday, promotion, or milestone in life. Georgia had stopped at one of the Ladurée shops on her way home from seeing Michel and selected a dozen macarons as a thank-you gift for Phoebe.

"You like citron, right?" Phoebe asked, holding out a bright canary yellow macaron. "Here you go. I'll share."

Georgia declined politely. She wouldn't be able to taste it, though she didn't tell Phoebe that.

"My mom left us when I was little," Georgia explained. "Just vanished for almost three decades. So why is she contacting me now? And what does she mean, come to San Juan Island if I want to know the truth about myself and our family? What truth? It just all seems so . . . strange." She wrinkled her brow, puzzled and a little skeptical.

"Seems pretty perfect to me." Phoebe nibbled the macaron as she reread the email on Georgia's phone. "This could solve everything! You can get away from Paris like Michel told you to and you can reconnect with your long-lost mom. Surely you've been curious about her? This is your chance to find out the truth. How is this not a good plan?"

"Maybe." Georgia hedged. She felt strangely reluctant. She couldn't quite wrap her mind around it. Star Stevens, her mother, was not only alive and well and living on an island somewhere but inviting Georgia to come for a visit? Just like that, out of the blue? She didn't know how to feel about it all. She had so many questions about her mother. Every time she thought of Star, she felt the familiar confused churning of anger, longing, grief, and resentment low in her belly, the same emotions she'd been harboring since she was a young girl. Star Stevens. There was nothing simple about that name. And yet, Phoebe was right. Georgia was curious, very curious. What did Star want to tell her? And why? There were so many questions.

"Frankly, what do you have to lose?" Phoebe asked, selecting a bright pink raspberry macaron from the box and nibbling it.

"Nothing I haven't lost already," Georgia admitted. "I just can't believe she contacted me after all these years. I know absolutely nothing about her. She's a stranger to me." She looked at the email on her phone again. "And where in the world is San Juan Island?"

"Sounds exotic. Let's look it up!" Phoebe whipped out her iPhone. A moment later, she squealed. "Ooh, look! It's in Washington State, north of Seattle. And it's *gorgeous*." She held out her phone to Georgia, flicking through a dozen photos. Deep blue water and emerald green islands capped by evergreen forests. Rocky bays and serene white ferries chugging past pods of orcas. A tiny town of quaint clapboard buildings painted in a rainbow of hues. A harbor clogged with bobbing sailboats. It looked idyllic, soaked in natural beauty. Serene. It was a world away from Paris, or Texas, for that matter. Georgia took the phone and studied the photos, mesmerized. She'd never seen anything like it. She felt a longing tug in her chest, something she couldn't quite articulate. Something was calling to her there. She had to go.

Phoebe took her phone back and read avidly for a few minutes. "It says here that San Juan Island is known for pods of orcas, kayaking, a lavender farm, cidery, vineyard, shellfish farm, restaurants with Pacific Northwest cuisine, and farmers markets." She put the phone down and looked at Georgia expectantly. "You've got to go," she urged. "Think about it. What better place to regain your spark than somewhere like that? And you can get to know your mom again and find out what she wants to tell you. It's a win-win."

Georgia bit her lip, considering. "It sounds pretty ideal," she admitted finally.

"Oh goody!" Phoebe clapped her hands. "It's the perfect time for you to have an adventure." She tipped her head and surveyed Georgia coyly. "Maybe you'll find more there than you bargain for."

"What does that mean?" Georgia handed the phone back.

Phoebe shrugged. "I don't know. A romance with a sexy fisherman or lumberjack? Something good you don't see coming. I just have the funniest feeling this is going to change everything for you."

Georgia wrinkled her nose. "No, thanks. After Etienne, I'm done with romance for a good long time."

She was only considering going to the island in the hopes

that she could get her sense of taste back, regain her spark in time to prove to Michel she was ready to have her own restaurant, and satisfy her curiosity about her mother. That was it. Perhaps going to the island and seeing Star would be a step in the right direction. Maybe regaining her spark was as simple as regaining her sense of taste. If she could regain her sense of taste, she hoped everything else would fall into place.

"So you're going?" Phoebe squealed.

"I'm going," Georgia decided in an instant. What did she have to lose? She sent a quick email reply to Star, one line letting her know she wanted to come and asking if she could arrive soon. She pressed the send button on the message before she could have second thoughts.

"This is so exciting," Phoebe crowed, almost bouncing with excitement. She loved drama of any sort. "What time is it in Washington State? It's early morning there, right? Ooooh, I hope she writes back soon."

"Me too," Georgia said, quietly sending up a petition heavenward. "Please help this not to be a mistake," she whispered.

Twenty minutes later when Georgia checked her email, there was a one-line reply from Star.

Dear Georgia,
Come when you can. I will be waiting for you.—Star

Below it she'd included her address, a place called Friday Harbor on San Juan Island. Georgia stared at the address, wondering what she would find there. Was Star married? Did she have other children? She could have another family and life Georgia knew nothing about. The thought was unsettling. What was she walking into? Many times over the years, Georgia had googled her mother's name, but had found no trace of Star on-

line. It was as though Star Stevens didn't exist. Except quite obviously she did. And if all went well, Georgia would soon be
face-to-face with her. The thought made her equal parts anxious and excited.

"Give me courage," she whispered, hoping Julia could help
her. "Please let this work out."

Phoebe shrieked when she heard the news and went to find
a bottle of champagne to celebrate while Georgia started looking for a plane ticket. A few minutes later, she'd located a one-
way ticket to Seattle, the closest major airport to San Juan
Island, leaving early the next morning. Everything was happening so quickly, but she figured why wait? It was better to go
as soon as she could. There was nothing to keep her here now.
She needed only to collect her belongings from her old apartment and she could be on her way in a matter of hours. She
blew out a breath, wincing at the exorbitant cost of the ticket
that would eat up much of her meager savings. Her finger hov-
ered over the "purchase" button for the flight. Was she crazy to
jump headfirst into this? What could happen if things went
badly? What if she didn't regain her sense of taste, didn't regain her spark? What if she and Star had nothing in common?
What if it all went horribly wrong?

She hesitated. It suddenly felt so risky, like closing her eyes
and jumping off a cliff. "Come on, Georgia, you can do hard
things," she murmured. She'd been doing them for years. Leaving
home at eighteen with a hundred dollars in her pocket and the
disappointment and disapproval of her father and aunt. Putting
herself through culinary school, learning to make gourmet meals
during the day and then going to work the overnight shift at
whatever minimum-wage job she could find. Eating only two
meals of peanut butter sandwiches and scrambled eggs in her
shared studio apartment every day to save money. Worming

her way into the restaurant scene in Paris and climbing the ranks through sheer talent and determination, as an American and a woman in the kitchens of Paris. It had been a Herculean effort. She had sacrificed and scrimped and worked her fingers to the bone to succeed. Now she was so close. She would do whatever she could to prove to Michel that she was the right choice. La Lumière Dorée could still be hers. She had to take the chance.

And while she was on San Juan Island, Georgia would finally reunite with the woman who had birthed her and abandoned her. The woman her family had refused to talk about after she vanished, the woman Georgia still longed for sometimes, waking muddled and forlorn with tears wetting her cheeks from a dream she could never remember. She was leaving Paris to try to regain all the precious things she'd lost. It was a risk worth taking.

"Let's toast to your new adventure," Phoebe trilled, returning from the kitchen holding aloft two champagne flutes.

"Just a second." Georgia took a deep breath and punched the "purchase" button for the flight. There was no going back now. She was really doing this.

"Bon appétit, ma choupinette!" she heard Julia chortle from somewhere in the back of her head, popping a chicken in the oven and waving goodbye.

7

"We are now approaching the Friday Harbor Ferry Terminal," a voice crackled over the loudspeaker of the Washington State ferry. "All passengers are asked to return to their vehicles at this time. All walk-on passengers will disembark from the car deck."

Georgia leaned over the top railing of the passenger deck on the double-decker white-and-green ferry and inhaled the fragrance of salty sea air and spicy evergreen needles as the large boat glided smoothly toward San Juan Island. She had never smelled air so fresh. It had been a grueling trip to get here—two layovers in Frankfurt and Dulles, and on all three flights she'd been crammed in the middle seat. But now after a shuttle from the airport to the ferry terminal and a jaw-droppingly beautiful hour-long ferry ride through the San Juan Islands, she was finally approaching Friday Harbor. Georgia swallowed nervously. It was time.

Retrieving her two rolling suitcases from inside the passenger area, Georgia followed the other passengers down onto the car deck. Her two heavy suitcases contained all her worldly possessions. After she purchased her plane ticket and toasted her new adventure with Phoebe, she had waited until late evening when she was sure Etienne would be at the restaurant. Then she and Phoebe had gone back to her old apartment to liberate her things. While Phoebe blasted the Spice Girls hit "Goodbye" on repeat and systematically emptied all of the bottles of expensive liquor from Etienne's Art Deco bar cart down the kitchen drain, Georgia had hastily packed up her belongings and said a final goodbye to her former home and the man she'd shared it with. It had felt brutal to leave that way. Although she'd had her doubts about Etienne over the course of their relationship, she never could have imagined that this was how things would turn out. The betrayal still took her breath away. But here she was, leaving Paris and oh so ready for a fresh start.

She shivered, nestling into her lined trench coat as the ferry entered the harbor. It was chilly here in April. The air on the front open ferry deck was bracing, sharp, and tinged with salt and rain. Although she was so exhausted she felt like she was floating a few inches off the ground, Georgia was almost giddy with nerves, every sensation clearer and sharper. She stood with the other walk-on passengers and watched the bright clapboard buildings of Friday Harbor grow closer. It was a quaint, small town made up of historic wooden buildings painted in a rainbow of colors. She felt like she'd stepped onto the set of a Hallmark movie. Not a high-rise or a scrap of litter in sight.

Once the ferry docked, Georgia walked up the ramp, scanning the waiting cars. She spotted a few with taxi signs on them and found one that was willing to take her to the address Star had sent her. The taxi was a butter yellow classic car, adorable but expensive. With a sigh, she slid into the back seat and pressed her face to the window as they wound through the tiny town filled with pubs, seafood restaurants, an ice cream shack sitting right at the edge of the harbor by the sailboats, a two-screen cinema, and an old-fashioned hardware store. It looked like something out of a postcard—quaint and nautical, a far cry from the stately grandeur of Paris. She found it utterly charming.

"Here for sightseeing?" the friendly cab driver asked as they headed down a rural road out of town. "The orcas went north earlier this morning, I heard."

"Visiting a . . . family member," Georgia replied. Her pulse quickened and she swallowed nervously as she pictured facing her long-lost mother in just a few minutes. She had sent an email letting Star know she was on her way and giving her flight details, but had received no reply before she departed Paris. In the email, she'd told Star that she'd find her own transportation to the house since she didn't know her exact arrival time to the island. She had no telephone number for Star and no other way to contact her. Hopefully, Star was okay with her daughter showing up at her doorstep on such short notice. Even if she wasn't, it was too late to turn back now.

Georgia stared out at the passing scenery, rolling hills dotted every so often with tidy farms and large swaths of evergreen forest. Occasionally, through the trees or across a field, she'd catch the gray-blue glitter of the sea. The island exuded tranquility and beauty. She'd never seen anything so peaceful in her life.

Nervously, she touched up her lipstick and fluffed her wild curls. Any minute she'd be face-to-face with Star, and she felt queasy with anticipation and nerves. What would Star be like? Would she be anything like the few hazy snatches of memory Georgia had clung to all her life? What if she felt like a complete stranger, one Georgia could not find anything in common with? Or what if Georgia was not what Star was expecting? What if Georgia herself was a disappointment? She had always suspected, somewhere deep in her heart, that this might be so. After all, Star had left and never come back. Why else would Star have left her behind when she disappeared? The thought of being a disappointment to her mother filled her with anxiety. Somewhere inside she still felt like that little girl, waiting at the window each evening at bedtime for her mother to return, eyes glued to that long, dusty stretch of driveway, yearning with every fiber of her little lonely being to know somewhere out there her mother still thought of her, still loved her. And yet she was not that little girl now. She was a grown woman who had learned years ago how to navigate a world filled with disappointments and questions left unanswered, but still she carried the ache of her mother's abandonment and broken promises in the softest part of her heart, nestled somewhere between anger and grief.

Georgia leaned her head against the car window and watched the scenery blur by, sending a little prayer heavenward. "Please let this go well with Star," she murmured. She desperately wanted Star to like her, for this reunion to be a happy one. If it didn't work, she had nowhere else to go. It made her feel vulnerable, to know so much was riding on such a huge unknown.

All too soon, they pulled up in front of a little white farmhouse with a steep green-gabled roof. Behind the house spread a beautiful bay of blue-gray water, ringed by evergreens. The house had a white picket fence lined with lavender bushes in full, riotous purple bloom. It was picturesque and serene. She loved it instantly.

Next to the road stood a small, simple wooden farm stand. A few jars of honey and some wildflower bouquets in Mason jars sat on a counter underneath. A sign hanging on a sturdy metal box said:

PAY HERE
HONEY $15/BOUQUETS $12
BE HONEST. KARMA'S A BITCH

"Is this it?" Georgia asked.

"Sure is," the cab driver confirmed. "This is Star Stevens's place. Used to be Justine Hardy's place too, till Justine passed away. Cancer, I think it was, a few years back." He turned to look at Georgia in the back seat. "Good folks, both her and Star. My wife likes to buy Star's honey and her heirloom tomatoes. Says she's got the greenest thumb on the island."

That information seemed reassuring, though Georgia wondered who Justine was. She guessed she'd find out eventually. Georgia got out and paid the driver, tipping generously even though the cost was already eye-watering. He unloaded her suitcases and shook her hand.

"Enjoy your time on the island. It's a special place," he said, then drove away in a puff of white dust, leaving her standing at the front gate, suddenly unsure. A moment later, her hesitation was broken by the sound of frantic barking as a streak of yellow shot from around the back of the house and cleared the gate in a single great bound. Georgia shrieked, throwing her hands up in self-defense as a large, barrel-chested yellow lab skidded to a stop at her feet. The dog jumped up and placed its paws on her chest, then began industriously licking her chin with a very pink, very wet tongue.

"Pollen! Pollen! Down, girl. Off! Off!" A wiry woman with long spirals of gray hair flew from around the side of the house in pursuit of the dog, scolding in a stern tone. Her commands had no visible effect on the animal, who was licking every square inch of Georgia's jaw and neck as she futilely tried to push the creature off of her.

"Urgh." Georgia squirmed backward, but the dog followed her movements on its two hind legs, as though they were dance partners doing a waltz. Pollen was very determined and very friendly.

"Sorry, sorry, she's just excited. She wouldn't harm a fly." The woman hurried through the gate and pulled at the dog's collar,

apologizing and scolding at once. "Pollen, get down. Stop licking strangers. It's rude." She caught a good look at Georgia's
face, and her voice died away.

"Georgia May?" she said, her expression turning from shock
to wonder in an instant.

"Mama?" Georgia said without thinking. She stared at her
mother with a sudden jolt of recognition. She remembered that
face. Star looked older, more weathered, but her eyes were the
same. A striking shade of pale gray-green, like the waters of Puget
Sound. Now they were filled with a mixture of hope and apprehension as she gazed at Georgia wide-eyed, as though she'd
seen a ghost. Self-consciously, Georgia smoothed down her rumpled white shirt and then launched into the speech she'd prac-
ticed a dozen times on the plane. "I'm sorry to surprise you like
this. I sent an email but I'm not sure if you got it in time. I didn't
have your number to call you. If it's not convenient, I can just
stay in a hotel or . . ." She let the sentence hang as she gazed at
her long-lost mother, waiting on edge to see what she would say.

Star let go of the dog and stepped forward, cupping Georgia's
face in her hands. Her fingers were gnarled and strong, the skin
of her palms leathery. The intimacy of the gesture took Georgia
by surprise, but she didn't pull away from the calloused warmth
of her mother's touch. Star's gaze searched Georgia's face, every
inch, as though looking at a rare work of art.

"I would know you anywhere," she murmured, her voice
warm and husky. It was the same voice from Georgia's memories. She felt a pang low in her belly at the familiar sound. It had
been so long. "Look at you. And that hair. You look exactly like
my grandma Emma." Her mouth turned up at the corners, and
she gave a surprised, delighted chuckle.

Georgia stepped back, feeling a little off-kilter at the intimacy,
and Star drew back immediately, brushing her hands together

self-consciously. "Look at me, getting carried away. There's time for all of that later. Come on in. You must be tired. Of course you can stay. I have room."

"Are you sure?" Georgia asked tentatively. "I don't want to intrude." But she was relieved. She couldn't afford a hotel for more than a few nights, and she couldn't go back to Paris for a while.

Star waved away her words. "You could never intrude. You're family. Besides—" She pointed to the yellow lab who was hopping from foot to foot excitedly and wagging her entire back end. She had a friendly, goofy face and was panting and whining joyfully. "Pollen would never forgive me if you didn't stay. She likes visitors. Come on, I'll make you some tea and toast. Everything in the world is better with toast."

With that, she grabbed the handles of both of Georgia's suitcases and hoisted them with a grunt, heading up the porch steps and into the house. Georgia looked at Pollen, who gave a little woof of agreement. She felt thunderstruck at the sight of her mother, dazed and elated and more than a little conflicted. So many questions crowded her mind, clamoring for attention, but Georgia pushed them all back. There would be time for that later. For now it was enough to just be together again. With one last look around, Georgia followed Star up the steps and into the house, feeling lighter with every step.

8

Five minutes later, Georgia found herself seated at a white painted table in a simple vintage farmhouse kitchen while Star bustled around making toast and tea. Pale afternoon light streamed in through a bank of windows looking out over a green lawn that sloped down to the bay. It was a gorgeous view. Georgia tried to imagine waking every day to that view. Did it ever grow old? She couldn't believe that it would. It was so peaceful here. The house radiated it, tinged with a hint of sadness. It was at odds with what Georgia remembered of her mother—a swirl of energy and color, like the sharp crackle of static electricity. The energy Star exuded now was one of quiet calm with an undercurrent of sorrow. There were grooves bracketing her mouth that spoke of suffering. She did not look like an addict or a liar or a witch, all things Georgia had heard whispered about her mother in the years since her disappearance. She looked like a woman who had lived a hard life and now finally was at peace with herself.

Georgia studied Star as she measured out dried leaves from a Mason jar and stirred them into a mug of hot water. She looked to be in her early fifties. A few inches shorter than Georgia with a slim build, she had a mass of salt-and-pepper curls cascading unbound down her back. She wore no makeup, and her bare face was gently lined, like someone who had spent years outside. There were crow's-feet at the corners of her eyes. She was wearing what Georgia thought of as standard-issue hippie clothing but with a twist—a short sleeve tie-dyed Grateful Dead T-shirt paired with a pebble-colored broomstick skirt. Long earrings with feathers and stones clicked slightly as she moved. On her right bicep, just visible below the edge of the T-shirt sleeve, was a tattoo. It looked like a skull wearing a crown of bright, blooming flowers. Georgia studied all this with interest. What did it say about the life Star had lived since she'd left? A toaster on the counter popped up a thick slice of toast, and Star buttered it and slathered it with honey from a pint glass jar.

"Here you go. This will set you right." Star placed a plate in front of Georgia, the toast dripping with golden honey and butter. She also set the mug of leaves in hot water beside the plate. "The honey's from my own bees." She gestured out the window. Off to one side of the lawn, backed up to a line of evergreens, Georgia spotted a row of beehives, each painted a different vibrant shade. Scarlet, tangerine, canary yellow, and turquoise. Georgia took a nibble of the toast just to be polite. The bread appeared to be homemade, and had the density and consistency of drywall. It needed more than honey to save it.

Georgia grimaced at the bitter taste of the toast and took a gulp of tea to drive down the dry crumbs of bread lodged in her throat. She'd always wondered where her culinary gift had come from. Aunt Hannah had been a decent cook, turning out hearty, nutritious meals that were edible enough. Nothing fancy, just plain American fare that would fill the bellies of hungry ranchers, but Aunt Hannah had made no bones about the fact that she did not enjoy cooking. There was no art for her in it. It was simply a chore, like weeding. Georgia had a few vague memories of being in the kitchen with Star and had always wondered if Star had been her early inspiration. After Star left, Aunt Hannah and her father refused to talk about her. Georgia had grown up hoarding the little scraps of memory and bits of information she could glean. But from the look of this bread, Star may not have been the inspiration either. Georgia poked surreptitiously at the bread, feeling surprisingly deflated. She'd always hoped and assumed that she and Star had shared a culinary gift. It appeared she was wrong.

Georgia took another sip of tea. It tasted bitter, but the aroma was good, strong and herbal. "What's in this tea?" When she saw Star's back was turned, she discreetly fed her slice of toast to Pollen, who was sitting by her chair, resting her head on Georgia's knee and raising her eyebrows beseechingly. Satisfied, Pollen dropped to the floor and gnawed at the crust like it was a rawhide bone.

"Oh, just a bit of this and that." Star joined her at the table with another mug of tea. "All things I grew in my garden. I'm a great believer in the power of herbs. You know each one has specific properties. This is my special tea blend." She swirled the leaves in her mug with a spoon. "Care to guess what's in there?"

Georgia sniffed the fragrant steam appraisingly. "Let's see. Definitely mint."

"For wisdom." Star nodded, taking a sip.

"And rosemary."

"For remembrance," Star confirmed.

"And . . ." Georgia sniffed again. "Tarragon?" She'd always liked tarragon. It was considered the king of herbs in French cooking.

"For devotion." Star looked pleased. "I call this clarity tea. I like to think when we drink it, the tea helps us remember what we've lost and what we've learned in life. It reminds us what's important to us."

"Sounds like powerful tea," Georgia murmured. She watched Star across the table, trying to reconcile the mature woman who sat before her with the few distant memories she had from before Star left. She knew this was her mother, but there were so many unknown years between them. How could they possibly cover all of them? How could they make up all the lost time and get to know each other again? What had happened in those lost years? Whatever it was, it had made them virtual strangers now.

Just then, the back door banged open. Pollen leaped to her feet, tail wagging, and woofed a greeting as a man stomped through the doorway.

"Star, I've got some fresh Manila clams for you," he announced, then snapped his mouth shut in surprise when he saw Georgia. He was tall, well over six feet, with dark windblown hair and a five-o'clock shadow. He looked to be about her age or a few years older, possibly mid-thirties, and was wearing an astonishing pair of bright orange rubber overalls that came up to his chest. It was the most ludicrous outfit she'd ever seen on a grown man. Georgia stared at him in consternation, and he gave her a similar look. He had a metal pail in one hand that was dripping on the floor.

"Cole, this is Georgia, my daughter," Star said simply. The man had bright blue eyes, and as he scanned her from head to toe, his gaze widened in recognition and then an instant later grew cold, like chips of glacial ice. His expression went from surprise to alarm to dislike in the space of a few seconds. Georgia sucked in a startled breath. What in the world had she done to warrant that look?

"Georgia, this is Cole. He's Justine's nephew. She was my best friend and my housemate for years before . . . before she passed. Cole lives here on the property in a little cabin down by the water and works next door at the Westcott Bay Shellfish Company," Star said by way of introduction.

That explained the overalls. What was even more surprising

was that he managed to look so good in them, as though he were some sort of catalog model for shellfish farm gear. She could picture him in an outdoorsy magazine somewhere, posed among the pines along a clear mountain stream, rugged and handsome and aloof in his bright orange rubber overalls. Oddly, he looked a little familiar but she couldn't place him. Where would they possibly have crossed paths? Maybe he just looked like an ad she'd seen somewhere. She straightened in her chair, summoning her poise to meet his obvious yet confounding dislike.

"Bonjour," she said coolly. She hadn't meant to greet him in French. It just slipped out. Usually, when she felt socially at a disadvantage, she would switch to French. She was fluent in the language, and in Paris it often gave her an edge in social situations. The French appreciated foreigners who could speak their language.

"Enchanté," he replied smoothly, looking warily at her. She blinked at him in surprise. His French was decent. What in the world was this French-speaking catalog model doing here on the island, harvesting shellfish?

"Your French is good," she commented in English. "Where did you learn?" Instantly, his expression shuttered and he turned to Star, ignoring Georgia's question. "I'd better get back to work. Enjoy the clams." He gave Georgia the briefest nod of acknowledgment and left abruptly out the back door.

Star cleared her throat and gave a nervous chuckle. "Cole's not one for small talk, but he's a good man." She rose and put the dripping bucket in the sink. "He was close with Justine, and he used to visit us here every summer when he was a teenager. After Justine got sick with cancer, he moved here permanently to help us. He's been a comfort to me since she passed."

"That's nice," Georgia murmured politely. Whatever this Cole person was, a source of comfort seemed unlikely. "Tell me about

Justine. You said she was your best friend?" Georgia took a sip of tea.

"Justine was like a sister to me, the truest, most loyal friend I've ever had," Star explained. She opened a pantry door next to the refrigerator and disappeared, popping out a moment later holding several potatoes and an onion. "She and I bought this place together years ago and lived here for a long time until she met Billy. He's the manager of the shellfish farm next door. After Justine and Billy got together, she moved in with him. He has a nice little bungalow on the far side of the oyster farm property." She set the vegetables on the counter and pulled a bunch of carrots from the refrigerator. "When she got sick, toward the end, she came back here to stay. Billy's job at the shellfish farm was too demanding. He couldn't give her the care she needed, so Cole and I took care of her when Billy was working. We did that all the way to the end."

"How long ago did Justine . . . pass away?" Georgia asked.

Star turned on the water at the sink and scrubbed the potatoes and carrots vigorously. "It's been almost five years now," she said. The tone of her voice was matter-of-fact, but Georgia heard the regret in it. "Some days it feels like forever and some days it feels like it was just yesterday. I guess that's the way grief is, when you lose someone you love," Star added.

"You're right," Georgia said softly. "They say time heals all wounds, but I don't think it's true. Not with everything." The words slipped out before she thought about them. Suddenly, it felt like she was sharing too much too soon. She glanced at Star uncertainly. Star shot her a quick look of understanding.

"Some wounds don't seem to heal no matter how long you give them," Star said, a peculiar expression on her face. It looked like regret. She set the scrubbed vegetables in the dish drainer and cleared her throat. "Here I am going on about the past and

I'm sure you're tired after your travels. Do you want to lie down or freshen up before dinner? I can show you to your room."

Georgia pictured clean sheets, her body sinking into them, and almost groaned. Tired was an understatement. "A nap sounds delicious," she admitted.

"Come on then." Star rinsed her hands and headed toward the living room, gesturing for Georgia to follow her.

In the living room, Georgia paused in front of a framed photograph on the wall. It showed Star standing by the front gate of the cottage beside another woman who was holding a wicker basket brimming with vegetables. Star was hugging a huge rainbow bunch of dahlias to her chest. Pollen sat at their feet looking up at them in adoration, tongue lolling.

"Is that Justine?"

Star peered over her shoulder. "Yes, that was taken right before she got really sick."

Georgia examined the two women with interest. Justine was broader in the shoulders and a few inches taller than Star, with a sleek salt-and-pepper blunt bob. Beside her in the photo, Star wore a smock and a cluster of long beaded necklaces. Her smile was sad but kind. Star. Her mother. For so many years just a memory. Now standing before her in real life. Georgia studied the photo, her mind racing. What had happened between then and now? Why had Star not contacted her before, and why had she chosen to do so now? How had she found Georgia? Why had she stayed away so long? And why had she left in the first place? Georgia had so many questions. She felt them bubbling up in the back of her throat, rolling forward on her tongue like tiny smooth stones, carried on a current of longing and confusion and anger, a muddled roil of emotions. She turned and saw Star watching her carefully.

"I know you must have a lot of questions," Star said softly, almost as though she could read Georgia's thoughts.

Surprised, Georgia nodded, clearing her throat. "I do," she admitted.

"I'll answer what I can," Star promised. "There are things you need to know, Georgia, big things that span back generations before you came into the world. But first come on upstairs and get settled. There's no rush. We have time for all of it." She headed up the stairs.

The second floor was simple—two bedrooms flanking a bathroom with a deep claw-foot tub and a small window that opened onto a panoramic view of the bay. Star ushered Georgia into the bedroom on the left and disappeared into the bathroom with a promise of clean towels. Georgia looked around. The room was painted a vibrant sunny yellow, awash with light even on this gray afternoon. A row of windows looked out over a small orchard of apple trees in full bloom. Another window gazed over the bay. A full bed with a colorful patchwork quilt faced the apple trees. There was little else in the room. A simple dresser and a small spindle-legged desk. A side table with a worn black Bible on it. It was plain and peaceful. Georgia sat down on the bed. The windows were open slightly, and a breeze slipped in, carrying with it the scent of salt and the heady fragrance of apple blossoms.

"Here are towels if you want a shower." Star set a stack of towels on the dresser, slightly threadbare but serviceable. She paused and gazed at Georgia, as though she could not quite believe she was there. "I'll come get you for dinner if you don't wake up."

Georgia nodded, already slipping off her flats and pulling back the quilt. "I'll just close my eyes for a few minutes."

"There's no hurry," Star said as she paused in the doorway.

"You're here now and that's all that matters. Rest now and breathe the island air. There's a touch of magic in it. Let it restore you." With that, Star gently closed the door.

Georgia meant to reply, but her eyes were already growing heavy. She wanted to stay awake, to squeeze all the secrets and answers from this place, but instead she slipped out of her tailored jeans, wiggled her toes in the delicious coolness of the cotton sheets, and fell headlong into a dreamless sleep. The last thought on her mind was not really a thought but a sensation, a feeling of cautious anticipation. As she drifted off to sleep, she kept picturing Star's face when she caught sight of Georgia for the first time standing in front of the cottage. The look in her eyes contained no disappointment or dismay. Star had gazed at her daughter like she held the sun, moon, and stars, Georgia thought drowsily, in surprise. Star had looked at her like she was the answer to a long-asked prayer.

9

Georgia awoke with a start at a soft knock on the door. She sat bolt upright, heart pounding, looking around her wildly in confusion. It took her a moment to remember where she was. San Juan Island. Star's cottage. It was early evening, the pale light starting to wash into shades of blue and gray. Outside the window, the apple trees looked pearly, like a bridal veil. Star spoke through the door.

"Georgia, soup's on. We'll eat in a few minutes."

"I'll be right there," Georgia mumbled, pulling the quilt farther up over her pink silk panties, trying to shake herself from a jet-lagged fog of exhaustion. She needed to get up, get downstairs, and start acting on the reasons she was here. She had questions, Star had answers. Napping the day away was not going to bring her any closer to them or to figuring out how to get her sense of taste and her spark back. She checked her phone, sending a quick text to let Phoebe know she had arrived.

Here on the island. So far so good.

Phoebe texted right back even though it was the middle of the night in Paris. She barely slept and was probably even now out at a club somewhere with colleagues from work.

How is it? Is your mom an axe murderer? Text me if you need a rescue. I want details!!!

Georgia bit back a smile.

She seems . . . great so far.

Georgia didn't mention the hostile, hunky-looking Lands' End model in the orange rubber overalls. Pulling her jeans back on, she splashed water on her face in the bathroom and took a moment to tame her unruly curls and reapply her signature red lipstick. There, she looked fairly presentable, though she still had dark circles under her eyes. She felt oddly refreshed by the nap, even after the long hours of travel. Maybe it was the sea air. Maybe there really was a touch of magic in it.

Shivering a little, she went back into the bedroom and un-zipped her suitcase, digging around for her cashmere sweater. The day was fading and the air was chilly. She found the sweater, wrapped around a heavy, bulky item. She unwrapped it care-fully, staring fondly at the big book with a turquoise cover and orange font. A vintage edition of Julia Child's *Mastering the Art of French Cooking* from the 1960s. It was the first cookbook she'd ever tried to make a recipe from. A tarte tatin that had managed to be both tough and disappointingly runny at the same time. It had been a failure, but she'd persevered nonethe-less. It was the only book she'd taken with her from the ranch when she left, and she'd brought it with her on every move since. Besides her necklace, it was her most precious possession.

"I couldn't leave you behind," she murmured, caressing the cover. It had been ripped and taped more than once, and the pages were spotted with butter stains. She flipped it open to the first page, her eyes catching on the name scrawled there: *Star Stevens*. She traced the name with the tip of her finger. For so long, her mother had been just this, a name attached to a handful of hazy memories. Now, if all went well, she was about to become so much more. Feeling a little thrill of anticipation and nerves, Georgia set the book carefully on her nightstand and went to find her mother.

As she headed downstairs, she could hear Star's voice and the deeper tones of a man coming from the kitchen at the back of the house. Curious, she tiptoed down the stairs and through the living room, pausing in the hallway and peering into the kitchen. Seated at the table facing her was the unfriendly oysterman, Cole. Georgia frowned. He was scratching Pollen's head, leaning back on the built-in white bench comfortably. He was sans orange rubber overalls, wearing a pale blue chamois shirt rolled up to the elbows with a white T-shirt underneath. His dark hair curled over the collar of his shirt. Goodness, the man was easy on the eyes. Too bad his personality seemed sour enough to curdle milk. She studied his face for a moment, trying to recall why he seemed familiar. She came up blank.

"I don't like it," she heard him say with a frown. "It doesn't sit right with me, Star."

Star stood at the stove ladling chowder into bowls. She turned and shot him a pleading look. "You promised me. I need you to trust me and keep your word about this. I'll tell her, just not yet. Please, Cole. I need more time."

Georgia leaned forward intently. Tell her what? Why did Star need more time? Cole crossed his arms over his chest and opened his mouth to reply, then caught sight of Georgia in the doorway. He shot her a startled look that melted almost instantly into an expression of wary dislike. What in the world was his problem with her? And what had he and Star been talking about? Curious, Georgia met his look with an arched brow and walked into the kitchen with her head held high. Whatever issue Cole had with her, she had no intention of letting it get in the way of her reasons for this visit.

"Georgia!" Star exclaimed warmly, shooting Cole a cryptic look. "You're just in time. You sit there." She pointed Georgia to a chair directly across from Cole. The air was warm and humid and smelled like slightly scorched soup. Star set a bowl of chowder in front of each of them. Reluctantly, Georgia slid into the chair, careful to not bump knees with Cole under the table.

"Bonjour." She raised her chin and looked him in the eye. After a second, he looked away, muttering a greeting in return. "Have we met somewhere?" Georgia asked him, tipping her head and considering him. "You look familiar somehow."

Cole gave her a cool, disinterested look. "Not that I'm aware of." He bent his head over his soup bowl, effectively putting an end to the conversation.

Star came over to the table holding her own bowl of chowder. "Now this is chowder made with clams from the bay right outside. Cole said he harvested them fresh today."

"That explains the overalls," Georgia murmured. Cole narrowed his eyes. He'd clearly heard her. She gave him a faux innocent smile.

"Now Georgia May, I forgot to ask. How long can you stay?" Star asked, spooning soup into a dish for Pollen and setting it at the foot of her chair as she sat down.

"Um," Georgia hedged, picking up her spoon. "I'm not sure. Right now I'm on a break from the restaurant where I'm the sous-chef, so my schedule isn't firm. I don't want to overstay my welcome, though." She stirred her soup and stalled having to take her first, bitter bite. She'd decided on the plane that she would not mention her loss of taste or the situation back in Paris to anyone. It made her feel vulnerable, and no good could come of it that she could see. Besides, she was hoping that with some rest, a change of scene, away from the pressure of Paris, she'd regain her ability to taste while she was on the island. If all went well, this lapse could soon be an unpleasant but brief memory and no one would have to know it had happened at all.

"Stay as long as you like," Star insisted. She turned to Cole. "Georgia's a chef in *Paris*." There was a note of pride in her voice.

"You mentioned that," Cole replied. His tone was flat. He bent over his bowl and ate silently. For someone so undeniably good-looking, he certainly knew how to dampen his own charms, Georgia thought with a frown. What in the world had she done to annoy him? Was he just antisocial? Or was he offended by her in some way? She'd never had a stranger react to her so negatively before. Puzzled and a little miffed, Georgia managed to get a few bites of the soup down, although it tasted, predictably, bitter and awful. To be fair, it smelled a little scorched and the texture was lumpy, so even if she'd been able to taste it, she had a feeling it wouldn't have been much better. She definitely hadn't gotten her culinary talents from Star.

"I was thinking I might stay a week or so, if that's okay?" Georgia asked tentatively.

She didn't want to intrude on Star's hospitality, but she didn't yet know how long she'd need to be on the island to accomplish all she hoped to, or when she would need to return to Paris for Michel to make his chef selection. She'd had no word from him since they'd parted ways at his villa. She planned to stay a week and see how it was going. She could always extend her visit if need be.

"Stay as long as you like," Star urged her. "We're happy to have you."

Cole put his spoon down with a clatter. He'd emptied his bowl in record time. "Excuse me." He stood, muttering, "I've got to check the oyster seed."

Without looking at her, he scooted out around the far edge

of the bench. "Star, thanks for the chowder." He shot Star a long, indecipherable look. She met his eyes, and her own look was almost pleading. He shook his head and sighed, but it seemed more like acquiescence than denial. Georgia looked from one to the other, trying to figure out what she was missing. Did it have to do with the exchange she had overheard when she came down the stairs? What did he not like? What was Star asking him to trust her about? Did Star have a secret? Without another word, Cole left out the back door, the screen door banging behind him.

"Did I do something to offend him?" Georgia asked, setting down her spoon. "He doesn't seem to like me very much." That was a polite way of putting it.

Star sighed, but her expression was fond as she looked in the direction of Cole's retreat. "Cole's a good man, but he's carrying a big burden," she said. "He doesn't take kindly to strangers, even beautiful chefs from Paris. Give him time. He'll come around." She scooped up a spoonful of chowder. "Pollen and I are glad you're here."

Hearing her name, Pollen thumped her tail on the floor and grinned, licking the last of the chowder from her jowls.

"Thank you for the soup," Georgia said politely. She laid down her spoon, hoping she'd eaten enough to not be rude.

"Oh, you're welcome. Makes me nervous, cooking for a trained chef." Star laughed a little bashfully.

"Home cooks are some of the best cooks in the world," Georgia replied. Star definitely did not appear to be in that category, but she didn't want to be rude.

"I never was much of a cook," Star confessed. "Justine did most of the cooking around here. When she got sick, I had to make do for the both of us, but it still doesn't come easy for me." She shook her head regretfully. "When you were little, I tried hard to learn to cook for a year or two. You and I would watch that Julia Child cooking show *The French Chef* together in the afternoons after your nap. I'd write everything down in a notebook and try so hard to make the recipes right. They never turned out the way Julia made them, though." She gave a grunt of amusement. "You showed more promise in the kitchen as a three-year-old than I ever did as a grown woman."

"Really?" Georgia leaned forward, surprised and intrigued. This was new information. She thought for a moment. "I remember . . . something about being in the kitchen with you. I remember rolling out pie crust. Is that right? You put your hands over mine on the rolling pin. I remember the pie crust stuck to the counter and we had to scrape it off with a butter knife." It was something she had not recalled before now. The heavy smoothness of the rolling pin under her fingers, Star's firm grip over her own. The memory surprised her.

Star chuckled. "Oh, that was a disaster. I was trying to make Julia's quiche Lorraine. It was my first time trying my hand at pie crust. Somehow, the crust turned out tough and the egg part was soggy. It was a mess. Your father opened up a can of cold beans and ate them for dinner instead. I never could quite master crusts, but I tried, Lord knows I tried so hard." She fell quiet, a look of regret passing across her face, then she glanced at Georgia and added, "But you always had the touch. I suspected you might have a special gift in the kitchen. That's why I gave my copy of Julia Child's cookbook to you. I had a feeling you'd make more use of it than I ever could."

Georgia stared at her mother in surprise. "You gave that cookbook to me?" She thought of the butter-stained volume sitting on the nightstand by her bed. She'd always assumed Star had just left the book like she'd left almost everything else in her life, abandoning it along with her family. After Star vanished,

Georgia had found the cookbook on the bookshelf in her room, wedged behind the white leather children's Bible she'd gotten from her Baptist Sunday school. She'd assumed Aunt Hannah had stuck it on the shelf while cleaning. Georgia had always loved that cookbook and often sneaked it into her bed to look at the fascinating and mysterious illustrations when she was supposed to be sleeping. She had never suspected that Star had meant for her to have it.

Star nodded. "I left it for you. I saved up all my egg money for a couple of months and bought it for myself for my birthday one year. I admired Julia Child so much. I thought she was the most strong, confident, independent woman I'd ever seen. She seemed like she was really in charge of her own life. She was my hero. I dreamed for years of getting to visit Paris. You and I used to play a game where we'd plan a trip to Paris. We'd look through the cookbook together and pick out what we'd eat when we got there. It gave me something to dream about. Gave us both something to look forward to. I hoped maybe Julia's cookbook would help me be more like her, but turns out some things can't be learned from a book." She looked rueful. "Did you ever try any of those recipes from the cookbook?"

"Yes." Georgia cleared her throat. She was dumbfounded by what Star had just told her. Star had not given her a culinary talent, but she had given her Julia and a dream of a life in Paris? How had she not remembered that before? It was a revelation. "Julia Child is why I ended up in Paris," she explained. "That cookbook shaped the course of my life."

Star looked surprised. "I'm glad to hear it," she said softly. "I guess I was right about something."

Georgia looked at her mother, astonished to discover this link between her past and her passion.

"Let me cook dinner for you tomorrow night," she offered

spontaneously, then bit her tongue when she remembered she couldn't taste a thing.

"Are you sure?" Star asked a little hesitantly. "I'd love to try your cooking if you're willing." She looked eager enough that Georgia didn't have the heart to backpedal.

"It would be my pleasure." Georgia smiled brightly, instantly regretting her hasty offer. It was intimidating to think of trying to cook without being able to taste anything, especially to cook an entire meal for her mother, who had never sampled anything she'd made. Too late now. She'd just prepare dishes she was very familiar with and muddle through somehow. Maybe she'd make something from Julia's cookbook. She knew many of those recipes by heart.

"Well then," Star said, looking pleased. "I'll let Cole know. We'll look forward to it."

Star stood and started to clear the table. Georgia stood as well. "Can I help with the dishes?" she offered.

"Oh no." Star was already reaching for the bowls. "It'll just take me a minute. You must be exhausted."

"Many hands make light work," Georgia insisted, gathering the water glasses. It had been years since she'd pulled a shift as a dishwasher, but it was like riding a bicycle. You never forgot how to scrub a pot. She was looking for any opportunity to learn more about her mother, and now seemed like a good time to start.

"We can do it together," Star acquiesced.

10

Side by side at the wide farmhouse sink, they fell into an easy rhythm. Star turned on the crackly radio to a folk station. The Mamas and the Papas were playing. Georgia smiled and hummed along. It had been years since she'd heard songs like these. She'd been fed a steady diet of French pop and classical music with Etienne, and the restaurant kitchen was often filled with driving European techno beats. She'd forgotten the soulful quality of American folk music. It fit the mood in the kitchen, quiet and contemplative.

Georgia washed and Star dried and put away. They watched the light fade over the bay, the water shining silver in the blue shadows of evening. Georgia thought it was one of the most beautiful things she'd ever seen. Down by the water sat a tiny log structure with a cedar shake roof. Georgia hadn't noticed it before. A light shone golden in the single window.

"That's Cole, probably reading German philosophy and wrestling with all the world's problems," Star commented with a smile.

"That's where he lives?" Georgia grabbed the dirty soup pot and squirted dish soap into it. The cabin looked hardly larger than a garden shed.

"Yes, for about five years now. I think he likes the simplicity," Star said, drying a water glass with a thin cotton dish towel. "He needed a place to land after things went pear-shaped for him. It was about the same time Justine found out she was sick, and it worked out well to have him here." She paused, looking out the window. "Justine passed pretty quickly. The liver cancer was in its last stages when they caught it. He was a great help to us in those final months, and ever since she passed, he's taken good care of me. This place has been my home for a long time, and I think it feels like home to him too." She carried the water glasses to the cupboard and put them away.

Home. The word held such a complicated mixture of emotions for Georgia.

"It's beautiful here. I've never seen anything like this island," Georgia commented. She vigorously scrubbed the scorched bits of clam chowder from the bottom of the pot with steel wool. "It's a world away from Texas or Paris." They were her only points of reference.

"It's a little slice of paradise, or as near as you can get on earth anyway," Star agreed.

Georgia rinsed the pot and handed it dripping to Star. "It feels like it," she said.

"It's more than that, though," Star continued. "This island is a safe spot for a lot of people. It's been a refuge for me." Star dried the pot, looking thoughtful. "Folks say there's a special kind of magic here, that it's in the land and the water. It has a healing energy, the kind of place that can soothe every wound and show you your true heart. This island can help lead people home."

Georgia listened but said nothing. Dishes done, she pulled the plug on the sink of soap suds and watched the gray water funnel down the drain. There was something about Star's description that made her feel her wistful, and she couldn't put her finger on why. Was it her current circumstances or something deeper than that, a longing she'd been living with like an ache in the center of her chest for years, almost as long as she could remember, a longing to be known, to feel like she belonged?

"Where's home for you?" Star asked, her pale gray-green eyes on Georgia, hesitant and curious. "Is it still Texas or do you feel like Paris is home now?"

"Neither," Georgia replied honestly. "I don't think I've ever truly felt at home anywhere." She scrubbed down the sides of the sink vigorously. The truth was that Texas and Paris had both in their own way been mostly home or almost home, familiar, but they had never given her a sense of true belonging. She'd stopped hoping for that years ago, deciding that some people must never quite belong anywhere. She had settled for familiarity, tried to be content with it, but sometimes she still found it cold comfort. She hadn't felt at home in almost thirty years. Not since the day she'd watched Star pull away in her Eldorado, leaving her in a cloud of red dust on that broiling August afternoon. Georgia remembered her tears making tracks in the grit coating her cheeks, running down to smudge the collar of her favorite dress, the one with rainbows on it and rickrack straps, the one Star had made just for her. The memory still stung, sharp as white vinegar on a cut.

If she were honest with herself, the last place that had felt like home was nestled in Star's arms, enveloped in the aroma that was so distinctly her mother, something she later pegged as a combination of herbs—anise, mint, and thyme—and cannabis. She could smell it now, standing so close to Star, and it made her feel off-kilter and nostalgic. Without thought, she leaned a little closer to Star, toward that remembered feeling of safety and belonging.

"I hope you know you always have a home here, Georgia," Star said gently, as though she could read her daughter's thoughts.

Georgia cleared her throat, feeling overwhelmed all of a sudden, unsure what to say. She simply nodded, then wrung out the dish cloth and hung it on the dish drainer. She stepped back, putting a little distance between her and her mother. She couldn't find any other words. She was overcome by what Star had told her about the cookbook, by the events of the last few days, by the unexpected turn her life had taken in the past forty-eight hours. Questions and conflicting emotions, revelations and the immediacy of her mother's presence. Her heart felt too full, like a cloud swollen with too much rain.

"I think I'll head upstairs and unpack," she managed to say at last. "It's been a long day."

"Of course." Star nodded, drying the last glass. "Sleep as late as you want. When you wake up, come find me in the garden."

Alone in her mother's old bedroom, in the warm glow of the bedside table lamp, Georgia sat on the edge of the bed and gently held the vintage cookbook in her lap. So Star had not simply left this behind. She had left it *for* Georgia. She had seen something special in Georgia and had left her this as a gift. Could she have known what a profound impact this book, Julia Child, and Paris would have on her daughter's life?

Georgia closed her eyes and saw again her little five-year-old self standing alone in that driveway watching the puff of dust that was her mother's car grow smaller and smaller on the horizon. Then she'd felt a firm grip on her shoulder. Aunt Hannah had turned her toward the house and away from that last glimpse of her mother.

"Come on, Georgia. Dry those tears," Aunt Hannah had told her, scrubbing her tearstained face with a cool washcloth in the bathroom downstairs. "You're a Jackson and that's all that matters now."

Then she'd stripped off Georgia's soiled dress and replaced it with a fresh one. Georgia had never seen her favorite dress with the rainbows again. Like everything else about her mother, it had simply vanished. No one spoke Star's name. From that day on, it was as though the family had erased Star from their world entirely. Aunt Hannah disapproved of Star, that much was clear. Every time Georgia asked about her mother, Aunt Hannah's mouth would pinch closed as though tasting something sour. "Never mind your mama," she'd say. "You're all Jackson now. Just remember that."

As Georgia got older, she had the impression that her aunt was keeping a close eye on her, vigilant for anything that might make her niece follow in her mother's footsteps and stray. Georgia's fascination with cooking and her dream of being a chef were mystifying to both her father and aunt. They regarded the entire thing with bewilderment and tacit disapproval. Georgia had spent all these years thinking that no one in her family had seen or encouraged her culinary gift. She had always felt so alone in her dreams and goals, but now she knew the truth. Star had introduced her to Julia and to Paris. Georgia's dream had started before she even remembered it. Star had given that to her.

Carefully, she traced the orange letters on the torn turquoise cover. What did it mean that her goal, her life's ambition, had been born of a dream she'd once shared with her mother? Suddenly, she was not the odd one out, the one always pulling against the weight of her family's expectations and disappointment. Once, someone had dreamed the same dream together with her. Someone had seen her talent, glimpsed who she could become, and encouraged it. She hugged the cookbook to her chest and lay back on the bed, tears springing to her eyes. For the first time in a very long time, she didn't feel alone.

11

Georgia awoke late the next morning, groggy and a little disoriented from the nine-hour time change. She yawned and glanced at the cookbook sitting on the nightstand. After the revelations of the day before, she was now even more curious about Star and the questions swirling around her disappearance and reappearance. But this morning those questions would have to wait. She had a dinner to prepare for, and she was determined to make it the best meal Cole and Star had ever tasted. She dressed hastily, slipping into her trusty tailored white button-down shirt and a pair of navy pants and pulling her hair back with a headband, à la Audrey Hepburn. Eyeing herself in the mirror, she sent up a quick request to Julia, patron saint of delicious meals.

"Help me make this fabulous today, Julia. I want to make a meal they'll remember forever."

She pictured Julia standing in her kitchen, attempting to flip a potato pancake in a large frying pan. She was wearing her signature blouse and string of pearls and concentrating hard. "When you flip anything, you must just have courage and simply go for it," Julia said and executed the flip. She bungled it, and gloppy mashed potato plopped all over her electric stovetop. "Oh, that really didn't go well at all." Julia looked puzzled.

Georgia frowned. That was definitely not what she was hoping for with this dinner. She wanted it to be flawless. She slicked on her signature red lipstick. "You can do this," she told herself, trying to bolster her courage, but she still felt a flutter of apprehension. Michel thought she had lost her spark, and she certainly had lost her sense of taste. She wanted to make a meal tonight that would prove Michel wrong. She'd try her hardest to make this the sparkiest meal she possibly could, even if she couldn't taste a crumb.

Julia scooped potato back into her pan, patted it flat, and then said brightly, "Well, if things don't go quite the way you'd like them to, it doesn't make much of a difference, really, because you can almost always fix whatever went wrong."

"Nothing is going to go wrong," Georgia said firmly. "Now first I'm going to need a lot of butter."

The kitchen was empty when Georgia went downstairs. The clock over the stove read almost eleven in the morning. Out the kitchen window, Georgia could see Star and Pollen behind the house in the middle of what looked like several large raised garden beds. Star was kneeling in the dirt amid a jungle of green vines while Pollen chased her own tail in a circle. Cole was thankfully nowhere in sight.

"Good morning," The screen door slammed behind her as Georgia headed toward Star. She patted a wiggling Pollen, who ran over and licked her hand, whining with joy. The grass was still wet with dew, although the sun was shining, and the air was crisp with the scent of salt water and freshly turned earth. She shivered, wishing she'd worn her blazer or a sweater.

"Morning, Georgia May." Star struggled up from her kneeling position, a dirt-caked trowel in her hand. "How'd you sleep?"

"Like a rock," Georgia said. It was true. She hadn't slept that well in longer than she could remember. Once she'd finally fallen asleep after three in the morning, it had been deep and dreamless.

"Good." Star dropped the trowel and removed a pair of flowered gardening gloves, slapping the dirt from them on her knee.

"Your garden looks amazing," Georgia observed, surveying the two large raised garden beds that sat a few yards away from the back door. It was only April and already they were a riot of green—cucumber vines curling in every direction with little dark green cucumbers peeking out beneath them; tidy rows of beans; tissue paper–translucent patches of lettuces; and tomato vines in cages, with small, ripening red globes hanging in profusion. Georgia studied the vegetables, puzzled. The produce looked like it was almost ready to harvest, but it was just the middle of April, far too early. What sort of climate allowed for ripe tomatoes already? Was the island some sort of gardener's utopia?

Star put her hands on her hips and surveyed the garden beds. "These are a mess. I usually sell my vegetables and honey at that stand out front, and I need to get things in shape now that the produce is starting to ripen. Truth be told, this whole property and house need a refresh. I've let some things go recently. It's high time I got everything in order."

"I'm happy to help while I'm here," Georgia offered. She squinted. Was that a fig tree with little purple figs on it growing in a pot near the back door? Those shouldn't be ready until late summer, surely?

Star swiped a curl away from her cheek, tucking it back into her low ponytail. "You probably don't remember this, but we used to garden together when you were young," she said. "You loved to harvest things. Weeding, not so much. You loved to dig carrots, if I remember right. Your eyes would light up like you'd found a treasure every time you pulled one from the ground." She chuckled at the memory.

"I remember the carrots," Georgia said. It had been years since she'd gardened, but she'd spent a lot of hours pulling weeds for Aunt Hannah as a kid. Star was right. She'd never warmed to weeding, but harvesting vegetables she always enjoyed. "I remember you showing me how to plant potatoes with the eyes facing up." She hadn't thought of that in years. Another piece of her history slipped into place. Little by little, she was filling in the blank spots. "I was wondering if I could borrow a car this morning?" she asked, changing the subject. "I was hoping to go to the store in Friday Harbor. I need to get some ingredients for tonight."

"Sure." Star nodded, wiping her brow with the sleeve of her shirt, leaving a smear of dirt across her forehead. "I've only got one client today, but I can go over there when you get back. I run a little business on the island planting and taking care of people's flower and vegetable gardens," she explained. "It's not the high season yet, though, so I just have a couple of places I visit every week. I can give you directions to the grocery store; it's pretty simple. Or if you'd rather wait, I can ask Cole to take you after lunch while I'm gone?" She looked questioningly at Georgia.

"Oh no, I can find my way. No need to bother him," Georgia demurred quickly. Enduring a car ride to town with a hot, glowering oyster farmer who seemed inexplicably to loathe her was definitely not on her agenda for the day.

"Can I get you some breakfast?" Star asked.

"I'm fine," Georgia hastened to assure her. "I had a protein bar." She'd stocked up on protein bars at the Dulles airport. Without being able to taste anything, she had little appetite but knew she needed to consume at least a modest quantity of calories just to keep up her energy. Protein bars, which the French chef in her shuddered to even consider food, were dense in nutrients. She could choke down a few bitter bites and call it a meal.

"Okay, if you're sure." Star looked doubtful at the mention of protein bars but didn't press the matter, just gave Georgia directions and tossed her the keys to her old green Subaru Forester.

Georgia drove to the grocery store with the windows down, the air smelling of sweet green grass and evergreen trees. The island was sparsely populated, mostly just rolling fields and dense patches of evergreen forest with the occasional house in the distance. She passed only a few other cars, and the motorists all waved. She waved back, feeling her spirits lift. She hadn't driven in years. In Paris, she took the Metro and didn't even own a car. But there was a forgotten pleasure in driving with the wind blowing through her curls, the Grateful Dead's greatest hits on the old CD player. She tried to switch to a radio station or stop the CD, but the CD player seemed jammed and the radio didn't work. She shrugged and let the music play. The sense of freedom was intoxicating, just her and the steering wheel and Jerry Garcia's voice and the gray ribbon of road rolling over the gentle hills. She couldn't remember the last time she'd felt so relaxed and free. She laughed out loud, surprising herself. She was even starting to look forward to the meal tonight.

In Friday Harbor, she found Kings Market easily enough and was pleased by the good selection of quality ingredients in the pint-size grocery store. She trailed her fingers over the French cheeses before choosing a Camembert. She had to make a couple of substitutions in ingredients for what she was going to make tonight. No fennel, but she found a surprisingly decent and affordable pinot noir from Burgundy and bought two bottles, one to cook with and one to drink with dinner. She didn't know how adventurous Cole and Star were with food, so she decided to stick with iconic French dishes, nothing too avant-

garde. She'd leave the tête de veau (boiled cow's head) for another day. The grocery total at the cash register was shockingly
expensive, but she swallowed hard and paid. It was worth it.
This was both a thank-you and a chance to prove herself. Neither of those came cheap.

12

Clad in a worn white cotton apron, Georgia was halfway through dinner prep by late afternoon. She was alone in the kitchen. Star was out making her visit to her client, and Georgia was enjoying the solitude. She had scrounged up enough pots and pans and kitchen instruments to make the dinner menu work and thankfully had her own knife kit with her to use. A chef never cooked without her own knives if she could help it. Now she was finally relaxing into familiar rhythms—chopping vegetables, cutting up a whole chicken and putting it to soak in a wine marinade. She had Édith Piaf warbling on her phone, a good pinot noir, and all the ingredients she needed. She was making magic in the kitchen.

Belting out the lyrics to the iconic "La Vie en rose" along with Edith and feeling a little homesick for Paris, Georgia cooked the bacon for the coq au vin in a cast-iron skillet until it sizzled brown and crispy. Faintly, she heard the kitchen door slam. She glanced up, expecting Star who had said she'd be home at about four, but instead, Cole stood in the doorway.

"That smells good," he commented. He sounded almost pleasant. He was wearing the ridiculous orange rubber overalls again. How in the world did the man manage to still look good wearing international orange—colored rubber overalls that came up TO HIS CHEST? His very toned, muscular chest. Under the overalls, he was wearing a tight waffle weave shirt that showed off his physique. She was determined not to be intimidated by his attitude or his sex appeal. She'd just been dating Paris's sexiest chef, and look where that landed her.

Georgia shot Cole an arch look and said dismissively, "Of course it smells good. It's bacon." She scooped the bacon from the skillet and set it aside to cool, then started braising the chicken segments in the bacon grease.

She hoped he'd leave, but instead he walked around her, reached for a glass and filled it at the tap, then drank deeply. She ignored him, sautéing carrots and onion in the Dutch oven while the chicken cooked in the skillet. She added garlic to the vegetables and inhaled the aroma deeply. It was one of her favorite scents. Too bad this delectable meal was going to taste horrible to her. But if it tasted half as good as it smelled, it would be a success. She had a good feeling about it so far.

Edith was trilling in the background, accompanied by an accordion. Cole raised an eyebrow, and Georgia gave him the side-eye. "Let me guess, you don't like French cabaret singers?"

"I didn't say that." He leaned against the sink, glass in hand, and looked amused. "It's a nice change from the Grateful Dead or those '60s social activist hippie feminist folk singers Star likes. I mean, don't get me wrong, I'm all for protests and social activism, but there are just so many versions of 'Blowin' in the Wind' with a tambourine accompaniment that a man can reasonably handle." The corner of his mouth twitched up slightly.

Georgia grinned in spite of herself and poured some wine marinade over the vegetables. "Oh, and what would you prefer instead? Some nice Johnny Cash, maybe? Does hearing 'Folsom Prison Blues' bring back a wave of nostalgia for you? Remembering the good times you had in the pokey?" Her tone was gently ribbing.

Cole glanced at her, surprised, and then laughed. He had a deep laugh, a little rusty, as though he didn't use it often. If his laugh were a liquor, it would be rye whiskey, she thought, dark and warm and ragged with a little bite at the end. The thought came out of nowhere, and she brushed it away.

"Leonard Cohen, actually," he said. "I like to listen to him while I'm whittling my shiv." He glanced at her from under his brows, his face deadpan, but there was a twinkle in his eye.

Georgia snorted in amusement. He was funny and self-deprecating. She hadn't expected that. She thought he'd leave, but he lingered, watching her. She found his gaze slightly unsettling. She nestled the chicken breasts and thighs in among the vegetables and tried to ignore the way his scrutiny made her pulse beat a little faster. She liked to be in control of her kitchen, not skittery under the gaze of a man dressed like a traffic cone.

"What made you want to become a chef?" he asked curiously.

Georgia considered her answer for a moment. "It was Julia Child," she replied. "I was looking for a way out of my family's ranch, and I found it through cooking. Julia inspired me. I adored her and wanted to be just like her. I used to watch her TV show every afternoon while I was supposed to be doing my homework." Georgia said it lightly, but there was a note of wistfulness in her voice. She could picture young Georgia in her jeans and T-shirt, sitting cross-legged in front of the old television in the front room every afternoon after school, eating graham crackers and cold milk and soaking up every word Julia uttered. She'd finish her homework in record time, then sit close to the screen with the volume turned down low so she didn't draw the notice of Aunt Hannah, who would switch off the TV and make her go out to do chores if she happened to walk into the room. Aunt Hannah disapproved both of watching TV during daylight hours and of Julia Child.

Georgia chopped a few sprigs of thyme, sprinkling them over the chicken and vegetables and covering the Dutch oven with the heavy lid. "Julia showed me a different life," she said. "She opened the world for me, beyond the hardscrabble existence on a Texas cattle ranch, beyond the borders of my little dusty town. Julia showed me another way to see the world, full of possibility. She showed me that life could be enjoyed, not just endured."

She glanced up. Cole was watching her silently. He took another sip of water. "All that from a cooking show?" His tone was mild, not mocking. He sounded like he genuinely wanted to know. Georgia nodded.

"I don't know how much you know, but Star left us when I was five," she said, surprising herself as she spoke. She never talked about Star. She'd been with Etienne for almost two years before she'd told him about her mother's abandonment. It was still a sensitive subject, all these years later, but somehow she felt comfortable opening up to Cole about it. Maybe because they were here, with Star just on the other side of the yard. He was part of it now too. She tossed the chopped mushrooms into the skillet with the bacon grease and turned up the heat. "After she left, our house was . . . sad. The ranch was prosperous enough, but there wasn't a lot of joy or laughter there. It was as though Star took all the happiness with her when she went. My dad worked long hours running the ranch. My aunt Hannah, my dad's sister, helped raise me. I know she loved me, in her own way, but she wasn't a particularly nurturing person."

She pictured her aunt—the tall, spare figure standing ramrod straight, her character forged of equal parts duty and determination. Georgia knew her aunt had cared for her and worked hard to provide a safe, stable home for her. There were always morally sound library books in a bin by the sofa and simple, nutritious meals in her lunch box. She had a warm bath every night, and her hair was braided every morning. On Saturdays, they'd do a jigsaw puzzle together. Her aunt had done the best she could to raise a child she could not seem to understand. Yet Georgia had been lonely, so very lonely, from the age of five onward.

"My family can't comprehend why I'm a chef," Georgia said, stirring the mushrooms. "They couldn't imagine why I'd want to go off to Paris to run my own restaurant. Julia was my inspiration. She gave me purpose, something to strive for. She showed me a different life." She paused, feeling herself flush. "I know that must seem so pathetic."

Cole cleared his throat. "Not pathetic. Understandable."

Georgia glanced up, surprised. "When I was ten, I swore I would do what Julia had done, go to Paris, make a name for myself in the world of cooking. I wanted to follow in Julia's footsteps. When I blew out the candles on Julia's Queen of Sheba Chocolate Cake that I'd made for my birthday, I promised I'd have my own kitchen in a Paris restaurant one day."

"And have you kept your promise?" Cole asked, looking interested.

Georgia hesitated. "Almost," she said at last. "We'll see." She gave a small Gallic shrug.

Cole drained his glass and eyed her thoughtfully. "It's rare to know from such a young age what you want out of life."

"Yeah, well the alternative wasn't great," Georgia muttered. "Roping and castrating cattle or driving a combine. It wasn't much of a choice for me. I picked what I wanted to do with my life, and I've spent every waking minute since that point trying to reach that goal." She gave the mushrooms a stir. She was surprised by how long Cole was lingering. Maybe she'd misjudged him and Star had been right. Maybe he just took time to warm up to people. Maybe he was warming. "What about you?" she asked. "What did you want to be as a kid?"

Cole's mouth curled up at the corner, a half smile, half grimace. "A superhero. An earth-saving, recycling, environmentally friendly superhero," he admitted. "My favorite show as a kid was *Captain Planet*, and I even made myself a Captain Planet costume. I found a green wig at a Halloween costume shop and wore a pair of red underpants over my sweatpants. I was convinced I was going to save the world from litter and pollution. I was a really cool kid." His tone was gently ironic.

Georgia laughed. "That's adorable," she said. "So did you do it? Save the world?"

Cole winced. Something flickered in his eyes. She'd hit a nerve. "No," he said shortly. "I'm just raising oysters." He set his glass down and gave her a brief nod. "I'd better get back to work." Apparently, the conversation was over.

Georgia watched him go with a touch of consternation. For a brief few seconds, she could have sworn they'd shared a moment, that he was enjoying her company. But then he'd shut down again. What in the world was going on with that man? Was he in hiding? In the witness protection program? Cooking up meth down in that little cabin?

With a shrug, Georgia hacked off a large piece of good-quality butter and sprinkled it with flour, starting to make the beurre manié. She had no idea what to make of Cole, the meltingly handsome yet strangely mercurial oysterman, but at least she could still make butter and wine, chicken and vegetables into a dinner he'd hopefully be tasting in his dreams. She'd started the day with doubts about her ability to make this dinner, but now she was feeling confident once more. She'd hit her stride, she could feel it. She could do this; she could still make magic in the kitchen even without her sense of taste.

"See, Michel," she said aloud, kneading the butter and flour together by hand. "I'm going to make sure this meal is the sparkiest thing they've tasted in their lives." She took a bitter, fortifying swig of pinot noir straight from the bottle and concentrated on the task.

"If you use enough butter, anything is delicious," Georgia heard Julia Child cheerfully chortle in her ear.

13

"Georgia, that was amazing." Star sat back in her chair under the apple trees and wiped her mouth with a cloth napkin. "Wasn't it, Cole?"

Cole muttered something unintelligible and sopped up the last of the coq au vin with a piece of buttered baguette, staring broodingly off toward the bay. The meal had gone beautifully despite the fact that Cole seemed to have switched back to being cold and stony. Apparently, their shared moment in the kitchen earlier had been an aberration. Maybe he'd temporarily forgotten to be grouchy for those few minutes earlier, a lapse in judgment he seemed to be making up for now.

"I'm so glad you enjoyed it." Georgia beamed, whisking away the serving platters from the table. Despite Cole's grumpiness, everything was going according to plan, and she could not be more pleased. She'd served dinner outside under the apple trees, assembling a mismatched selection of old silver, china, and glassware she'd scrounged from the cabinets. The table was lovely, surrounded by a bower of white, fragrant apple blossoms and facing out to the tranquil bay. Georgia had propped her iPhone in the fork of a nearby apple tree, and Nina Simone was crooning "I Want a Little Sugar in My Bowl" in her honey rich voice. Georgia could not have asked for better ambience. And the food . . . from the way those two had tucked in, it seemed to have been a huge hit. She was feeling very satisfied indeed, buoyed by the knowledge that even if she could not taste, apparently, she could still cook. Maybe Michel was wrong and she hadn't lost her spark after all. The thought brought sweet relief.

"I've never had green beans like that before," Star said, marveling over the haricots verts. "And that chicken stew. What was it called. Cock a what?"

"Coq au vin," Georgia replied with a smile. She gathered their dinner plates and cutlery and balanced them precariously on top of the serving platters. "Don't go anywhere," she said over her shoulder, steadying the wobbling dishes. "Dessert is coming."

Inside the house, she quickly unloaded the dishes onto the counter and pulled the little glass canning jars of Mousse au Citron out of the refrigerator. It was an easy recipe, but so bright and luxurious tasting with fresh squeezed lemons and whipped cream. It was one of her favorite dessert recipes and always a crowd-pleaser. Humming along with Nina Simone, she carried the mousse outside, the grass cool and damp against her ankles, the breeze fresh off the bay.

"Here you go." Georgia set jars of mousse in front of Cole and Star, laying a tiny silver spoon over the lip of each one. "Mousse au Citron, one of my favorites." She sat down at the end of the table and took a sip of water. Thankfully, it tasted of nothing. She watched contentedly as Star spooned up a dollop of mousse and took the first bite. An instant later, Star's eyes widened and she made a horrible gagging sound.

Georgia gasped in dismay. "Are you okay? What's wrong?"

Star shook her head, then grabbed her water glass and gargled, spitting the mouthful of soggy mousse onto the grass. Cole gingerly tasted a spoonful of the mousse and promptly spit it out too. "Tastes like pure salt," he said in a strangled voice. He took a swig of water and swished it around in his mouth, looking pained.

"What?" Georgia watched them in horror. "No!" She ran through the simple recipe in her head. It should all be perfect.

"I'm afraid so. Here." Star looked sympathetic and held out her glass jar and spoon. Georgia hesitated but didn't take the mousse. It would do her no good to try to taste it.

"I'm so sorry," she said, mortified. "I don't know what happened." It had been a glorious dinner, seemingly perfect. And now this. She felt crushed. Unexpectedly, tears prickled behind her eyelids. She glanced up to find Star watching her with a look of compassion. Georgia blinked the tears back fiercely. She was tough. She'd made kitchen errors before. Salty mousse was not a reason to cry. But she felt humiliated regardless. This was about far more than salty mousse. This was the loss of her dream. She had so wanted to prove to herself she could still cook well regardless of her ability to taste. Apparently, that was simply not true. Georgia looked at the little jars of inedible mousse with a sinking heart. Michel was right. She had lost her spark.

"It's okay, Georgia. The rest of that dinner was perfect. It was just a little hiccup at the end," Star told her comfortingly.

"I ran out of sugar in the kitchen sugar bowl and found a big paper bag of what I thought was sugar in the pantry," Georgia explained, cheeks burning with humiliation. "It must have been salt."

Star nodded. "I buy everything in bulk, and sometimes I'm not good about labeling the bags."

"You didn't think to taste it before you cooked with it?" Cole asked skeptically, pushing the jar of mousse away from his place at the table in distaste.

Frustrated, Georgia shook her head. "It wouldn't have done any good. I can't taste anything," she said without thinking.

"What?" Cole and Star stared at her in mutual surprise.

Georgia glanced away and didn't answer, wishing she could slip those words back into her mouth. She gazed across the wide sweep of grass, out over the rippling silver water of Westcott Bay. She felt utterly deflated. How in the world could she even think about competing to win Michel's approval, much less running her own restaurant, if she couldn't even tell that her mousse was mostly made of salt? She blinked hard.

"What do you mean you can't taste anything?" Cole asked again, his gaze assessing.

"Nothing." Georgia waved away the question. "I made a mistake. A really stupid mistake."

"Come on, Georgia May," Star coaxed. "Everyone makes mistakes. It's not the end of the world."

Georgia shook her head. "This might be the end of mine, actually," she said bluntly.

A long, silent moment stretched across the table. Star and Cole exchanged a quizzical glance.

"Georgia," Star said slowly. "What's going on?"

Georgia looked from one to the other and hesitated. She had two choices. She could try to convince them all was well and bluff her way through this visit, or she could swallow her pride and come clean. She frowned, considering. She glanced at Cole, who was watching her skeptically, one eyebrow raised. It seemed a little late to pretend all was well. Clearly, something was amiss. She was going to have to tell them the truth.

"A few days ago, I found out my boyfriend of two years, a brilliant chef who also happened to be my boss, was cheating on me with our new pastry chef," she admitted. "In the heat of the moment, I did something very stupid in retaliation and afterwards I quit my job."

Star winced and Cole muttered, "Ouch."

"It gets worse," Georgia told them. "The next morning, I woke up and I'd lost my sense of taste."

Star leaned forward in her chair, perplexed. "You couldn't taste anything?" she asked.

"Everything tastes bitter," Georgia amended. "No matter what it is. It all tastes the same to me, like burnt coffee grounds." She made a futile gesture. "My mentor, Michel Laurent, is opening a new restaurant in Paris, and up until a few days ago I was his top choice for chef. Running the kitchen at La Lumière Dorée would be my ultimate dream come true, but after what happened with Etienne, he's reconsidering."

"Oh, Georgia." Star looked sympathetic.

Georgia sat back and scrubbed her hands through her curls, vexed. "I moved to Paris when I was twenty-one, and I've spent years working my way up the ladder. It's been brutal, absolutely brutal. To be a woman and an American, two strikes against me. I've had to work harder, longer, and more than anyone else around me. And I'm so close. After all these years, I'm so, so close to getting what I've worked so hard for, but I can't run a restaurant if I can't taste the food I cook. Tonight was an experiment, to see if I can still cook well even if I can't taste, which clearly I have failed to prove." She sniffed, inhaling the crisp evening air, apple blossoms, and the brine of the bay, then exhaled disappointment. Tonight's failure was humiliating. Airing her dirty laundry like this felt even more vulnerable. "Michel advised me to get away for a while, to let everything settle down," she explained. "So when I got your invitation to come here, it seemed like the perfect opportunity to get out of Paris. I was hoping I could regain my sense of taste somewhere peaceful and beautiful, somewhere without the pressure of working in a kitchen." She glanced at Star. "That's not the only reason I accepted your invitation, though. I wanted to come meet you," she assured her mother. "I wanted to see you again." She paused, waiting for Star's reaction.

The table was silent for a moment, then Star took a big breath. "Well," she said, "that explains a lot. But it doesn't change anything, not from my end. I wasn't sure you'd want to have anything to do with me," she admitted. "When I wrote, I wasn't even sure you'd answer. You being here is a gift to me, even if you had other reasons to come." She studied Georgia and frowned. "You can stay as long as you need to, and I'll help in any way I can. Do you have any idea how to get your sense of taste back?"

"I have no idea," Georgia admitted. "I've seen specialists. They've run tests. No one has any idea what is wrong or how to fix it." She paused, then swallowed her pride. "If you have any bright ideas, I'm open to trying anything."

Silently, Cole reached over and poured a generous glass of pinot noir, then slid it over to her. Surprised, she took it gratefully and sipped. Bitter, but she liked how it warmed the center of her chest. Georgia set down her wineglass and looked from Star to Cole and back. They both watched her. Star had a thoughtful expression on her face, like she was mulling something over. Cole sat back with his arms crossed, his expression remote. She couldn't tell what he was thinking. Pollen came and licked Georgia's hand under the table. She petted the dog's soft, floppy golden ears and took another gulp of wine.

"I'm going to think on this," Star said slowly. "I have some ideas, but I want to make sure you're ready."

Georgia raised her eyebrows. Ready for what? That sounded intriguing.

Star reached across the table and took Georgia's hand in her strong, sinewy fingers. "Georgia May, I'm sorry it's been so hard for you. I wish I could wave a magic wand and make it all turn out okay, but I can't. I hope your time here on the island will be just what you need. Remember, the island has its own sort of magic. It's a place that can make you whole."

"I hope you're right," Georgia said. She felt humbled by Star's generosity. The dinner had not gone according to plan. She had meant to impress them, not spill her entire sad, sordid story. It was embarrassing to admit failure, and yet she felt strangely hopeful somehow. Maybe here on the island, with Star's help, she could still figure out how to save her dream.

14

Georgia awoke to a text from Michel. The night before, she'd sent him a photo of the dinner she had made for Star and Cole, laid out under the apple trees in bloom. It was a gorgeous shot.

I took your advice. I'm trying to find my spark again, she captioned it, sending the text before falling asleep. No need to mention the salty dessert debacle. She wanted Michel to know that she was doing the work she needed to. She wanted to stay fresh in his mind. The next morning, his reply was waiting.

Excellent. Keep up the good work. The competition for head chef will be held in one month. I'm considering you and two other chefs. I'll send details as I have them. Au revoir, Georgie.

Still in bed in her pajamas, Georgia stared at his text with a mixture of relief and panic. Four weeks. That gave her a little breathing room, but the time would go quickly. She had work to do. She set down the phone and considered her next move. She needed to get started. Now she knew there were two other chefs in the running, two chefs who were presumably super talented AND still had their sense of taste. She didn't have any time to waste. From here on out, there was a ticking clock hovering over her island visit. Four weeks. She could feel it starting the countdown now; from this moment on every minute mattered.

She glanced out the window at blue sky and pale sunshine. Her phone said it was almost ten a.m. She hopped out of bed and headed for her suitcase. She would get ready for the day and then call Phoebe. She needed her friend's perspective.

Fifteen minutes later, clad in skinny jeans, a white fitted T-shirt, and a navy-blue blazer with leather ballet flats, Georgia stood on the edge of Star's property, looking out over the bay. Phoebe answered on the first ring. "Georgia, babe, hiii!"

Georgia leaned over the picket fence bordering Star's yard.

"Hi, Phoebs." Georgia exhaled with relief at the familiar sound of her friend's voice. "Where are you?"

"I'm down in Saint-Tropez with this group of Serbian models who are all aspiring swimsuit designers," Phoebe told her in a loud stage whisper. "We're doing an evening shoot. They've rented us this enormous villa and there's a swimming pool and buckets of vodka. It's completely mad and loads of fun."

"Sounds wild." Georgia grinned.

"We're going to film the models in their own swimwear designs doing flaming vodka shots in the pool, balancing on giant inflatable ice cubes," Phoebe confided.

"How could anything could go wrong with that scenario?" Georgia deadpanned, gazing out at the water. The day was cool but clear, and a light breeze was ruffling the surface of the bay. Georgia spotted Star down by the beehives wearing some sort of baggy white outfit that looked a bit like a hazmat suit. Pollen was prancing around her heels, barking. At that moment, France and Phoebe's glamourous world of high fashion felt a million miles away.

"I've only got a minute. Tell me more about this Cole," Phoebe demanded. "He sounds dreamy."

Georgia and Phoebe had been texting off and on since Georgia's arrival. Last night, after the salty mousse incident, she'd casually mentioned Cole in a text. Instantly, Phoebe had responded with a dozen heart-eyes emojis and the words "CALL ME!"

"I only texted you his name last night," Georgia protested. "How could you possibly get that he's dreamy from just his name?"

"If he weren't dreamy, you wouldn't have mentioned him," Phoebe said sensibly.

"That's not true," Georgia argued, but then admitted, "Okay, he is ridiculously good-looking . . . but he's weirdly hostile. He really doesn't like me and I have no idea why." Georgia wrinkled her nose. "He works on the oyster farm next door and wears these ridiculous orange rubber overalls." She didn't add that he somehow made those rubber overalls look good.

"Who could not like you?" Phoebe protested. "You're a strong, independent, gorgeous woman . . . from PARIS. And a natural redhead! What's not to like?" She sounded genuinely baffled.

"Maybe he doesn't like redheads?" Georgia hypothesized. "Maybe a redhead broke his heart? I have no idea. He's acted like he loathes me from the moment he laid eyes on me. I don't like him either. The dislike is mutual."

"Ooh, maybe he's secretly in love with you," Phoebe exclaimed, sounding inordinately excited by the prospect. "Maybe you'll fall in love with each other. Ooh, it's exactly what you need. An island romance with a mysterious, sexy oysterman." She gave a high-pitched giggle. "After all, orange rubber overalls are *so* sexy."

Georgia made a *pffft* sound of dismissal. "You're dreaming. I just got my heart ripped out by Etienne, remember? I'm not looking for love anytime soon." Georgia closed her eyes at the momentary pang his name brought.

"Oh, Etienne, he was all wrong for you and you know it,"

Phoebe scoffed. "Your pride is more hurt than your heart. You knew what he was."

For a moment, Georgia was taken aback, but she had to admit Phoebe was right. She had resisted Etienne for so long, for years, actually, so drawn to him, so tempted, but knowing deep down that he was careless with women's hearts, a man to be admired, desired even, but not trusted. But he'd won her over against her better judgment, and she'd let herself fall for him in the end. She'd given in to the temptation, but she'd been right all along. It still hurt, though. Phoebe was wrong about that. Her pride was hurt, but so was her heart. Even though she'd known the danger, she'd given a little piece of her heart to Etienne, and now that piece was smashed.

She thought of Cole, and for a brief moment, she let herself wonder about him. Was he harboring some secret hurt? Or was he just a prickly hermit living in a cabin? For some reason, her mind flashed to his hands, strong and long fingered, sliding that glass of wine over to her last night. It had been an unexpected gesture of kindness. She wondered for a brief instant what those hands would feel like skating across the bare skin of her shoulder, tangling in the curls at the nape of her neck. She shook off the image. Not happening. Not in a million years.

"Phoebs, I got a text from Michel this morning." She steered the conversation back into safer and more pressing territory. She told Phoebe about the competition time frame and the two other competitors.

"What are you going to do?" Phoebe asked soberly.

"I don't know yet," Georgia admitted. "But I've got to figure out how to get my spark back soon. I'm running out of time."

"You'll figure it out," Phoebe told her comfortingly. "You always manage to come out on top, Georgia." Then she switched topics. "How are things going with your mom?" she asked. "Has she told you the big secret?"

"Not yet, but I found out something interesting." Georgia briefly told Phoebe about Star's connection to the cookbook and to Julia Child and the City of Light. "She said we used to dream of Paris together, to plan what we'd do when we went there."

"Oh my gosh, babe," Phoebe exclaimed. "That's so amazing! So you and your mom had this dream but you grew up not knowing she shared it with you? But it shaped your whole life? That's so beautifully tragic." She sighed dramatically. "It's like a Shakespeare play."

In the background, Georgia could hear someone calling Phoebe's name. Phoebe yelled, "I'll be a minute. Just rub them all down with baby oil. Yeah, front and back." She came back on the phone. "Sorry, I'm going to have to go. So do you have any idea what this big thing is that she wants to tell you?"

"No." Georgia hesitated, looking down toward the beehives at the small white-clad figure of her mother. "But I'm curious to find out what it is." She narrowed her eyes and thought of Star's initial email.

There is something I need to tell you, something that could change your life . . .

That line was stuck in her mind. What did it mean? What did Star know that could change Georgia's life?

"Babe, I have to go," Phoebe said apologetically. "They're done inflating the giant ice cubes. We've got to start the shoot."

"Get back to your swimwear models," Georgia said fondly. "And be careful with flaming vodka, okay, Phoebs?"

"Snog that oysterman for me," Phoebe retorted with a giggle. "Have fun!" And then the line went dead.

Georgia slipped her phone into her pocket and looked once more at her mother and Pollen. Star knew something that she felt was important enough to call Georgia to the island, something she claimed could change Georgia's life. What was it? Could it help her now?

"Maybe it's time to find out," Georgia murmured, and headed toward the beehives.

"Is it safe to come closer?" Georgia picked her way through the dewy grass toward Star and the beehives. She really needed more appropriate footwear for an island, she reflected, feeling the moisture from the grass soak through the thin leather of her flats in a matter of seconds. Pollen galloped up to her and woofed a greeting, wagging her tail so hard her entire back end wiggled. Georgia scratched the dog's head, and Pollen grunted happily.

"Morning, Georgia. You can come closer but move slowly. I'm almost done," Star instructed in a calm tone. Clad in her voluminous white suit and a wide-brimmed hat with a black mesh veil, she had the top off one of the beehives and was puffing smoke from a metal can that looked like the Tin Man's oil can from *The Wizard of Oz.* Her movements matched her voice, quiet and steady, almost sleepy, as though she were in slow motion. Georgia presumed it was so she didn't upset the bees. The veil on Star's hat was draped over the top of the brim, though, leaving Star's face exposed. She also wore no gloves. Her hands were bare, and she was doing something with the hives.

Georgia approached cautiously and gave the hives a wide berth. "What are you doing?" she asked curiously.

Star slid one of the square sections of the hive out and examined it closely. Bees thickly coated both sides of the panel. "Inspecting the hives to make sure the bees are happy and healthy and have enough to eat. It's finally warm enough for me to do an inspection. It's too cold over the winter. But now things are warming and blooming and the bees are ready to get busy making honey through the summer." Star slid the panel back into the hive.

"There." She stepped back from the beehives. "Want to help me label the honey from last season? I need to get more jars ready to sell at the farm stand."

"Okay," Georgia agreed. Maybe that would be a good opportunity to ask Star about her email. She followed her mother to the table under the apple trees. Star slipped out of the beekeeper outfit. Underneath, she was wearing a worn pair of soft blue denim overalls and a shirt the color of moss.

"Grab a seat," Star instructed. Brushing apple blossoms off a chair, Georgia sat down. On the table were a dozen or more glass Mason jars of honey lined up in rows, as well as scissors, labels, markers, and rough twine. Star sat across from her, and Pollen collapsed at their feet under the table with a heavy sigh and drifted off to sleep.

"I'll make the labels and stick them on the jars. Can you tie a twine bow around each of the necks?" Star asked, reaching for a sheet of labels.

"Sure." Georgia picked up one of the jars. Inside, the honey looked like liquid gold, thick and viscous and the most beautiful amber color.

"I harvested this honey last August," Star explained. "The bees like the lavender out front of the house. Gives the honey a lovely flavor." She scribbled *San Juan Island Lavender Honey—$15* on a label.

"Star?" Georgia asked, deciding to be brave and ask the question she was so curious about. She picked up the ball of twine and turned it in her hands. "When you sent me the message inviting me to the island, you said there was something you needed to tell me, something that could change my life. Can you tell me what that is?"

Star set down the labels and gave Georgia a thoughtful look. "Are you sure you're ready to hear it?" she asked quietly.

Georgia hesitated. "Do you think it could help me?"

Star pressed her lips together and considered. "Yes, I think so, but I think it will do far more than that."

"Then tell me," Georgia said firmly.

Star surveyed her for a long moment, so long Georgia grew uncomfortable under her assessing gaze. She glanced down at the twine in her hands.

"What do you feel when you cook?" Star asked finally. "When you touch ingredients, when you create a dish?"

Around them, the air was filled with the contented hum of bees buzzing from the hives and gathering pollen from the apple blossoms. The scent of the blossoms was heady and luscious.

Georgia considered for a moment. "I guess I feel more alive, like everything is in Technicolor. It's exhilarating." She hesitated. "I know this will sound crazy, but when I touch ingredients, it's like all my senses intermingle. I can taste and see and hear elements of the ingredients. I instinctively know what each dish needs, how everything fits together. It's a gut intuition, a sense of . . . rightness. At least that's how it's been up until recently." She glanced sideways at Star. "That probably makes no sense, right?"

Star smiled. "It makes perfect sense. You're a Stevens woman, after all."

Georgia was puzzled. "What does that mean?"

Star ignored the question. "And how do people respond when they eat the food you cook for them?" she asked. Her tone was conversational, but Georgia had the feeling that somehow her answers mattered a great deal.

"I . . . I don't know. They respond positively?" No one had asked her that question before.

"I'm sure they do," Star agreed, cocking her head and studying Georgia. "But more specifically, when you cook a meal and someone eats it, what happens? How does your food make people feel?"

Georgia was stymied. She knew she was a talented cook, and that food could touch people on a deep, primal level. Her food seemed to do that particularly well. But she'd never really thought about it before. She considered for a moment.

"My mentor in Paris said that my cooking filled him with a sense of wonder, of possibility, that it gave him joie de vivre," Georgia said slowly. "He said that with every bite it was as though he could taste a better future, full of possibilities, that he could see things more clearly, could glimpse a better world. He said it gave him hope, and that it felt . . . sublime." She looked down at the scattered apple blossoms on the grass under her feet and blushed, feeling awkward to be singing her own praises. But they were Michel's words, not hers.

"And do other people feel the same way about your food?"

Georgia looked up to find Star watching her intently. She furrowed her brow and considered the question. Looking out over the bay, she thought back over the years and kitchens and meals. Memories and moments came to her in brief flashes. A grown woman tasting a spoonful of Georgia's Mousse au Citron at a late afternoon lunch, then suddenly standing and announcing that she needed to reconcile with her estranged sister before it was too late. She'd hastened away, leaving her coat, one hundred euros to pay the bill, and the mostly uneaten mousse at the table. After devouring Georgia's beet and goat cheese tart one bitter winter evening, an American man with an engagement ring nestled on top of a slice of Georgia's cherry clafoutis looked across the table at his girlfriend and said later that he could suddenly see clearly that she was not the love of his life. He'd hastened back to the kitchen to remove the ring from the dessert where it was waiting to be served at the right moment. They left the restaurant with the ring in his pocket and his girlfriend in tears. There had been others. Many others, now that she thought of it. It had been a bit of a joke among the kitchen staff, that Georgia's dishes could cause more breakups and engagements and family feuds and reconciliations than the restaurant had ever seen. She'd never really put it all together before, but now that she thought of it . . .

"I think my cooking might give people clarity somehow," Georgia said in surprise. She told Star about the instances she could remember. "I never put it all together before," she admitted. "I guess I just figured it was normal, that people connect over food and sometimes that leads to big life changes, but now that I think about it, it does seem like an awful lot of customers' big life moments happen over meals I've made." Quite a lot of them, if she were honest.

"Have you ever eaten something another chef prepared that gave you that sense of clarity, that changed the course of your life?" Star asked, pausing to write out another label. A small smile played around her mouth. That smile made Georgia pause. What did Star know that she wasn't saying?

"Never," Georgia admitted, unfurling a length of twine from the ball and snipping the end. "I've eaten amazing meals in my life, things that make me happy to be alive, to enjoy every morsel. But I've never eaten a meal that changed the course of my life. Not once."

"And there you have it," Star said matter-of-factly. "That is your gift, Georgia May, and the true mark of a Stevens woman. Your cooking gives people clarity about their own hearts." She finished the first sheet of labels.

"What do you mean the mark of a true Stevens woman?" Georgia asked, mystified.

Star leaned forward in her chair and clasped her hands. "The women in our family each have . . . a special gift," she explained calmly. "Call it magic, call it a deep connection to the earth. It can be labeled many things, but the fact is that every woman in the Stevens line has had some special ability. Your great-grandmother, my grandma Emma, could bake pies that inspired people to tell the truth. One bite of her apple streusel crumb pie and a man would confess to an affair. A forkful of her peach cobbler and feuding siblings would apologize for their mistakes and make up. I'm told her cherry pie was especially popular for making shy beaus finally declare their true love and propose to their sweethearts." Star chuckled. She peeled off a label from the sheet, then reached over and carefully stuck it on the front of a Mason jar.

"Grandma Emma was famous in her small Georgia town for her ability," Star continued. "Now my mama, Helen's, gift was something different. She could heal any small ailments or injuries just by her touch. Growing up, we never suffered from cuts or scrapes or sore throats. I remember coming in crying as a child with a scraped-up elbow. I'd fallen off my bike. Mama bent down and kissed the wound, bloody and dirty with pieces of gravel in the scrapes, and when she lifted her head, the skin on my elbow was pink and smooth, and the hurt was gone."

Georgia listened, wide eyed and astonished. Star's pale eyes turned suddenly sad. "She couldn't heal everything. She couldn't save my grandma Emma from kidney failure, or heal herself of breast cancer, but she could soothe the little aches and pains of life with just a touch. She always had the gift, as long as she could remember." Star met Georgia's gaze frankly. "So when people tell you that your food brings them clarity, that it has a touch of the sublime, I don't find that strange at all. You're a Stevens woman, carrying on the line with your own unique gift. And that gift is to bring clarity to people's hearts through the food you cook."

Georgia stared at her mother, dumbfounded. "You're telling me that every woman in our family was what, some kind of a witch, and I am too?" She couldn't have been more shocked if Star had announced she was an alien visiting earth from outer space.

"No," Star said firmly with a shake of her head. "We're not witches. My grandmother was a devout Catholic. My mother was Lutheran. I came back to my own place of faith when I got sober in AA. We have a gift. It's a blessing, not something we control with incantations or spells." She stuck another label on a jar. "Our gifts are often misunderstood by those around us, but each of us has a unique gift, and we use it to bring joy to those around us. We use our gifts for good, and as our gifts bring blessings to others, they bless our own lives as well. We find purpose and delight in using our gifts to help others. It is a virtuous cycle." She paused, waiting for Georgia to process her words.

Georgia felt completely blindsided. Of all the secrets Star could have shared, this had never crossed her mind. It was ludicrous. Yet she had to admit it was also strangely compelling.

It occurred to Georgia that she knew little of Star. What if there was a history of mental illness that she'd never been told about? What if her mother wasn't quite in touch with reality? Because what other explanation could there be? And yet, when Star had described the women in her family, Georgia felt instinctively that she fit right in. She'd known for years that what she felt when she touched food was different, that *she* was different. She just didn't know why. What Star said made sense, although it felt far-fetched at the same time. Of course, she didn't believe it. Except it would explain so much . . .

15

"*If what you're* saying is true, then what's your gift?" Georgia asked skeptically. She wrapped a length of twine around the neck of a honey jar and tied a neat bow.

"This." Star reached up and snapped an apple twig from the bough above them. It was laden with small white buds not yet blossomed. "Watch." She cupped it in her strong-knuckled hands. Before Georgia's eyes, the buds began to slowly open, their blooms unfurling into delicate white starbursts. Soon Star was holding a branch laden with fragrant white blossoms in full bloom where a few seconds before there had been only tightly closed flowers. It had taken no more than a minute. Star looked at her and smiled knowingly.

"Impossible," Georgia breathed in astonishment, eyes wide.

"I have a green thumb," Star said, offering the blooming twig to Georgia. "That's my gift, to help things flourish and grow. I can make tomatoes ripen all year round, harvest peaches so juicy they're bursting on the trees in the dead of winter. I can coax life from any plant at any time."

Georgia took the twig gingerly and looked up at her mother in disbelief. It sounded like a fairy tale, like wishful thinking, except she'd just seen it happen with her own eyes. "But how?" She struggled to form the words.

Star shrugged. "I don't know. It's always been that way, since I was a little girl. Just like my mother with her gift, just like you, I don't know how or why I can do it. It's just a part of me, as your gift is a part of you."

"That explains the gardens," Georgia said, glancing back at the garden beds near the house. She'd been right. It *had* been too early for the verdant riot of vines and plants—the cucumbers she'd seen peeking out from under vines, the red globes of the tomatoes swaying in the breeze off the bay. The ripe purple figs . . . She'd chalked it up to a long growing season, some sort of bizarrely mild island microclimate, when in reality it was all Star's gift. She sniffed the apple blossoms. Each silky white bloom was filled with a heady sweet fragrance. "This is amazing," she whispered, stroking the delicate silky petals.

Star smiled. "And so is your gift. I left when you were so young, I wasn't sure what your gift was yet. Your daddy's family viewed my gift with suspicion, as a bad thing. They thought I was using witchcraft, that I was consorting with the devil. I didn't fit into the box of what they could comprehend about how the world worked, so they feared and rejected me. I was worried that they would never encourage you to use your gift if they knew you had one. I wasn't sure how you would feel about your gift either, if you were even aware of it. When I heard you'd gone to Paris to be a chef, I was pretty sure that cooking had something to do with it. I'd sensed it when you were a child too, but you were too young for me to be certain. But yesterday, when I tasted the dinner you made for us, it confirmed what I'd suspected all along. I could taste it in your food."

"You could taste the magic?" Georgia said with a touch of skepticism.

"The gift," Star said simply. "It's not hocus-pocus, not fairy tales, Georgia May. It's just a special little extra something we get to give to the world. And that's a gift no matter how you slice it." She pushed a few labeled jars across the table toward Georgia.

Georgia looked down, a little chagrined. "Sorry," she said quietly. "This is all just very new and unexpected."

"I wouldn't believe it myself if I didn't see it with my own eyes, if I didn't feel it coursing through my fingers," Star agreed. "But we don't need to understand something fully to know it is real. We can know something is true without understanding all the whys and hows, can't we? You've experienced the gift, haven't you? You've sensed it even if you didn't know what to call it?"

"Every time I touch a carrot or crack an egg or peel a tangerine," Georgia admitted. "I just thought I was a little crazy. Aunt Hannah always seemed suspicious of my cooking. I think it disturbed her when I'd talk about how I could feel the ingredients with all of my senses. I remember being little and helping her peel apples. I told her I could hear their colors. She sent me out of the kitchen and never encouraged my interest in cooking again. I think it scared her." Georgia suspected now, thinking back on it, that perhaps Aunt Hannah had been worried Georgia would somehow take after Star. She'd wanted to keep her a Jackson and forget all about the Stevens half of her heritage.

"People are afraid of things they don't understand," Star agreed. She slid a labeled jar across the table to Georgia.

"I grew up thinking my brain was just wired a little differently, that I was weird somehow. I think Michel sensed my gift from the very beginning, though," Georgia said thoughtfully. "My mentor in Paris. He calls it my 'spark,' but I think he's talking about the same thing. That's why he told me to leave Paris, because he said I'd lost my spark and needed to figure out how to get it back."

Star paused. "He said you'd lost your spark?"

Georgia nodded. "I thought maybe he was just picking up on me losing my sense of taste, but now I wonder if it's more than that. I wonder if I've lost both my sense of taste and my gift? Maybe they're connected somehow?"

"I tasted something last night," Star said, looking thoughtful. "I could sense your gift in the food you made us, but I tasted something else as well, especially in the salty mousse. It tasted bitter to me."

Georgia looked surprised. "Bitter? That's weird." There was nothing that would be bitter in that recipe. "What do I do?" she asked. "How do I get my gift back if I've lost it?"

Star frowned. "I don't know," she admitted. "When did you first notice something was wrong?"

"It happened gradually," Georgia explained. "I started noticing it maybe six months ago. I couldn't sense the ingredients like I've always been able to. Sometimes an ingredient would taste completely wrong, or I couldn't taste anything at all. I even went to see specialists, but they told me everything was fine. And then after the blowup with Etienne, I woke up and all I could taste was bitter. That's when I went to see Michel and he told me to leave Paris and try to regain my spark."

"Hmm," Star murmured. She tapped a marker against the corner of her mouth. "So why can you still taste bitter?"

Georgia looked mystified. "I don't know."

"Tell me, since you started sensing something was wrong, how has it felt to cook? Do you still have that same sense of wonder and delight?" Star asked, her eyes intent on Georgia, assessing.

Carefully tying the twine in a bow around the neck of one of the jars of honey, Georgia thought back, her mind flicking through hundreds of hours in the kitchen, weekends and late nights, the exhaustion and intensity, Etienne's moods, small disasters, the daily grind that had turned into the weekly and monthly grind that had become her life. She couldn't say when it had happened, but she could see it clearly now. Something had changed. What had once brought her delight no longer did.

"No," she said honestly. "I haven't felt delight or wonder or joy when I cooked in . . . weeks, months, maybe longer." How long had it been? Certainly not since her sense of taste had started to fail her. She could not remember that last time she'd felt delight in cooking. It was a skill, something she was very good at, and performed with precision, but somewhere along the way, cooking had turned into a task, a competition, a set of steps she had to execute efficiently to achieve a result. She hadn't even realized it until now.

It had not always felt like that. Even when she'd joined the kitchen at La Pomme d'Or she could remember the feeling of elation every time she set foot in the gleaming space. But now . . . the wonder had gone from it so gradually she had not even been aware of its absence. The thought filled her with sadness. It felt like such a loss.

"What about in the rest of your life?" Star asked. She stuck a label on another jar, smoothing it across the curve of the glass. "What brings you joy?"

Georgia tried to answer and drew a blank. She had been consumed by the kitchen for all of her years in Paris, and even before that, she'd been driven since she'd left the ranch at eighteen. There had been moments of wonder and delight—when she'd first reached Paris, she'd felt as though she were walking on clouds for weeks. And for many years, setting foot in a professional kitchen had given her a thrill unlike anything she'd ever experienced. Biting into the chewy center of a Ladurée macaron always brought a smile to her face, and strolling to work through Paris in the spring, with sunshine on her skin and the chestnut trees blooming in the Jardin du Luxembourg usually felt like a benediction to her. But lately . . .

"It's not just cooking. I haven't felt delight in anything in my life for a while," she admitted. "I've been so focused on achieving that I think I forgot to do anything else."

Star sat back. "What if everything tastes bitter to you now because that's what your life has become?" she asked, her eyes bright with sudden inspiration.

"What do you mean?" Georgia asked. She picked up the twig of apple blossoms and twirled it in her hands.

Star explained, "You are a Stevens woman. Our gifts bring us delight when we are doing what we were meant to do and blessing others. It's how I feel when I'm in my garden. Growing things brings me more delight than anything else on earth. When I put my hands in the soil, when I touch green and budding things, I feel such a sense of joy and of wonder. It feels like I am doing what I am meant to do on this earth. And the things I grow bless others, they nourish people, and that brings me deep joy. But it sounds like you've been so busy living by a list, trying hard to achieve your goals, that you forgot the entire purpose of what you do—to delight in your unique gift and to bless others with it. What if you've slowly starved yourself of delight, of wonder, of a purpose for living? What if that's what's made you lose your spark and your sense of taste? What if all that was left after all that stress and striving was the bitterness of life? Maybe if you rediscover your joy in food and in the kitchen, you'll reignite your gift and your sense of taste will come back too."

Georgia considered her mother's words. They made sense to her. "But how can I fix it?" Georgia asked.

Star stared at the rows of honey jars on the table between

them, her brow furrowed in thought. "Our gifts are meant to be just that, gifts. Not a job or a task, but a sense of rightness, of being in the right place and time, doing the thing we were gifted to do. What if regaining your spark isn't about trying harder. What if it isn't about trying at all?"

"You're saying I should stop trying to get my spark back?" Georgia clarified, looking dubious.

Star nodded. "Maybe if you stop trying so hard to *do* and spend more time allowing yourself to just be present and enjoy, you'll make space for delight to grow and your gift to flow again."

"Hmm." Georgia looked dubious. It went against every code she had. For as long as she could remember, she'd been striving hard. And yet it seemed that the harder she tried, the less she was able to access her gift. The delight and wonder had faded from her life the harder she strived. Could Star be correct? It felt like a gamble.

"I don't know how to not try," she admitted. "And if I do manage to stop trying, what if you're wrong? I could run out of time to figure this out and lose any chance I have for La Lumière Dorée." The thought made her heart palpitate just a little.

"It's a risk," Star agreed. "Then again, what has trying so hard been getting you?"

"Nothing so far," Georgia admitted.

"Well then," Star said. "What have you got to lose?"

Georgia hesitated. There was a certain logic to Star's words. What she had been doing didn't seem to be working. What if she gave Star's method a try? Just for a day or two, to see if anything changed.

"Okay," she said firmly. "I'll attempt to NOT try and see what happens."

Star sat back, looking delighted. "Great," she said. "I've got an idea. What if we tried to help you regain your sense of delight and wonder by sending you to some of the most beautiful places right here on the island, places that are uniquely tied to our local food? If you can just relax and enjoy yourself, maybe the island will work its magic and you'll regain your spark and your sense of taste." She shot Georgia a speculative look.

"It's worth a shot," Georgia agreed. "What have I got to lose?"

Star nodded. "That's the spirit. Hold on. I'll be right back." She jumped to her feet and pulled out her ancient flip phone from the front chest pocket of her overalls, then headed down toward the beehives. Georgia finished cutting twine and tying bows on the rest of the honey jars while she waited. She was still astounded by Star's revelation about her family legacy and struggling to wrap her mind around the implications. Would Star's plan work? Only time would tell.

Five minutes later, Star was back. "It's all settled," she announced, tucking her phone away. "I've arranged the first stop on your tour of local delights. Cole's waiting over at the oyster farm for you, but you have to go now before the shellfish farm opens up for business at eleven thirty. It will get busy quick after they open."

"Cole?" Georgia squeaked in surprise. "I thought I'd be doing this with you."

"Cole's the expert on oysters," Star demurred. "And I've got a few clients to take care of in the next couple of days. Cole's agreed to drive you and show you all the places on the list I'm making for you to visit this weekend. Tomorrow, he'll take you to our local winery. You'll have fun."

Georgia's heart sank. Being ushered around the oyster farm

or anywhere else by Cole sounded like about as much fun as going to the dentist for a filling, maybe less, but she couldn't think of a graceful way out of it. She was stuck now. She glanced over toward the oyster farm and sighed reluctantly. She'd just have to go and make the best of it.

16

As she headed through the line of evergreen trees toward the shellfish farm, Georgia couldn't decide which was less appealing. Eating what was almost certainly going to be a horrible-tasting oyster or having to eat that oyster while in the unpalatable company of the man most likely to win both sexiest and grouchiest shellfish farmer on the planet. It was a toss-up. But she was determined to do whatever she could to get her life back on track, and not even a grumpy oyster farmer was going to get in her way.

The oyster farm was rustic and quaint, with a handful of wood-clad buildings encircling an outdoor eating area with wooden picnic tables and plastic crates half-full of empty oyster shells. Beyond the graveled eating area, the land gently sloped down to the beach and the wide span of the bay beyond. A long pier stuck out into the water with a small wooden shack at the end. Georgia looked around, spotting two figures in bright orange overalls doing something at the end of the pier. Cole was at the far side of the eating area, splitting wood with an axe like some sort of lumberjack commercial. She didn't see anyone else around.

Pausing by a picnic table, she made herself slow down and take a deep breath. It was difficult to cultivate wonder and delight while marching single-mindedly toward a goal. That sort of behavior was what had gotten her in trouble in the first place, most likely. Her mind was still reeling from Star's astonishing revelations, but she tried to calm herself and focus on the moment. She looked around and tried to imprint the beauty of the setting onto her mind. "Relax, enjoy," she told herself. Then reluctantly, she headed toward the sound of chopping wood.

When Cole saw Georgia, he grimaced and set down the axe, tossing the split wood onto a tall pile near a stone firepit.

"Good morning." She tried to smile brightly.

He gave her a curt nod and turned away, gesturing for her to follow him. "Let's get this over with," he said gruffly.

She rolled her eyes behind his back. "Lead the way."

What was his problem? They'd shared a nice chat yesterday afternoon while she was cooking dinner, but then he'd been distant and silent again during the meal. Now he was looking at her like she was a boil on his backside. His very tight backside. He filled out a pair of jeans well. She tried not to notice. Too bad he had the personality of a wet sock, she thought uncharitably.

"This place is beautiful," she said.

He grunted in reply. "Westcott Bay Shellfish Company is one of the only family-run aquaculture farms in the San Juan Islands," he explained. "We farm oysters, clams, and mussels right here in the bay. It's an environmentally friendly way of farming that actually improves the water quality and overall health of the bay and provides fresh shellfish daily to customers and local establishments. It's a solid operation."

"Sounds wonderful." Georgia looked around her in appreciation. She knew next to nothing about shellfish farming but was enchanted by the peaceful serenity of the farm, the sunshine glistening on the bay, the scent of evergreen needles, the call of gulls.

Cole led her to a tall, open wooden shed-type building closer to the water and stopped at a deep stainless-steel trough filled with water. The bottom of the trough was piled high with oysters, their rough, gray ridged shells tumbled haphazardly over one another.

"I'm assuming you've had an oyster before?" he asked.

She raised a brow. "I've lived in France for the last twelve years."

He nodded once. "Okay then, pick out the one you want."

She dipped her hand into the water and gasped aloud. It was ice-cold. Her fingers instantly went numb. She grabbed a large oyster and brought it dripping to the surface. Cole slid on a pair of thick leather gloves with flared cuffs and reached out for her oyster. She handed it to him, watching as he expertly shucked it with a deft twist of the oyster knife at the hinge of the shell. She had always found culinary competence sexy, and watching him effortlessly shuck the oyster was no exception. A moment later, he held it out to her, fresh and creamy and glistening on its half shell.

Without thinking, Georgia leaned forward, putting her lips to the edge of the oyster shell and tipping her head back, letting the plump oyster slide into her mouth. She saw Cole's pupils widen in surprise. For an unguarded instant, something flickered across his face. She could have sworn it was admiration, or maybe even desire. That was unexpected. She met his eyes in a silent challenge, sucking down the brine. The oyster was everything it should be—fresh and cold, creamy with a little crunch. For a split second she thought she might be able to taste it, but then it hit her. The bitter bite at the end. Horribly, revoltingly bitter.

"Oh." She shuddered, pulling back.

He tossed the empty shell into a nearby plastic crate half full of shells and stepped back from her quickly. "No good?"

She shook her head, trying to tamp down her disappointment. "No." Worse than no good. Horrible. And horribly disappointing. She'd hoped it would work. Had she not been present enough? Not enjoyed enough in the moment? Maybe she should have savored it more.

"Sorry it wasn't what you were hoping for," he said stiffly. He glanced at the woodpile. "I should get back to work."

Georgia nodded but didn't move. "Thanks anyway," she said. "I appreciate you trying to help me."

"I'm not doing it for you," Cole replied evenly.

"Oh." Georgia understood. He was doing it for Star. She just happened to be the favor Star was asking of him.

"Well then," Georgia retorted crisply. "Thank you for the oyster."

"My pleasure." His tone said it was anything but. Without another word he headed toward the woodpile and picked up the axe again. Georgia snorted. *My pleasure.* They both knew that was a lie. On impulse, she followed him.

"Look," she said, stepping directly in front of him, ignoring the fact that he was wielding an enormous, sharp wedge of metal near her face. "I know you don't like me, and that's fine. I'm not everyone's cup of tea. I get it. I'm not sure what I've done for you to dislike me so quickly, but if we're going to be spending any amount of time together while I'm here, I'd like us to be civil at the very least. Pleasant would be even better. Pleasant strangers. Otherwise, I'd rather chew glass than spend a minute more with you." She gazed at him defiantly.

He was watching her with a look of surprise that quickly melted into a chagrined amusement.

"You think this is funny?" Georgia demanded. She crossed her arms and stared him down. She was fuming and could feel her cheeks flushing a telltale red. She blushed when she got mad.

It was very inconvenient. "I have never met a ruder human being and I've lived in PARIS for over a decade. You don't even know me. I don't know if you hate women or just redheads or if you've got something against me personally, but let's just try to be civil to each other, especially since it appears we will be forced to spend time together this weekend, okay? And then after I leave the island, we can go back to being strangers who will never, ever have to see each other again. Which I'm assuming will suit both of us just fine."

He was trying to keep a straight face, but there was a glimmer of a smile playing around his mouth. She wanted to slap it off. "Boorish behavior isn't funny," she snapped.

"You're right," he said unexpectedly. He rested the head of the axe on the ground and leaned on the handle, looking her steadily in the eye. "Through no fault of your own, you've stepped into a . . . complicated situation. I've been churlish. I'm sorry."

Georgia was taken aback. "Oh." She didn't know what to say. She hadn't expected this glimpse of humanity from Cole. She wondered what complicated situation he was referring to? And who on earth used the word "churlish"? The same man who spoke French, read German philosophy, and worked on an oyster farm in the middle of nowhere, apparently. What was this guy's deal? This island was harboring more than one secret, she had a feeling.

"Pleasant strangers, huh?" Cole said, raising an eyebrow at her. She cocked her head and surveyed him. With that light in his eyes, in this brief moment of levity, she had the strangest feeling of déjà vu once more. She could have sworn she'd seen him somewhere. But what were the odds their worlds had collided before? She brushed the sensation away.

"Pleasant strangers," she confirmed. Cole stuck out his hand and she clasped his. It was even more calloused than her own, strong and firm. She glanced up to find him giving her a searching look she couldn't decipher. It sent a little shiver through her backbone, right down to her toes.

"See you tomorrow, stranger," Cole said lightly and let go of her hand.

17

At one minute to noon the next day, Cole pulled up in front of the cottage in an old baby blue Land Cruiser, Kansas blasting loudly from the open windows. Georgia hopped inside to the strains of "Carry On Wayward Son." Cole leaned forward and turned down the music.

"This is your car?" she asked.

"Hello to you too," he replied dryly.

"No, it's amazing. I feel like I just stepped back in time." Her seat was a little bouncy, and everything smelled like old vinyl and what she assumed was Cole—a pleasing combination of pine sap, coffee, and soap. He smelled wholesome, clean. What she imagined a grown-up Boy Scout might smell like.

"Her name is Martha," Cole said.

"My father wanted to name me Martha," Georgia commented, buckling her seat belt. "After his grandmother."

Cole glanced at her. "It suits the car better," he deadpanned.

"Is that a compliment?" Georgia teased.

"Take it as you will," he said evenly, but she saw the corner of his mouth twitch up. He was wearing worn jeans and a dark waffle weave shirt, pulled tight across his chest, and a pair of aviator sunglasses. She felt like she was in a commercial for something. Gin maybe? Or expensive sunglasses?

"What's on the agenda for today?" Georgia asked.

"Star made a list." Cole nodded to a piece of paper sitting

on the dash. Georgia leaned forward and picked it up. In bold, slanted handwriting it said:

Georgia's List of Island Delights
Winery
Cidery
Bakery in Friday Harbor
Lunch at Anemone

"That all sounds very . . . filling," she commented, glancing over the list. So much to eat and drink. Star had told Georgia that she was planning a culinary tour around the island for her, but thinking about an entire afternoon related to food felt more daunting than delightful at the moment. Georgia knew Star was hoping that these experiences would spark something in her, that they would act as a catalyst to help her get her gift back, but looking at the list, Georgia saw so many ways she could fail. "Try to enjoy this," she admonished herself under her breath. The goal was to not have a goal. She could do that, right? But she wished Star had included some other island highlights that were less food-related. The island was small, and there were not many attractions that weren't linked to food, Star had told her. An alpaca farm, a lavender farm, and some historical sites and parks were about the sum total of it. Georgia sighed, deciding to make the best of it. This was her chance to prove she could still find delight in just being, and she was sure that anywhere on the island would be beautiful and peaceful, regardless of the culinary situation. She could do this.

"We'll hit the winery first," Cole said. He shifted into first gear, and the whole car jerked forward, bouncing over the gravel onto the road.

They drove in silence with the windows down, the cool, fir-

scented air gusting into the car, classic rock music as their
soundtrack. The day was gorgeous with peeks of sun through
fluffy white clouds. The roads they took were long, winding rib-
bons rolling over hills, passing dark stands of evergreens and
bucolic pastures dotted with sheep and a few cows on either
side. There wasn't another car in sight, just Martha and the sunlight and the beauty around them. The entire island was steeped
in a tranquility so different than Paris, which was always humming with activity, always aware of itself. Georgia had expected
she'd miss Paris, but she found she hardly thought of it. The realization surprised her.

   She leaned her head out the car window, feeling the cool
air ruffle her curls. This was more like it. She closed her eyes and
grinned, drinking in the moment, letting her cares melt away.
She was determined to put aside all thoughts of Etienne and
Michel, of the restaurant and Paris, of getting her spark back,
and just enjoy the day. She was on an island. With a handsome,
almost tolerable stranger who was taking her to a winery. Life
could definitely be worse. When she opened her eyes, Cole was
watching her. She flushed, pulling her head back into the car,
shaking out her curls and adjusting her scarf.

   She'd taken care this morning with her appearance. A Breton
striped shirt, a pair of ankle-skimming dark pants, her trusty
leather flats, and her favorite scarf tied around her hair like a headband. It was her Hermès scarf, an extravagant gift from Etienne
on their second anniversary. She knew she should probably get
rid of the scarf and exorcise the memories it evoked, but she
couldn't bear to part with it. Not because Etienne had given it
to her, but because she loved the orange geometric design and
how she felt in it. When she wore it, she took her place in Paris
and in the world. She was her best self in that scarf.

   Barely contained by the scarf, her curls spiraled around her

face in a burnished halo, wild and free. Her hair liked the cool
humidity of the Pacific Northwest. Her curls were going crazy.
She took a deep breath, smiling wide in the sunshine, and sneaked
a glance at Cole. He was driving with one arm casually balanced out the open window, looking competent and completely
relaxed. With his aviators and scruff and corded forearms, he
seemed very manly and in control. He also looked almost
pleasant, the corners of his mouth curving ever so slightly up-
ward. It was a good look for him.

"We're here," Cole announced, turning into the San Juan
Vineyard's property. Georgia gazed around her. The setting for
the vineyard was charming. A little white-steepled building
that looked like a chapel sat framed by rolling meadows. Rows
of grapevines climbed in orderly rows up the hill behind the
property.

"The tasting room's there." Cole nodded toward a modern,
rustic white wooden building with a covered outdoor seating
area. He parked and got out of the car, slamming Martha's door.

"I keep feeling like this entire island is too good to be true,"
Georgia commented, hopping down from Martha. "Like it's all
actually a movie set I've accidentally wandered into."

"It definitely has its charms," Cole agreed. "Islanders think
it's the best place on earth." He led the way to the tasting room.
"I've been a lot of places in the world, and I can't say I disagree.
This place is special."

"Oh, you've traveled? What were your favorite places?"
Georgia asked, intrigued by this glimpse of his life. What had
he been doing all over the world?

Cole held the door open for her. "I liked Japan. Paris was
great."

"Paris? When were you in Paris?" Georgia was curious.

"Years ago," Cole said evasively.

"Did you ever eat at a restaurant called La Pomme d'Or?" Georgia asked as she entered the tasting room, Cole close behind her. Was that why he seemed vaguely familiar? Had they crossed paths somehow in Paris?

"No," Cole said briefly.

Georgia looked around at the warm wood interior and long white marble counter where staff stood at the ready. Cole approached the counter and perused the tasting menu. "They grow the Siegerrebe and Madeleine Angevine grapes here. I'd recommend you try one of those."

"Not that it's going to matter," Georgia said with a sigh. Bitter was bitter no matter the grape. Still, she tried to think positively. "I'll try the Siegerrebe."

Cole ordered a glass for her and a bottle of Perrier for himself.

"You aren't having wine?" Georgia was surprised.

"I don't drink," he said briefly. "Sober five years next month."

"Oh." She felt embarrassed. "I'm sorry. I didn't know. We could have gone somewhere else."

"It's fine. It's not hard for me to be around it. I've been here before. I know these folks." Cole brushed off her apology. She thought back to the dinner she'd served, recalling that Cole had stuck with water that evening. She hadn't really paid attention to it then.

The girl who helped them, a cute blonde in her early twenties, flirted with Cole as she handed him their drinks. "Anything else I can get for you?"

"This is fine. Thanks, Kelsey," Cole replied, either oblivious to the girl's flirtations or ignoring them on purpose. He paid cash and took both their drinks. Georgia grabbed the napkins the girl handed them and started to follow him, but the girl leaned over the counter and stopped her. "Is he your boyfriend?" she asked wistfully, eyeing Cole as he headed out the door.

Georgia stifled a laugh. "No, definitely not."

Kelsey perked up at this news. "Really?" She grabbed another napkin and scribbled her name and number on it. "Can you give him this then?" she asked, handing it to Georgia.

"Sure." Georgia took the napkin, amused.

"Do you know who he really is?" Kelsey asked conspiratorially, her eyes never leaving Cole as he found a table outside and set their drinks down.

Georgia paused. "No, do you?"

Kelsey leaned closer and confided. "There are lots of theories about Cole. Some people think he was in the CIA. My best friend swears he was in this big TV show about vampires. She said her older sister used to watch it all the time. I guess it was an old show, popular like five or six years ago, but she's sure it was him. He's still really hot for an old guy, though, right?"

Georgia bit the inside of her cheek to keep from laughing at the characterization of Cole as old. "Yeah, I guess he's not bad for an old guy," she admitted. "Thanks for the napkins." She went out to the patio where Cole was sitting, intrigued by Kelsey's comment. Was it possible one of the theories was true? Could Cole really be CIA or some sort of famous TV star? If so, what in the world was he doing working at an oyster farm on San Juan Island?

Cole had found a quiet spot under the covered pavilion looking out at the grapevines. There were several other groups of customers clustered at tables on the patio. Most looked like tourists, many of them middle-aged, dressed in Lands' End vacation attire, snapping selfies with their glasses of wine. Georgia sat down in a chair across the small table from Cole and handed him his napkin. "Kelsey left this for you," she said with a sly smile. Cole blinked and tucked the napkin under his Perrier bottle, face down. He looked uncomfortable. "Does that happen to you often?" Georgia asked. She was enjoying goading him a little.

"More than I'd like," he responded, taking a sip of his Perrier. His eyes were hidden behind his aviators.

"Must be hard to be so irresistible," she said with mock sympathy.

"Look who's talking," he muttered.

Georgia tasted her wine. Predictably bitter. "What do you mean by that?"

"Oh, come on, a talented, gorgeous woman like you in Paris. Don't tell me you don't get your fair share of attention." Cole shot her a skeptical glance.

Georgia pinked. He thought she was talented . . . and gorgeous! "Mostly old French men offering to make me their mistress," she conceded. "On a bad day at the restaurant, I have to admit it was sometimes almost tempting."

Cole chuckled, then changed the subject. "I know this place isn't French, but the wine here is good, or so I've been told. They've won a few awards, gained some recognition."

Georgia set down her glass. There was no point in drinking any more, which was a pity. She loved good wine. It was one of the joys of living in France. Instead she looked around. The spot was beautiful, the day pleasantly warm. She could think of far worse places to be at the moment. Gazing at the orderly rows of twisted grapevines, the picturesque white chapel, the smattering of other patrons, she tried hard to relax. Then she smiled wryly as she realized the effort she was putting into *not* making an effort. She was terrible at doing nothing. It wasn't in her nature.

She was used to working hard, focusing, and succeeding. She wasn't quite sure how to succeed by NOT making an effort. Relaxing in order to accomplish her goals felt counterintuitive.

"How's it been going with Star so far?" Cole interrupted her thoughts.

"It's been . . ." Georgia hesitated, her mind immediately going to her conversation with Star about the Stevens women and her gift. "Unexpected."

Cole raised an eyebrow. "Unexpected how?"

Georgia studied Cole for a moment. How much did he know? Did he know about Star's gift? He'd lived in close proximity to Star for years. Had he figured out there was something different about her by now? Surely, ripe tomatoes in January must have tipped him off.

"Have you ever noticed anything . . . unique about Star?" she asked carefully.

Cole stilled, his face a careful blank, eyes hidden by the sunglasses. "Unique how?" he said, his tone a touch wary.

"For starters her lush off-season garden," Georgia replied. "She has the greenest thumb I've ever seen." She paused, waiting to see if he would pick up on what she was saying. His shoulders relaxed instantly.

"Oh, you mean the fact that she can make anything grow, any time of the year? That green thumb? Yes, I've noticed."

Georgia exhaled in relief. "So you know about her gift?" Briefly she noticed that he'd relaxed when she'd mentioned Star's gift. Almost as though he'd expected her to ask about something else. She wondered if Star had more than one secret.

Cole nodded. "She told me eventually. It took me a while to figure out that it wasn't the island that was producing ripe plums for Thanksgiving and making roses bloom for Christmas. I've never seen anything like it. Star is . . . special."

Georgia nodded. "She is."

"And you're okay with that?" Cole asked evenly.

Georgia wrinkled her nose and stared straight ahead, at a group of tourists taking photos by the grapevines. "Well, it turns out I'm . . . special too."

Cole tipped his head, surveying her. "Really?" He sounded intrigued. "You have the same ability she does?"

"Not exactly." Georgia swirled the wine around in her glass. "Apparently, the women in our family each have a gift. Hers is her very green thumb. Mine is cooking food that gives people clarity when they eat it." Matter-of-factly, she told him the story Star had told her, starting with Star's grandmother Emma. She wasn't sure why she was confiding in him. Perhaps because he knew about and embraced Star's gift. Or perhaps because she just wanted to tell someone who wouldn't think she was crazy.

Cole gave a low whistle when she was done. He looked impressed. "So that explains why after the dinner you cooked the other night I went home and reconsidered all my life choices." He smiled wryly, but she wasn't entirely sure he was kidding.

Georgia laughed, relieved. She'd said the truth out loud, and Cole wasn't treating her like she was strange or wrong somehow.

"You believe me?" she asked a touch hesitantly. "You don't think I'm crazy?"

"You forget I've eaten Star's ripe watermelon for Valentine's Day," Cole remarked. "So no, I don't think you're crazy. I think you have a gift no one understands, and that's a very different thing."

Georgia didn't know what to say. She was touched. Someone saw her, knew the thing that had always made her different, and called it good. He didn't seem to think it strange or wrong. He was acting as though it were just what Star called it, a gift.

"I've known since I was very young that I was different,"

Georgia admitted. "But I didn't understand why. Growing up I was made to feel that there was something wrong with me, and I think I've carried that feeling around for a very long time. My dad and aunt always acted like the Stevens side of me was something to be wary of. It's strange to think that the very thing I was made to believe was a flaw—the Stevens half of me—might truly be a gift after all."

Cole nodded, listening carefully and watching Georgia through his sunglasses. "You Stevens women are extraordinary," he said softly. "Don't let anyone tell you differently."

Touched, Georgia cleared her throat and glanced down at her wineglass. She felt confused and a little embarrassed to have gone so deep so quickly with a man who half the time seemed like he could barely stand her. But here he was, looking at her with what seemed like respect and admiration. It confused her. She'd always felt she had to work to prove herself valuable. From the time she was small, she'd been striving to prove her worth, to succeed and show the world she had merit, that she mattered. But now when she could not taste or cook with excellence, the very things that had always been her ticket to recognition, Cole was looking at her like she had value just because she existed, as though her very person was a gift to the world. It was unexpected, and she didn't quite know how to feel about that. It made her a little uncomfortable, to be valued for herself and not what she produced. It felt too good to be true.

Sudddenly the moment was interrupted by a cry of greeting from the parking lot. "Hey man, no way!" Cole glanced up, startled. A young man in a new-looking Patagonia fleece and a very pretty brunette in expensive athleisure wear had just jumped out of a gleaming Mercedes SUV and were making their way toward him from the parking lot.

"Remember me? Tyler Perkins?" The young man exuded a

cocky confidence as he approached their table, the brunette in tow. "We were on that panel together at that enviro tech expo in San Jose? What happened to you, man? Word is you fell off the face of the earth after you won that big award." He stuck out his hand. "Sorry, I'm blanking on your name."

Georgia glanced at Cole, whose face had lost all expression. He didn't grasp the man's hand, just left him hanging. "You seem to have me confused with someone else," Cole said flatly. "I'm an oyster farmer here on the island."

Only Georgia seemed to notice that Cole was gripping his Perrier bottle so hard it looked like he might crack the glass. The young man dropped his hand and stepped back, looking uncertain.

"You sure?" The young man looked quizzical. "Wait a minute, let me look up that panel. You look just like a guy that was on there, a real biotech legend. Here, I'll show you." He pulled out his phone.

Cole pushed back his chair, his expression annoyed. "Sorry, I think you've got the wrong guy." He stood. "Guess I just have one of those faces." He shrugged, then nodded to the brunette. "Enjoy your time on the island. The whites are particularly good here." And then without another word, he headed toward the parking lot.

The girl flicked her hair and tugged on the man's arm. "Come on, I'm thirsty." She pulled him toward the tasting room. The man followed reluctantly, tucking his phone in his pocket and glancing back toward Cole with a confused expression on his face.

Georgia stood. It seemed their winery visit was over. Cole was already almost at the car, his strides long and determined. Georgia left their drinks on the table and headed for Martha. She practically had to jog to catch up with Cole.

"What was that all about?" she asked as she hopped into the passenger seat and buckled her seat belt.

"Nothing," Cole said shortly, starting the engine and pulling out of the parking lot in a spray of gravel. "Just a case of mistaken identity."

18

As Cole pulled out onto the road, Led Zeppelin's "Ramble On" came blaring through the speakers. He reached out and turned up the volume, keeping his eyes straight ahead, his expression stony. Georgia watched him, puzzled. What was going on? She had no idea about his past. Star had told her he'd been on the island for almost five years. What had he done before that? Who was he? She didn't even know his last name. And he obviously didn't want to discuss any of it.

"Do you mind if we skip the distillery today?" he yelled abruptly over the music. "There's something else on the island I think you should see."

"Sure, I'm game," Georgia yelled back, trying to lessen the tension in the car. They drove in silence until they passed a sign welcoming them to Friday Harbor. Georgia recognized the quaint painted wooden-framed buildings as they passed—the vintage-looking Palace Theatre cinema, the charmingly bookish window display of Griffin Bay Bookstore. They parked outside Kings Market and Cole jumped out. "I'll be back shortly." He slammed the door. Georgia waited in Martha, content to people watch. Ten minutes later, Cole came back with a paper bag of groceries in hand and they headed out of town.

"Where are we going?" Georgia asked after a few minutes.

"How do you feel about orcas?" Cole asked.

"As in whales?" Georgia was puzzled.

"Technically, they're in the dolphin family, but yes."

"I'm . . . for them?" she said hesitantly.

"Good. Word around town is there's a pod in the area. If we're lucky, we can see them as they head north." He sounded genuinely excited by the prospect.

Ten minutes later they pulled into a parking spot at Lime Kiln State Park, and Cole led her down a trail to a historic white lighthouse with a red roof. The lighthouse was perched on a jut of rock sticking out from a line of high black cliffs that ran raggedly along the sea. From where they stood on the cliffs, a dozen yards below the water gleamed a swirling silver in the sunlight. It made her a little dizzy to look down at the churning depths. Cole came to a halt at the lighthouse and shaded his eyes. "Current's going north now. They'll probably come from the south. They usually follow the current, chasing the salmon." He led her down a narrow dusty sliver of path along the cliffs' edge to a weathered picnic table sitting under a twisted red madrone tree. There was no one else around, just the two of them amid the vast panorama of cliffs and sea and sky.

"Oh look," Georgia cried, delighted to see the friendly face and shiny black head of a creature pop up from the water below. It looked like a puppy.

"That's a harbor seal," Cole said, opening the paper bag. "The cliffs drop steeply right offshore here. These kelp beds are hundreds of feet deep. The salmon like the kelp beds, and the orcas like the salmon. And the seals like to sit on the rocks to rest."

As Georgia watched the seal, Cole pulled a baguette, a pat of Camembert, a tiny jar of olives, and a few other tasty morsels out of the bag. "I know you can't taste anything, but I got us a few things for a picnic," he explained. "It's what you do here. People come and wait for the orcas and have a picnic. So I thought we'd give it a try. Want some wine?" he asked, taking a cold bottle of white out last. "It's a local one."

"Sure." Georgia sat down on the picnic table bench, facing the water, and took a sip out of the paper cup he handed her. He'd thought of everything. The wine was still disappointingly bitter, but she took another sip, this time focusing not on what she could not taste but instead on what she could glean from her other senses. The wine was cold and refreshing on her tongue, sliding down her throat like a mouthful of winter air. She closed her eyes and sniffed the bouquet. Ripe apricots smashing open on gray rocks, the smell of cut grass. She still could not taste anything but bitter in the wine, but she could feel it, feel where it had come from. She turned the bottle around and read the description, smiling at the words "ripe stone fruit" and "mineral complexity." She gave a little hum of satisfaction and leaned forward, resting her elbows on the table, paper cup in hand. The vista was spectacular.

Cole sat down next to her and laid out the picnic. He offered Georgia some of everything, and she accepted, focusing not on the bitter taste, which was still there, but on the creamy fullness of the cheese, the gritty seeded texture of the fig jam, the crisp crunch of the baguette's crust. She found that if she concentrated on other things, the bitter taste wasn't as bad.

They sat in companionable silence, eating and enjoying the view. For the first time in a long time, Georgia felt herself start to relax completely. It was delightful, this sensation of letting herself be in the moment. She was always striving, always thinking one step ahead. She awoke each morning already in motion. Productivity and efficiency were her golden rules. To be still, to savor—how long had it been? She was ashamed to say she had no idea. Perhaps not since those magical early days in Paris. They had been brutal—so much rejection, so many refusals—but she had tasted the beauty and the newness of the city and it had been intoxicating. She had felt so alive, every sense heightened, every corner revealing some new delight. When had she lost that, the ability to be so wonderfully surprised? She had missed the feeling without even knowing it was gone.

She tipped her head back and closed her eyes, luxuriating in the knowledge that she had nowhere to be and nothing to do at this moment. Her job at present was to just . . . be present and try to find delight, to open herself up to wonder. Her eyes popped open, and she found Cole watching her intently. Embarrassed by the scrutiny, she sought a diversion.

"Did you grow up by the water?" Georgia asked, seizing the opportunity to turn the conversation toward him. After all, she had just spilled her life secrets at the winery; the least he could do was give her some small crumbs of personal information. She reached for an olive and nibbled it. Still bitter, but she ate it anyway, enjoying the rubbery squeak it made against her teeth.

"No." Cole helped himself to an olive. "I grew up in Phoenix, Arizona. Pretty much the exact opposite of this." He stretched his long legs out in front of him, a glass bottle of San Pellegrino in his hand. He looked like he belonged here, a part of the rugged, striking landscape.

"Do you miss the desert?" Georgia asked, wondering how much he would share with her. Prying information from Cole often felt to her like shucking an oyster from its shell. He was closed tight. Her mind flashed to Kelsey's comment. Could he be someone famous? Or a government spy?

Cole took a swallow of his mineral water and stared out at the horizon. To her surprise, he answered the question. "Sometimes. I miss going out into the desert with Aunt Justine. My dad split before I was born, and my mom raised me alone. She was the hardest-working woman I knew, but we were always struggling to keep our heads above water financially. She worked as a receptionist at an insurance agency in Phoenix and also took some night shifts at a bar down the street from our apartment. She kept a roof over our heads, but there wasn't much time or money left over. I was a lonely latchkey kid who watched *Captain Planet* and dreamed of saving the world." He frowned. "Then Aunt Justine came to stay, sleeping on our couch for a week that turned into a lot longer. She wasn't the cuddly or maternal type, but she was kind in her own way and sharp as a tack, and she had time for me, which was the biggest thing."

He chuckled, his gaze distant. "She appreciated me, her nerdy little nephew with my oversize glasses and obsession with recycling and superheroes. She'd take me on walks, and we'd pick up litter or sometimes we'd check out books from the library on plants and animals of the Southwest. On weekends when Mom was working, Aunt Justine would drive us out into the desert in her old beater car, and we'd spend all day out there, seeing how many plants and animals we could identify. She helped me feel less alone and gave me a sense of purpose, even as a kid. She told me I could make a difference in the world, and that's a powerful message for anyone to hear." He shifted on the hard picnic table bench and took a swallow of water. "My mom passed away when I was in my early twenties, and Aunt Justine was all the family I had left. She and Star gave me a place to call home here on the island. I'm grateful for that." He gazed out at the horizon contemplatively.

"I'm sorry," Georgia said, wondering what it would feel like to be so alone in the world. She might not always see eye to eye with her dad and aunt, but she knew right where they were, and she knew if she needed to, she could always go home.

"Where were you before you came to the island?" Georgia asked.

"California," he said shortly.

"Star said you've been here five years?" Georgia pried.

"About that," he said reluctantly. "I . . . needed a career change, and when Aunt Justine got her diagnosis, I came to help and just . . . stayed."

"Do you think you'll stay here permanently then?" Georgia asked. She half expected him to clam up at any moment, but he seemed easier out here alone, less closed off. Maybe it was because she'd been vulnerable with him earlier. She wasn't sure. But whatever the reason, she liked learning about Cole. He intrigued her.

"I won't go back to California," he said firmly. He scanned the horizon to the south intently. "There's nothing for me there anymore. And I like it here. The islands are a special place. The ecology is like nowhere else on earth. The biodiversity is amazing."

"Maybe you can live out your dream of being Captain Planet here," Georgia said with a smile.

"Pretty sure that ship has sailed," Cole remarked. He didn't glance her way, but she saw a shadow pass across his face, a look of profound regret.

"Look." Cole straightened suddenly, shading his eyes. "See that splashing?" He pointed out over the water.

Georgia peered in the direction he was pointing.

"What is it?"

"Orcas." He stood. She felt a thrill race through her body. Together they made their way to the edge of the cliffs, watching the pod of orcas draw closer. At first the creatures were simply distant splashes, disturbances in the shimmering silver of the water, and then she could make out the sharp black point of a dorsal fin, then another and another.

"I see them," Georgia cried, clapping in excitement. "Oh, they're incredible."

The animals were magnificent, cutting through the water gracefully, their speed and dexterity astonishing. Georgia was transfixed. There were more than a dozen of them racing through the water toward where they stood, turning and splashing, chasing the salmon. They were sleek and stunning, impossible to look away from in all their gleaming black-and-white glory.

"Look!" Georgia shrieked. Without thinking, she grabbed Cole's arm. He was all muscle under her hand, but she barely noticed. She was focused on a mother orca and her calf swimming toward them. She heard the snort as they cleared their blowholes. The mother hopped up vertically from the water, her top half visible above the gentle waves.

"That's called spy-hopping," Cole informed her. His face split into a wide grin. When he smiled, it transformed his whole demeanor. He was always handsome. He'd probably be handsome drooling in his sleep, but when he grinned, he looked younger, not so guarded and remote, almost boyish. It was endearing.

Georgia laughed in delight as she watched the baby orca play in the waves with its mother. How long had it been since she'd felt this euphoria, the sensation of wonder? It was pure magic.

They watched the pod of orcas until the last one was a tiny dot heading north. Only then did Georgia realize she was still holding on to Cole's arm. He was warm and taut beneath her hand, and for a moment, she froze. Etienne had been slim and strong but small framed, just a little taller than Georgia. Cole was much bigger. And he was ridiculously toned. Oyster farming must really provide a good workout. She glanced up to find Cole watching her with an inscrutable expression. He almost looked like he was in pain. Flushing red, she released his arm.

"Sorry. I got carried away by the whales."

"Dolphins, but yeah, they'll do that to you. No problem."
He took off his aviators, and his expression was almost indulgent as he gazed toward the distant orcas. She realized she and Cole were standing very close together on the edge of a cliff. One step to her left went straight down into the swirling waters of the kelp beds. One step to the right went straight into Cole's chest. She didn't know which felt more dangerous. "I think we'd better head back," she said softly.

Neither of them moved. Georgia swallowed hard. This afternoon had done something to her. It had loosened something that had been so very tightly wound for so long. She could breathe easier. Without conscious thought, she started to move past Cole and head back toward the picnic table, but her foot slipped on a loose patch of rocks. She gave a little cry as she lost her footing, flailing instinctively for a handhold. Instantly, Cole was there, his strong hands gripping her upper arms as he jerked her back away from the cliff edge. Unfortunately, he lost his footing too and landed with a thump on his back on the ground, pulling her down on top of him.

"Oof." Cole grunted. They landed hard, their faces very close together. For an instant, Georgia froze. She could feel Cole's heart beating wildly against her rib cage. She saw his eyes dip down to her mouth, and then he released her arms like she was a hot frying pan. She scrambled off him, mortified.

"Are you okay?" she asked anxiously. He winced as he got to his feet.

"Just bruised my tailbone and my ego," he said with a grimace. "I've done worse." He retrieved his sunglasses, which had flown a few feet away in the grass when he fell.

Georgia brushed dust and bits of dried grass from her clothes, her face flaming. *Smooth, Georgia*, she chided herself. She'd gotten carried away by the day and the orcas . . . and maybe his pheromones. Whatever the cause, it was embarrassing to be rescued and then rejected. He obviously did not want to be that close to her, and that was just fine with her. She did not want to be attracted to any man, not with Etienne in the walk-in refrigerator so fresh in her mind. Not with Michel's deadline looming. Even if Cole thought she was special . . . and gorgeous . . . he obviously didn't want to do anything about it. And she didn't need a rebound or a distraction. She needed to regain her spark and regain her life. She needed to keep her priorities straight. She shook her head, trying to shake some sense into it.

"Thank you for breaking my fall," she said stiffly, moving away and putting a few yards of distance between them.

"My pleasure," he said. They faced each other in awkward silence, the spell of the afternoon broken. "I guess we should get going," Cole said, hastily packing up the picnic supplies and slipping his aviators back on.

"Good idea." Georgia followed him up the path, carrying the mostly full bottle of wine. The car ride back was silent. She stared straight ahead. Out of the corner of her eye, she could see him doing the same. Gone was the easy camaraderie of a few hours before. Now he turned up the radio and ignored her.

When they reached the cottage, he pulled up to the gate but left Martha running. He cleared his throat as she hopped out, not looking at her. "I'll pick you up at one tomorrow. Star is insisting I take you to Anemone. It's the best local restaurant on the island. I think she's hoping the environment will inspire you."

"Fingers crossed she's right," Georgia said awkwardly. "Thank you. See you tomorrow." She turned to go into the house, but then for some reason stopped and turned back, watching Cole as he pulled away toward the oyster farm. She could still feel the imprint of his strong fingers wrapped around her upper arms. She hugged herself and gave a little shiver. And as much as she tried to stop herself, as she watched him disappear down the road, she couldn't help but wonder what Cole would taste like if she kissed him.

19

COLE

Oh boy, he was in trouble. Cole pulled his truck into the parking lot of the oyster farm and found his usual parking spot beneath a spreading oak tree. With a groan, he cut the engine, then leaned forward and rested his head on the steering wheel. He swore softly to himself. It was just his luck that Star's daughter would turn out to be so wildly appealing. So confident, cultured, and ballsy at the same time. He was drawn to strong women with grit and gumption, and she had it in spades. And redheads. He'd always liked redheads. Georgia looked like Rosie the Riveter with Titian hair. Exactly his type of woman, which was making this far more difficult than he'd anticipated.

When Star had first brought up the idea of asking her long-lost Parisian chef daughter to come to San Juan Island, he'd told himself that it couldn't possibly be the same woman. What were the odds? It had been more than seven years ago, after all, and an entirely different continent. There was no way it was her. But he'd taken one look at Georgia, standing there in the kitchen, fresh off the plane, that fiery hair and arch look, and he'd known instantly. It was the same woman. Dammit.

He'd vowed to keep his distance from her, but Star seemed determined to throw them together whenever possible. What was she playing at? He swore again, irritated at Star for putting him in this position, but more than anything, mad at himself.

The problem was that he'd enjoyed his time with Georgia today . . . too much. She was funny and fiercely intelligent and kept him on his toes. She was . . . extraordinary. No two ways about it.

It had been so long since he'd felt this way about anyone. Not since he'd met Amy. That had been so long ago, and look how that had ended. Now he couldn't seem to keep away from Georgia, but he had no choice. When she found out who he was, what he'd done, that would be the end of her interest. And besides, she had made it clear that her life and dreams were in Paris, far away from here. There could never be a future for them.

"Get ahold of yourself," he murmured to himself. "Just avoid her as much as you can." But he couldn't seem to make his heart agree.

He sat back in the seat with a scowl and looked around. Today, the parking lot was packed with cars as tourists enjoyed oysters at the outside eating area. The grill was going. He could see Billy manning it down by the picnic tables, barbecuing oysters in a variety of sauces. The air was pungent with the meaty, smoky scent of the grill. Cole didn't get out. He didn't work on Saturdays and tried to avoid interacting with customers if at all possible. He liked tending to the oysters better.

Cole sighed heavily, feeling the ache of the past. It had been five years since he'd lost Amy. It was the little things he missed the most. Rolling over in bed and fitting himself against her back like a pair of nesting spoons. Sharing a big bowl of ramen at their favorite Japanese restaurant, dipping their chopsticks into the rich broth and play fighting over the last of the noodles. He always gave her the soft-boiled egg, and she picked out all the scallions for him.

The pain was no longer fresh, more like a dull ache in his

belly when he thought of her. He missed her still, though. Even now, five years on, he was living like a monk devoted to her memory. Only in the last year had he even allowed himself to date casually, going to a pub in Friday Harbor a handful of times out of boredom and loneliness. Never the same woman, and never anything too serious. But with Georgia, it was different.

"Don't do this," he warned himself aloud. "There's no way it will end well."

A few more days, that's all he needed to handle. Keep his head down and grit it out for a few more days. Then Georgia May Jackson would swan off to Paris and he'd do what he'd been doing for the past five years—work hard, keep out of trouble, and avoid any complications to his new life or his heart. Surely, he could manage that. How hard could it be?

20

"Star?" Still on a high from the amazing afternoon, Georgia wandered through the house looking for her mother.

"In the garden," she heard Star call out faintly. Pollen met her at the back door with a happy woof and a wagging tail. She had dirt on her muzzle. "Hey, girl." Georgia scratched her blocky head affectionately. "What have you been up to today?"

"How was the winery?" Star straightened up from a patch of vines, her hands filled with cucumbers. The air was filled with the rich, loamy scent of the soil and the sharp freshness of growing things.

"Short," Georgia said frankly. "And unexpected. The wine still tasted bitter, but I think I made progress, and the rest of the day was incredible . . ."

She told Star the broad strokes of everything, only leaving out the part about her almost falling off a cliff and Cole saving her and then the awkward ride home. As she talked, Star harvested vegetables and Georgia took whatever Star handed her and piled it on the back steps. Remembering the odd interaction at the winery with the young couple who thought they knew Cole, Georgia glanced toward the cabin. There was no sign of life down there. She wondered where he was.

"Do you know what Cole did before he came to the island?" she asked casually.

"Yes." Star stopped and arched her back with a slight groan

and a popping sound. "I do, but that isn't my story to tell. Cole is a very private person. He'll tell you when he's ready." She surveyed Georgia. "If you want to help me pick the vegetables, I'd be happy for the extra hands. The lettuce is coming on strong right now."

"Of course." Disappointed, Georgia obliged. She was just going to have to find out about Cole some other way. The day was drawing toward evening, the light turning blue over the bay. It was growing chilly, and Georgia shivered. Through the pines, she could just catch a whiff of smoke and the smell of roasted food. The faintest sound of music and laughter drifted from the oyster farm. She hesitated at the edge of the vegetable beds. "I don't really have the right footwear," she confessed. Italian leather flats did not do well in mud.

Star glanced at her shoes and nodded toward the porch steps and a pair of green rubber clogs sitting by the door. "You can wear my gardening clogs," she said. "Looks like we're about the same size."

Georgia slipped off her shoes and slid her bare feet into the clogs. There was something in the toes. She pulled one off and shook it. To her surprise, out fell a shower of four-leaf clovers.

"What's that?" Star asked, wiping her brow with her sleeve.

Georgia picked one up off the cement steps, holding it out for Star to see. "Four-leaf clovers," she said. "I've been finding them everywhere, in the oddest places."

Star stepped out of the garden bed and gently plucked the clover from Georgia's hand, pinching it between her fingers. "Well look at that," she said softly. She glanced at Georgia. "My grandma Emma was Irish, raised near Galway—that's where our red hair comes from—and she loved four-leaf clovers. Always felt they connected her with the country of her birth. Every time I brought her a four-leaf clover when I was little, she'd give me a piece of candy and tell me the four leaves stood for faith, hope, love . . ."

"And luck," Georgia chimed in. "I remember." Her fingers went to the charm at her throat. Star saw the movement and stared incredulously at the little tarnished four-leaf clover in Georgia's hand.

"Is that the necklace I gave you all those years ago?" she asked, bending forward to get a better look.

Georgia nodded. "You gave it to me the day you left," she said softly. "I've worn it ever since. It's my good luck charm."

Star pulled back, looking stunned. "Not just luck," she said, clearing her throat. "That charm may have a little luck to it, but it carries far more than that." She met Georgia's eyes. "Grandma Emma gave it to me when I turned twelve years old. It was the only thing I had from her after she died. My mama passed away three years later. I was fifteen at that point, and things kind of fell apart for me after that." She said it matter-of-factly, but her mouth twisted slightly as she spoke, like the memory still hurt her. "When I left home in my teens, that charm was the only thing I took with me, that and my guitar, and two hundred dollars I stole from my stepfather." She frowned. "At the time, it seemed a small repayment for what he'd already taken from me. Years later, after I . . . left the ranch in Texas, I stopped at a very dodgy roadside tattoo parlor in Santa Fe and got this." She turned and pulled down the shoulder of her sage green smock. Georgia caught a whiff of Star's familiar scent, the faintest hint of anise and mint and the dusty underlay of thyme. On the lightly freckled skin of her shoulder was a small, emerald green four-leaf clover tattoo.

"It matches the charm," Georgia murmured in surprise.

Star nodded and slipped the smock back up over her shoulder. "Georgia May, I gave you that charm to remind you of who you are," she said firmly, "so that even if you didn't know it, you were holding all of us close to your heart, all the women in your family. I gave it to you so that you would always carry a part of me and a part of Grandma Emma and my mother, Helen, with you no matter where you went. I wanted it to remind you to have faith, to never give up hope. I wanted you to always feel my love, even when I wasn't with you. And yes, I guess I hoped it might bring you a little bit of luck as well." She looked at Georgia intently, her pale gaze steady.

Georgia twisted the charm on its chain. It meant the world that Star had given it to her as a way to connect them, and yet it made her wonder even more. Why had Star left in the first place? The question sat there, lodged in her throat where it had been waiting for almost thirty years. She had wanted to ask it for so very long. Suddenly she didn't want to wait any longer.

"Star." Georgia screwed up her courage.

Star glanced up. She saw something in Georgia's face. "Oh," she said, then, "Yes?" She looked as though she were bracing herself, as though she knew and feared what was coming.

"Why did you leave us?" Georgia asked softly. As soon as the words were out of her throat, it felt like she could breathe again.

Star hesitated. She looked down at the ground. Her face constricted. "Because I made a promise," she said quietly. "Because I had no choice."

Georgia furrowed her brow, staring at her mother in confusion. "What promise?" she asked. "What choice?"

Star shook her head. "I'm so sorry, Georgia May, but I can't tell you that." She met Georgia's eyes, her own deeply apologetic.

Georgia stared at her mother in disbelief. Here she was, finally asking the question that had defined her life for almost
thirty years, and the answer she got was no answer at all?

"I deserve to know the truth," she said sharply, feeling a
flash of anger at her mother's avoidance.

Star nodded, looking miserable, her shoulders slumped. "You
absolutely do," she agreed. "and I wish more than anything that
I could tell you, but I've kept my end of the bargain for thirty
years. I can't break my promise now. I'm so sorry, Georgia." She
gently tucked the four-leaf clover into the pocket of her smock.

Georgia stared at her mother in astonishment and indignation. What in the world was Star talking about? What promise
had Star made, and to whom?

Star shifted uncomfortably. "I'll tell you anything else I can,"
she said humbly. "Anything you want to know, but I can't tell
you the reason why I left. I know that's probably small comfort,
but please believe me, I don't have a choice." She glanced at
Georgia, her own gaze pleading for understanding.

Stymied, Georgia didn't know what to say. In all the years
she'd imagined having this conversation, she had never dreamed
it would go this way. So many times she'd imagined what Star
might say, the reasons or explanations she might give Georgia
for her long absence. Some were terrible, some heartbreaking.
But never had Georgia considered that she might get no answer
at all. Obviously, there was far more to the story, but Star seemed
determined to stay silent. So where did that leave her? Still wondering. More than a little frustrated.

"I need a minute," Georgia said tightly. She stalked away,
putting some distance between her and Star, heading down toward the apple trees. She needed a little space to think. Under
the spreading bower of blossoms, she stopped, mind whirring,

feeling almost dizzy with anger. She crossed her arms and stared out at the rippling water. Her heart was beating fast, and her jaw was clenched. She felt so betrayed. She had no idea where to go from here. She had asked the question, but had received no answer. So now what? Where did that leave her? She glanced at Star then whirled to face the bay. She was too angry to go back to Star. She stood there for a long time as the light faded into evening, feeling again those many years of hope and heartbreak, all the questions and unknowns, the sense of abandonment and confusion. Everything leading to this moment, to her facing Star and asking the question and again getting no answers. She felt powerless once more. It was infuriating. She clenched her fists as angry tears fell. Long minutes later, as darkness slipped softly over the bay, she wiped her eyes and took a shuddering breath. Her anger cooled slightly and a sense of calm slipped over her like a breath of fresh air. She glanced back again. Star was still in the garden bed, working under the glow of a back porch light. Watching her mother's small figure, Georgia felt her anger lessen a little more. It was not Star's choice to keep silent, Georgia sensed. Something or someone was holding her back from telling the truth.

But what did that mean for Georgia? Was she willing to live without an answer to that most important of questions? Could she move forward without knowing the why? It was such a huge question mark in her life. She blew out a sharp breath, considering. Could she still have a relationship with Star if this question were not answered? She reached up and touched the four-leaf clover charm. Faith, hope, love, and luck. She needed more than a little of each right now. She wavered for a moment. She thought of the tattoo on Star's shoulder, of her mother's desire to keep them connected across time and distance.

There was a tangled mystery at the heart of their relationship, one that Star could not explain to her for some reason. And yet, and yet . . . Georgia believed Star loved her, had always loved her. Something had driven her away and kept them apart for all these years. Something was keeping her silent now.

Georgia hesitated, considering. She had just found Star. She did not want to lose her mother again. She had so many questions still, so much curiosity to know the woman Star had become. Maybe for now it was enough to just reconnect, to get to know each other as adults. She had waited for so long. Perhaps she could wait a little longer for answers to Star's long-ago disappearance. Decision made, Georgia slowly made her way back to Star. When she reached the garden beds, Star glanced up, looking worried.

"Okay." Georgia cleared her throat. "I'll wait, but can you promise me that someday I'll know the whole truth?"

Star nodded slowly. "Yes," she agreed. "Someday." She looked at Georgia, her expression hovering between heartbreak and hope.

Georgia took a deep breath. She could live with someday. She'd been living with it for a long time already. To her surprise, she realized that the unanswered question did not weigh quite as heavily on her heart as it had before. Star was here, standing before her, offering love and acceptance. Whatever terrible thing had happened all those years ago, it did not erase the reality of the good thing that was happening now. Being with Star felt redemptive. Georgia stepped into the garden bed and leaned over the patch of tissue paper–thin baby lettuce.

"Tell me about what happened after you left Texas," Georgia said. "How did you meet Justine?"

Star smiled, her eyes crinkling at the corners in relief. "We met in Phoenix, Arizona, in an AA meeting of all things." She picked a handful of lettuce. "It was a couple of years after I headed out of Texas. I spent a while bumming around out West, making a mess of things—petty theft and always either drunk or high, anything to keep myself from feeling the pain of all my bad choices. I ended up in Phoenix. Justine had been sober for a few years by then, on the back of a marriage gone bad. She was living with her sister and nephew, Cole, in Phoenix, working at a golf course. She loved Cole but hated Arizona. She was always dreaming of the rain and having her own place one day. And one afternoon, I came into her AA meeting. I was just passing through, but I hit a wall in Phoenix, and I knew I needed help." She straightened up with a little groan and stretched out her back for a moment, her hands full of lettuce. "The AA meeting was all bad coffee in disposable cups, industrial carpet, and fluorescent lights at the local Methodist church. And in I waltzed. I was what people kindly called a free spirit and more accurately called a loose cannon." She gave a dry chuckle, stepping out of the garden box and carefully piling the lettuce on the steps. "Justine told me later she thought I was high, but I wasn't. I was stone-cold sober. I sat down next to her. I still remember I was wearing patterned vintage bell-bottoms I'd made out of an old patchwork quilt. My hands were trembling so bad I spilled my coffee. I was going through the early stages of withdrawal. And Justine looked straight at me and asked me if I needed help. And I said, 'I've been running for a long time, but I can't run any longer. Either I get clean starting today or I'm going to die trying.' God love her, Justine opened her mouth, I think without even meaning to, and said, 'I'll help you.' And that was that."

"That was what?" Georgia held handfuls of lettuce out to Star, who took it from her and put it on the pile.

"I got clean," Star said simply, stepping back into the garden box and bending over a row of lettuce again. "Justine helped me. I've always been stubborn. We both were. I put my mind to it and I did it. Together we did it. It was hell for the first few weeks, but I got clean and then we left Phoenix soon after. Worked our way up the California coast till we hit the Pacific Northwest and then poked around until we found the islands. We were looking for a haven, a place we could live quietly, make our own way. The moment we set foot on this island, we knew this was it. We scrimped and saved, working whatever jobs we could find around here just to get by. When Justine's mom died, she left her a little money and we were able to get this place. We settled here almost twenty-five years ago. I have a lot of regrets in my life, but a lot I'm grateful for too." Star straightened and looked around, at the gardens and orchard and bees, down across the bay. "This place saved me, gave me a second chance. It helped heal me when I thought I'd be broken forever. I think of all those years I wasted numbing my pain, and I think of my life now, and even though I have regrets, I'm truly grateful. It could have ended up so differently."

"Why did you decide to get clean when you did?" Georgia asked curiously. "In Phoenix. What prompted you to do it?" She met Star's eyes, questioning.

Star smiled and then said simply, "Every decision I made—getting clean, finding the island, building this life—all of this"—she swept her hand over the yard and pointed to herself—"wasn't just for me. It was for you, Georgia May." She looked at her daughter steadily, her gaze soft and vulnerable. "I did all of it hoping that someday there would be a day like today, where we would be together again. I did all of it for you."

21

Later that night in the upstairs bathroom, Georgia scrubbed the dirt from under her fingernails and brushed her teeth, letting the events of the day settle in her mind. There had been so much, her head was still spinning. She thought of Cole, picturing his face when she'd told him about her gift. It was still such a novel thought that perhaps what she carried as a Stevens woman was a gift and not a curse. She'd grown up believing that the Stevens half of her was lesser, shameful, and wrong somehow. This lie was the unspoken narrative her family had instilled in her young heart, that the Stevens side was a defect she had to overcome to be a good citizen, worthy of the Jackson name. But now what she had learned about Star and the Stevens women turned that belief on its head. She was a Stevens through and through, and that, she was beginning to see, was a good and beautiful thing.

She thought too of the puzzling conversation she'd just had with Star in the garden.

"Georgia?" She heard Star's footsteps in the hall. "I left something in your room for you."

Surprised, Georgia hurriedly blotted her face dry. "Oh, thank you."

A pause, then, "Sleep tight."

"Don't let the bedbugs bite," Georgia responded instinctively, then froze. She hadn't completed that phrase in thirty years. Right then and there, her past and present collided. She was thirty-three, standing two feet away from her mother with a bathroom door between them. She was three years old, giggling and pink from the bath, pressing her face to Star's, and they were nose to nose, whispering the saying to each other over and over until they dissolved into peals of laughter.

"Good night . . . Mama," Georgia called through the door. She had not said that name since her arrival, when it had slipped off her tongue by accident. Since then it had felt awkward to call Star by her given name or use any term related to Star as a mother, so Georgia had avoided calling her anything at all. Now somehow it finally felt right again.

Star paused. "Good night, Georgia May," she said gently.

Wrapped in a silk robe she'd bought with her first pay raise in Paris, which felt insubstantial against the cool, wet air of the island, Georgia padded out of the bathroom and into her room. She clicked on the bedside table lamp and spied a plain white envelope sitting on her pillow, her name written in big, slanted handwriting. Georgia picked up the envelope and slid under the covers hastily, shivering in the chill. She carefully opened the envelope. Immediately, she was met with a waft of anise, mint, and thyme and the skunky underlying hint of cannabis. Star. She inhaled deeply, trying to seal the scent of her mother in her brain, to preserve it for later when she was back in Paris.

From the envelope she withdrew a stack of photographs, tattered at the edges and soft with wear. She examined the first one. Three women stared back at her. She flipped the photograph over. In Star's handwriting it said *Emma, Helen and Star Stevens.* Curious, Georgia studied the photo. Three generations of Stevens women stared back at her. The photograph looked like it had been taken in an old farmhouse kitchen, with Formica countertops and white painted cabinets. The oldest woman, Georgia guessed she was Emma, was wide hipped and green-eyed, with her long red hair pulled back in a low bun. She stood wearing an apron and holding a rolling pin in her hands, caught in the act of rolling out pie dough. Georgia studied her face. There were echoes of her own reflection there in the older woman's brow and the slant of her nose. A younger woman with Emma's same wide brow but with short, curly dark hair stood next to her. Helen, Georgia thought, looking at the laughter crinkling the corners of her eyes. My grandmother. And then little Star. Georgia stared at her mother's face in fascination. It was like looking at a slightly distorted mirror image of herself—same riot of red curls, same slanted cat eyes and snub of a nose. But Star's nose was a little longer, and her skin was lightly freckled. She was sitting on the edge of the counter, wearing a pair of light denim overalls and a pumpkin-colored turtleneck. It looked like the late '70s from the turtleneck and Helen's teal bell-bottoms. Around her neck was a thin chain, and suspended from it, the four-leaf clover charm. Georgia's hand went instinctively to her neck. She touched the charm reverently. Seeing this picture made her family history feel so real somehow.

Georgia studied every square inch of the photo with forensic intensity. This was her heritage, her family. As she stared at it, she felt a long-missing piece of her heart click into place. The Stevens women did not look heroic or saintly or angelic. They were simply women. Helen with her dark hair curling around her face, laughing into the camera lens. Emma, her mouth pinched, but a quirk of a smile as she concentrated on her pie crust, ignoring the camera. And Star sitting on the edge of the counter, legs caught by the camera mid-swing, so carefree and happy.

This was the missing half of Georgia, the half she had been told was bad and wrong, weak and to be shunned. But these women were none of those things. They were just women, with quirks and flaws and dreams. Women who had known where they belonged, who carried within them the legacy of their gifts. And they were a part of her. She was a part of them. Gazing at that photo, she had the strongest sensation that she was not alone, that she was being cradled in the embrace of three generations of Stevens women and the heritage she'd always longed for yet never known. She touched the charm at her throat.

"Faith, hope, love, and luck," she whispered. And then she added a fifth element, just two words, but they meant the world to her. "And family."

She didn't realize she was crying until a warm tear splattered the photograph. Quickly, she wiped it away. Carefully, she tucked the photo back into the envelope and picked up the stack of remaining photographs. The next one was wallet sized. Georgia flipped it over and gave a gasp of startled recognition when she saw what it was. She was staring at her own kindergarten face. Aunt Hannah had given her a terrible haircut right before school picture day, a pyramid cut of ringlets with bangs that frizzed. She'd worn her favorite overalls with a Scottie dog print T-shirt underneath. It was a truly terrible photo. But what in the world was Star doing with it?

She hastily rifled through the other photos in growing astonishment. They were all of her, one for each grade. She stared at little first grade Georgia with one giant adult-size front tooth that made her look like a chipmunk and one empty space where a new tooth was just coming in. Her fourth grade photo when she'd been convinced she looked great in mustard yellow (patently not true). She cringed at the photo of herself at her high school graduation in her cap and gown, sporting an embarrassingly large zit on her chin. Thankfully by that point she'd learned to use mousse and had refused to let Aunt Hannah

come near her hair with scissors, so at least things were looking up for her stylistically speaking.

She lined up each photo on the bed in front of her. Thirteen
years of photos, kindergarten to high school graduation. There
were also two additional photos, both ones she recognized as pictures she'd sent her dad and Aunt Hannah. One was her graduation from culinary school, which no one from her family had
attended. The other was of her standing in front of La Pomme
d'Or in her chef's whites, grinning and wide-eyed as a frightened
rabbit. She had been so elated and so terrified her first day there.

She studied the photos in bewilderment. Although Aunt
Hannah and her dad refused to talk about Star, the underlying
narrative Georgia had picked up through mean comments by
kids at school or things adults would insinuate was that Star
had abandoned them all, selfishly flown away to live her own
footloose, drug-induced life. Georgia had been led to believe
she had simply disappeared, but why, if that was true, did Star
have these photographs? Where had she gotten them? Georgia
frowned, trying to put the pieces together. Obviously, either Aunt
Hannah or Buck had known where Star was all these years.
They'd been sending her photographs of Georgia. That much
seemed clear. But why? Why had they kept in contact with her
secretly and never told Georgia about Star's whereabouts? Why
had they acted as though she didn't exist?

Georgia thought of the conversation she'd just had with Star
in the garden. The answer when she'd asked Star why she had
gotten clean. *It was for you, Georgia May. I did all of it for you.*

Something was not adding up.

Georgia stared at her own younger face, another realization
dawning on her. Star had kept track of her year after year, but
she had never come for her, never made contact until now. All

these years, even when Georgia was grown and in culinary school and in Paris, Star had known where Georgia was, but she had chosen not to reach out. So why had she done so now? Georgia had a feeling there was something more at play, something she didn't know yet. There was a reason Star had contacted her now. She just didn't know what it was.

Gently, she gathered up the photos and tucked them safely back in the envelope. So many little Georgias all with the same ginger hair and stubborn streak, all carrying the same question in her heart, the question no one would answer. Why had her mother left? But now she added another question to the mix, one which felt almost as important. Why had Star decided to reach out to her now? She set the envelope carefully on the nightstand and snuggled under the quilt. As she finally drifted off to sleep, she made a promise to herself. She'd find the answer as soon as she could.

22

Four a.m. and Georgia was wide awake after a few hours of sleep, her brain whirring. Cursing jet lag, she clambered out of bed and switched on the light. She was not going back to sleep anytime soon, that was clear. Going to the window, she lifted the sash and leaned out. It was drizzling, the night dark and cloudy. Off to her left, the apple trees gleamed white in the rain, flowers resplendent like a fairy bride. And down by the bay, she could see Cole's cabin. A warm yellow light shone through the windows. He was up too. She ducked her head back inside and shut the window. She didn't want him to look out and think she was spying, although that was exactly what she was doing. There was a peculiar feeling in her chest when she thought of Cole, a golden tickle like champagne bubbles. Their time together the day before had sparked something in her, something unexpected.

"Oh no. This is just what you do not need, Georgia May Jackson," she muttered, climbing back into bed and switching off the light. "You can't afford to get distracted." But as she lay there in the dimness, futilely waiting for sleep, she kept picturing his face. The way his pupils had dilated when he'd pulled her from the cliff's edge, those ice-blue eyes locked on hers. When she made him laugh, she felt like she'd won some sort of hard-earned prize. And then, over and over, she kept picturing the alarm on his face when that couple had approached him at the winery. There was something about that interaction that was niggling at her. Cole had not handled it like a normal person who had accidentally been mistaken for someone else. When that happened, people generally laughed it off and went on with their lives. But he had practically fled the scene. In short, he had handled it like someone who had something to hide.

"Who are you?" she whispered into the darkness. She reached for her phone and checked the clock, calculating the time change in her head. It was one p.m. in Paris. She called Phoebe. It was high time to find out more about the mysterious Cole.

Although she was at work, Phoebe was instantly on board when she heard the reason Georgia was calling. "Oh, this is so exciting!" she squealed. "Hold on. I'll go on my lunch break. We can Google stalk him together." Georgia could hear rustling on the other end of the line and then Phoebe popped back on. "Okay, so what info do you have about him?" she asked breathlessly.

Georgia listed off everything she knew about him. The details were scanty. "His name is Cole. I don't know his last name. And he worked in California, but he's been on the island for the past five years." As she said it, Georgia realized it was pathetically little to start with.

"Anything else?" Phoebe asked dubiously. "That's not a lot to go on."

"He was raised in Phoenix," Georgia sighed. "And there's speculation on the island that he worked for the CIA or that he was an actor on some popular vampire show a few years ago."

"Ooh, a vampire show? That's a good tip," Phoebe said approvingly. "Let's see!" Georgia could hear her tapping away for a few minutes. "No, no good. I'm not getting any leads. Do you have a photo of him?"

Georgia sent her one she'd snapped covertly the previous

afternoon at Lime Kiln. In it, Cole was standing on the cliff's edge, looking broodingly out at the water, watching for orcas. He hadn't noticed her snapping photos of the beautiful setting, or of him. The wind was ruffling his hair, and his jaw was set beneath his permanent five-o'clock shadow.

"Ooh la la," Phoebe purred. "You were not joking. He's sexy. Look at that jawline. He does have that broody vampire vibe going. Okay, let's see what we can find about our mystery hottie."

It turned out there were a surprising number of vampire shows to sort through. They looked through cast lists for almost an hour to no avail.

"Maybe I'm wrong," Georgia finally said reluctantly. It was surprising how many gorgeous dark-haired men there were in show business who were *not* Cole with no last name. Although they had both concluded that if Ian Somerhalder ever needed a stand-in, he was in luck. Cole could practically be his twin. "If only we had a last name . . ." Georgia snapped her fingers, remembering something her cab driver had mentioned when she'd arrived at the cottage. "Wait, his maternal aunt's last name was Hardy. Justine Hardy. See if you get anywhere with that information."

Tap. Tap. Tap. A few seconds of silence and then Phoebe let out a squeal.

"Georgia May, I found him! And you are not going to believe this!"

Georgia's phone pinged with a text. She opened the image Phoebe had sent and stared at it in astonishment. It was Cole all right, standing on a red carpet wearing a tuxedo, looking broodingly handsome as ever with one arm around his aunt Justine. Georgia recognized her immediately from the picture in the living room. On his other side, Cole was flanked by none

other than King Charles of the United Kingdom, who was beaming at Cole and handing him a medal of some sort.

"Who ARE you?" Georgia breathed.

"His name is Cabot Cole Montgomery," Phoebe said excitedly.
"Dr. Cabot Cole Montgomery. He's not an actor." She sounded
vaguely disappointed by this information. "Nothing about vampires at all, actually. And he's not a medical doctor. It looks like
he won some sort of major sustainable technology innovation
award ten years ago. That photo is of him getting the award from
King Charles—at that time he was Prince Charles." She paused,
her tone a touch awed. "Georgia, your oyster farmer is a bona
fide genius scientist."

"Anemone is considered the best restaurant on the island,"
Cole told Georgia when he picked her up at one in the afternoon later that day. "It's a little hidden gem."

Then he turned to the road, set his jaw, and didn't say anything more. They drove in awkward silence. Cole seemed to be
totally ignoring her, which suited Georgia just fine. She studied
his profile, trying to reconcile what she'd learned in the early
hours of the morning with the man seated next to her. Nothing
made sense. What was he doing here? After she'd hung up with
Phoebe, she'd stayed awake until sunrise googling everything
she could about Dr. Cabot Cole Montgomery. She'd watched
interview clips on YouTube, pored over his Wikipedia biography,
and scrolled through dozens of pictures of him. What Phoebe
had told her was just the tip of the iceberg. Dr. Montgomery
held a master's degree from UCLA in something biotech related
and a PhD from Berkeley in Environmental Science, Policy, and
Management. He'd founded a start-up in San Diego developing
some exciting new renewable energy source that used algae.

Georgia's eyes had started to glaze over when she got too far into the technical language about algae, but she'd watched some interviews with him. It was Cole all right, with shaggy hair and adorable chunky glasses, looking like a movie star playing a geeky but brilliant scientist, but apparently he really WAS a geeky, brilliant scientist. She'd found a number of articles mentioning how promising his innovations were. Top people in the field were interviewed about his work.

"This could be a major breakthrough as a source of clean, renewable energy," his PhD adviser at Berkeley said in an interview with CNN.

"It could change how we harvest energy from the earth," the head of a major biofuel company commented in the same interview.

An article in the *New York Times* about him was titled, "Can This Man Keep the Lights On and Save the Planet at the Same Time?" and he'd been named one of *Time* magazine's 35 under 35 entrepreneurs to watch. A tech billionaire had invested heavily in his start-up. Then in 2017, Cole had won a prestigious global sustainable technology innovation award. His star was rising, but just as he seemed poised to become a giant name in biotech and renewable energy, there was a terrible car accident. A woman identified as his fiancée was gravely injured. Shortly thereafter he'd sold his start-up to a major biotech firm and seemingly vanished from public view. After 2018, Georgia found a few online forums asking where he was now and conjecturing everything from his early demise by suicide to sheep farming in Argentina. Then nothing. Dr. Cabot Cole Montgomery had become a ghost.

A ghost who was currently sitting next to her in Martha, driving her to lunch. It boggled her mind. Georgia shook her head and sat back. The world was indeed a strange place. She was wildly intrigued by what she'd learned, but not sure if she should broach the topic with him. He seemed grouchy. Again. She decided to bide her time. When it felt right, she would tell him that she knew about his secret identity. For now she was going to enjoy the rare sunshine and the spring day.

Determined not to let his mood affect her, Georgia reviewed her goal for the day—don't try too hard and focus on cultivating wonder and delight. Star had given her a pep talk at breakfast when Georgia confessed she was feeling a little nervous to visit a restaurant again. The debacle at La Pomme d'Or was still so fresh in her mind.

"Just give it a try and see what happens," Star urged Georgia. "You spent so many years of your life in restaurants. It's a big part of who you are and how you shared your gift with the world. Maybe if you're back in a restaurant again, a good restaurant that's doing things the right way, it could spark something for you."

Pushing aside a flutter of apprehension, Georgia reluctantly agreed. After all, it was just lunch. What was the worst that could happen? Even if she couldn't taste anything, maybe Star was right. Perhaps being back in a restaurant as a guest and not a chef would remind her of why she'd fallen in love with restaurant life in the first place. It couldn't hurt to at least go and see, she supposed.

Now, driving to Anemone, her stomach rumbled even though she knew the food would taste awful. Star had made her chia pudding that morning, and she'd eaten most of it, but it was hard to make herself eat enough when everything tasted bad. And the chia pudding, though it was packed with nutrients, had the unfortunate consistency of frog eggs. Determined to enjoy what she could, Georgia rolled her window all the way down as they drove up the east side of the island. She put her hand out the window and let her fingers surf the breeze. She had a feeling she'd never tire of this fresh island air, salty and spicy with evergreens. It was euphoric.

Anemone was a wood-clad restaurant perched on a cliff wedged between a thick stand of evergreens and the sea. It was small, with fewer than a dozen tables and a live edge wood bar that seated another six people. The inside was rustic and airy with a high cathedral ceiling, a whimsical round window at the peak, and a nautical theme—old fishing buoys, a weathered wooden boat suspended from the ceiling, and oars hung on the walls.

The real star of the show was the view, however. The entire back wall of the restaurant was glass-paned windows looking out over the water toward smaller evergreen-capped islands. The panorama was wild and remote and breathtaking. Georgia sat down with Cole at their cozy table for two and gazed out at the slate gray water. Their server, a young man who introduced himself as River, set a menu in front of her, and Georgia perused the options. Local lamb grown on the island with herbs and root vegetables the restaurant grew in their own gardens. Pork belly with homemade sauerkraut and applesauce from heirloom apples. A few seafood dishes—house smoked salmon on a bed of locally grown potatoes and foraged mushrooms, Westcott Bay clams in white wine from the winery, raw oysters on the half shell in a cider mignonette using locally pressed cider from the cidery. Georgia's mouth watered at the descriptions.

She looked around. Many of the tables were taken up by what appeared to be a tour group of middle-aged Korean ladies. They were snapping photos and chatting animatedly with another server, a waifish young woman wearing what looked like hand-knit wool pants and a matching vest. A family of four with two tweens sat at another table by the wall of windows. All four were dressed head to toe in hiking gear. A balding man in a wool fisherman's sweater sat at the bar nursing a pint of beer and working his way through a large bowl of steamed clams.

"The whole ethos of Anemone is using locally sourced food from the Pacific Northwest, both from farmers and artisans on the island and also foragers," Cole explained to Georgia. "They source their shellfish from Westcott Bay Shellfish Company, and Star sells them her honey. It's simple food, not fussy, just good, well-prepared island fare. They pride themselves on being ecologically responsible too. I know the owner, Myra. She grows a lot of the produce they use here. She's great."

Impressed, Georgia ordered the house smoked salmon with potatoes. Cole ordered the clams. Georgia kept sneaking glances at him, trying to reconcile all she'd read last night with the man sitting across from her, frowning over the menu. How was this the same person? Brilliant PhD scientist innovator to . . . remote island oyster farmer? It was perplexing. Her phone pinged with a text from Phoebe.

Have you told him you know about his secret sexy scientist identity yet? Phoebe included no less than a dozen question marks with her text and several puzzling emojis including an eggplant, flames, and a beaker.

Working on it, Georgia typed back, hitting send and glancing at Cole surreptitiously. She wasn't quite sure how to broach the subject. How would it change their dynamic if he knew she knew who he was? Theirs felt like a fragile peace, and she wondered if he'd retreat into his shell. But she was wildly curious to know how he'd ended up here, going from running his own start-up to working at an oyster farm in orange rubber overalls. She was going to ask him at some point soon. Her curiosity was getting the better of her.

Deciding to just be forthright and see what happened,

Georgia leaned forward and met his eyes. "So this morning I woke up way too early with jet lag and spent some time poking around the Internet, and look what I stumbled across." She held her phone out to him, zeroing in on the image of him accepting his prestigious award. "Your first and last name. Hello, Dr. Montgomery."

He froze, staring at the photo. "How did you find that?" he demanded. He looked visibly shaken.

"So I guess you're not that actor from *The Vampire Diaries*, huh? Kelsey is going to be so disappointed," Georgia said lightly.

Cole said nothing. His face had gone blank, no emotion.

"You want to say anything about this?" she invited.

"No." Nothing more. It was like talking to a brick wall.

She sighed and clicked off the phone, putting it in her purse. She leaned across the table, talking in a low voice so the other diners wouldn't hear. "What in the world are you doing working on an oyster farm?" she asked. "You won the world's most prestigious sustainable technology award and then just disappeared off the face of the earth?"

Just then, River approached their table wearing an apprehensive expression. "Uh, folks, there's been an incident in the kitchen." He cleared his throat nervously.

Georgia and Cole both looked up. "What kind of an incident?" Cole asked. He sounded relieved to be off the conversational hook.

"Um." The young man glanced back toward the kitchen and lowered his voice. "Our new cook, uh, well. She just chopped the top of her finger off slicing scallops."

Cole winced and Georgia sucked in a breath. Out of the corner of her eye, she saw three people rush out the back of the restaurant into the parking lot. One of them was wearing chef's whites and cradling her hand while the other two supported her. Georgia recognized the server with the knitted garb as she helped the injured chef into a car, then jumped into the driver's seat, and sped off. They left behind a small, distraught-looking dark-haired woman who watched them go.

"I'm really sorry, folks, but your meal is not going to be able to be served," River said. "We don't think we can get another chef in today. We apologize for the inconvenience. All drinks you were served are on us." He turned to go.

"Wait a minute," Cole called, flashing Georgia the briefest hint of a smirk. River paused. Georgia didn't like the look of that smile. Oh no, surely, he wasn't going to . . .

"This is your lucky day, pal. Because this lovely woman right here is a professional chef in Paris," Cole told him.

Georgia shot him a dirty look just as River asked, "Really?"

"Yes, it's true," Cole said helpfully. "And she's got a heart of gold. Loves to volunteer her time to help others in need."

"Just a minute, let me go get Myra," River said and he loped off, looking hopeful.

Georgia rounded on Cole. "What do you think you're doing?" she hissed.

He shrugged with faux innocence. "Helping you out. You said you needed to get your spark back. What better way to do it than to help this local restaurant out of their difficulty?" He took a slow sip of water. "After all, one good turn deserves another, isn't that how that saying goes?" He gave her an arch look.

And just when she was starting to warm up to him . . .

"You are intolerable," Georgia murmured hotly. But there was no backing out now. Here came River with the small, harried-looking woman from the parking lot. The woman gave a tired smile when she saw Cole, and he raised a hand in greeting. "Hey, Myra."

Then she saw Georgia, and her face lit up like she'd just glimpsed her salvation. "River tells me you're a trained chef?" she asked tentatively.

"In Paris," Cole supplied helpfully. "Her restaurant has a Michelin star."

"Two stars," Georgia corrected, "but I'm only a sous-chef." No one acknowledged either correction.

"Oh, thank goodness." The woman let out a huge sigh of relief. "I'm Myra Yoon." She stuck out her hand. She was a lean, petite woman who looked to be in her early forties, with an earthy vibe, the kind of person who undoubtedly wore natural deodorant and composted. "Can you, do you think . . . could you step in for us, just for today?" Myra gave her a pleading look, then rushed to explain. "I know it's a lot to ask and you're probably on vacation and I totally understand if you can't, but we're booked solid for lunch and dinner and we can't really afford to lose a day of customers." She trailed off, looking so hopeful . . . and tired.

Georgia softened. In Myra's eyes, Georgia recognized a kindred spirit, a woman passionate about food, trying to make a go of it in an industry heavily biased toward men. Women in the restaurant industry were a sisterhood. They had a responsibility to lift one another up, Georgia firmly believed. She owed it to Myra to help her if she could.

"Okay, I'll see what I can do. Don't expect much," she warned with a sigh, standing and pushing her chair back. "I'm not very experienced with these ingredients, and cooking in a completely new kitchen is a tall order."

Not to mention that she couldn't actually taste any of the ingredients or dishes. She looked around at the other tables, at the family with tweens and all the middle-aged ladies in the Korean tour group. Now the entire restaurant would be waiting for her to whip up a culinary miracle. Her stomach did a flip. What if she failed? What if she made another salty mousse sort of mistake?

Myra heaved a huge sigh of relief. "Thank you so much. You don't know what this means to us. I'm not a chef, but I know my way around the kitchen. I've been helping out while we look for a sous-chef anyway, so I can sort of guide you through the recipes. And I think that together River and I can handle serving all the tables today. I'm fluent in Korean, so I can take this tour group, and River can handle the rest of the lunch reservations. If we work together, I think we might be able to manage this." She cast an anxious look in Georgia's direction.

"Okay then, let's get going," Georgia responded graciously. As she followed Myra toward the kitchen, she turned and flipped Cole the middle finger. He smiled grimly and called out, "Have fun, honey. I'll come back to pick you up at closing."

Georgia pivoted and surveyed the room. "Excuse me," she said loudly. Every eye swiveled to her. The Korean tour group ladies fell silent. The tweens looked up from whatever they were doing on their smartphones. "If you're thinking that the handsome gentleman at the table right over there by the window looks familiar, the answer is yes. He is that famous and very sexy actor from *The Vampire Diaries*. And he loves meeting fans, so today only, he's going to be taking selfies with anyone who wants to. Don't be shy, just go ahead and approach him." She pointed to Cole, shooting him a big, bright, evil smile.

Immediately, both the tweens started snapping pictures of Cole from across the room while a few of the middle-aged Korean ladies reached for their selfie sticks and pushed back their chairs. The balding man in the fisherman's sweater kept eating clams, watching the commotion with interest.

Cole shot her a look of pure loathing as he jumped to his feet and practically bolted from the restaurant. Feeling marginally victorious, Georgia resolutely put all thoughts of Dr. Cabot Cole Montgomery, mysterious vanishing brilliant scientist / current oysterman / all-around pain in the ass from her mind and followed Myra into the kitchen. She had bigger fish to fry. It was time to make some magic. And she was absolutely terrified.

23

"Julia, help me, please! How am I going to pull this off?" Georgia whispered, looking around the unfamiliar kitchen. She was scared to try to cook in a new environment when she couldn't taste anything but bitter. What if she failed and made Anemone look bad? What if her cooking reflected poorly on Myra? Georgia paused for a moment, trying to quell the panic fluttering like a trapped bird in her chest. And then softly in her ear she heard a whisper, her mentor's voice giving timeless advice. "To be a good cook you have to be adventurous," Julia reminded her. "You should try your hand at new recipes, learn from any mistakes you make, determine to be fearless, and most of all, have fun." Georgia drew a deep breath, steadied. Julia's words were just what she needed to hear.

"Okay," she whispered firmly. She stuck out her chin. "I can do this. Adventurous, fearless, and fun."

"That's the spirit," Julia said with a wink and an encouraging smile.

What followed were the most intense, chaotic, creative nine hours of Georgia's life. After taking a quick inventory of the kitchen, she dived right into cooking the orders that were already waiting. The kitchen was compact but well equipped, and she was soon more or less up to speed on where everything was. With Myra's help, Georgia quickly stripped down the menu and served only the dishes she felt confident in making, like the smoked salmon with potatoes and the mussels in white wine. A few of the more fringe items—seaweed salad with scallop crudo, for instance, they quietly shelved for another day. Together she and Myra worked with an almost frantic efficiency, and with River's help, they managed to keep the dining room service moving along more or less smoothly. Myra tasted each thing Georgia cooked and suggested tweaks if it wasn't quite right. The preparation of each dish took longer than it should have, but the end result was better than expected.

Gradually as the day wore on, Georgia settled into the rhythm of the kitchen. As she relaxed, she started to notice something happening to the ingredients beneath her fingers. As she touched them, poking and prodding, kneading and caressing, the sensations she used to feel when she cooked started to return. She could feel the icy gurgle of the salt water against weather-beaten black rock as she tossed a handful of local mussels into a pot of butter and white wine. She chopped a foraged mushroom and inhaled the damp, loamy soil of the forest spicy with ferns and dripping with cool humidity. She grinned, buoyed by a wave of relief. At least for tonight, her Technicolor senses were in full swing. With a satisfied sigh of contentment, she spooned Star's honey over local goat cheese on rounds of sunflower seed crackers, hearing all around her the nectar-drunk buzzing of the bees. It felt like pure joy to handle these ingredients. She was where she wanted to be, doing what she most loved. The realization brought her up short. This was what Star was talking about. This was delight. How long had it been since she'd felt it in a kitchen?

"Your food is getting rave reviews," Myra told her as she returned from the dining room. She looked harried but pleased. "One customer told me she'd forgotten fish could taste that good. She said her meal reminded her of her childhood in the countryside outside of Seoul, catching fish with her grandfather. She actually teared up when she told me. She said it made her remember how much she had loved her visits with him. And a couple of our regular customers told me it's the best meal they've ever had here!"

Hearing those words, Georgia remembered what Star had said to her about using her gift, how it was a blessing to be shared with others. At least for the moment, her gift seemed to be working. And it felt wonderful. This was how she was meant to live, she thought as she plated a pork belly dish. She was doing something that brought her delight and was a blessing to others. It felt exactly right.

Many busy hours later, long after dark, Myra ushered the last customers out the door and came back to the kitchen. Georgia glanced at the clock, surprised to find it was past eleven. The time had flown by.

"You're amazing. So much better than the chef we have now," Myra said frankly. She looked frazzled but happy. "Our previous chef retired to Florida in September, and we've been trying to find a good replacement ever since. This last one was from Portland and had good references, but she just isn't working out well. Frankly, I think she may be high half the time. You're not looking for a job, are you?" she asked hopefully.

Georgia laughed as she tidied up her work area. "No, I'm heading back to Paris soon. But I've enjoyed today. Thank you for letting me experiment. I haven't had so much fun in a kitchen in . . . well . . . a long time." In truth, she'd forgotten cooking could feel like this. It almost felt like she was back in Texas under the big loblolly pine tree out back of the ranch house, playing pretend in her toy kitchen, whipping up imagined delicacies from pine needles and dust and weeds she collected. That's it. Today had felt like play.

"You saved us," Myra said. She heaved a huge sigh of relief. "How can I ever repay you?"

"No need," Georgia said lightly. "I enjoyed myself. Today helped me as well, more than you know."

Her phone pinged with a text message. It was from a number she didn't recognize. She opened it.

Myra texted me. Coming to pick you up in 5 min.—Cole

Oh, this was going to be interesting. She'd gotten so caught up in cooking she'd forgotten how strained they'd left things.

She grabbed her bag and bid farewell to Myra and River. River gave her a sweaty, fervent handshake, and Myra squeezed her in a tight, grateful hug.

"Do you think . . ." Myra pulled back and hesitated. "Would you be open to filling in any more for us?" she asked, hastening to add, "Just until we can figure out something else? I'll pay you for your time."

Georgia considered. She'd enjoyed herself, but was it the best thing to do? Was it going to help get her where she needed to go?

"Let me think about it, and I'll call you in the morning," she promised.

Carrying two bottles of cider and a giant jar of homemade pickles that Myra had insisted she take home, Georgia let herself out into the cold, wet night, shivering a little. The kitchen had been hot, and she had not brought a jacket to the restaurant, since the day had been warm. Now, alone in the dark under a clear sky bright with stars, she took a deep breath and exhaled. Today had been exhilarating. She was still shaking a little from the pure adrenaline. She felt like her feet were floating a few inches off the ground. She closed her eyes and breathed in, letting the silence and the night settle around her.

A few minutes later, Cole pulled into the parking lot in a spray of gravel. Dusty Springfield was wailing "Son of a Preacher Man" through the closed windows. Georgia climbed inside. Without a word, Cole reversed onto the road as she was buckling her seat belt. She glanced at his profile, at his hands gripping the steering wheel hard. He looked so stern and remote it was almost intimidating. Almost. But she wasn't easily intimidated. She'd stared down irate customers and volatile chefs for years. She was a woman who rose to a challenge, not shrank from it.

"Care to talk about it?" she asked lightly.

"Nope." Nothing more. His jaw clenched and he drove fast, taking the turns a little too hard. She sat back and looked out the window. After a minute, he surprised her by asking, "How'd it go today?"

"It was . . . amazing, actually," Georgia admitted, breaking into a smile at the memory of the busy, happy hours. "It's been a lot of years since cooking's felt that fun. I'd forgotten it could feel like that."

He grunted. "That's good."

She said nothing, and a stilted silence fell between them.

"Cole, what are you doing here on the island?" she asked finally. She'd been wondering what his story was since the moment she first saw him, standing in the kitchen in those ridiculous orange rubber overalls, a dripping pail of clams in his hand.

She let the questions hang in the silence. He said nothing for a long time.

Finally, he sighed. "You're not going to let this go, are you?"

"Can you blame me for wondering?" she replied honestly. "Now that I know who you are?"

He didn't reply, but turned the wheel sharply, taking a hard right onto another road. After a couple of minutes, she saw the cottage fly by.

"I think you just passed the house," she remarked.

"We're not going home," he said evenly.

Surprised, she watched in the rearview mirror as the road unspooled behind them in the red glow of the taillights. For a brief, irrational instant, she felt a little thrill of alarm. Where was he taking her? No one knew where she was. They could be headed anywhere in the night. But then she brushed away the thought. She trusted Cole. Despite his surly demeanor, he was an honorable man.

"Let's play Twenty Questions," she said. "I'll start. Are you going to take me somewhere remote and murder me?"

He snorted. "No. I'm taking you to Roche Harbor. Since you seem determined to pry my life story out of me, I figured we should go somewhere pleasant for the interrogation." He sounded resigned.

"Oh. Well, good . . ." Feeling satisfied, she stared out into the darkness. After a moment she added softly, "You don't have to tell me if you don't want to."

He didn't respond. Instead he asked with a touch of incredulity, "Did you really think I was going to murder you and what, feed you to the seals?"

"Well." She shrugged. "A girl can never be too careful. Now that I know your secret."

"One of them," he muttered.

"What?" She turned to him curiously.

"Nothing." He stared straight ahead. "And seals don't eat people. Next question."

"Are you wanted by the FBI or Interpol?"

"No."

"Are you in the witness protection program?" She was starting to warm to the game.

"Seriously?" He shot her an incredulous look. "Me being on the island has nothing to do with international crimes or espionage. It's strictly self-imposed."

They drove into Roche Harbor, and Georgia forgot her questions for a moment. "Oh, how adorable!"

The tiny town of white-framed buildings and picture-perfect Craftsman houses spread below them in a semicircle around a beautiful marina and bay. Yellow lights twinkled on the dark water, and white sailboats and yachts bobbed gently in the breeze.

"Yes, it is. A playground for every rich guy with a yacht on the West Coast," Cole explained with a touch of irony. "It used to be a company town with a lime kiln over a hundred years ago. Now you can get a fifteen-dollar omelet and rub elbows with retired Microsoft executives all year round."

"It's like a postcard," Georgia said, thoroughly charmed. "Can we walk around a little?"

Cole pulled into a parking spot near the tiny town center. There was a diminutive grocery store called the Company Store, a historic hotel and restaurant, a real estate office, and a few boutiques that looked like they catered to a high-end clientele. In front of the Company Story stood a line of white painted booths, closed now, that Cole told her was a local artisans market.

"Star sells her honey there on Saturdays in the tourist season," he said. He turned off the ignition, and they got out of the car. She shivered, and Cole reached behind his seat, pulling out a bulky old fleece and handing it to her.

"Thank you." She put it on gratefully. She was constantly surprised by how cold the island could be in spring. The fleece smelled like Cole, that soap and pine sap scent with a hint of dark roast espresso. Delicious. She wanted to bury her nose in it but instead snuggled up and tried to get warm. Streetlights illuminated the tiny town center, but they were the only ones out and about at this late hour. In one or two of the houses up the hill there were lights on, but otherwise, everything was quiet. Georgia looked around her, delighted by the quaint charm of Roche Harbor, like a throwback from a hundred years ago. They wandered toward the marina, walking side by side in silence. It felt like they were the only two people in the world.

24

To her surprise, Cole jammed his hands in his pockets and said, "You asked what I'm still doing here? Hiding, I guess."

"Hiding from what?"

"Success. Failure. The biggest mistake of my life." He sounded morose. They passed the darkened grocery store and a tiny, tidy park with flowers in the center of the town.

Intrigued, Georgia waited.

Cole sighed. "I told you about how I grew up, right? Dreaming of being Captain Planet." Georgia nodded and Cole continued. "Aunt Justine always supported those dreams, even though they seemed far-fetched for the kid of a single mom who struggled month to month just to get by. But I had two things going for me. I was smart, really smart, and I was persistent. I knew how to work hard against long odds. I'd seen my mom do it my whole life. After high school, I got a full scholarship to the University of Arizona. I double majored in environmental science and applied biotechnology."

"Smarty-pants," Georgia murmured, impressed. They stepped onto the long wooden pier that jutted out into the dark water of the marina, wandering past a half dozen good-sized yachts. Most were dark and quiet. Light spilled from a few others. Through the glass sliding back door of one she saw a paunchy man doing a crossword puzzle at a table. The wooden planks creaked under their footfalls, and the slap of the water against the hulls of the boats was the only other sound.

Cole looked a little embarrassed by her praise. "It was Aunt Justine who fostered a love for nature and care for the earth in me. At school I was naturally good at what I chose to study, and I was also motivated. I really wanted to make a difference in the world. By twenty-six, I was on track to a career that would make Captain Planet proud. I got my master's degree at UCLA and my PhD from Berkeley. While I was doing my research for my PhD, I traveled to Europe and Asia—France, Korea, Japan. And I uncovered some really exciting scientific data during those research trips that no one else had stumbled on yet. It was potentially a huge breakthrough in the area of biotechnology and clean energy. It got me a lot of job offers, but more significantly, it brought me an angel investor. A tech billionaire named Bruce Hannigan wanted to back my research. He told me to assemble a team and gave me free rein to continue my work down in San Diego where there is a lot of algae and biofuel research already going on. It was a dream come true."

"Sounds like it," Georgia said. She knew nothing about his area of research, but it sounded impressive. They passed a sleek red sailboat, and a black Lab barked a greeting at them from the deck, tail wagging.

"My research had the potential to change how we use biofuels, to develop new ecologically responsible biofuel technology that could change the landscape of energy," Cole explained. "We were working on developing a new kind of clean energy. It was exciting and cutting-edge. And then I met Amy."

His tone of voice changed, suddenly wistful. He stared out across the dark water pensively as they passed a slew of moored boats. "She was my angel investor, Bruce Hannigan's oldest daughter. She was the daughter of a billionare but the most normal, well-adjusted person I'd ever met. She worked at Chick-fil-A in high school, and when I met her she still drove this old white beater Toyota Camry she'd bought with the money from that job. She worked hard and didn't take things for granted. She was whip-smart and funny, such a firecracker. She'd been crowned Miss California right out of high school, and she used her platform to champion girls in STEAM careers. She wanted to be a social worker. We just clicked."

Cole came to a halt under a light pole on the pier and Georgia stopped beside him, afraid that if she even swallowed he'd stop talking. She wanted to know more. She wanted to know everything about Cole and Amy and what had happened to bring him to this place. She'd seen a photo in one of the articles about the crash. Amy had been very pretty, an all-American blonde with a wide, winning smile. As wholesome and sweet as apple pie.

"Amy was the best thing that ever happened to me," Cole said, and his voice held a rasp of longing. He looked down and scuffed the toe of his shoe across the rough, weathered boards of the pier. "She normalized everything for me—the intense world of research and development and biotech and the California lifestyle, the money and the politics and the big business. She made me feel like I didn't have to be consumed by my work. I'd been pushing hard since high school. I barely had a life outside of research—no hobbies, no free time. She gave me a reason to change all that. She liked to go hiking, and we'd sometimes slip away and road-trip up the coast, see the redwoods, camp under the stars. She made life fun again, and it had been a lot of years since I'd had that."

He sighed, more of a groan, and shook his head, then walked on, past piers that branched off the main arterial, like tree limbs off a trunk, past dozens of sailboats and tugboats and Pacific trawlers.

"Everything was great for a while, and then I won the Pierce-

Morton award. It's a globally recognized award, given every two years for outstanding advances in sustainable technology innovation. All of a sudden, I was in the public eye. It got crazy fast. Job offers were flooding in. There was an article in the *New York Times*."

"I saw that one," Georgia confirmed, skipping a little to keep up with his long-legged stride.

"I got mentioned in *Time* magazine."

"Not the best photo of you, but a good article," Georgia commented.

Cole paused and shot her a skeptical look. "What did you do, google my entire life story?"

"Pretty much," Georgia admitted. "It's amazing what you can find on the Internet if you really poke around."

"Then why am I even telling you this?" Cole scowled.

"Because I still don't understand how you got from algae innovation's golden boy to incognito oyster farmer," Georgia explained.

Cole grimaced and paused by a tugboat called *The High Tide*. "Success ruined me," he said bluntly. "For a guy who just likes to be left alone to geek out and research, the high-profile publicity was a nightmare. I started experiencing pretty severe anxiety, and my doctor put me on meds to calm me down and help me function. I felt trapped in the spotlight. All these people clamoring to see advances in our research and the product, people trying to buy the company, offer me jobs, interview me, steal our research. It was a circus. I felt like an animal in a zoo. I wanted to leave San Diego, go somewhere quieter where I could do research and not be hounded. I had been offered an interesting opportunity in Korea and was seriously thinking about it, but Amy wanted to stay. San Diego was her home." He exhaled in exasperation. "I felt trapped. I loved her. We'd gotten engaged a few months before I won the award, and we were starting to plan the wedding. She was the best thing about my life, but we didn't have the same vision for our future. I can see that now, but at the time I couldn't. I couldn't think about leaving her, and she couldn't think about leaving San Diego, and I was burning out and starting to spiral." He paused at the end of the pier and Georgia stopped next to him. He peered out at the dark, calm water, but she could tell he wasn't really seeing what was in front of him. He was somewhere else entirely.

"The research was promising," he continued quietly, "but we needed time and money to develop it. I just wanted to go away, find somewhere where I could think. Everyone wanted results, and all I could give them were promises that we were doing the best we could. And that wasn't enough. Even Bruce was getting antsy. It felt like the walls were closing in. I was working all the time, desperate to somehow get ahead of things, but I couldn't seem to do it. I was always one step behind." He was riffling his hands through his hair, looking distraught. She could see his jaw clenched in the dim glow from the overhead lights on the pier.

"You don't have to tell me more," she said quietly, alarmed by his obvious distress, but he shook his head.

"No, you can't stop the story here." He shut his eyes. When he spoke, his voice sounded flat. "I have to finish it. But I don't blame you if you don't want to have anything to do with me when you know everything."

"Try me," Georgia countered softly.

Cole looked at her, his face doubtful, then continued with his story. "My mom had passed away a few years before, when I was doing my research in Japan. It was pretty quick, a heart attack, and I didn't make it home in time. That really ate away at me. She was so proud of me, and I knew she understood why I wasn't with her when she passed. I was on a 747 over the Pacific, flying as fast as I could to get to her in time, but I didn't make it. Even though I knew I couldn't have done anything differently, I still felt like I'd abandoned her. So when Aunt Justine got her diagnosis, I felt like my entire life was crashing down once more. She was in the late stages when they diagnosed her. It was terminal. There was nothing they could do. She was my only living relative. The day I got the news, I'd just had a huge fight with Bruce. He'd told me if we didn't have something tangible soon, he was considering pulling our funding. I went from that meeting to getting the call from Justine about her diagnosis. It just all felt like too much."

He trailed away, his voice going jagged at the end of the sentence.

"I'm so sorry," Georgia said softly. She could hear the pain underlying his words, as though it had happened only recently, not five years before. She reached out instinctively, wanting to put her hand on his arm, to offer comfort, but then stopped, unsure. He stood woodenly next to her at the end of the pier, staring out across the black water. The moon was high in the sky, making a trail of light over the surface of the sea. "I don't remember exactly what happened, but from what the police and doctors pieced together later, they think I took several times the amount of the anxiety meds than I was supposed to. And then followed that up with a few shots of Jim Beam neat. I didn't even like whiskey," Cole admitted, laughing mirthlessly. "I just wanted to dull the panic and the pain. I was so angry and scared thinking about losing the funding, but truly, I was shattered inside thinking about losing Justine." He paused. Somewhere nearby a dog barked and out in the water, a seal popped up and looked at them for a moment, then dived back down below surface.

"By the time Amy found me at the lab, I was pretty cognitively impaired, but neither of us really realized how much." Cole's voice was quiet, confessional. "Later she said she knew something was off, but figured it was the stress and anxiety, maybe lack of sleep. And I didn't realize how not okay I was. She convinced me to come home." Cole swallowed hard. "She'd made pasta carbonara. She wanted to show me wedding invitations she liked. I finally agreed to go with her, and then I made a really terrible mistake."

He squeezed his eyes closed as if to keep from remembering. When Cole spoke again, his voice was hoarse with regret.

"It was July twelfth. Six forty in the evening. Not even dark yet. It was only a few blocks to our apartment. We'd rented an apartment close to the lab so we'd see more of each other, even if I was working crazy hours, which I always was. When we got to the car, she had an urgent message from work, so she asked if I'd mind driving home. I should have said no, but neither of us realized how under the influence I was. We got into her Camry. I remember Ed Sheeran was playing on the radio. She loved Ed Sheeran. She wanted to dance to "Perfect" at our wedding. We left the lab and she was on her phone, emailing work. Two blocks from our apartment, I drove her Camry into a telephone pole. It was a stupid accident. Entirely my fault. The doctors suspect I may have blacked out for a moment. I went through an intersection and lost control. I was fine, just a little bruised and sore, but Amy wasn't. Her side of the car was the one that hit the pole. She was paralyzed from the waist down. She was in the hospital for a month, and she never regained sensation in her legs."

"Oh, Cole," Georgia breathed. She'd read about the accident and Cole being cited for a DUI, about Amy's injuries, but it was different to hear the story from him, to see his face twist with grief and remorse.

"I took the best part of my life, and in one careless moment I destroyed it. I destroyed her life and I destroyed us." His voice sounded so raw, his expression anguished as he gazed out over the quiet harbor. "I will never forgive myself for what I did to her," he said bluntly. "All the best parts of my life ended that day."

Georgia had so many questions. What had happened after Amy came home from the hospital? Amy had lived, so why were they not still together? But as she glanced at his face in profile, seeing his ravaged expression, she did not press further. It was still so fresh for him, she could sense. Years may have passed, but in some way, Cole was still back in the wreckage of that accident. She laid a hand on his arm, offering wordless comfort. He glanced down as though surprised to find her with him.

"I'm so sorry," Georgia said, watching his face. He looked . . . broken. And so resigned.

He nodded. "Me too."

They stood in silence for a moment, then Georgia asked quietly, "What happened after the accident?"

Cole exhaled heavily. "Bruce pulled my funding after the accident, not that I blame him. That effectively shut down my research. I could have gotten funding from somewhere else, but . . . I just couldn't continue. The week Amy got out of the hospital, I stopped the research project. I'd lost the desire to keep going. Nothing else mattered except Amy and trying to help her get better." He frowned. "I gave Bruce what we'd done so far, and he sold it to a big biotech company that had been trying to get us to work with them for years. Then I devoted myself to caring for Amy full-time. But a couple of months after the accident, she broke off our engagement." His stopped and swallowed. She could feel the tension radiating from him in the muscles under her fingers. "When she called it quits I'd just finished my requirements with the state of California for my DUI charges from the accident. After she left there was nothing for me in San Diego. I packed up my apartment the next weekend and came up here to help Justine. I never went back."

Georgia didn't know what to say. It felt like such a pointless tragedy.

"And you've been hiding out here ever since? Where no one knows who you really are?"

Cole gave a mirthless laugh and gazed at her bleakly. "Cabot Montgomery is a loser, a man who ruined everything he touched. Why would I want to still be him? At least here I can hold down a job that does some small bit of good in the world. I can help grow oysters that clean the water and feed people. And no one looks at me with judgment or expectations or pity. The only way I can live with what I did is if I can leave who I was in the past."

Georgia bit her lip. "That's the saddest thing I've ever heard anyone say," she told him honestly.

"I did it to myself," Cole responded with a tired shrug. He turned and faced her. "And now I have to live with the consequences for the rest of my life." He looked so resolute and hopeless standing there, hair tousled by the wind. Georgia felt her heart break for him. What a terrible waste of a life.

"I think we'd better head back," Cole said, checking his watch. "I've got an early morning at the farm washing the oyster seed."

Silently, they walked back to Martha. Georgia glanced at Cole as they retraced their steps, her heart hurting for all he'd lost. She wanted to comfort him but didn't have the words. Much as she might wish to ease his burden, she sensed she could not fix him. He was trapped by regret and shame in a cage he'd built himself. If only he could find a way to set himself free.

25

Clambering into Martha in the Roche Harbor parking lot, Georgia settled into her seat and reached for her seat belt. Just then, her stomach rumbled loudly. Key poised over the ignition, Cole looked over, startled, and Georgia blushed. "I forgot to eat today," she explained. "Too busy." Cole's lips quirked in a small smile as her stomach gurgled again. The sound lifted the sadness lingering between them. Georgia glanced down at the goodies Myra had given her.

"Want a pickle?" She hefted the large pickle jar onto her lap.

"Are those Myra's?" Cole asked.

"She insisted I take them with me." Georgia unscrewed the lid. "Here." She fished a fat pickle out of the jar, shook off the brine, and handed it to him.

"Myra makes the best pickles." He took a big, crunchy bite.

Georgia held another dripping over the mouth of the jar. The sharp odor of vinegar and dill stung her nose. She screwed the lid on the jar tightly, set it at her feet, then leaned forward and nibbled the end of the pickle. It was nice and crisp, the brine mouth-puckeringly sour. She paused, then took another small bite, chewing slowly. It wasn't her imagination.

"I can taste it," she whispered in disbelief. "Cole, I can taste the vinegar."

"Really?" He looked at her in surprise.

"Really!" she shrieked. "I can taste the sour! Not the pickle itself, but I can taste the sour tang of the vinegar in the brine."

She stared at him, stunned. "I think I may be getting my sense of taste back!" She ate the rest of the pickle happily, bouncing up and down on the seat, doing a little dance of joy. She was smiling from ear to ear with gratitude and sheer relief. Cole chewed his pickle and watched her, a faint smile playing around his mouth.

"What?" she demanded.

"Nothing. I've just never seen anyone get so excited about a pickle."

She rolled her eyes and batted his arm. "You know it's more than that."

"I know. I'm really happy for you." He took another bite.

"Thank you," she said fervently, meeting his eyes.

"For what?" he asked cautiously.

"If you hadn't been a complete turd today and volunteered me to work in the kitchen at Anemone, this wouldn't have happened," she told him.

He laughed dryly, a deep rumble of amusement. "Happy to oblige."

She leaned back against the door and looked at him in the dim light. "Really, though," she said. "I think cooking at Anemone is what did it. I think somehow it connected me to something I'd forgotten for too long. So thank you, even though it was a dirty trick to play."

"You want to talk about dirty tricks," he snorted. "I'm now in half a dozen tween and middle-aged Korean ladies' vacation photos. They all think I'm some famous vampire actor."

"Wait, you actually took pictures with them?" Georgia asked, delighted by the thought.

"I didn't have the heart to say no," Cole admitted. "The tweens followed me out to the parking lot and demanded I take a selfie with them. And then I'm pretty sure some of the tour group ladies were snapping pictures of my ass while I was climbing into Martha."

Georgia burst out laughing. "Somewhere on the island there are a bunch of tourists who firmly believe they just met Ian Somerhalder."

"And some now even have pictures of his ass." Cole grinned. "They're going to be really disappointed if they ever find out those are just photos of a washed-up ex-scientist who rakes oysters for a living." Cole turned the key in the ignition, and Martha's engine roared to life.

"It's a great ass, though," Georgia replied teasingly, buckling her seat belt. "Ian Somerhalder would be proud."

"Er, thanks." Cole looked embarrassed. She thought he was blushing. They pulled out of the parking lot and wound up the hill out of Roche Harbor. Cole shot her a quick sideways glance. He seemed relieved. There was less tension in the set of his shoulders. "Okay, so now that you've heard my entire tragic life story, I have some questions for you," he told her.

"That seems fair," Georgia agreed. She reached down and grabbed the pickle jar, unscrewing it and finding another pickle. She took a big bite. "What do you want to know?"

"What happens if you don't get your sense of taste back?" Cole asked as they drove past dark and silent Craftsman cottages and an old-fashioned gas station with a single gas pump.

"I don't know," Georgia confessed. "I can't go back to my old job. Not after what I did."

"What did you do?" Cole looked curious.

Georgia hesitated, staring out the window as they passed an avant-garde outdoor sculpture park set in a field near the grassy runway of the tiny Roche Harbor airport. A moment later civilization gave way to a jagged inky dark line of evergreens against a starry sky and the empty ribbon of road in the headlights. There was not another car in sight. She felt a million miles away from that horrible night in Paris. How much should she tell him? Cole had just laid bare the biggest failings of his life to her. Was she brave enough to offer him the same level of vulnerability? She took a deep breath and confessed everything. To her surprise, it felt like a relief.

When she was done Cole said, "In my opinion, the sexiest chef in Paris sounds like a real grade A jerk. He had it coming."

Georgia turned to him in surprise. "How do you know about Etienne being voted the sexiest chef in Paris?" she asked. She had not mentioned that detail.

"You're not the only one who can google," Cole admitted a touch sheepishly.

"You googled me?" Georgià demanded, then remembered she'd done the exact same thing. "I guess that makes us even." She sat back, mollified.

"So what are you going to do now?" Cole asked.

"Go back to Paris and try to win the position of head chef," Georgia said. "I can't give up, no matter what. This is everything I've worked for. I'm so close. Tonight at Anemone, I remembered why I love to cook. It felt . . . fun. It's been a long time since I enjoyed it that much. And not only that, but tonight my cooking seemed like it was helping people like it used to. At dinner a couple visiting from Toronto decided to elope in Vegas while they were eating the meal I served them. It's been a while since that happened. That gives me hope that I'm on the right track. I *think* it's working. I think I'm getting my spark back. I'm trying so hard to not try. I'm attempting to just be present and open myself up to wonder and delight again. That's what Star thinks I need to do." She heard the vulnerability and hope in her voice. She so desperately wanted this to work. And today, for the first time since that first bitter bite of pastry in Phoebe's apartment, something had shifted. The pickle was proof of that. The realization filled her with sweet relief. She rolled down the window in a rush of crisp air, sticking her hand out into the night and feeling the cool darkness trail between her fingers. She felt so light she almost believed she could float.

When they pulled up to the cottage, everything was silent and dark.

"Thank you for the ride," Georgia said quietly, putting her hand on the door handle. "And thank you for making me cook today. I hated you for it, but I think it was exactly what I needed."

Cole looked a little embarrassed. "Honestly, I was just trying to get a rise out of you."

"I know." Georgia gave him a wry smile. She could just barely make out his face in the dim glow from Martha's headlights. "You can trust me with your secret identity, you know," she said, sobering. "I won't tell."

He nodded. "I know. I try to keep a low profile. The islanders don't care who you are. This island is full of folks with stories. Former CIA agents, writers, felons, even a celebrity or two. No one cares as long as you're a good citizen here and work hard. It's the tourists I worry about, like that guy we saw at the winery yesterday. I did know him. He works for a big biotech company in San Francisco. We ran in similar circles."

"Why are you so worried about someone recognizing you, though?" Georgia asked. "You're not a fugitive or famous. I mean, if you really were Ian Somerhalder, I'd understand, but does anyone really care about a research scientist? No offense."

Cole scrubbed a hand over his face, over the five-o'clock shadow he seemed to always have. "I care," he said at last. "I'm ashamed of who I was, of what I did to Amy, of what I let myself become under all the pressure. I left it all behind when I came here. Dr. Cabot Montgomery is dead and buried. I'm just Cole now. I don't want any reminders of the mistakes I made. I don't want anyone looking at me and seeing who I really am."

"And is this all you want?" Georgia asked searchingly. "To work on the oyster farm and read German philosophy in your cabin alone every night?"

"There are worse things," Cole said, his tone a touch defensive. "Is this all I want? It's not the life I imagined, but it's a good, honest way to live. And I can help Star. I couldn't leave her, not now. So I guess my life is as good as it's going to get." He sounded so resigned.

Georgia found his answer terribly sad. She surveyed him for a moment. He was so much more complex than she'd assumed at first. A deep well, Star had called him once. And he was certainly that, filled to the brim with guilt and duty, grief and kindness, hating himself for a mistake that had cost him and the woman he loved so much. How could he forgive himself for destroying everything he cared about? Evidently, he could not.

"You said that your former life was one of your secrets," she said. "Are there others?"

He smiled humorlessly, a brief turn of his lips. "None that are mine to tell," he said almost gently. "I think you've asked enough questions for tonight. Time's up." He reached across her and opened her door. She got the message.

"By my count, I've still got at least a dozen questions left," she told him, unbuckling her seat belt.

"I would expect nothing less," he said, a low note of amusement rippling through his voice. "You are quite a woman, Georgia May Jackson." It sounded like a compliment.

She got out of the car, laying his fleece across the seat.

"Don't forget your pickles," he reminded her, grabbing the jar as he opened the driver side door and jumped out.

"You keep them," she said.

He came around the front of the car, and they lingered for a moment in the bright wash of the headlights. She hesitated. She was reluctant to end the evening. She had started off the day viewing Cole as a slightly antagonistic enigma and now found that he felt like far more than that. He felt almost like a friend.

Spending time with Cole didn't feel like it had with Etienne, who had wooed her against her better judgment, who had enjoyed the chase. She'd felt like she had to always be on her toes with Etienne, always trying to be smarter, bolder, sexier, brasher— the most vivacious version of herself at all times just to prove her worth. But with Cole, it felt different. She felt like he saw her, saw who she really was, the flaws and desires of her heart, her courage and hot temper and determination, her soft underbelly of vulnerability and failure, and yet he did not seem to judge her for any of it. He simply listened, not trying to fix anything, not turning away. The thought made her smile. She was used to having to impress, to put her best foot forward and hope it was good enough. She'd been doing it since she was a child, fighting for every bit of attention and encouragement. But not with Cole. With him, she could be real and raw. She had never felt more exposed, and yet she had never felt more accepted. It was re-markable. He was remarkable.

"You're wrong, you know," she told him.

"On what subject?" He sounded a little amused. "There are a lot to choose from."

"You said if I knew your story I wouldn't want anything to do with you, but you're wrong."

He stilled, searching her face, then nodded. "I'm glad," he said softly.

"Should I call you Cole or Cabot, which is, by the way, a very cool name?" she asked, taking a step closer to him.

Cole considered for a moment. "Let's stick with Cole. That's how people know me here, and honestly, I've always preferred it. It reminds me of Aunt Justine. She was one the who always called me by my middle name, and it just sort of made sense to keep it once I came to the island." He leaned back against Martha's hood. "But it's . . . nice to have someone know my full name again."

"Okay then. Bonne nuit, Cole," she said. On impulse, she stood on tiptoe and planted a soft kiss on his cheek. Then she opened the white picket gate and started down the crushed oyster shell path.

"Good night, Georgia May," he called out. Through the darkness, his voice sounded a little huskier than normal. He didn't budge while she walked up the path. As she mounted the steps to the front porch, she could sense him behind her, waiting. When she turned at the door, he was still there, leaning against Martha's hood, cradling the giant jar of pickles in one arm and watching her intently in the silver bright moonlight.

26

COLE

Cole watched Georgia all the way up those porch steps. The spot where she'd kissed him burned like a brand on his cheek. This was a very bad idea. He could not fall for Georgia May Jackson. It was true that she had surprised him tonight. He'd told her who he was and what he had done. He'd laid his failures bare, and she had not rejected him. He'd been honest, expecting the worst, but she'd surprised him with her acceptance and compassion.

But she had also made her own priorities quite clear. She was intent on returning to Paris. Her life was there, everything she'd worked so hard for. And he could not see himself ever leaving the island. No, their lives were too divergent. Getting close to her was playing with fire.

And what would happen when she found out the secret he was privy to, the one that wasn't his to tell? He had a feeling things might go very badly when that happened. And it would sooner or later. The truth, in his experience, had a way of making itself known whether you wanted it to or not. And on this island, things came to light. He didn't believe the island had a special sort of magic, not like Star did, but there was something about this place . . . hidden things didn't stay hidden long. He was amazed he'd managed to get away with his own secret identity for as long as he had. The island didn't like secrets. It was only a matter of time until this last hidden thing would be revealed.

He sighed and pushed himself up from Martha's hood as soon as Georgia was safely inside the house, then drove the few hundred feet to the oyster farm and parked in his usual spot. As he headed through the trees toward his little cabin down by the water, he forced himself not to look toward Star's house. He knew he should keep his distance from Georgia and keep his feelings in check. Fat chance of that now.

He let himself into the cabin and shut the door behind him, instantly enveloped by the silence and the calm. The little one-room space was rustic and smelled faintly of seaweed, but it was free and weathertight and a place to call his own. When he'd come five years before, it had been a refuge, a place of solace. The simplicity had felt almost monastic to him, as though he were taking personal vows of poverty and chastity in living there. It had been healing for him as he struggled through those first hard years. But now . . . tonight, it just felt a little lonely.

He set the giant jar of pickles on the simple pine table. It made him smile, picturing Georgia biting into that big pickle and shrieking that she could taste the brine. She'd looked exhausted from nine hours on her feet cooking in a strange kitchen, and yet she'd been positively vibrating with energy. Hermès scarf askew, cheeks flushed, a nimbus of curls around her face, her green eyes bright.

"You don't want to go there, buddy," he muttered to himself, but it was too late. Telling her his story today, seeing the compassion in her face as she listened without judgment or pity, had cracked open some sealed portion of his heart. Georgia had touched some tender place that had been closed tight since Amy's accident. He cared about Georgia May Jackson. It was as simple as that. Watching her open up with that heartbreaking mixture of honesty, pluck, and vulnerability, he'd felt protective of her. He wanted to reassure her that she was more than enough exactly as she was. He wanted to do more than reassure her. If he was honest, he wanted to bury his hands in her glorious riot of curls, put his mouth on hers, and kiss her until her knees buckled, until they both came up gasping for air.

"You're an idiot," he told himself in disgust. "This is what happens when you live like a monk for five years."

It was cool in the cabin, but he was feeling too warm, a little irritated and feverish. He paced restlessly for a few minutes. It made him feel guilty to talk about the accident and Amy, then think about kissing Georgia. It felt wrong, disloyal to Amy, although he knew she'd long since moved on with her life. But he couldn't deny that Georgia was filling his thoughts more and more each day. Cole shut his eyes, but all he could see was the pale scoop of Georgia's neck where it met her clavicle, the half-moon scar on her thumb as she reached up and pushed her curls out of her eyes. He had the strongest desire to brush his lips against the pulse in that pale, soft hollow of her neck, to press her against the side of Martha and . . .

"Get a grip on yourself," he admonished, annoyed by his heated thoughts. He shrugged out of his shirt and jeans and opened the cabin door, picking his way down to the edge of the bay in his boxer briefs. The water was shining black in the silver moonlight, still and calm. The shore was sharp with oyster shells and rocks. He winced and waded in a few yards, then dived down shallow, the icy temperature of the salt water making him come up gasping for air. He swam out farther, staying in as long as he could stand it, until his body felt like he was being electrified with a thousand little icicles, until he couldn't quite draw a deep breath. He stayed there until his heartbeat slowed to normal, until his blood was no longer boiling with longing for something he couldn't ever have. Then he swam back to shore, feeling once more in control of his emotions.

"Don't make this situation any harder than it already is," he muttered. He rinsed quickly at the outdoor shower, then pulled on a pair of flannel pajama pants. Inside the cabin, he reached for a book, Heidegger's *Being and Time*, from the crab trap he was using as a nightstand. Perfect. Heidegger was quite a buzzkill. Nothing like a dense German treatise on existentialism to cool any errant thoughts. He sprawled shirtless across the scratchy wool army blanket on his bed and started reading the heavy work, resolutely trying to put all thoughts of Georgia May Jackson out of his head.

"She's going back to Paris and you're going . . . nowhere," he told himself firmly. "Stay the course, and everything will be back to normal before you know it."

But he knew as he spoke that he was lying to himself. Georgia very well could be returning to Paris, but there was no way his heart was going to return to normal anytime soon.

27

The next morning, Georgia wandered downstairs in her paja-mas and robe, barefoot and tousled and grinning like a fool from the events of the night before. So much had happened—rediscovering her joy in the kitchen at Anemone, the revelations about Cole, and the sour delight of tasting that briny pickle. This morning, for the first time since she'd left Paris, she felt a warm glow of anticipation in the center of her chest where there had only been a cold, leaden dread. Pollen came padding up to her as she entered the kitchen and sniffed Georgia's knee, wag-ging her entire backside. The room reeked of paint fumes. Georgia wrinkled her nose. "Star?"

"Georgia, there you are." Star popped out from behind the refrigerator, which had been pulled out a couple of feet from the wall. She was holding a paintbrush and wearing an old pair of denim overalls, liberally splattered with paint. A blue bandanna was tied over her hair. The raspy strains of Bob Dylan and his harmonica filled the room. "How did it go at Anemone?" Star asked. "I got your text that you were filling in as their chef. That was kind of you. Myra's a good, hardworking woman."

"It was amazing!" Georgia said. She felt a little giddy from the events of yesterday. There was so much to say. Where did she start? She wanted to jump right in and grill Star about Cole, about what had happened between him and Amy, but she also was eager to tell Star about Anemone, and then there was the crunchy, sour taste of the pickle . . . so many things to say.

"Tell me all about it," Star said, sliding back behind the refrigerator. "I'm repainting the kitchen, so don't bump the walls. They're still wet." Her warning was muffled by the bulk of the refrigerator.

"Is there anything you're not freshening up?" Georgia asked, glancing around her. Since Georgia had arrived, Star seemed to be in constant motion, pruning, weeding, tidying, and painting.

"Just sprucing things up. A lot got neglected over the past few years," Star replied quickly, casually, popping her head out around the refrigerator but not looking Georgia in the eye. "This old place needs a little love and attention. But enough about that. Tell me everything."

Sitting at the table, munching a dish of tiny gherkins she found in the refrigerator, Georgia recounted the events of the day, starting with Anemone and culminating in her ability to taste the sour flavor from the pickle. As Georgia talked, Star painted the kitchen a clean, bright white, using a roller for the big swaths and cutting in around the edges with a smaller brush. Bob Dylan accompanied Georgia's story, wheezing his poetry in the background. When Georgia finished, she was beaming from ear to ear.

Star stopped painting for a moment and grinned, holding a wet paintbrush, eyes bright. "Sounds like our plan is working," she said, looking pleased.

"It seems so," Georgia confirmed. "I still need to regain the rest of the flavors, but sour is a good start. So far I've got bitter and sour. Now all I need are sweet, salty, and umami." She gazed at Star, dazed and happy. "I'm so relieved," she admitted.

Star balanced her brush on the lid of the paint can and wiped her hands with a damp rag. "I'm so glad, Georgia May," she said with a smile. "The sky's the limit for you now."

"Never mind the sky. I'll settle for Paris," Georgia said, taking a sip of tea. Star picked up her brush and started painting again.

"Cole told me his story last night," Georgia said casually after a few minutes of silence.

"Oh, did he?" Star glanced over at her in surprise.

"He told me about Amy and the accident."

"Hmm." Star nodded. "That was a real tragedy for both of them." She painted carefully along the edge of the kitchen doorway.

"What happened after her accident? Why aren't they together now?" Georgia had not wanted to pry further when she saw how painful the past still was for Cole, but she was so curious to know what had happened between him and Amy.

Star sighed and tucked a long curl back into her bandanna. "I guess since he told you his story, he won't mind me telling the rest. She left him," she said bluntly. "After the accident, they tried to make it work, but she just wanted to move on, and he was stuck with such a huge load of guilt. He was trying to do everything perfectly, I think, to make it up to her somehow, but how do you make up such a huge loss to someone you love when it's your fault? She wanted to forgive and just move on, but he couldn't." Star shook her head and frowned. "So she left him. She told him she had to keep living her life even though it looked different than she'd imagined. She told him that his endless apologies and guilt were suffocating her. She told him she forgave him, and then she returned the engagement ring he'd given her and left. A few days later, he showed up here with a duffel bag and a whole load of hurt. I've never seen a man so smashed by grief and guilt."

"What happened to Amy?" Georgia asked. Pollen wandered over to the table, gave a deep sigh, and slid down to settle her warm bulk on Georgia's feet.

"She turned lemons into lemonade." Star stood on tiptoe on a small step stool to reach the top of the doorframe, painting the wall above it. "She became a motivational speaker. You know, one of those folks that goes around telling their story to inspire other people? She's real successful."

"Wow, that's impressive." Georgia digested this news. So Cole was the only one stuck in the tragedy, it seemed. Amy had been able to move on. The accident had taken her ability to walk, but it had taken Cole's ability to get on with his life. How sad was that?

"Guilt's a tricky thing," Star said contemplatively, dipping her brush in the gallon of paint. "If you can't forgive yourself, you get stuck; everything around you moves on but you can't. You're trapped back in that moment, hoping and waiting and wishing for a different outcome that can never happen. You can't go forward in life. Believe me, I know."

Georgia looked at her mother, struck by Star's words. She knew Star felt guilty for leaving. She'd said so herself. But was she still paralyzed by guilt for leaving Georgia? Was Star stuck? Georgia sensed not. Whatever had happened when she left Texas, Star had managed to find her way through to a place where she could still grow. She had deep regrets, but she wasn't stuck. It seemed a much better way to hold the past than how Cole was dealing with it.

"You think Cole is stuck?" Georgia asked.

"I do." Star came off the step stool and brushed her hair back from her face, leaving a smudge of white paint on her cheek. "And it's a shame, because he's such a good man—kind and considerate and so darn intelligent. And Lord knows he's easy on the eyes." She gave Georgia a meaningful look. "You two seem to be getting friendly."

Georgia waved off the observation, trying to look casual, but she felt her face flush. "More like we're finally getting cordial," she corrected, hoping her flaming cheeks didn't betray her. She ate the last gherkin in the dish. "Myra asked me if I'd consider helping out more at Anemone, until they get a new chef," she said, happy to change the subject.

"What did you tell her?" Star asked. She started to cut in under the upper cabinets in the kitchen, twisting her body like a pretzel across the counter to reach the spot.

"I told her I'd let her know today," Georgia said. "I wanted to talk to you about it, see what you thought."

"Well, do you want to do it?" Star asked with a grunt from under the cabinets.

Georgia thought about it, about the hours of sheer panic and adrenaline she'd felt yesterday, but about the exhilaration too. She glanced down at the empty dish of pickles. Maybe her newly regained ability to taste sour was a direct correlation, maybe not. But the thought of going back to Anemone gave her a nervous, happy thrill. "I think so, at least for a little while until they can find a new chef," she said. She hesitated, feeling suddenly shy. She had told Star about the text from Michel, but she had not asked if she could stay longer at the cottage. Now, faced with the opportunity to spend more time at Anemone, she found she was not ready to leave the island or Star yet. "Would it be okay if I stayed here until I need to go back to Paris?" she asked hesitantly. "It would be probably another couple of weeks . . ."

Star popped out from under the counter like a jackrabbit from a hole, her eyes creasing into crescents of happiness. "I'd love that," she said simply. "This is your home now too, Georgia May. Stay as long as you like."

A few minutes later in her bedroom upstairs, Georgia got dressed for the day. Now that she'd made the decision to stay and help out at Anemone, she felt excited to get started. Who knew what might happen in the extra days or weeks she was going to spend on the island? It was thrilling to contemplate the possibilities. For so long, she'd had her path laid out for her, working her way through her life like a paint-by-number coloring book, always striving for the next thing, working hard to color inside the lines and always connecting the dots, one to the next, to painstakingly create the life she'd dreamed of. To not know what was going to happen next, even for a few days, made anticipation bubble up in her chest like a glass of Veuve Clicquot. The unknown felt unexpectedly liberating.

While she got ready, Georgia poked around YouTube on her phone, searching for a video. In a few seconds, she'd found it, an inspirational talk by paralyzed former Miss California Amy Hannigan. She watched the video while she brushed her teeth and tried to tame her curls at the bathroom sink. Amy was as cute as ever, with peppy energy and a gleaming smile as she addressed a group of high school students from her motorized wheelchair. Georgia watched the entire clip avidly, marveling at the woman's ability to overcome adversity. She really was inspirational. Georgia could see why Cole had loved her so deeply. Maybe still loved her. The thought brought an unexpected pang to her heart. She brushed it away. She was concerned for Cole as a friend, she told herself firmly. Nothing more. But she could still feel the rasp of his cheek against her mouth. She pressed her finger to her lips, in remembrance or admonition, she couldn't quite decide. A few moments later when the video was over, she clicked off her phone. It was painful to watch Amy in her wheelchair getting on with her life, doing something productive in the world while Cole was so very stuck.

On impulse, she slid open the bathroom window, leaning out until she could see Cole's cabin down by the bay. She won-

dered what he was doing, shamelessly picturing him shirtless
with those great abs, reading German philosophy, all brooding
and conflicted. For a moment, she was half-tempted to march
across the grass to the cabin, knock on his door, show him the
video of Amy, and demand that he forgive himself and move on
with his life. The other half of her was tempted to go down
there and simply throw her arms around his neck and kiss him
until he forgot the hurt and the grief, until his arms and thoughts
were so full of her that he had no room to carry guilt or shame.
But as soon as they came, she squashed both inclinations . . . It
was not her job to fix Cole. Only he could do that. And no matter
what she felt for him, she told herself firmly as she shut the window, the truth was that she was headed back to Paris soon.
These feelings could go nowhere.

28

The next two weeks passed in a happy blur. Each morning, Georgia spent an hour or two with Star, having breakfast and tea, puttering around the cottage and grounds, helping with repair projects, and gardening. As they worked, they shared about their lives. Star told her more stories of her early years—of growing up with Emma and Helen, and her memories of Georgia as a baby, a toddler, a precocious preschooler. A few times, Star briefly alluded to her stepfather, comments that chilled Georgia to the bone with their matter-of-fact reference to things no child should have to go through. Every day, Georgia walked away from their time together with a much clearer picture of her own lineage, her mother's life growing up, and some of the wounds Star still carried from her past. But now Star held them with grace, peacefully, like old broken bones that still ached but did not cripple. They did not talk about the reason Star had left Texas. Georgia still held the question in her heart, but found she could move forward in getting to know Star with it still unanswered, at least for now.

In turn, Georgia told Star more about her life after she left the ranch—culinary school, those hard early years in Paris, all the kitchens she'd worked in, the quirks and foibles of the kitchen staff at each place, her happiest memories. Star especially loved hearing about Paris, and Georgia told her everything she could think of, aware that she had gotten to fulfill a dream that had never come true for Star. Slowly but surely, they filled in the gaps for each other, getting to know the contours of the years they had missed. Those morning hours felt suspended in time—precious and fleeting. They both were well aware that Georgia's days on the island were numbered.

At the end of her first week at Anemone, Georgia texted Michel a gorgeous photo of one of her entrées, a plate of fermented potato gnocchi with local salmon fillet and house-made seaweed kimchi on the side.

A few minutes later, Michel replied with Ça a l'air délicieux. Translation: "It looks delicious."

Georgia studied his brief text. He gave no update on the competition or when she needed to return to Paris. The clock was still ticking down the minutes and hours and days until the competition, but surprisingly, she found she did not mind not knowing any more details. She wanted to preserve this time for as long as she could—the simple, easy mornings with Star followed by the exhilarating, exhausting lunch and dinner shifts at Anemone. She had barely seen Cole since their night in Roche Harbor. He was at work when she was with Star, and then she was at Anemone until late every night, coming home exhausted to fall straight into bed. Star had lent Georgia her Subaru to drive to and from the restaurant, so she did not need to seek him out for a ride anymore. They were on different schedules, and there didn't seem to be any good reason for their paths to cross. Which disappointed her more than she was willing to admit.

Despite not seeing Cole, Georgia was having a ball, cooking every day with Myra and the staff, experimenting, finding her footing. She felt a strange sort of reluctance when she thought of it all ending. She chalked it up to how badly things had gone when she left Paris. Of course, it made sense to be a little nervous thinking about returning to the scene of her disgrace.

"I'll wait to think about leaving until I hear details from Michel," she told herself. "For now, I'll concentrate on getting the last three flavors back."

If she could do that, she would be ready for the competition. Then she could go back to Paris and get on with her life.

On Georgia's first Monday off, Cole showed up for dinner with Billy, Justine's former partner and the manager of the shellfish farm, and a large pail of glistening blue-black mussels fresh from the bay.

"Miss Georgia, it's a pleasure to finally meet you," Billy told her, shaking her hand enthusiastically. He was short and stout, clad in butterscotch-colored Carhartt bib overalls that strained over his tummy and a fisherman's hat pulled low over his brow. He looked about sixty with wiry gray hair sprouting from under the cap and a bushy beard to match. "Cole told me you were here visiting Star." He eyed her shrewdly. "I'm glad you're here. She needs all the help she can get at a time like this."

Puzzled, Georgia opened her mouth to ask Billy what he meant, but Star interrupted them, requesting volunteers to help with dinner prep.

They all pitched in. Billy whipped up a simple but delicious-smelling supper of mussels in white wine while Georgia contributed a loaf of crusty leftover bread she had brought home from Anemone and made a French balsamic dressing for the green salad Star put together. Cole set the places, and they ate clustered around the kitchen table while Billy regaled them with wild tales of his younger days on an Alaskan fishing trawler. Pollen lay under the table, hopeful that someone would drop a mussel or a bite of bread. Georgia forced down a few mussels in broth to be polite, and devoured a dish of pickled onions, capers, and peppers. It was still a struggle to make herself eat anything that tasted bitter, but she comforted herself with the knowledge that at least one more flavor had come back. She had never eaten so many pickled items in her life, relishing the taste of the sour brine each time.

It was an easy, pleasant evening, the kitchen windows steamed over from the fragrant, briny broth, rain pattering on the roof. Since he walked in the door, Georgia had been overly alert to Cole's presence. She tried to act casual, to avoid glancing in his direction, but she was achingly aware of his every word or movement. She had missed him.

Stop it, she scolded herself. *This can go nowhere.* But it did no good. She might as well have been a radio tuned to the "Dr. Cabot Cole Montgomery" station.

After dinner, Billy challenged them to a game of Scrabble. They quickly cleared the table.

"It's been years since I played this," Star said, laying out the Scrabble board.

"It was Justine's favorite game," Billy noted. "We played most evenings together when the oyster season was slow. She always managed to beat me."

"I never won a game against her," Cole confessed with a rueful smile. "We'd play every time I visited and I finally just resigned myself to always losing."

They crowded around the table and began the game. Star was a decent player who usually managed to score at least ten points. Cole deliberated far too long on every turn, but came up with obscure words like "qat," which turned out to be a shrub from Africa, and "fozy," which meant puffy or fat. Star or Georgia challenged him every time, but he was never wrong. Georgia, for her part, struggled to recall words in English. She'd spent too long learning French vocabulary for English to come easily to her anymore. She scored pitifully, although she was enjoying herself. If she were honest, she was just enjoying being a scant yard away from Cole. Billy proved to be an expert Scrabble player. He had the official two-letter-word list memorized, and despite using the smallest and simplest words, he scored the highest every turn, which pleased him to no end. "Sometimes the simplest things are best," he explained, hitching up his overalls and happily scoring twenty-two points for the word "za."

On Cole's second-to-last turn, he placed the word "crave" on the board, glancing at Georgia and quickly away. She looked down at her tiles, feeling a telltale warmth flush her cheeks. Surely, that was a coincidence? Star played and then it was Georgia's turn. She took her time, deliberating. It was cozy in the kitchen, redolent with wine and garlic, the sound of spitting rain hitting the windows. There was a sense of good-natured competition around the table. She was reluctant for the evening to end. She laid down her tiles. Cole's gaze flicked down to her word, then up at her sharply. She'd played the word "kiss."

"My, this game is heating up," Star commented, shrewdly glancing between Cole and Georgia.

Cole hunched over, running his fingers through his hair. Finally, he put down the word "ache."

"Could be talking about arthritis," Billy joked. "My knees ache every morning." He played another high-scoring two-letter word. Star raised her eyebrows and looked at Georgia but said nothing. She got a measly six points for "hat."

Georgia bit her lip. Then she laid her tiles out for her final word, "gone." She hazarded a glance at Cole, finding his ice-blue eyes pinned on her with a peculiar pained expression. She looked away, caught off guard by the directness of his gaze.

"And that's the game," Billy said happily, laying out his last word, another two-letter high scorer. Star tallied the points. Cole was watching Georgia across the table, his gaze intent. It made her self-conscious.

"Billy wins by a landslide," Star announced.

Cole stood abruptly. "I think I'll head out," he murmured. "I've got an early morning." With that, he excused himself.

Georgia didn't see him for days afterward. She told herself it was for the best, but each day that passed brought a little ache between her ribs. She ignored it, but it didn't change the fact that she could not deny it was there.

On a bright Saturday morning two weeks after she'd first set foot in Anemone, Georgia awoke and checked her phone to find a sweet, slightly off-key voice text from Phoebe singing her the "Happy Birthday" song in French with a heavy Scouse accent. Georgia blinked in surprise. She had, in truth, forgotten it was her birthday. Usually, she was working on her birthday. Etienne would get her a luxurious gift, often French lingerie (which in hindsight seemed more like a gift for himself, now that she thought of it). On her way to work, she would always swing by Ladurée and select a box of macarons for her birthday treat, but that was the extent of the fuss made about it. No macarons this year, she thought with a touch of regret. There was another text, this one from Michel.

> The competition is in two weeks on Saturday at eleven at La Lumière Dorée. Bring your best inspiration. After that I will make my decision.

Georgia's stomach dropped. *Bring your best inspiration.* In two weeks it would be decided. Her best shot at a kitchen of her own.

She texted back.

I'll be there. Hard at work on inspiration. Who else
are you considering?

Thirty seconds later she received a response.

Gerard Boucher and Leonie Alarie

She frowned when she saw the names. Gerard Boucher was
not really a threat. Pompous, arrogant, he was a good chef, but
unimaginative and cooked with a heavy hand that leaned toward
the classics. She was surprised Michel was considering him at all.
It wasn't the direction Michel wanted to take La Lumière Dorée,
she was sure of it. But Leonie Alarie was a different story, a significant threat. Originally from the South of France somewhere
near Marseille, she had come to Paris a year or two after Georgia
and had been climbing the ranks as fast—okay, Georgia hated
to admit it—faster than Georgia had. They shared a similar drive,
a tireless work ethic, and the same fire and determination. Leonie could hold her own against Georgia, and her fresh, modern
twist on French cooking would work well at La Lumière Dorée.
Georgia worried her lower lip, thinking. She'd heard a rumor that
Leonie was going to be named head chef at a Michelin-starred
restaurant in Nice. Apparently, she'd heard wrong. She felt a flutter of apprehension. She was really going to have to step up her
game to beat Leonie.

She reread Michel's text. Two weeks before she needed to
be back in Paris and ready to dazzle Michel with her newly restored spark in the kitchen. A spark that was partly revived, but
not entirely. She felt a frisson of panic skitter up her spine. What
if she wasn't ready? She was doing all she could—nurturing her

sense of wonder, trying to cultivate delight, making progress at not being so goal oriented, not trying so hard to keep everything in line. And she had seen the good fruit of those choices. She licked her lips, remembering the joy of tasting the sour flavor that now dominated her palate. Could she design an entire menu of bitter and sour if she didn't regain any of the other three flavors in the next two weeks? That sounded horrid. She shuddered. She needed to regain the other flavors to have a prayer of winning. That was all there was to it.

She glanced out the window, down to the little cabin by the bay, and caught a glimpse of a figure in bright orange overalls walking up toward the house. Cole. Her stomach flipped. She felt a peculiar bittersweet tug of regret when she thought of him. She knew it could go nowhere. In two weeks she would be back in Paris where she belonged, but still . . .

She shook off the sensation. She had two weeks left. She had to make the best use of them. Maybe today would be a lucky day. Maybe she'd get a little birthday miracle.

"Georgia," Star called up the stairs. "Breakfast. Cole's here."

"Be right there." Georgia hurriedly dressed. As she grabbed her favorite navy blazer from a hanger in the closet, a shower of little green plants fell out of the pockets and scattered across the floor.

"What on earth?" She shook the blazer, and more fell out from under the collar. She bent over and picked one up, already knowing what they were. Four-leaf clovers. Dozens of them.

"What are you trying to tell me?" Georgia murmured, gathering up the four-leaf clovers and setting them on the nightstand. She gave her blazer a final shake and slipped it on over a good-quality fitted tee. With one final puzzled glance around her room, she went down to breakfast.

Five minutes later, Georgia was seated at the table across

from Cole as Star stirred oatmeal at the stove. Georgia and Cole kept covertly glancing at each other, and every time their eyes would snag, both would hurriedly look away. Georgia cleared her throat uncomfortably. How many points could she get in Scrabble for the word "awkward," she wondered? Or "ridiculous crush"?

"Here you go." Star set a plate down in front of Georgia. "Happy birthday!" It had a single lit pink candle stuck in a giant dill pickle. Georgia laughed in surprise and glanced up at her mother. She certainly had not expected any sort of acknowledgment.

"Thank you." She was touched that Star had remembered her birthday. This was the first birthday Star had acknowledged in almost thirty years, she realized with a pang.

"Blow out the candle and make a wish," Star urged. "You don't need to eat the pickle unless you want to."

"A wish." Georgia stared at the lit candle. She cleared her throat, not sure what exactly to wish for. To get her spark back completely? To regain the last three flavors? To win the competition for La Lumière Dorée? To have all her questions about Star finally answered? And that didn't even include the fact that her stomach did a backflip every time she laid eyes on Cole. She fixed her gaze on the cheery little candle flame and avoided looking in his direction entirely. She was going to need a lot of birthdays to make all her wishes come true.

She closed her eyes, threw caution to the wind, and made a single, silly romantic wish, then blew out the candle. When she opened her eyes, Cole was watching her across the table. "Happy birthday," he said, his eyes catching hers for a long moment.

She concentrated hard on removing the birthday candle from the pickle, not looking at him. "Thanks."

"Are you excited about the Oyster Shuck tonight?" Star asked, ladling scoops of oatmeal into bowls and bringing them to the table.

"The oyster what?" Georgia asked, mystified. She took a tiny taste of the oatmeal, making sure to get a bite of apple and honey. Still bitter. Resigned, she speared the dill pickle with a fork and gnawed at the end of it. No birthday miracle yet.

"Didn't Cole tell you?" Star looked reprovingly at Cole, who was quietly eating his bowl of oatmeal and staring fixedly at a knot on the painted table. "You're going with us to the Oyster Shuck tonight."

"Slipped my mind," Cole murmured, shifting in his chair and looking uncomfortable.

"Well, you can't miss it," Star declared. "It's the annual oyster festival at the seafood farm. It's tonight. There's live music and line dancing and barbecued oysters and carnival games. Practically the whole island comes. It's quite the party."

"That sounds . . . lively." Georgia hesitated. "But I have to cook at Anemone."

"No, I talked to Myra and got you the night off," Star reassured her. "Myra says, 'Happy birthday and have fun.' I guess their regular chef's finger is healed up enough that she may be able to take over the kitchen again when you go back to Paris. They're using tonight as a trial run, see how it goes."

"Oh, well that's perfect timing then," Georgia said. Surprisingly, the idea of the former chef's return to Anemone felt like an intrusion, but why should it bother her? Myra would have to hire someone when she went back to Paris.

"You'll have fun tonight," Star assured her. "It's an island tradition."

Georgia hesitated. "It sounds fun, but I don't know if I should spare the time. I got a text from Michel this morning about the competition. It's in two weeks." She told them all she knew about it. "So it might be better for me to spend this evening brainstorming inspiration for my menu."

"What happened to you letting go and being in the moment?" Star pressed, raising one eyebrow. "Let yourself have this one night. You can brainstorm tomorrow. It's a good way to celebrate your time on the island, especially since you'll be leaving us soon. Think of it as a send-off party." She looked a little wistful as she said the words.

Georgia sighed and caved. "What time should I be ready?" This Oyster Shuck seemed important to Star. It was the least Georgia could do. One more night wouldn't make that big a difference, would it? She hoped she was right.

Star turned to Cole. "Come get us at seven."

"Okay." Cole nodded curtly, then dropped his spoon in the empty bowl and rose. He washed his bowl quickly but thoroughly in the sink and left without another word. Georgia watched him go, then glanced up to find Star looking at her with a knowing smile.

"What?" Georgia said, a touch defensively.

"Nothing." Star held up her hands, placatingly, but she was still smirking ever so slightly. "Looks like I'm not the only one sad to see you go."

Just then, Georgia's phone pinged with a text. She glanced at it, surprised. It was her dad.

Happy birthday, Georgia.—Buck Jackson

Georgia rolled her eyes and smiled at his habit of signing his full name to a text to his own daughter. It was so Buck. He texted by jabbing the keys with his forefinger like he was trying to subdue them. Sort of like Star did, come to think of it.

Georgia started to respond with a quick "thank you" but

stopped. She thought of the row of her school photos Star had left for her to see, a year-by-year chronicle of her childhood. She thought of Star's insistence that she could not share why she had left. Someone had been complicit in making Star leave and in keeping her silent all these years. And Georgia was willing to bet money her father had something to do with it. She decided to poke the hornet's nest and see what happened. She wanted him to know where she was and who she was with.

She texted back.

Thanks, Daddy. Look who I found!

Then she sent a selfie of Star and her that she'd taken out at the garden beds a few days before. They were both sweaty and disheveled but grinning, their arms looped around each other's shoulders. In the photo, they looked so alike it was almost uncanny. Pollen was splayed at their feet, tongue lolling happily.

Three dots appeared almost instantly.

I see she got ahold of you. How's she holding up?

Georgia stared at the text in puzzlement.

"What do you mean 'holding up'?" she texted back. "She's great. We're making up for lost time." She waited for the reply, but it never came. Buck was a man of few words. Sometimes too few.

"Everything all right?" Star asked.

"Fine," Georgia replied. "Just Daddy wishing me a happy birthday." She clicked her phone off, confused and a touch uneasy at her father's text. What did he mean, *how's she holding up?* She scrutinized Star surreptitiously. Was there something she was hiding, something she was not telling Georgia about? And how in the world did Buck know that something was going on with Star? The mystery deepened. She had a feeling she may have just unwittingly poked a different hornet's nest altogether.

"You want some tea?" Star asked. Shaking off her sense of unease, Georgia nodded. Star stirred her special herbal blend into two mugs of hot water and set one before Georgia, sitting down across the table from her.

"Thanks." Georgia frowned, thinking about Buck. Her relationship with her father was a muddle of love and annoyance and irritation and the constant feeling that she was disappointing him just by being herself. It was easier to stay away, and so she had. She knew he loved her in his own way, but his disappointment sometimes drowned out his affection. It had never been easy between Buck and her. She scrutinized Star for a moment longer. Buck must be mistaken. Star looked calm, centered, and perfectly fine. Georgia picked up her mug to take a swallow of tea. As she did so, she saw something peculiar floating amid the mint and tarragon leaves. A sodden four-leaf clover.

"What are you doing in there," she murmured, fishing it out.

"What's that?" Star asked curiously.

Georgia showed her the drooping clover stem.

"I'm finding them everywhere."

Star looked thoughtful. "Any idea why?"

Georgia blotted the clover on her cloth napkin. "Not a clue."

Star reached over and picked up the clover stem, twirling it between her fingers. "Maybe the island is trying to tell you something," she suggested.

"Like what?" Georgia said with a note of skepticism.

Star pondered for a moment. Her expression was serious. "I

don't know, but there's a little bit of magic in this place, remember? It's a place where secrets are revealed and where lost things find their way home." She set the soggy clover in front of Georgia. "You should ask the island what it's trying to tell you," she said at last. "Maybe you'll be surprised by the answer."

29

Georgia could hear the bluegrass music drifting over the lawn as she walked through the evergreens toward the shellfish farm, flanked by Star and Cole. Star was holding up the hem of her patchwork peasant skirt as it brushed the dewy grass. Cole, looking particularly striking in an ink blue wool fisherman's sweater and jeans, took long, silent strides. He'd said only one word to her since coming to pick her and Star up, a muttered, "Ready?" But she'd seen his eyes widen in surprise when he first spotted her.

She'd eschewed her little black dress, the standard-issue Parisian outfit for almost every special event, and instead pulled out a dress she had only worn once, on a brief trip to Cannes with Etienne. It was a gorgeous silk emerald green cocktail dress with a full skirt and a sweetheart neckline. She'd adored it the moment she'd seen it in a vintage shop in Paris, but Etienne had not liked her in it. Too garish, he said when he saw it on her the first time she'd worn it, so she'd put it away for another occasion. That occasion was tonight, she'd decided. She'd paired it with her soft cashmere cardigan as the evening was growing chilly and low black peep-toed heels that always made her want to dance. She'd worn her good black lace bra too, the one that made her breasts look extra perky. She'd done her hair in soft waves, the glamorous starlet look she favored for events, and slicked on her signature red lipstick for the final touch. She knew she was probably overdressed for an outdoor oyster festival, but she didn't care. Screw Etienne, she thought, as she walked through the damp grass. Georgia felt like a million bucks. It was her birthday and she was leaving the island soon and she wanted to celebrate in style. For tonight, she was going to forget all her unfinished business and simply enjoy.

"Oh, look," Georgia exclaimed as she spied the shellfish farm through the trees. "It's magical!"

The entire property had been transformed for the party with strings of white lights crisscrossing overhead in the eating area, and lanterns illuminating the pathways. Every picnic table was filled with islanders and tourists in their party clothes, chowing down on fried and barbecued oysters and beer and wine. Over in one corner was a live bluegrass band with a stand-up bass and fiddle and banjo, already plucking a lively tune. There was a dance floor set up in front of the band, and a few intrepid couples were whirling and dipping each other more or less in time to the music. She spied several carnival-type booths set up in the grassy area behind the main building, children and teens gathered around them, cheering one another on in games of skill and chance. The place was packed, buzzing with happy, festive energy, the air thick with the smell of charcoal and fried oysters. It was mouthwatering. Georgia looked around and grinned, glad now that she'd worn the party dress. This felt like the perfect way to finish out her birthday.

Georgia spied Billy talking to an older white-haired woman seated at a picnic table. They waved and Star said, "There's Barbara and Billy. I'm going to go say hi. I'll see you two later." She peeled off from them, leaving Georgia alone with Cole.

"Come on," Georgia invited, grabbing Cole's hand and dragging him toward the line for food and beverages. "I'm going to try a fried oyster. Who knows, maybe I'll be able to taste it this time around."

COLE

Reluctantly, Cole stood beside Georgia in the line. She was pressed close to him in the crowd. Her hair brushed his arm, and he could smell her perfume, something that reminded him of the delicate scent of cherry blossoms, a warm Paris evening, the freshness of growing things. He leaned a little closer, savoring the memory and the warmth of her against him. She was leaving soon, and the thought filled him with regret. It scared him, how fast his feelings were growing for her. It had been a long time since he'd felt this attracted to someone. Not since Amy. Not since he'd destroyed everything. He was leery of love. He had not deserved it the first time, and he was certainly not worthy of a second chance.

But Georgia would be gone in a few days, he reminded himself, and with that knowledge, he let down his guard a little. What was the harm of savoring being close to her when the odds were high that he would never see Georgia May Jackson again? Might as well let himself enjoy the evening, a bittersweet farewell before she swanned out of his life for good. The thought of her departure gave him an unexpectedly sharp twist of pain right in the center of his chest, the place that had felt hollow since Amy left him. It surprised him to feel anything in there. He had felt numb for so long.

"One white wine, one Coke, and a dozen fried oysters, please," Georgia said confidently when it was their turn at the shellfish farm's walk-up order counter. She glanced at him. "Want anything else? My treat."

"I'm good." He shook his head. She paid and then turned quickly, almost bumping into him. He was standing so close, too close. *Back off. Don't make this weird*, he chastened himself, taking a step back. What was it about this woman that made him keep edging closer?

"Here you go." She handed him the Coke and a paper tray of fried oysters. Miraculously, they snagged two empty stools made out of cut rounds of logs. A few had been scattered around the open area near the beach for extra seating. Cole dragged their seats a few yards away from the other revelers, giving them a bit of privacy. Then he sat down and took a long swig of his Coke. Georgia sat across from him, holding her little paper tray of fried oysters and a plastic cup of white wine, looking around with a delighted smile.

Right then, in the glow of the lights overhead, with the strains of the fiddle and the mournful voice of the lead singer wailing about the girl he loved so true, Cole didn't think he'd ever seen someone so beautiful. She was saying something to him, but he was distracted by the curve of her full lips, with that scarlet shade of lipstick she always wore. Her curls tumbled loose, brushing her neck, and when she threw her head back and laughed, his mouth went dry.

He didn't want her to leave, plain and simple. He wanted her to stay. He wanted to hear her voice calling sleepily to him in the darkness of a rainy winter night. He wanted to feel the curve of her hip against his as she shifted in sleep. He wanted . . . her. And it petrified him. He took another swallow of Coke and gazed out at the dark water of the bay, trying to steady the battering ram thud of his heart in his chest. She was going away soon. Back to her life in Paris, back to the life she'd always dreamed of. And he and Star . . . what would become of them?

You have to tell her, his conscience urged. *You can't let her walk away without knowing the truth. It could change everything.* He owed it to her. She deserved the truth.

"Georgia."

"Yes?" She turned to him, eyes bright. He opened his mouth to tell her, but stopped, picturing Star's face, the hope and sorrow mingled as she swore him to secrecy and told him about her plan to bring Georgia to the island. It was not his secret to tell. It was Star's, and although it affected all of them, he could not break a confidence. He'd promised Star, and he was a man of his word.

He snapped his mouth closed. "Nothing. You look beautiful tonight. I like your dress."

"Oh." Her cheeks flushed pink and she looked pleased. "Thank you." She took a sip of wine and grimaced. "I wish this tasted better."

"It's probably not that good even if you could taste it," he assured her. "Billy always goes cheap with the wine at these events."

She laughed, looking back toward the party, watching the dancers and listening to the music. He drank in the sight of her for a long moment, trying to remember every last detail, an inoculation against her absence.

"Let's dance." Georgia stood and held out her hand.

He shook his head. "I don't dance. Two left feet."

She shot him a pretty little red-lipped pout. "It's my birthday and I want to dance. That means you can't say no." With a grin, she grabbed his hand and pulled him up, tugging him toward the dance floor. He protested but she insisted. She could be very persuasive.

Georgia was having a ball. It had been years since she'd felt this free. Cole turned out to be a surprisingly good dancer. He seemed to have a strong sense of timing and moved with a contained sort of grace that made it easy to follow him. He made it look sexy and effortless at the same time. Georgia, however, kept bumping into him, getting distracted by his nearness and forgetting to follow his lead. Was it his pheromones that were making her clumsy or the wine? She couldn't tell. The band was doing a slow dance number, and Cole pulled her close, surprising her, his arm encircling her waist snugly. She hesitated, then gave herself to the music and the moment, wrapping her arms around his neck and leaning in. He smelled the same, that soap and salt and coffee scent. They were dancing very close together, their faces inches apart.

"I still have at least a dozen questions left to ask in our twenty questions game," she said coyly, "and since it's my birthday, you have to answer truthfully."

Cole gave her an amused half smile. "Is that how this works?"

"Absolutely." She threw him a flirtatious little smile. "Here's the first one. Why were you so hostile to me when we first met?"

He hesitated. She saw the indecision in his face. "You have to tell the truth," she reminded him.

"You want to know the truth?" he said, swaying slowly with the music. He looked resigned. "I was afraid you'd recognize me."

"Really?" She pulled a face. "Come on. I don't really keep up with hot nerdy genius award-winning science types. Not really my scene."

"Not because of that," he replied. "Because you were right when you said I looked familiar. We've met before." He looked her in the eye frankly.

"What?" Georgia pulled back a little and stared at him. "When?" Her mind was racing, trying to figure out when their paths would have crossed. "I knew it! I knew you looked familiar! But you told me we'd never met."

He had the grace to look embarrassed. "I lied," he admitted, spinning them in a slow circle. "We met in Paris about seven years ago. I was being honored by the academic community for some research I'd done when I was studying in France for my PhD. There was a cocktail reception before the awards ceremony, and they'd hired some fancy chefs to make hors d'oeuvres."

Understanding bloomed in Georgia's face. "I remember that event," she exclaimed. She gave him a startled look. "You were there for that? That was a terrible night."

He nodded. The music and other dancers swirled around them languidly as they kept pace with the rhythm. "It was the first award I'd ever received, and I was sweating through my rented tux," Cole told her. "And then I saw you. You were making some sort of savory crepe things with a Texas twist."

"Pork belly barbecue crepes," Georgia corrected him, grimacing at the memory.

"I thought you were the most beautiful woman I'd ever seen."

"That's sweet of you to say," Georgia replied, "but that evening was a disaster. I got fired halfway through the evening because some pompous idiot insulted me and I . . . responded strongly." She looked incensed by the memory.

"I know." Cole winced. "That was me."

"No." Georgia's eyes widened in disbelief. She stepped back, dropping her arms from his neck. "You're kidding! That was YOU? No wonder I thought you looked familiar. How could you?" Her surprise was starting to melt into outrage.

Cole stopped dancing too and looked mortified. "I didn't mean to insult you, Georgia. I'd had three glasses of champagne, for liquid courage, which was a stupid idea. This was before I knew Amy. I was awkward around women. I had a bad haircut and a rented tux. I'd been practicing my French all evening just so I could approach you. I just wanted to ask if you'd have a drink with me after the awards ceremony."

"You propositioned me and called me a crude term for a whore," Georgia protested, putting her hands on her hips and glowering. "In very bad French."

Cole looked embarrassed. "That's not what I meant to say. Some of the tech guys I was with at the ceremony spoke French. They told me the right phrase to say to compliment you. But it turns out they were playing a practical joke on me, and it wasn't a compliment at all. It was a horrible mistake."

Georgia looked slightly mollified. "I thought you were just being an entitled jerk," she confessed. "It happened all the time at those sorts of events—too much alcohol and men think they can get any woman into bed with them. I was so tired of it. You were the fifth geeky science guy who hit on me that night. Your crude and offensive proposition was just the last straw."

"I guess that explains what happened next," Cole mused. "I will never forget the look on your face when you took a big spoonful of barbecued pork, leaned over the table, and very carefully shoveled it into the breast pocket of my rented tuxedo." Despite himself, Cole chuckled. "And then you looked up at me, all wide-eyed and innocent, and said in that cute Texas twang of yours, 'Bon appétit!'"

Georgia groaned, covering her face with her hands. "I got fired immediately for that."

Cole smiled. "I deserved it. Was it worth it?"

Georgia glanced at him through her fingers with a wicked grin. "Yeah," she admitted. "It was totally worth it."

"I had to pay a two-hundred-euro cleaning fee when I returned the tux," Cole told her. "I doubt they ever got the smell of barbecue sauce out of that pocket."

Georgia looked at him for a long moment and then she burst

out laughing. Cole looked surprised, and then he joined her. They stood facing each other, laughing until tears ran down their faces while the bluegrass band wailed and the dancers swirled around them like currents of water.

When they'd laughed themselves out, Georgia straightened and took a deep breath. "So that's why you were so nasty to me when I got here?" she asked. "Because you thought I'd remember you from that night?"

Cole nodded, looking bashful. "When Star told me about her chef daughter in Paris, I thought it couldn't possibly be the same person. What were the odds? But then you turned up. I took one look at you and knew it was you. I was worried you would recognize me and figure out who I was and hate me for it, not just for my misguided French compliment but for what came after, for Amy, for all of it." He fell quiet, his face flushed with shame. "I was ashamed. I'm sorry."

Georgia sobered. "Cole," she said gently. "It was a mistake, what happened to Amy. A big, terrible mistake that you have to live with for the rest of your life. But you didn't mean to do it. And one big mistake doesn't mean your life is over. You are a kind and loyal person, Cole. And you still deserve goodness and love in your life."

Cole looked down at the dance floor, scuffing the toe of his boot on the hard surface. "You say it, and I wish I could believe it," he said quietly.

Georgia nodded. "I know. I hope someday you can." She tilted her head and looked at him. "Now that your French is better," she said, trying to lighten the mood, "you could try that compliment again." She cocked a brow at him playfully, a tacit invitation. "Just don't ask for help from your frat bro friends this time."

Cole studied her face and then took a step toward her with an expression she couldn't quite read. Slowly, he reached out and circled her waist, gently tugging her to him. Her breath caught in her throat. He didn't start dancing again, just stood still with her clasped in the circle of his arms. She twined her arms around his neck.

"What did you mean to say to me that night?" she asked him. Her eyes were unexpectedly soft.

He leaned forward until his lips just grazed the shell of her ear, his breath warm against her skin, his hands firm around her waist. "I meant to tell you that you were the pluckiest, prettiest girl I'd ever seen." He paused. "I still think that."

She pulled back a little and looked at him with surprise. "Really?"

He nodded. "Georgia May Jackson," he said, his ice-blue eyes boring into hers with a look of such open longing it made her catch her breath, "I have never met someone like you. I think you hung the moon."

Georgia stared at him open-mouthed with astonishment for a second, then she bridged the few inches between them, pressing her lips against his. He made a noise of surprise, and then his hand slid up the back of her neck and his other arm pressed her against him. He was kissing her under the lights with the wail of the fiddle and the thrum of the bass. The world fell away as Georgia closed her eyes and let herself sink into the moment. She wasn't thinking about Paris or Star or the competition. She wasn't thinking at all. She ran her fingers through the wavy hair at the base of his neck, feeling the rasp of his stubble against her cheek. He knew what to do with that gorgeous mouth of his. He was kissing her with utter concentration, as though it were his sole purpose in life. She felt her knees buckle just a little, but he held her up with one strong arm. He tasted of fried oysters, rich and savory, his mouth warm and insistent against hers. Their kiss deepened. All of a sudden, she gave a little gasp and broke away, stumbling back, putting her hand to her lips.

"I can taste you," she whispered.

He stared at her, eyes a little unfocused and glazed. "What?"

"I can taste you," she repeated. "The oysters, the umami flavor. Cole, I can taste it!" She stared at him in wonder for a moment and then she shrieked in glee, hurling herself at him. He caught her and she wrapped her arms around his neck and her legs around his waist, giddy and exuberant and laughing so hard she almost cried. He spun her slowly, laughing with her, as the lights and the music whirled around them in a perfect, dazzling blur.

30

"*Now that was* a party," Georgia declared dreamily. It was almost midnight, and she was a little tipsy from several glasses of sauvignon blanc she'd consumed with a dozen fried oysters during the remainder of the evening. Cole put his hand under her arm to steady her as they wove their way by moonlight away from the remnants of the party and through the evergreen trees to the cottage. Star had gone home some time ago, leaving them to dance the evening away. Behind them, the band was packing up, the dance floor was empty, and the barbecue grill was growing cold. Billy was wandering around with a giant black trash bag, whistling and collecting rubbish from under the picnic tables. The Oyster Shuck was over for another year.

But what a night it had been. Georgia was incandescent with happiness, giddy with the joy of being able to taste another flavor again and the unexpected delight of kissing Cole. Quite a lot of kissing, in fact. Since that moment on the dance floor, there had been many kisses, each one better than the last. She closed her eyes, humming the final tune the band had played. Tonight . . . tonight had been pure magic. The lights and music, the wine and oysters, and Cole. She glanced up at him and found his eyes on her. Her heart felt like butter gone soft at the edges, starting to melt from the heat between them. Her gaze went to his mouth, that gorgeous mouth. She loved a man who knew how to kiss like he meant it.

Cole's confession of his feelings for her changed everything. He cared for her, and she cared for him back. But what could they do about it? Would he be open to moving to Paris? It seemed highly unlikely. He loved the islands, the nature and quiet and anonymity. He seemed to belong here. She sensed he would be miserable in Paris. But Paris was her dream, one she could not imagine giving up for anyone or anything, not even someone who kissed like it was his calling in life, not even for Cole. She frowned. There were no easy answers. They walked in silence toward the house, and Georgia determined to think about it all later. Tonight she was giddy and smitten and a little tipsy. It had been the best birthday she'd ever had. She wanted to enjoy it just a little bit longer.

At the back door to the cottage, they paused. She could see through the kitchen door that there was a light on in the living room, although the kitchen was dark. Star must still be awake, or else she'd left a light on for Georgia. "Thank you for tonight," she said softly. He was standing very close to her, just a dim outline in the midnight blue.

"My pleasure," he said. She could hear the smile in his voice.

She stood on tiptoe and pressed a kiss against his cheek, raspy and warm in the cool night air. "Good night, Cole."

"Good night, Georgia May," he replied. For a moment, he pressed his forehead to hers, their noses almost touching. He inhaled once, roughly, then opened the kitchen door. "Can I walk you in?" he asked. She nodded, taking his hand and leading him into the house. She didn't want the evening to end just yet. She was not ready to say good night.

Holding hands with Cole, she led him through the darkened hallway and into the bright lights of the living room, then stopped in utter shock.

Her father was sitting in the living room.

"Daddy?" Georgia gasped, halting so abruptly that Cole bumped into her from behind.

"Hello, Georgia May." The tall, rawboned figure of Buck Jackson was seated in the lone armchair in the corner. He had his Stetson balanced on his knee, his arms folded across his barrel chest. His blond hair was cropped close in his signature crew cut, and even in spring he was slightly sunburned. For a wild moment, Georgia wondered if he had come all this way for her birthday. But then she noticed him scowling at Star, who was huddled on the opposite end of the couch, as far as she could get from Buck, still wearing her party outfit and looking equal parts defiant and nervous. Pollen sat at her feet, looking from one to the other and whining uncertainly.

Cole peered around Georgia, saw Buck, and stopped short. "Who are you?" he demanded.

"Buck Jackson." Buck raised an eyebrow. "Georgia's daddy and Star's ex-husband. Who are you, son?"

Cole glanced at Georgia in surprise. She nodded, flabbergasted to find her father sitting in the living room. "What are you doing here, Daddy?" Georgia stammered. She had not seen her father in years. What in the world was he doing sitting in the living room at midnight on her birthday? She moved into the room a few steps, glancing between her parents. There was a palpable level of hostility radiating between them. They could have boiled water with the heat of their animosity. What in the world was going on?

"Georgia May," Buck announced, slapping his hat on his knee and standing. "That woman is a liar." He gestured toward Star. "She is not to be trusted. Come on, get your things. I'm taking you out of here."

"What?" Georgia exclaimed at the same time as Star protested, "Buck, no!"

"You promised me a long time ago you'd stay away from our daughter, and for all these years you kept your promise," Buck said firmly, jabbing a finger in Star's direction. "Until now." He looked at Georgia. "She contacted me a few weeks ago with this sob story about a bad prognosis, saying she's so sick and doesn't have much time left. She begged me to let her get in touch with you. She said she wanted to tell you herself before it's too late. Against my better judgment, I agreed and gave her your email address. But then you texted me this morning, said she was fit as a fiddle. I decided I'd better come out here and sort this all out, see what she was up to." He rounded on Star accusingly. "You lied to me, Star. And this is the last time."

"It's not a lie!" Star cried. Every head in the room swiveled in her direction. She swallowed nervously.

Georgia stared at her mother in consternation. "What does he mean a bad prognosis?" she asked, her voice shrill in her own ears. "Are you sick?"

Star shot a single panicked glance at Cole, who raised his hands and took a step back. "You knew she'd find out eventually, Star," he said, his tone weary. He glanced at Georgia with sympathy. That look sent a cold tendril of dread spiraling through her heart.

"Find out what?" Georgia asked. She glanced around the room. What were they not telling her? How was she the only one who didn't know what was going on? She felt her temper flare. She was tired of people keeping things from her. "Someone tell me the truth!" she demanded. "What is going on?"

Star deflated. "It's not a lie," she said finally, reluctantly. "What I told Buck is true. I got the diagnosis a month ago."

"What diagnosis?" Georgia suddenly couldn't breathe. All the air had been sucked from her lungs.

Star swallowed hard and met Georgia's eyes. "I have a disease called Lewy body dementia," she said. "It's sort of like Alzheimer's and Parkinson's combined. It's in the early stages, but it often progresses pretty fast after a diagnosis. Most people only live a couple of years after they're diagnosed. There is no cure." She looked resigned. "I'm so sorry, Georgia."

"No," Georgia whispered, tears springing to her eyes. "This can't be happening." Star was sick with a disease that had no cure? She had just found her mother only to lose her again. It was too horrible to be true.

"That's why you contacted me," Georgia said in a small voice, all the pieces clicking into place. Star had reached out because she was sick. That was the secret Star had been hiding. It all made sense now. The timing of Star contacting her, Billy's cryptic comments, the tense conversation between Star and Cole she'd overheard the day she arrived.

Star blew out a breath and nodded. "I reached out to you because I'm running out of time," she admitted, "and I wanted to see you before . . . before things got too bad. My symptoms are manageable right now, not so obvious most people notice. I'm starting to get a little forgetful now and then, and I'm having some insomnia and sleep problems. But soon it will get much worse. Within a couple of years, I'll lose a lot of cognitive function and short-term memory and some motor control. I don't have a lot of time left before things are going to get bad."

Georgia looked around her in disbelief. This evening had been so perfect, and now it felt like she had plummeted into some horrible nightmare. "Isn't there anything the doctors can do?" she asked, hating the pitiful note of pleading in her voice.

Star shook her head. "I'm on medications that can slow it,

but the reality is that at some point this disease will catch up to me. It's just a matter of time." She looked sadly at Georgia.

Georgia closed her eyes. She felt nauseated. Just when she felt like she was finding her way back to hope and happiness, everything came crashing down again.

From the doorway, Cole cleared his throat. "Tell her everything," he said.

"There's more?" Georgia asked in alarm. She could not handle any more bad news.

Star looked pained. "I'm selling the cottage," she said quietly. "Before my condition gets any worse. It's just too much for me to keep up, even with Cole's help, and I am going to need the money for my care. I'm putting it on the market in a few weeks and planning to move to a care community out on Lopez Island. It's a safe place where I can get the help I need as my condition gets worse."

Georgia was stunned. In these past few weeks, she felt as though she'd gained a mother, a legacy, even a place to call home. Now everything was crumbling around her, disinitigrating in the space of a few minutes.

"I . . . I can't believe this is happening," she murmured finally, shaking her head in confusion, wishing she could rewind time an hour or two and be back at the Oyster Shuck dancing and kissing Cole, not here watching her entire life dissolve like a sugar cube in water. In an instant, everything good was vanishing in front of her eyes.

"Georgia . . ." Star began.

"No." Georgia put up a hand to stop the words. "Just no. Not tonight." She couldn't handle any more. Her head was fuzzy and she felt sick with dread and grief. She wished she hadn't drunk those glasses of wine. A headache was throbbing right behind her temples.

"Georgia?" Cole reached out and clasped her arm lightly, but she shrugged him off.

"You." She rounded on him in sudden indignation. "You lied to me."

"I never lied." He looked at her steadily, his expression pained. "I just didn't tell you the truth."

"That's not any better." She scowled. "Leave, please, Cole. Just . . . go."

Cole looked at her for a long, searching moment. "Is that what you want?" he asked slowly. He looked hurt. She nodded miserably, deliberately turning away from him. Without another word, Cole turned and walked through the kitchen and out the back door.

The room was silent for a long moment.

"I should go." Buck tapped his Stetson on his knee. "Star, I'm real sorry to hear about your health condition. I'll get out of your hair now, let you have your time with Georgia." He looked uncomfortable.

"No," Georgia snapped suddenly. Both of her parents glanced at her in surprise. "Neither of you are going anywhere," she announced. "I can't handle any more revelations tonight. But tomorrow we are going to have a talk, the three of us. You both have some explaining to do. No one leaves until we have a chance to talk, is that clear?"

Star and Buck exchanged a look. Surprisingly, neither of them protested. "You can sleep on the couch if you need a place," Star told Buck grudgingly.

Buck looked surprised and discomfited. "I appreciate the offer, but I'll be fine in the car." He nodded toward the front where a shiny black rental SUV was parked by the produce stand.

"I'm going to bed," Georgia announced. "I'll see you both in the morning." She turned toward the stairs wearily. Her feet felt leaden, dragging her down with every step. She thought she might be able to hear her heart breaking.

"Georgia . . ." Star called after her in a tone pinched with worry.

"Save it for the morning," Georgia said, not looking back. Then she headed up the stairs alone.

Upstairs in her room, Georgia quietly locked the door. Her head was throbbing, and there was a lump in her throat the size of a plum. Star was sick. Star was losing her memory. It was just a matter of time . . .

With a little sob, Georgia kicked off her shoes and sank onto the bed, the full skirt of her emerald green party dress splayed out around her. What had been a magical night was now broken beyond repair. All her joy had been leached away by the knowledge that the mother she had just found was going to leave her once more and there was absolutely nothing she could do about it. It felt so crushingly tragic, so massively unfair.

Gulping back tears, Georgia shrugged out of her cardigan and unzipped her dress, letting it puddle on the floor. The evening had been so deliciously sweet—Cole, the oysters, the kisses—but now it all felt hollow with disappointment and loss. Georgia stepped out of the dress, shivering in her underwear in the chilly air. She hurried into her pajamas and hung the dress in the closet, then picked up her cardigan. As she did so, a handful of four-leaf clovers scattered across the wood floorboards. She stood staring at the little green plants in bewilderment, then kicked at them in a sudden burst of frustration, crushing them with her bare feet.

"What are you trying to tell me?" she whispered fiercely.

Silence.

With a sigh, she knelt down and gathered up all the clover she could find. She held the smashed little plants in the palm of her hand. Frowning, she stared down at the four leaflets of the clover. Faith, hope, love, and luck. They were in short supply tonight. Nothing felt charmed about her life right now. Instead it felt like a cruel trick had been played on her. Everything had been going so smoothly until the revelation about Star's illness blew a gaping hole in the center of everything good. How could she cope with losing her mother just when they'd found each other again? The shock of it left her breathless.

Dumping the clover in the trash, she climbed into bed and pulled the worn cotton sheets up to her chin. "Julia," she whispered to her patron saint. "Help! I feel like I'm drowning here."

Julia's voice, practical and chipper. "My dear, all I know boils down to this one truth—nothing in life is ever really wasted. Somehow it will all be used for good."

Georgia closed her eyes in resignation. "How can this possibly be good?" she muttered sadly. "I need a miracle."

"One of the secrets I've learned about cooking," said Julia conversationally, pouring hot rum over a puffy dessert soufflé and setting it alight, "is that you must learn to correct something if you can, but if you cannot, then you must learn to bear it with honesty and courage. And remember, if you're afraid to cook with butter, you can always use cream."

"Honesty and courage," Georgia murmured, her eyes welling with tears. "Butter and cream." She didn't fully understand Julia's advice, but she drifted off to sleep feeling comforted nonetheless.

31

Georgia woke at the crack of dawn, feeling resolute and oddly calm. As soon as she opened her eyes, she knew what she needed to do. She dressed hurriedly, throwing on her chef's whites and pulling her hair back with her Hermès scarf. It was the outfit she was most comfortable in, and she wanted to be wearing it when she finally got the answers she'd been waiting for all these years. And she intended to get those answers as soon as possible.

Downstairs in the kitchen, she grabbed some leftover rice from the refrigerator and set a medium-sized saucepan on the stove. She put Édith Piaf on her phone, keeping the volume low. She needed to hear Édith's voice. Correct what you can, and bear the rest with honesty and courage, Julia had told her. Georgia was trying to do just that. Dumping the rice, a cup of cream and a dab of butter, some sugar, and a pinch of salt into the pan, she turned on the burner. While the rice mixture warmed, she sprinkled in some cinnamon and a dash of nutmeg, and threw in a handful of raisins. She stirred the rice pudding as it heated.

"Come on, please let this work," she murmured. She was a welter of conflicting emotions. Her heart felt leaden at the reality of Star's condition, yet overlaying the grief was a quiet mounting frustration with both of her parents. She was determined to get answers from them once and for all. But she didn't just want answers. She wanted more than that. She wanted to help fix things, to bring clarity to a situation that had been hidden and toxic for too many years. She was going to try to correct what she could the only way she knew how. Through using her gift and cooking for those she loved with the help of a little butter and cream.

When the rice pudding was warm, Georgia stirred in a bit more cream, one beaten egg, and some vanilla extract, then spooned the warm pudding into three bowls. Rice pudding had been a staple on the Jackson dinner table ever since she could remember. It was Buck's favorite dessert. No reason it couldn't be breakfast this morning. They would need all the warm comfort pudding could muster if this conversation was going to be anything short of a disaster.

"Help this bring clarity to the unknown places." Georgia whispered the words like a prayer, sprinkling in an extra dash of nutmeg, just the way Buck liked it. "Show us what we need to see."

Taking a spoon from the drawer, she tasted the pudding, bracing herself for the bitter taste of disappointment. But to her surprise, the instant the creamy warmth touched her tongue, she could taste the sweetness. She gasped, then licked the spoon to be sure. It was true. She could taste the sugar, the cinnamon, the hint of vanilla.

"Oh." Georgia sagged back against the counter in sheer relief. "Thank you," she murmured aloud. Why today of all days would she get her sense of sweetness back? What strange timing. But she was grateful. At least one thing in her world was being set right this morning. Now she needed a miracle for all the rest too.

Georgia glanced up when she heard footsteps in the hall. Star stood uncertainly in the doorway, Pollen at her heels. She was wearing a bulky knit cardigan in cream wool, a pair of worn linen drawstring pants, and a Grateful Dead T-shirt. Her hair curled around her shoulders in a silver cloud.

"Morning," Star said, her tone a little hesitant. She looked tired. She walked past Georgia and filled the electric kettle at the sink. Georgia studied her mother. How could this woman be suffering from a disease that was stealing her memories, stealing her functionality? How could it possibly be true?

"Why didn't you tell me?" she asked quietly.

Star grabbed a mug from the cupboard and turned to face her daughter. "Because I wanted a chance for us to get to know each other again without my diagnosis standing between us," she said frankly. "When people hear the word 'dementia,' it changes how they see you. When they know you have a disease, it stops people from being able to see who you still are. I watched it happen with Justine and the cancer. They stop seeing you as a whole person and just see you as your sickness. I hadn't been with you in twenty-eight years and I was desperate for a little window of time where you saw me as I am now, just Star, not a woman with a terrible disease slowly consuming her brain. I just wanted . . . a little time together before I told you the truth." She met Georgia's eyes, her own pleading for understanding.

Wordlessly, Georgia stirred the pudding. She didn't know what to say to Star. Was she asking for absolution or simply understanding? Georgia understood, but it did not lessen the pain she felt over Star's duplicity or the reality of her disease.

"You should have told me," she said finally.

Star nodded. "You're right," she admitted. "But would you have come if I did? Would we have been able to get to know each other like we have these past few weeks?"

Georgia hesitated. What would have changed if she'd known earlier? She would still have come to see Star, surely, but would she have treated Star differently? Would she have protected her heart and kept her mother at arm's length? Would she have missed out on the gift of these precious weeks together where it had just been the two of them each morning, talking and reconnecting?

"I thought we had more time," she said quietly, grieved.

"I was trying to give us more time," Star said, spooning some tea leaves into her mug and adding hot water from the electric kettle. "Cole kept telling me that I had to come clean with you, but I kept delaying telling you. I wanted just one more day with you. Every day I wanted just one more day. I knew it was wrong to not tell you, but I was so afraid that if I did, you'd disappear, or choose to keep me at a distance." She looked up at Georgia. "You have every right to be angry with me, but honestly, I wouldn't trade these few weeks with you for anything on earth. They've been the happiest of my life."

Georgia nodded. "They have for me too," she admitted. She blinked and looked away, trying to swallow the lump in her throat. She kept stirring the pudding, more for something to do than because it needed it. She was going to make it mushy if she kept it up.

A moment of silence stretched between them. Pollen lifted her head and gave a low "woof" just as they heard the heavy tread of a man's footsteps in the hall. A moment later, Buck came into the kitchen. He looked like he'd slept in his Levi's and his battered ranch hand leather jacket. His hair was growing sparse, Georgia noticed when he removed his hat. Her father was getting older. The realization hit her with a sharp little twist in her gut. He was still vigorous, but there were new lines in his weathered face, and his shoulders were a little stooped. He still filled a room when he entered it, though, with a firm authority and a strong presence.

"Ladies," he greeted them, then stood awkwardly in the doorway, turning his Stetson in his hands. "I should be getting on the road." He glanced over his shoulder toward the door with a touch of longing as though he couldn't wait to get out of that kitchen. "I've got a flight back to Texas this afternoon. I need to be getting back to the ranch. It's the busy season."

"No one is going anywhere yet," Georgia said firmly. "Not until you both tell me the truth. So I suggest you get comfortable. I made you breakfast."

Buck opened his mouth in what looked like surprise or protest, but Georgia pinned him with a fierce glance. "I have been waiting for almost thirty years to understand what happened to my mother," she said, her tone steely with determination. "I know you two kept it a secret from me, but that ends today. No more secrets. I deserve to know."

Buck scratched his head and glanced at Star, who spread her hands wide. "I would have told her years ago," she said.

Buck sat down heavily in a chair. "Okay then." He sighed. "Is there any coffee? Sounds like I'm going to need it."

Five minutes later, Buck was sipping a cup of coffee, strong and black as tar, just the way he liked it. Across the table from him, Star nervously clutched her mug of tea. Pollen whined and put her head on her paws, lying on the floor, eyes shifting back and forth between Star and Buck. Georgia slid bowls of rice pudding in front of her parents.

"Eat this before we talk," she ordered.

Star took the bowl slowly and cocked her head at Georgia, eyeing her thoughtfully. Georgia ignored her. She took the chair at the end of the table where she could see both of them easily. She couldn't believe they were all here, sitting at the same table. It felt surreal. For so many years, she'd had questions that went unanswered. Now before her were the two people who she suspected held the keys to every question. And she intended to make sure they finally told her the truth. She was not going to budge until she got answers.

After a few minutes of clinking spoons and quiet slurps, when their bowls were almost empty, Georgia looked from Star to Buck and asked, "I want you to tell me what happened to our family." She folded her arms and fixed her parents with a determined gaze.

Star shot Buck a look and raised her eyebrows. "You swore me to secrecy," she said. "And I've kept my end of the bargain all these years. It's up to you to end it."

Buck frowned, considering for a moment. Then he slapped his hand down on the table and sighed in resignation. "I guess we're past the point of secrets now," he said. He looked at Star. "Do you want to tell her or should I?"

"I will," Star said quietly. She looked steadily at Georgia. "I was nineteen and headed west, running from a mean step-daddy in Georgia, the one I told you about, when my car broke down in the middle of nowhere in West Texas. I was in trouble, though it took me a while to realize it. It was so hot, no water anywhere, and foolishly, I had nothing with me but an empty takeout cup of gas station coffee." She looked down at her mug and toyed with the handle, her voice soft with remembering. "There were no cars coming by, nothing in sight except the scorched earth and the sweltering sun. I lasted for a couple of hours before I started feeling like I was going to pass out."

"It was heatstroke," Buck interjected. "When I found her, she was suffering from heatstroke."

Star nodded. "I was sitting in the shade of my broken-down

car, trying to keep cool in the broiling heat, when here came your daddy in his big Ford truck. He saved me, towed my car to the ranch, made me lie down on the sofa in front of a fan and take little tiny sips of water." She smiled at the memory. "I fell in love with him right away. He was so big and strong and capable, so upstanding and honorable. I'd never met a man like him in my life."

Buck looked surprised. "Well I'd never met a woman like her either," he admitted, clearing his throat self-consciously.

"I was wild then," Star explained to Georgia. "Beautiful and reckless. And your daddy looked at me like I was some rare creature. We were from two different worlds, but each hurt bad in our own ways. Our wounds fit together, just like we did somehow. We fell into bed before the weekend was out."

At that, Buck made a noise of discomfort. Georgia glanced at him to find him staring fixedly at the ceiling, looking embarrassed. "She doesn't need to know the particulars," he said gruffly.

"A week later, I moved in," Star said, ignoring him. "We had so little in common, but somehow we couldn't seem to keep away from each other."

Buck grunted in assent but said nothing more.

Star smiled sadly, a brief twist of her lips. There was a faraway look in her eyes. "The Jackson clan pitched a fit when your daddy introduced me to them," she admitted. "I wasn't what they wanted for their eldest son. I knew I wasn't good enough for him. I had spent years lying and stealing just to survive. I was using drugs when I met Buck, trying to drown out a lot of things that had happened to me as a young girl. I'd been used and abused by a lot of men by the time I stumbled onto the ranch. But when I met Buck, I knew he was one of the good ones. And I tried so hard to be good enough for him, for all of them." Star looked regretful. "Then I got pregnant with you. His family hated me even more when they found out about the baby, thinking I was trying to trap him, but it wasn't like that. We both thought of you as a gift, Georgia, right from the very start."

"That's God's honest truth," Buck interjected.

"His family threatened and cried and prayed until they were hoarse," Star continued, "trying to get him to leave me, but he was steadfast. He asked me to marry him, and I did. We eloped one weekend when I was four months pregnant. I stopped using drugs as soon as I saw that positive pregnancy test, just quit cold turkey. I loved your daddy, and I loved you, even when you were no bigger than a kidney bean. So we lived together on the ranch while my belly grew big as a watermelon."

Star stopped and took a sip of tea.

"And then I had you," she said simply. "And you were the most beautiful thing I'd ever seen in my life. We both adored you. We thought the sun rose and set on your face, Georgia May. You were all the best parts of us both, put together in one perfect little girl." She smiled softly at the memory. Georgia glanced at Buck and was surprised to find him looking at Star. There was an expression on his weathered face she'd never seen before, a tenderness and a sadness that surprised her. He caught her eye and cleared his throat, taking a big gulp of coffee and looking away.

"For a while after you were born, I managed okay," Star said. "We kept Buck's family at bay best we could, although they tried to meddle in anything they could. They were worried sick about him and about you. They'd found out about my gift by then and labeled me a witch. They thought I was using black magic on your daddy. It was the only way they could understand why he'd be with someone like me."

"Now that isn't quite fair," Buck protested. "They had concerns, and they were worried about you. And they had good reason to be, as it turns out." He crossed his arms and leaned back in the chair. Star pressed her lips together, but she did not contradict him.

"We did all right for a couple of years, but when you were three or four, the cracks started showing through," she continued. "Buck wanted me to fit into the community more. I didn't, and I couldn't. There was no place for a woman like me. We . . . fought a lot." She glanced at Buck, who was staring down at his coffee cup silently.

He nodded. "We fought like feral dogs," he confirmed ruefully.

"His family still hated me and tried to undermine me any way they could. They knew what I was, a broken girl trying to fit somewhere she didn't, and they weren't wrong." Star frowned. "This is the part that's hard for me to say," she admitted. "I loved being your mama, but the life I was living in Texas started feeling suffocating. Every time I had to go to town for diapers or groceries, I'd panic. I wasn't sleeping, wasn't eating. It felt like the walls were closing in. I wasn't cut out for ranch life, for the heat and the isolation and the dust. I tried, but everything I did turned out wrong. I was struggling. Nowadays they'd probably diagnose me with some sort of severe depression and PTSD from the trauma I'd endured before I met your daddy, but I didn't know enough to call it that back then, and there wasn't anyone that could help me. Buck did the best he knew how, but he's a man who knows how to sledgehammer problems out of his way. He had no idea what to do with a fragile, depressed woman he could not fix."

Buck made a noise. Georgia expected him to protest, but he only commented. "I tried my best, but nothing seemed to help." He shifted heavily in his seat. "I didn't know what to do."

Star took a deep breath. "It was a miserable time. I was trying so hard to be a good mom to you, to be enough for Buck, but I never seemed to quite measure up. And then I made a terrible choice, one that destroyed our family."

32

Star grew quiet for a moment, and Georgia was afraid she would stop the story. "What happened?" she prompted.

Star looked down at her hands on the table. "I started using again," she admitted. "Heroin this time." She closed her eyes, seeming to shrink in upon herself in shame. "There was a man in town who could get it for me. He worked at the meat counter in the grocery store, so it was easy to hide our deals. I'd order a few slices of bologna, and he'd slip it to me in the brown paper wrapping. I told myself I was doing it so I could cope, and in a way that was true. It was a bad way to cope, but the only way I knew." She swallowed hard. "I kept it hidden as best I could for almost a year, but sins and secrets don't stay hidden long." Star stopped and looked pained.

"Who found out?" Georgia asked. She was on the edge of her seat. It felt like watching a car accident in slow motion, the mounting sense of horror as you see things go terribly wrong. But she didn't feel like a spectator. She was watching the events unfold, knowing that what was about to happen was going to hurt her terribly too.

Star shook her head. "I can't tell this part," she whispered hoarsely. "You tell it, Buck." Her hands were clenched around her mug so hard her knuckles were white.

Buck cleared his throat. "For a while I'd suspected she was using again, but it took me some time to confirm my suspicions. When I finally found out what she was doing, I confronted her.

She swore she'd stop, but then a month later she started back up. It became a cycle. We hid it from everyone, trying to make things work, but we were in a bad way." He took a swig of coffee and set the cup down hard on the table. At the sound, Pollen raised her head and uttered a concerned woof.

"Hannah suspected something was wrong," Buck continued. "She started dropping by, staying to watch you for the afternoon at least once a week so your mama could rest. By that point, Star wasn't taking very good care of herself or sometimes of you. Often I'd come home at the end of a long day out on the land to find the stove cold and the refrigerator almost empty. Once or twice, I found Star passed out sleeping in bed and you were playing outside alone." He paused, his brow furrowed. "I knew Star needed help, but I didn't know how to fix her, and I didn't want to admit it to my family because they were so against Star. We fought a lot, your mom and I. I'd confront her and she'd swear she'd change, and I'd give her another chance, except the chances always ended the same way. I didn't understand much about addiction, about the cycles and the lying and the trying to do better but failing. I didn't understand why she couldn't just stop."

"I tried," Star interrupted, her voice hoarse. "I tried so hard. I wanted to stop, but I couldn't. I'd get clean for a few days or weeks, sometimes a month or more, but I always slipped up again. I hated myself for what I was doing to Buck and how I was failing you, Georgia. But I couldn't seem to stop."

"What happened then?" Georgia asked. She had a funny flutter of apprehension down low in her belly, a whisper of a memory, something she couldn't quite recall.

"One day you disappeared," Buck said bluntly.

Star made a little grunt, like someone had just punched her

in the stomach. Pollen poked her head up from under the table, then laid it in Star's lap, shifting her eyebrows in concern.

"It was August. You had turned five a few months before. I remember it was about noon when Hannah came and found me up at the north field," Buck said, his expression grave. "I've never seen anyone look like that, before or since. She was white-faced and terrified. Immediately, I knew something terrible had happened. She said she'd come over to check on you, and found Star passed out on the couch, the TV turned to that cooking show you two liked to watch together, but you were gone. Vanished." He shook his head, blowing out a long breath. "We didn't know where you were or how long you'd been gone. It took us two hours to find you. Those two hours were the worst of my life, Georgia May. We gathered the ranch hands and called the neighbors and formed a search party. The neighbors brought their hound dogs. We even called the sheriff. We all knew what can happen to a child lost out in the wilderness in the summer heat in Texas." He reached out and took a big gulp of coffee. "It still gives me nightmares just thinking about what might have happened to you, what nearly did happen to you."

Georgia was both horrified and fascinated. She had a vague memory of walking alone down an empty road, of being thirsty and hot and feeling a little scared. She remembered carrying the little rainbow purse Star had knit for her and singing to herself to keep up her courage.

"I was going to the grocery store," she said suddenly. "I remember we were watching Julia Child on TV. She was making floating islands. I wanted to make them, but we were out of sugar. So I took my pocket money and decided to walk to the store. I was going to buy sugar."

"You didn't have any idea the store was twelve miles away,"

Buck confirmed. "And when we found you, you were headed in the wrong direction. You'd turned left instead of right out of the ranch driveway, away from town. You'd made it a couple of miles into the middle of nowhere."

Georgia was silent, trying to recall the rest of the memory. It was lost in time. "What happened? Who found me?" she asked.

"I did," Buck said simply. "I've never been more glad to see anything in my life than when I caught sight of your bright pigtails on that empty stretch of road. You were dusty and thirsty and sunburned, but you were alive."

Georgia looked from Buck to Star. "And then what happened?"

"That was the last straw," Buck said heavily. "When we got you home, I told the sheriff that Star had just dozed off, that she'd been feeling poorly, but I knew something had to be done. I covered it up because I didn't want the gossip and the shame that a scandal would cause our family, but I knew this was the end. We could have lost you. Dehydration, heatstroke, snakes, or someone coming along that stretch of road with bad intentions." He shuddered. "After everyone left, Hannah got you clean, fed, and tucked into bed, then she confronted me and demanded I tell her what was going on. When I did, she turned the house upside down . . ."

"Until she found my stash," Star admitted, breaking into the story. "Then she and your daddy confronted me. I confessed everything and begged for forgiveness, but this time was different. I felt so ashamed. I loved you, but I wasn't capable of being a good mother to you. I knew it. I was so full of hurt and so broken that I couldn't care for anyone else. I couldn't even take care of myself." Star glanced at Buck. "Your daddy is a good man, but he can be a hard man, as you know. His integrity is like iron, strong and unyielding. Hannah was like that but even harder. I begged for their forgiveness, and for the first time . . . Buck said no."

"I told her she wasn't a fit mother for you," Buck interrupted. Even all these years later, his face was darkened with anger at the memory. "You could easily have been killed, Georgia May. She couldn't keep you safe."

"He was right," Star admitted, wincing. "I was trying my best, but it wasn't enough. As much as I loved you, I couldn't take care of anyone, not even myself."

Buck glanced at Star, his expression like flint, and Georgia felt a qualm in her heart. She could see the scene playing out in front of her, the impossible combination of a woman who could not stop her destructive behavior, and a man whose sense of duty and concern for his daughter could not allow him to soften or show mercy.

Georgia swallowed hard. The truth she had wanted for so long was more painful to hear than she had imagined. She didn't know exactly how she was supposed to feel about Star's confession. She had thought it would feel like a catharsis or an epiphany, but instead it felt like a tragedy all the way around. She felt sick with the knowledge.

"What happened next?" she asked softly.

"I gave her a choice," Buck said, shifting in his chair. He looked resigned.

Star winced. "Hannah wanted to have me arrested for child endangerment. With the addition of the heroin possession, I would have gone to prison for a long time."

"But I said no," Buck interjected. "Star was still your mother and my wife, the woman I had loved. So I gave her a choice. Leave immediately and don't ever come back. Leave the ranch and our marriage . . . and leave you. It broke my heart to do it, but I couldn't trust Star anymore. It was the only way I could think of to make sure you were safe."

"And you said yes?" Georgia asked, turning to Star. Here it was, finally, the truth about why Star had left and never returned.

Star hesitated. "It was an impossible choice," she said, her voice catching on the words. "Buck said I could leave of my own free will, but if I did, I had to swear to disappear and stay away completely. I was giving you up for good. And if I didn't go, Hannah told me she would turn me in to the sheriff and I'd go to jail for drug possession and child endangerment and I'd lose you anyway."

"Hannah cared for you, Georgia May," Buck interrupted. "You were her blood, and she was trying to protect you."

"She saw me as a threat and was trying to keep you safe," Star continued. "I was trapped. I knew if I'd fought them I would end up in prison and I'd lose you for sure. At least if I left voluntarily, I thought I would still get to see you through the photos and letters Buck promised to send. I thought if I went willingly, if I got clean and sorted out my life, I might have a chance to connect with you again when you were older."

"So you chose to leave," Georgia said bluntly.

Star nodded, looking down, her face twisted in shame. "Leaving you was the hardest thing I've ever done, Georgia May. I felt like my heart was getting ripped from my body when I drove away. I could see you in the rearview mirror, your forlorn little face, and it hurt so bad I couldn't breathe. I couldn't imagine how I was going to live without you even for a day. I thought about trying to steal away with you, to keep you with me, but I knew your daddy would move heaven and earth to find you and then they'd take you away permanently. I'd never have a chance to see you again. And deep down I knew I was failing you as a mother. You deserved better. I could not keep you safe, not from my own demons. I knew your daddy and Hannah could give you a better life than I could. I knew they could give you every-thing I couldn't—stability, respectability, a family name. So I took the best bad option there was and I left. I left because I loved you."

Georgia made a little sound of protest. "But you didn't come back," she exclaimed. "You got clean and built this life for yourself, but you never sought me out. You never contacted me. Why?"

Star gave her a sympathetic look but pressed on. "Your daddy and Hannah and I made a pact before I left. They promised to cover up why I left to protect you and the Jacksons from scan-dal and me from jail time. And in exchange, I promised to never talk about what happened and why I disappeared. We all took that vow of silence. It was to protect all of us, and you. And I promised them I'd stay away from you until you were old enough to make your own decisions."

"I'm thirty-three," Georgia burst out. "Why did you wait all this time?"

Star glanced at Buck, doubt and frustration flickering across her face. "Because they told me you didn't want to see me."

"What?" Georgia whirled on Buck. "Tell me that's not true."

Buck shifted uncomfortably in his chair. "Well now, Georgia May . . ." Uncharacteristically, he seemed at a loss for words.

Star interrupted. "Buck and Hannah sent regular photos and updates, just like they promised. I could see you were growing so well, so beautiful and confident and strong. Every so often, I'd ask them if you ever asked about me, if you remembered me, and they said no. They told me you were happy, and later, when you were older, they told me that you didn't want any contact with

me. I wrote a letter to you when you turned eighteen, asking if
you wanted to meet me. They told me you didn't even open it."

Georgia darted a sharp look at her father. "Is she telling the
truth?" she demanded. "I never saw a letter. Did you tell her I
didn't want any contact with her?"

"Uh." Buck scratched his head, looking like he would rather
be anywhere but where he currently was. "I think we did tell
her something like that," he admitted, then hastened to explain,
"but we thought we were doing the right thing. You have to understand, Georgia. You were doing well in school, you had plans
and your entire life in front of you. We didn't want Star to mess
things up for you, especially if she was still struggling with the
drugs. We didn't know if we could trust her, so it seemed safest
to just keep her away from you. We were trying to protect you."

"I'd been clean for years. I told you that," Star protested
angrily.

Georgia was speechless. "You had no right to speak for me,"
she cried indignantly. "You lied to both of us."

Buck looked chagrined. "I can see why you'd be upset," he
agreed. "But we were just trying to keep you safe."

"By not telling me the truth and keeping my own mother
from me for almost thirty years?" Georgia said hotly. She looked
at Star. "I didn't know," she explained. "They never told me anything about you. After you left, it was as if you didn't exist. I
only had a few memories of you and then . . . nothing. No photos, no one would even say your name. It was like you vanished
into thin air. I grew up thinking you left because you didn't
want me, that you'd left us of your own free will."

Star flinched and closed her eyes. "Georgia May, my heart
has yearned for you every second of every day for the last
twenty-eight years. Leaving you was the toughest decision of
my life. It about killed me. I left my heart behind, held in your

sweet little hands. The only thing that kept me going was the knowledge that you were safe and loved and thriving. I did everything I could for you. I got clean for you and built a stable, good life, all in the hopes that one day we might get to be together again. I stayed away all these years because I thought it was what you wanted, Georgia May, but I never gave up hope." Her jaw trembled and she pressed her hand to her mouth, trying to steady herself. "And then when I got the diagnosis, I knew I couldn't wait any longer. Even if you didn't want to see me, I had to try. I was out of time. When I got your reply to my email saying yes you were coming, it was the closest thing to a miracle I've ever seen." She looked at Georgia, her gray-green eyes brimming with tears. "When I saw you standing there in front of the cottage that first day, so grown-up, so beautiful and confident, only then did it feel like my heart was back where it belongs. Finally, after all these years, my heart feels whole again."

Tears sprang to Georgia's eyes hearing those words. Finally, finally, she knew the answer to her questions. For twenty-eight years, she'd been trying to piece together the reason Star had left her. Now she held the truth. She looked from her father to her mother. It was a heartbreaking story of a family shattered by addiction and dysfunction, marriage troubles and human failings, deception and secrets. She thought she'd feel relief, that finally hearing the reason Star had left would bring her peace, but instead she just felt a deep sense of grief—for all that was broken, for the two flawed humans who had made her and then made such a mess of their lives and hers. They had lost so much time. They could never get it back. The enormity of the loss took her breath away.

She looked from her father to her mother once more. Their failures had cost her so much. They had cost her a mother all her growing-up years. Star's struggle with addiction had driven her from Georgia as a child. Buck's misguided effort to keep Georgia safe had kept Star from her for far longer. She closed her eyes, remembering so many birthdays when she'd blown out the candles and wished for Star to come back. So many days and weeks and lonely years longing for her mother's advice and love and acceptance . . . believing somehow she was to blame.

"I thought it was me," she said softly, opening her eyes and looking at Star, her voice breaking on the words. "I thought I was the reason you left. You promised me you'd come back, and you didn't. I waited for you to come for me. I waited for years, with a little girl's absolute trust that what her mama says is God's honest truth. And then little by little, that hope wavered and died, and the only thing I could think was that there was something bad about me, wrong with me, that you would leave me behind and break your promise to come back for me. It was the only way I could understand a mother leaving her child." Star winced, but Georgia didn't stop, the words spilling out of her in a rush.

"So I determined that I had to do better, *be* better. I had to prove myself to everyone—Daddy, Aunt Hannah, the world, *you*. Everything I've done I did to prove myself worthy, to prove that I was worth something, that I was good enough." She shook her head, looking between Star and Buck with astonishment. "All these years, I believed that somehow I was the reason our family fell apart. That lie defined my entire life. I've been trying to prove myself to you and to the world ever since. And now, all these years later, I see that this wasn't about me at all. All the broken promises and lies and secrets, what you've done, or failed to do . . . This was about you two all along."

A moment of silence, the ticking of the clock. Star and Buck both sat wordlessly. Star had her head bowed and hands clasped before her on the table as though she were making a supplication or a prayer. She was crying quietly. Buck tapped his hat on his knee, frowning uncomfortably.

Georgia looked from Star to Buck, feeling angry and helpless and suddenly so tired—tired of holding the weight of their failures and foibles. She was tired by her own efforts to make herself worthy, to prove she was enough. It was exhausting. She had been carrying the burden of her family's dysfunction for so long. She just wanted to put it down now. She wanted to be free.

She glanced at the kitchen clock. If she hurried, she could still make a flight out to Paris by this evening. The thought brought instant relief. She could pack quickly and call a taxi. By tomorrow, she could be back in Paris, away from the pain and mess of her fractured family, away from everything that was causing her such grief. She felt the confusion and helpless anger lift with the thought of leaving the island.

"I've got to go," she said, not an apology but a statement of fact.

"Where are you going?" Star asked in alarm. There were tears making tracks down her cheeks. She looked devastated.

"Back where I belong," Georgia said firmly, and then she headed upstairs to pack.

33

Georgia was throwing all of her belongings into her suitcases with a determination that bordered on desperation when someone knocked on the door to her room.

"Come in," she said warily, a pair of leather boots in her hand. She expected Star, but it was Buck who opened the door.

"Daddy?" Georgia was surprised.

He ducked and came in, his tall form filling the doorway. "I just came to say goodbye, Georgia. The ferryboat's leaving soon and I've got a plane to catch. I've got to get back. Hannah's been having some trouble with her heart, and I can't let her carry the load of the ranch for too long. It drains her."

"Oh." Georgia straightened. "Okay." She hesitated for a moment, then went back to packing. She didn't want to talk to him. She just wanted him to leave.

Buck waited a moment, then nodded. "Well then, I guess I should get going." He hesitated, turning the brim of his Stetson around in his hands. In the silence, she could hear the rasp of the fabric against his chapped skin.

"You should have told me the truth," Georgia said abruptly, facing him, her anger blazing up in an instant. She held a folded jacket against her stomach like a shield. "My mother didn't just vanish into thin air, but you and Aunt Hannah acted like she had. That was wrong. You decided something for me, and it shaped the course of my life. You should have at least told me she was alive and answered my questions about her. And when

I got older, you should have given me the chance to make my own decision about if I wanted to see her. Now she's sick and it's too late. You've cost me . . . so much. All the years we could have had together." Her voice broke and she cleared her throat, trying to regain her composure. She didn't want to cry in front of her father. She wanted to stay strong. She steeled herself and raised her chin defiantly.

Buck nodded. "I see that now," he admitted. "All this time, I thought we were doing the right thing." He looked regretful. "I was so angry with your mother for so many years. I made her solely responsible for ruining our family and, if I'm honest, for breaking my heart. I've never loved another woman like I loved her. I was so angry when she couldn't stop hurting herself and you and me. I thought she could choose differently, that she didn't love us enough to choose us over the drugs. But I see now that it was more complicated than that. Her hurts were so big she couldn't make the right choices, even though she wanted to. And that's a shame." He shook his head, his expression sober. "In a way, I think I wanted to keep her away from you, away from us, because it felt like she'd made her choice and she'd chosen her addiction over us. It was easier that way, to erase her from our family history. It hurt less if I just ignored her entirely. But I see now that was a mistake. I'm sorry I kept your mama from you like a secret. I made that choice for you. I was wrong. I'm sorry, Georgia girl." He cleared his throat awkwardly.

Georgia stared at her father in wary amazement. She had never heard him apologize for anything in her life. To her surprise, she found his words weren't nearly enough. "Sorry doesn't give me my life back," she said sharply. "Sorry doesn't give me those years I could have had with my mother. Sorry doesn't replace the truth you kept from me or the choices you made for me." She threw a stack of shirts into her suitcase. The little hot coal of anger that had been glowing steadily in her stomach for so long ignited into a righteous indignation, fueled by all the hurt and injustice, the lies and secrets her parents had kept for so long.

Buck nodded, his face sober. "You have a right to your anger, Georgia May. No question about that. But be careful. I spent a lot of years holding on to rage and blame against your mama. And that anger and hurt I'd carried for so long, well, after a while it starts to harden into something ugly, something mean. As the years pass, you either soften or you calcify. I see now I've been making the wrong choice for far too long. I'm a hard man, Georgia, and I've been carrying a heavy load, all this resentment and self-righteousness. I'm tired of carrying the weight of it. I'm getting too old for this now. It's time to lighten the load, so I guess I'm going to lay down this old grudge against Star." He sighed heavily. "It's about time to let things go. You might want to remember that, Georgia. Star has made her share of mistakes, but she loves you and she doesn't have much time left."

Georgia stared at her father in astonishment. She'd never heard her father put that many words together or been that self-reflective. Apparently the rice pudding she had made had actually worked. Was it possible that it was bringing her parents clarity after all these years?

"I'll think about it," Georgia said stiffly, hearing his words but not willing to bend just yet. She folded a pair of jeans and stashed them in her suitcase, then added, "That's the first positive thing I think I've ever heard you say about Star."

Buck gave a rueful smile. His face wasn't used to smiling; the creases around his mouth ran in the wrong direction. "Well, I guess maybe folks can always find some common ground over a bowl of rice pudding," he admitted gruffly. "We may not have agreed with each other on much of anything in life, and the good Lord knows we were about as mismatched as two people could be, but we always loved you and tried our best to do right by you. That we can agree on." He looked uncomfortable. It was the most sentimental speech Georgia had ever heard her daddy give.

"Looks like you're headed somewhere?" Buck slapped his hat against his thigh briskly, changing the subject to the safer territory of practicalities.

Georgia nodded. "Back to Paris," she said, then reluctantly added, "I just booked a flight for later today. I have a competition coming up soon and I need to be back for it. If I win, I'll have the chance to run my own kitchen in Paris."

"Well, I know that's what you've been aiming for," Buck said. "I hope it goes well for you, Georgia May." He hesitated. "You need a ride to the ferryboat?"

Georgia shook her head. "I have to finish packing. I'll take a later boat. My flight isn't until tonight. You go ahead."

Buck nodded. "Okay then. Guess I'd better get going." He paused and cleared his throat. "Georgia, If you ever want to come back to Texas, you know the door is always open to you. Hannah and I would welcome you for as long as you want to stay."

Georgia nodded but didn't say anything to his invitation, just folded a T-shirt and tucked it in her suitcase. "Thank you for coming to check on me," she said grudgingly. The fact that her father had dropped everything at the ranch immediately to catch a plane and come make sure she was okay was not lost on her. When he'd thought Star was deceiving Georgia, he'd braved an airplane, city traffic, a ferry ride, and his loathed ex-wife to make sure his little girl was safe. He was not a demonstrative man, but his actions spoke volumes. He might have made plenty of mistakes, but deep down, she knew her daddy loved her.

Buck looked pleased and a little uncomfortable. "When

you're a daddy, your little girl is always a little girl, even when she's grown. I've always been trying to protect you, Georgia, the best I knew how."

Georgia nodded. She felt her anger toward him soften just a notch. They'd had their share of differences, but here was proof that he loved her. Despite his many failings, he had always tried to take care of her. That counted for something.

"Tell Aunt Hannah I hope she feels better," Georgia said at last. It was an olive branch. She was still furious with him, but her anger was tempered with a touch of understanding.

Buck smiled. "I sure will." He hesitated, then walked over and kissed her cheek, put on his Stetson, and left.

Quickly, Georgia finished packing and got dressed. Her favorite Breton striped shirt, a comfortable pair of navy pants, and her leather flats. She adjusted her Hermès scarf and as a final touch slicked on more of her signature red lipstick. She checked her phone. She'd already booked a one-way ticket to Charles de Gaulle Airport and ordered a taxi to pick her up at the cottage. It would be here in thirty minutes. But first . . . she clattered down the stairs to the kitchen, checking to make sure she didn't run into Star. She was not ready to face her mother just yet. Instead, she scooped the last of the rice pudding into a bowl and headed out the kitchen door. There was one more conversation she needed to have, and then she could leave all this behind her.

34

"You deceived me," Georgia accused as soon as Cole opened the door. She briefly registered that he was bare chested, dressed in a faded pair of jeans. A few streaks of shaving cream dotted his face, and he held a razor in his hand. She pushed past him, ignoring his ridiculously defined abs. She was holding the last bowl of rice pudding in her hand, still slightly warm and fragrant with cinnamon. She was tired of lies and half-truths. Her relationship with Star and Buck was complicated by time and history and family, but Cole was a different story. She had fallen for him, trusted him, opened up the most vulnerable parts of her heart to him only to find out that he had not been honest with her. Now she was hurt and angered by his silence and what felt like a betrayal. She was ready for some truth telling. She was ready for a confrontation.

The cabin was sparse and clean, furnished simply with a pine table and two chairs, a camp stove and mini fridge, a single cot with a wool army blanket and a crab trap as a nightstand piled high with books. It was cold enough to make her shiver and smelled faintly of seaweed.

"I didn't deceive you," Cole countered, shutting the door behind her. "I just didn't tell you everything."

"You withheld information from me that changes my entire life," Georgia protested. She whirled on him, temper flaring, bright and hot as a struck match. "You've been keeping this huge secret from me this whole time. You and Star both." She looked at him accusingly.

"Star made me promise to keep quiet," Cole said calmly, carefully. "It wasn't my secret to tell." He took a towel from the sink in the corner and wiped the shaving cream from his face, then went over to the camp stove and pulled an enamel coffee-pot off a shelf above the table. "Coffee?" he offered.

Georgia shook her head. She stood in the middle of the room, holding the bowl of pudding, fuming with indignation and trying to keep her eyes off his bare chest. A flash of memory from last night crossed her mind, him pulling her close, swaying in time to the bluegrass band, his mouth on hers, warm and hungry. She'd thought it could be the start of something wonderful. She didn't know he'd been keeping such a devastating secret from her the whole time. The truth of that hurt more than she cared to admit.

"I thought it was a terrible idea when Star first told me her plan," Cole explained, filling the coffeepot with water from the sink. He lit the stove and put the kettle over the flame. "I spent a good week trying to talk her out of it. But she was desperate to see you before her health got worse. She just wanted time with you, for you two to get to know each other again. And in the end, how was I going to say no to that?" He grabbed a black T-shirt from the bed and slipped it over his head. Georgia glanced away.

"I just wish I'd known sooner," she muttered.

"What would it have changed?" Cole asked with a frown.

"I don't know, but it was wrong to keep it from me," Georgia said stubbornly.

Cole nodded. "I agree. And I've regretted it every day since I promised Star I wouldn't tell you. She begged me to go along with it, said it was her final wish. I'm sorry." He looked at Georgia frankly. "You deserved to know."

Georgia was brought up short by his apology. She softened just a little, but not enough to let him off the hook. Not yet. "You kissed me while keeping a secret like that," she said bluntly. "Were you going to let me go back to Paris without knowing the truth?"

Cole looked uneasy. "She promised she'd tell you herself before then."

"And if she hadn't?"

"It wasn't my secret to tell," he repeated reluctantly.

"So the short answer is yes, you would have let me leave this island and go back to Paris without ever knowing my mother has an incurable, debilitating neurological disease." Georgia pinned him with a pointed look.

Cole looked uneasy and a little trapped.

"I'll take that as a yes," Georgia said shortly. Her eyes flashed. "I expected more from you, Cole."

He crossed his arms, his expression stony. "In what way?"

"I thought I could trust you to be honest with me."

"I've been honest with you," he muttered. "As honest as I could be without breaking a promise."

Georgia looked at him. It was not just about him not telling her about Star's condition, she realized. What rankled her was also something else. Something about him, and the two of them, and the future that could never be. She saw that clearly now.

"I understand why you didn't tell me Star's secret," she admitted. "I don't agree with you, but I understand your reasons. But there's something else too. When you kissed me last night, I felt . . ." Georgia paused. What had she felt? "I felt like it could be the start of something wonderful. I see now I was wrong."

"What do you mean?" Cole asked cautiously. "Wrong how?"

"I was fooling myself," Georgia said. "You're not ready to start something new with me or anyone else. Look at this." She gestured around the cabin. "You're wasting your life out here in this little cabin hiding from your mistakes and your past life. You're trapped by shame and regret. It's tragic, because you have so much to give, but you won't even try because at some point in the past you made a mistake, a big mistake, and someone you love got hurt, and you can't forgive yourself."

"I ruined the life of the woman I loved," Cole said sharply. "To move on would be . . . callous." He faced her, his jaw set in a stark, belligerent line.

"But that's just the thing," Georgia countered. "You didn't ruin Amy's life. Is she unable to use her legs because of an accident that was your fault? Yes! But her life is not ruined. Far from it. I've watched her interviews. She's amazing. She's not wallowing in self-pity. She's living a full, vibrant, meaningful life while you've exiled yourself to this fishy little cabin. That accident ruined only one life, and it wasn't Amy's." She stared him in the eye defiantly, aching at the sight of him. What a waste of a brilliant, beautiful man, she thought, looking at him. It broke her heart.

Cole met her gaze, his own expressionless. The kettle started whistling, and he took it off the heat and turned off the flame. "That's not true," he said flatly. "This isn't an exile."

"Oh, really?" Georgia challenged. "You have a PhD from Berkeley. You won a major international award for ecological innovation, the very area you've always dreamed of making a difference in, ever since you were a kid. You were this close to becoming Captain Planet." She pinched her fingers so they were a scant inch apart. "You were poised to make a huge difference in the world, and yet now you're hiding out here, working on a shellfish farm raising oysters, convinced this is somehow what you deserve, some penance. You're pretending to be someone you're not, and you're letting your life go by, wasting it by not spending it on the things that are so important to you. If you don't think this is an exile, you're lying to everyone, most of all yourself."

Cole was stirring heaping spoonfuls of coffee grounds and boiling water into a French press with controlled ferocity. At her last words, he went very still. "You don't understand," he said tightly. "It's more complicated than that."

"Life always is," Georgia agreed, her tone softening. Her heart hurt for him, for how trapped he felt, for the wounds that he couldn't let heal. "You have to forgive yourself. It was a mistake, Cole. A mistake with terrible consequences for someone you loved. But instead of accepting it and trying to turn it for good somehow like Amy has, you've hidden away and let yourself be trapped by this terrible load of guilt. You could use your skills and talents in so many amazing ways, but you're wasting everything because you're afraid you haven't paid enough penance. You said you wanted to make the world a better place. You could be doing so much more than raking clams in orange overalls, but your guilt won't let you move on. You can't bear to live again because you feel you don't deserve it."

"You make it sound so easy," Cole said, his tone taut.

"I never said it was easy," Georgia argued. "It's not easy to let that guilt go, to forgive yourself and let yourself start to live again, to let yourself love again. But there's a big difference between easy and right. And I don't think you're doing either."

"I think you've said enough," Cole said stiffly. His face was impassive, but she could tell he was angry.

"Fine," Georgia retorted. This entire conversation felt like talking to a brick wall. Cole was unmovable. "You can't hide from the truth forever," she warned him. "It will find you, even here. What did you tell me? The island doesn't like secrets. It's only a matter of time until you're going to have to face yours." She set the bowl she was holding down on the table, hard. "Enjoy your pudding."

And then she turned on her heel and walked out the door, slamming it behind her, leaving Cole and his kisses and his guilt and secrets behind her.

"Georgia. Georgia, wait!"

Georgia looked up as the taxi driver loaded her two big suitcases into the back of the cab. Star was hurrying down the walkway, Pollen at her heels.

Georgia hesitated. "Give me a minute," she told the driver.

She reluctantly went through the gate in the white picket fence, under the arbor of climbing roses that were already a riot of orangey yellow blooms so early in the season. How had it only been a few weeks since she first walked through this gate? So much had happened since then. She was leaving changed, brimful with what these weeks had brought, the good and the bad, the bitter and the sweet. Mother and daughter looked at each other in silence.

"Georgia, I never meant to hurt you," Star said. She looked distressed. "I know it doesn't make it better, but I'm so sorry. I just need you to know that before you leave."

Georgia nodded, not trusting herself to speak. In her chest was a ball of grief and hurt and anxiety that was making it hard to draw a breath. She felt torn about leaving the island, but staying felt impossible. Her dreams were in Paris, and right now the island held a complex tangle of sorrow and secrets and contradictions. Behind her she heard the taxi driver clear his throat impatiently. She glanced at the taxi. She had to go or she'd miss the ferry.

Star clasped her hands together in front of her anxiously. "I can't make up for all the years you waited and wondered about me. I had no idea you were even thinking about me." She looked at Georgia, her eyes shining with tears. "Your daddy and I made choices that hurt each other and hurt you. I'm so sorry, and if I could fix it, I would. But life doesn't work like that. We don't get a do-over. All I can do is try to make it right going forward. You were always the most precious thing in the world to me, I want you to know that. I made so many mistakes, but never once did I stop loving you."

Georgia nodded again. If she opened her mouth she would burst into tears. Star straightened and looked Georgia firmly in the eye. "Georgia May, I want you to know that you do not have to prove anything to anyone. You are enough, just by being you. When I held you in my arms for the first time, I imagined who you might become, but you are more and better than I ever could have dreamed. You are strong and courageous and so beautiful. You are gifted beyond what you understand yet. And wherever you go, you will make the world a better place." She spoke with quiet confidence. It almost felt like a benediction, a blessing. "You may not believe me and you may not be able to forgive me, but I want you to know that no matter where you go or what you do, I am so proud of you. I love you, Georgia May Jackson. You are a gift to me and to the world." Star's voice broke on the last word, and she swiped at her eyes with the woolly sleeve of her cardigan.

Georgia blinked fast. She had waited so long to hear those words. She'd been waiting her whole life. She closed her eyes against the prickle of tears, balling her fists. Suddenly, she was five years old, standing at the window every night hoping to see the headlights of her mother's old brown Eldorado come bouncing down the drive. She was turning ten, vowing to move to Paris and cook like Julia, to make her mother proud. She was seventeen, pinning her own hair up for the junior/senior prom and imagining that her mother stood behind her, helping her with each curl. She was thirty-three, reading the email from Star, realizing that her mother was indeed alive and allowing that tiny spark of hope to ignite once more in her chest. For a moment, she was tempted to stay, to turn away from Paris and run into Star's embrace. But the truth of the matter was complicated. Star loved her. But Star was leaving her again.

"I have to go," she said at last, her words thick with emotion. It was better this way, that she be the one leaving this time. Paris was waiting. Her dreams were waiting. If she stayed here, it would just be to face another agonizing goodbye. She couldn't do it again.

Star nodded, not quite able to mask her disappointment. "I hope you find what you're looking for, Georgia May," she said quietly. "I wish all the best in the world for you."

Georgia reached out and scratched Pollen's knobby head. "Goodbye, Mama," she said. And then she got in the taxi and drove away.

35

Paris welcomed Georgia with open arms. On her way to Phoebe's apartment from the airport, she watched as the streets of her beloved City of Light slid by the taxi window. The sight filled her with nostalgia and relief. She was back where she belonged.

"Georgia! Come on up, babe!" Phoebe's voice rang over the intercom onto the street when Georgia alighted from the taxi and pressed the buzzer for Phoebe's apartment. A moment later, the door to the building clicked open. When Georgia stepped out of the elevator on Phoebe's floor with her two big suitcases bumping behind her, Phoebe flung open her apartment door. She was dressed in an outrageously pink silk dressing gown trimmed in ethereal marabou feathers. She looked like a starlet from the 1930s. A sort of Jean Harlow vibe.

"You look awful," Phoebe announced, pouncing on Georgia. "Come inside. I'll make you a coffee."

Georgia had told Phoebe nothing except that she was coming back to Paris. She wanted to share everything face-to-face. There was a lot to catch up on.

"I don't go into work for another hour, so we've got loads of time," Phoebe said, sliding an espresso in front of Georgia at her tiny kitchen table for two and handing her a grease-stained paper bag from the boulangerie.

"You are a saint," Georgia said fervently, opening the bag. The smell of fresh, buttery pain au chocolat wafted out temptingly.

Her stomach rumbled. The plane food had been predictable—miniscule and mediocre, and all she wanted was to sink her teeth into this pastry and then nestle into Phoebe's marginally comfortable futon for a nice long nap. Now that she could taste sweet again, a French pastry was exactly what she needed. She still couldn't taste salty, so everything she ate seemed a little bland, but she was relieved to have four of the five flavors back. Hopefully, salty would return before the competition.

Phoebe sat down across from Georgia and pulled a croissant from the bag. "I'm starving," she announced, taking a big bite. "I was clubbing all weekend in Saint-Tropez with a bunch of Moldovan models. They hardly eat anything." She pulled a face. "Now, tell me everything."

Georgia broke the flaky, knobby end off the pain au chocolat and inhaled. Bliss. She nibbled the buttery bite. "There's a lot to tell," she prefaced.

Phoebe waved away her statement like a pesky gnat. "Skip the boring bits. Tell me what happened with your hunky oysterman scientist?" Her eyes gleamed.

"Nothing happened." Georgia thought briefly of Cole, and her face flamed, recalling their evening of passionate kisses at the Oyster Shuck. The memory made her feel both sad and indignant. Now there was an ocean between them. An ocean and his silence and his inability to move on from his tragic past. "Well, not quite nothing. I kissed him," she admitted. "Or he kissed me. We kissed . . . a lot."

"AAAGH! I KNEW you were going to snog him!" Phoebe crowed jubilantly, pumping her fist into the air in a victory gesture. "Tell me everything. Is he a good kisser? He is, right?"

"I don't kiss and tell," Georgia demurred, then relented almost immediately. "Okay, yes. When he kissed me, I completely lost my equilibrium," she confessed. She stopped, remembering the sensation. The world had tilted on its axis. "I've never felt that way with anyone before." She dropped her gaze and toyed with her espresso cup. "And then right afterward, I found out that he and Star had been keeping a secret from me. A big one."

"Oh no." Phoebe took a sip of espresso, eyes widening in alarm. "What happened? Give me all the details."

"Star has a degenerative neurological condition called Lewy body dementia. That's why she contacted me out of the blue, because she's sick and running out of time." Georgia heard the plaintive edge to her voice as she told Phoebe all about the night of the Oyster Shuck, the shock of walking in to find Buck sitting there, and the aftermath—the revelation of Star's illness. When she paused for breath, Phoebe was staring at her aghast.

"Oh. My. Word. Babe, that is so heartbreaking." Phoebe breathed. "And what awful timing too. I'm so sorry."

"But wait, there's more," Georgia said miserably. And then she told Phoebe about the next morning, about finally getting an answer to her long-held questions surrounding Star's disappearance, about discovering the terrible reason her mother had left and why their family had fallen apart.

When she finished, Phoebe sat back with a dramatic sigh. "That's epically tragic, Georgia, for all of you. Poor Star. So she's been watching you from afar all these years, loving you but not able to be a part of your life?"

Georgia nodded. "It feels like such a waste, all that time we could have had together. And my dad and Aunt Hannah keeping the truth about why she left us from me for so long and telling her I didn't want to see her." She shredded part of her croissant into tiny flaky bits with suppressed fury. "I'm so angry with all of them for what they took from me. First Star because she couldn't be a good mom to me, and then later when she got clean, my dad and Aunt Hannah wouldn't let her near me."

Phoebe looked thoughtful for a long moment. "Yeah," she said slowly. "I see your point. Of course you're angry that your dad and aunt kept these big things from you, and it makes sense that you're hurt that your mom failed you. I'd feel the same way . . ."

Georgia heard the hesitation in Phoebe's voice. "Is there a 'but' coming?" she asked warily.

"Just that at the end of the day, it sounds like your family really still loves you," Phoebe said carefully. "I mean, yes, your mom couldn't take care of you and left you when you were little, which is awful. But she never stopped loving you. She made some really bad choices, but then she tried to do the right thing, even when all her options were terrible options. She didn't leave you because she didn't love you. She left you BECAUSE she loved you. She left because she thought it was the best thing for you. And then she turned her life around and waited all these years, hoping for the day you two could be together again."

She picked at her French manicure and said wistfully, "It's kind of beautiful, honestly, in a really tragic way. I think my stepmother would be happier if I just didn't exist, like if I vanished from the planet she would not mind at all. And frankly, I'm not sure my dad would notice if I did." She glanced at Georgia, her pretty face suddenly sad. "At least your mom still loves you. And your dad flew all the way from Texas to make sure you were okay. You have a family that cares about you, and that counts for a lot, even if they did mess up pretty epically. No family gets everything right, but it sounds like they keep trying to love you, and that has to count for something."

Georgia gazed past Phoebe's pink silk shoulder, out the tall French doors leading from the kitchen onto the tiny balcony, looking contemplatively over the rooftops of Paris.

"Maybe you're right," she admitted. "I know they love me,

but they failed me in such big ways, I don't know if I can forgive them. And even if I could, how can I stand to lose my mom again just when we found each other? It feels impossible. I don't think I can bear it." She was quiet for a moment. If she just kept away, went back to rebuilding a life for herself in Paris, maybe it wouldn't hurt quite so much. "My life is here," she said at last, with conviction. "What I want is here. I need to concentrate on that now."

Phoebe nodded reluctantly. "If you're sure . . ." she said, then paused and changed the topic. "Tell me what else happened while you were there. Did you get your spark back?"

"Yes, and even more than that," Georgia told her honestly. She thought of those wild, exuberant days at Anemone, of her sense of taste returning flavor by flavor, of the sensation of delight she'd managed to capture once more. She recalled the revelation about her gift and the legacy of the Stevens women. That had changed everything for her. And although the conversation with Star and Buck had been painful, at least she knew the answers to the questions she'd been asking for almost thirty years. They may not have been what she hoped for, but at least she knew the real story now. That was something, right? Plus, she had done as Michel had asked. She'd gone away and rediscovered her spark in the kitchen. Even more than regaining her sense of taste, she'd regained her ability to find delight in life again, to find joy in watching for orcas, digging in the garden with Star, playing a game of Scrabble, waking to the scent of flowering apple blossoms and the sea. Her time on the island had been life-changing.

"I feel like on the island I learned how to live again," she confessed.

"Babe, that's amazing!" Phoebe reached across the table and squeezed Georgia's hand. "I can't believe so much happened for you there. It was everything you hoped for! Plus getting a snog from a super sexy scientist turned oysterman. Pretty epic if you ask me."

"Pretty epic," Georgia agreed. Phoebe was right. The snogging had been very, very nice. She couldn't deny that. She thought of Cole and grimaced. There was a sharp twist in her heart when she recalled how they'd left things.

"Well,"—Phoebe pouted—"I have to get ready for work in a minute, but first, what are you going to cook for Michel?"

"I haven't decided yet," Georgia admitted, relieved to turn her attention to less emotionally fraught topics. "I thought I'd take a walk through the Marché des Enfants Rouges today and then on Thursday browse Marché Richard Lenoir and see what inspires me."

Paris was legendary for its delectable covered and open-air food markets where local farmers and artisans sold a mouthwatering assortment of cheeses, cured meats, and fresh produce and baked goods. Wandering through the markets was sure to be inspiring.

"Ooh, sounds like a yummy plan," Phoebe agreed. She stretched languorously. "I've got to get to work. Make yourself at home. You know where everything is."

Georgia nodded. Suddenly she was so tired she just wanted to lie down and sleep forever.

"Phoebs, thanks for letting me crash here until the competition." She took the final sip of her espresso and dabbed up the buttery croissant crumbs with her finger.

Phoebe waved her hand. "You can stay as long as you need to. You know that, but of course you're going to win the competition and be the new head chef at La Lumière Dorée and then you can live anywhere you like. Paris will be your oyster."

Georgia felt a pang of longing at the word "oyster." It conjured up very different images than Paris. The gray-blue waters of Westcott Bay and a strikingly handsome man in orange rubber overalls deftly twisting a shucking knife at the hinge of a closed oyster. She brushed away the images. She had left the island behind, and with it the frustrating puzzle of Dr. Cabot Cole Montgomery and his stubborn, broken heart. This was where her heart was. Paris was where she belonged.

And yet, as she washed the breakfast dishes after Phoebe left for work, Georgia couldn't help but think of the island, so many miles away. For a moment, she could have sworn she smelled the pungent spice of evergreens and the sweetness of apple blossoms. Unexpectedly, she felt tears spring to her eyes. She tried to blink them away. Instead, a few rolled down her cheeks and into the corners of her mouth. Surprised, she licked at them. They tasted salty as seawater.

She froze, her hands in the soapy dishwater. She could taste them. She could taste the salt! Hastily drying her hands, she grabbed the saltshaker from Phoebe's cupboard. She scattered a few grains of salt into her palm and licked them. No doubt about it. She could taste salty again. Slowly, she set the saltshaker down and leaned against the counter, overwhelmed with a feeling of almost euphoric relief. She had regained all the flavors just in time. She closed her eyes, feeling profoundly grateful. It was possible her sense of taste might vanish again as it had before, but she had a hunch that it wouldn't. Not as long as she was pursuing wonder and delight, not if she continued to use her gift to bring joy to others. She thought of the upcoming competition and smiled. Now she could enter with confidence.

Later, as she unpacked her suitcase in search of her pajamas, she found her chef's whites. They were wrapped around something small and heavy. Puzzled, she pulled out the bundle. As she did so, a shower of tiny, fresh four-leaf clovers fell to the floor. She brushed the bits of clover away and unfurled the chef's whites. Wrapped up in the double-breasted jacket was a jar of Star's lavender honey. Attached to the jar by a piece of twine was a note scrawled on a slip of paper. In Star's handwriting it said simply:

Georgia May,
For when you get hungry.
Your mama, Star

Georgia held the jar up to the light, gazing at the dark golden color of the honey, remember the buzzing of the bees, the fragrance of the apple orchard laced with the briny scent of the sea.

On impulse, she twisted the lid off the jar and swirled her finger through the honey. She licked it clean. She could just catch a hint of lavender in the creamy goodness. She scooped up another little dollop. Strange. Somehow, the honey tasted like love, like the answer to a question, like coming home.

For the next week and a half, Georgia allowed herself to luxuriate in Paris. She had no obligations on her time until the competition other than planning her menu for Michel, so in the mornings, she wandered the city, indulging in espresso and pastries, meandering through gardens and squares, into and out of museums. She visited the Musée d'Orsay and took the elevator up to the top of the Eiffel Tower, sat before the resplendent Monet water lilies in the Musée de l'Orangerie, and listened to the nuns sing at Sacré-Coeur high above the city. One day she picnicked with one of her old roommates for a long lunch, sharing wine and a fresh crusty baguette and a pat of Camembert under the chestnut trees in the Luxembourg Gardens. One evening she met up for drinks with Phoebe and a handful of casual friends who were not connected to the restaurant world. Almost every day, she treated herself to lemon, pistachio, and orange blossom macarons at Ladurée, delighting with every bite in her ability to taste again. As she walked and sat and ate and soaked in the beauty, art, and culture, she remembered what had drawn her to Paris in the first place. It was a sublime city.

Yet for all its charms, she found herself unexpectedly longing for something entirely different. For the spicy smell of evergreens in loamy soil, for the briny air blowing in from the bay, for the homey simplicity of the kitchen table, the buzz of Star's happy bees. It took her by surprise, and it was several days before she could finally name the pangs in her heart that accompanied these brief snatches of memory. She was homesick.

Surely not, she told herself in surprise, standing in front of the glass pyramid at the Louvre trying to talk herself out of longing for the quiet rolling hills of the island, for the silver shimmer of the water on Westcott Bay, for a sometimes prickly dark-haired oysterman, for a slightly worn-out hippie who smelled of cannabis and herbs and who made her feel so loved. How could she be homesick for a place and people she'd known only a few weeks? How could anything be better than Paris? It annoyed her, and she tried to push it away, but the feeling remained, sneaking up on her at the oddest times. She dressed like a Parisian, ate like a Parisian, spoke her most polished French, but she could not stop her traitorous and unruly heart from longing for something she'd left an ocean away.

Cooking proved to be unexpectedly complicated as well. Every day after lunch, Georgia trawled the local food markets of

Paris, bringing home bags brimming with ingredients. She had planned to make her signature cuisine—classic French with a Texas twist—but instead found herself straying toward the type of dishes she'd cooked at Anemone. Instinctually, she sought out salmon and oysters, seaweed and apples, instead of leeks and fromage. It surprised her that she would draw such inspiration from somewhere she'd been for so short a time. But the island had captured her culinary imagination. There was no denying it.

She tried to get herself back in line, cooking a perfectly adequate cassoulet with a side of fresh ramps for dinner one night with Phoebe and a batch of gougères for a snack the next day. But she had to admit, her typical French dishes lacked inspiration. They were sufficient but did not thrill.

"Julia, what do I do?" she asked in exasperation, poking one of the gougères and grimacing. The cheese puffs should be light and airy. There were a little doughy and too dense.

"The trick," she heard Julia confide in her ear, "is to discover something you're truly passionate about and then to simply keep doing it."

Georgia looked at her cheese puffs. They were not interesting. She remembered the thrill she had felt cooking at Anemone. She wanted to feel it again.

"Okay," she said aloud, capitulating. "I get it."

And so, with just a few days to go before the competition, she gave up and embraced her creative spark. She stopped trying to force herself to cook the way she had before she'd been on the island and simply acknowledged the truth. Her time on the island had changed her. She had regained her spark there, and she didn't want to risk squashing that precious gift again.

"I'll cook whatever delights me," she announced to Phoebe's empty kitchen. She would choose the ingredients that intrigued her, even if she wasn't quite sure what she would do with them. She sent up a little petition for help to Julia, praying that this path would lead her toward the culmination of her long-held dream and not into some sort of last minute spectacular culinary disaster.

"Please let this be the right thing and not a mistake," she whispered.

"When you make a decision, you must then go forward with confidence and courage," she heard Julia say bracingly. "Nothing good was ever accomplished in the kitchen by a cook being faint of heart."

Confidence and courage. Georgia squared her shoulders. Julia was right; this was not a time to be faint of heart. And on Saturday, she would find out if her leap of faith was going to pay off.

36

The Saturday of the competition dawned fair and warm, a perfect blossoming day in May. Georgia was a bundle of nerves. Everything felt off-kilter except the ingredients in her hand. She packed her supplies in two wheeled trolleys and donned her chef's whites. Michel had texted her detailed instructions the week prior, so she knew what to expect and what she needed to bring with her. At the last second, she wrapped her Hermès scarf around her hair and applied her signature red lipstick.

Sending lots of love and luck today —xoxo, Phoebe texted. She was at a photo shoot in the gardens of Versailles. Georgia kept checking her phone, but no other texts came through. She felt a twinge of disappointment. What had she expected? She'd left the island in a fit of pique. She'd burned all her relational bridges behind her. It was not a surprise that no one had reached out to her since she'd left.

There was no one to see her off, so she let herself out of the apartment and took an expensive taxi to La Lumière Dorée. It was too unwieldy to haul all her ingredients on the Metro single-handedly. The taxi got snarled in traffic, and she arrived a few minutes late, feeling a little harried and off-kilter. Michel was waiting for her at the door. He greeted her with the customary kisses on each cheek and stepped back to survey her.

"The island agreed with you," Michel said, looking her over

approvingly as they walked. "I see you have regained your joie
de vivre."

Georgia paused, surprised by his perception. "I think so,"
she said, smiling brightly and trying not to think of Star and
Cole and the island. "So sorry I'm a little tardy. I'm ready."

"Good." Michel looked satisfied. "The others are already
here." He gestured for her to follow him and headed back to
the kitchen. She glanced around eagerly as they passed through
the dining area. It was a beautiful space, intimate and perfectly
appointed with a sleek, understated elegance. Outside the main
room, live trees grew in a beautiful little courtyard with tables
dotted around the stone patio. She spied a fountain with a lion's head set in one of the patio walls. The inside of the restaurant reminded her of nearby Sacré-Coeur, serenely white and
bright and dignified. It was a gorgeous restaurant. And after
today, it could be hers to helm. Strangely, the thought did not
thrill her. She brushed aside the sensation, chalking it up to
nerves, and followed Michel.

"Your place is there." Michel motioned to the far end of the
kitchen. The space was a good size for a Paris restaurant kitchen,
far larger than that of La Pomme d'Or. It was also brand-new,
all gleaming stainless-steel surfaces and high-quality cookware.
Now it was set up almost like one of those televised cooking
competitions, but far more bare-bones. There was a giant gas industrial cooktop that the contestants would share, three stainless-
steel prep tables arranged in a U shape to fit in the kitchen
space, and essential kitchen items for each contestant. Nothing
fancy and unnecessary like a frozen yogurt machine or an air
fryer. Those were for American TV, not quality French cooking.

The other contestants, Gerard Boucher and Leonie Alarie,
greeted her politely. They were already setting up their stations.

Georgia swallowed hard, feeling a flutter of nerves. What if she panicked and couldn't get her dishes made in time? What if she forgot an important step or did something stupid again like substituted salt for sugar? What if she failed completely? She took a deep breath and closed her eyes.

"You can do this," she told herself. Not only could she taste everything again, but she knew who she was. She was Georgia May Jackson, the next in a long line of Stevens women. She had a gift to give the world. This was her moment, the opportunity she had been working toward since she was a child. She opened her eyes.

"Julia, help me win this, please," she whispered. "Today is the day I've been waiting for almost my whole life." She waited, hoping for a word of inspiration from her patron saint.

"Just remember, nothing is more important than the people who love you. Relationships are the most important thing—not a career or work, or success—people who love you are the greatest gift," Julia trilled earnestly in her ear.

Georgia blinked, a trifle taken aback by the sentiment. "That's not helpful right now," she protested under her breath. Julia said nothing.

"Many thanks for being here today." Michel started the competition with a gracious little speech. "You are each here because I believe you can bring something fresh and exciting to the Paris culinary scene. And so today I am not looking for technical brilliance but for that spark of inspiration, that touch of curiosity that leads to true revelation for those who eat the food. I am not looking to be impressed. I want to be enthralled. Please complete your three-course meal in a timely manner. I will enjoy each of your preparations on the patio in three hours. Then I will decide." He gave a little nod, and Georgia's heart leaped. This was it. It was time to shine.

She saw Gerard and Leonie spring into action. For an instant, she froze, panicked, then spied the leafy green fronds of celery root poking out of the top of her bag, and all of a sudden she could breathe again. She knew what to do. Follow her heart and cook what delighted her.

"Follow the wonder, find the delight," she murmured, and reached into the trolley for her ingredients.

The next few hours passed in a blur. Later, Georgia couldn't remember much about that time. She vaguely recalled Gerard swearing explosively in French after burning himself on a hot pan. And Leonie working across from her with silent, laser-like focus. After her initial spurt of panic, a strange sort of calm descended on Georgia. She worked quickly but smoothly, dicing and chopping, sautéing and whipping with a metal whisk. She let the ingredients speak to her. She was not just cooking, she was inventing a little too, and it felt light and fun and a touch nerve-racking. Her menu was simple—she worried that it was perhaps a little too simple, but she had found her spark and she didn't want to extinguish it under the weight of elaborate dishes and complicated techniques. She wanted the food to sing, to inspire with its fresh simplicity. So she put aside her worries and tried to recapture the joy she'd felt at Anemone, the sensation of delight, like child's play.

Beside her, Leonie was muttering instructions under her breath like a mantra. Across from her, Gerard dropped a knife and cursed aloud in French. Georgia closed her eyes and concentrated on the sensations of the island—the bracing, spicy scent of evergreen needles, the briny creaminess of an oyster still in its shell, the chewy, viscous luxury of Star's honey on the comb, the light acidity of a local cider. And then she cooked what she felt, that sense of wonder, the lightness and clean sea salt air. A sprinkle of salt, the crispness of fresh vegetables, the unctuous luxury of good olive oil. Finally, as if from far away, she heard the bell ding. Her time was up.

She came to as if out of a trance, finding herself standing in the kitchen at La Lumière Dorée once more. She looked around in surprise. Michel was waiting on the patio.

Gerard served his menu first, a decent-looking bleu cheese soufflé followed by seared lamb chops in a cognac and mustard sauce accompanied by potatoes dauphinoise and a light salad of wild spring greens. For dessert, he served a Sauternes custard with bitter caramel. It was technically well executed, Georgia could tell as she watched the dishes go by, but his menu lacked creative imagination, and the food was heavy. As Gerard served each dish, Georgia and Leonie crowded close to the window overlooking the patio, watching Michel sample each course.

"He doesn't like it," Leonie observed in French.

Georgia secretly agreed. She knew Michel well, and although he kept his face smooth and blank, he did not look surprised as he took each bite. He also did not savor it, just ate as though it were his duty. She exhaled in relief. One down. One to go. The odds were more in her favor now. Surprisingly, the thought did not bring her the thrill of joy she expected.

Then it was Leonie's turn. Her dishes were perfectly executed and technically complex, with a surprising twist. She was an exceptional chef, Georgia had to admit. She stood at the window with a sulking Gerard. They both watched as Leonie brought out her three courses. First, a delicate velouté of chilled asparagus sprinkled with tarragon, the vivid green hue of spring grass. She followed this by a second course composed of a beautiful Lyonnaise potato salad redolent with pickled herring, accompanied by crab-stuffed deviled eggs topped with a silky dollop of hollandaise sauce and tiny medallions of pepper-crusted veal.

Her dessert was a simple but decadent chocolate ganache torte with an olive oil crust and blackened pistachios.

This time, Michel lingered over each bite. And the sliver of torte he finished completely. Not a good sign, Georgia thought with a frown. Not a good sign at all. He had enjoyed that.

"Georgia?" Leonie tapped her on the shoulder. "It is your turn. Bonne chance." She spoke the words without a trace of rancor.

Georgia nodded and smiled. "Merci. He liked yours," she affirmed.

She swiftly returned to her prep station and served the first course to Michel on the patio. Scallops crudo made with scallops sourced from Normandy drizzled with preserved lemon-infused olive oil and a side of seaweed salad. Michel cut a tiny piece of the raw scallop and tasted it, dipping it in the preserved lemon olive oil. He ate a bite of the seaweed salad. Georgia held her breath. He closed his eyes, chewed, swallowed. Looked at her. "Daring."

She exhaled, relieved. He liked daring. That was a good sign. She served the second course. She had opted for a light menu, perhaps too light. She placed the plate in front of him. Rounds of roasted apple and celery root liberally smeared with a chèvre and toasted walnut spread and topped by a nest made of strips of candied salmon.

Michel studied the plate a moment, then glanced at her and raised his eyebrows. She gave a small, chagrined shrug. "I told you I found my spark on the island," she said.

"Hmm." He poked at the candied salmon, which was deliciously chewy, heavily smoked, and cured with sugar and salt, then tried a bite of the dish, careful to get a taste of every layer. "Fascinating."

He set down his fork and took a swallow of water. Georgia was disappointed. Fascinating, but not good enough for him to want to eat the rest. She glanced over at the window where Gerard and Leonie were keeping an eye on the proceedings with a studied air of disinterest. She knew they were dissecting every gesture and glance. She felt a little sick with the strain. One last course to go.

Her dessert was so simple she hoped it would not seem offensive. A little cup of light-as-air meringue filled with tiny wild strawberries and drizzled with Star's lavender-infused honey. It had felt right to use something from the island today. It was because of Star that Georgia had found her spark again. Now here she was standing before Michel, her dream finally within her grasp.

Michel made a little sound of appreciation as he looked at the meringue, diminutive and pretty as a still life. Georgia served it with a tiny silver spoon, the bowl of it no bigger than a quail's egg. Michel cracked the meringue and nodded approvingly. He scooped up half the meringue with a few wild strawberries and ate the bite, then quickly devoured the other half.

"Where did you get this honey?" he asked, scraping up the last golden drizzle with the edge of the spoon and licking it clean. "It's divine."

"From my mother. She keeps bees," Georgia admitted.

Michel shot her a speculative look. "Interesting," he mused. He set the plate aside. "Merci, Georgia. Now I will consider. Please let the others know I will have an answer for all of you shortly."

Dismissed, Georgia returned to the kitchen. Gerard and Leonie looked up anxiously as soon as she entered. She delivered Michel's message.

"How do you think it went?" Leonie asked. "He enjoyed your dessert."

"Meringue lacks imagination," scoffed Gerard under his breath. "Even a monkey can make a meringue."

Leonie sent him a look of pure disdain.

"Perhaps, but he ate all of it, unlike some other dishes," Georgia said tartly. Leonie giggled and Gerard scowled.

"Come, let's look around," Leonie said, gesturing for Georgia to follow. She did. They surveyed the dining room—the fine linen-covered chairs, the sleek zinc bar and airy elegance—then explored the back of the restaurant more thoroughly.

"Can you imagine?" Leonie asked, a touch of longing in her voice, looking around the kitchen. "To be at the helm of this place. It's the most talked-about restaurant opening of the year in Paris. It could very quickly get its first Michelin star. It will be a success, and whoever is the chef, they will steer that success. It would be an honor to be the chef here."

Georgia gazed around, trying to picture herself in the gleaming new kitchen, serving the upper echelons of Paris. She thought of the hours she would spend here. This would be her life, more home than anywhere else. But try as she might, every time she pictured it, she could summon no enthusiasm. Instead, her mind kept skipping to the kitchen of Anemone, the sheer terror and delight she'd felt during her days there, two sides of the same coin.

"Georgia," Leonie hissed, bumping her shoulder. "Michel is asking for you."

Michel was at the door to the patio, gesturing to her. She went out, and he offered her a seat across from him. He crossed one leg over the other and leaned back, surveying her, looking calm and collected in a navy jacket, slim trousers, and very expensive leather shoes.

"I have before me a difficult decision," he said without preamble. "On the one hand, I have a French chef of significant talent and drive. Leonie would make a fine chef for La Lumière

Dorée. And on the other hand, I have you and this spark you have rediscovered. It is thrilling, what has reawakened in you. I have glimpsed it before, but now it has come to fruition. You have come into your own. You are in love, no?"

Georgia startled, thinking for a wild moment he was talking about Cole. "I barely know him," she protested, wondering if Michel might see something she did not.

"Not with a man." Michel laughed. "You are in love with a place. It has captured your imagination and your heart. Whatever happened on that island, it has brought back your spark. Such a thing is precious and rare. You found your spark, but I think even more than that you found your heart again. I knew it as soon as I tasted the first bite. I could sense it immediately. You have come more fully into your gift, and make no mistake, it is a rare gift that you have, Georgia."

He paused, steepling his fingers and considering her.

"Those few bites of your food transported me to places, memories, emotions I have not felt in years. Your dessert . . . filled with such sweet longing. It has made me decide to take a long overdue trip to see my mother next month. That dish reminded me that time is precious with those we love. It urged me not to waste a second. Now your spark is brighter than ever, Georgia. However, something gives me pause. Do you know what it is?"

She shook her head. "What?"

He looked at her, assessing. "This restaurant is in Paris. We are in Paris. But tell me, Georgia, is Paris where your heart still wants to be?"

Georgia sucked in a breath, opening her mouth to give a pat answer, the obvious and correct answer. But Michel was watching her with a calm, curious expression, and Georgia hesitated, his question bringing with it a whisper of doubt. Was Paris where she wanted to be? For a moment, she was overcome by the remembered taste of honey and herbs, the salty scent of the sea, the warmth of Cole's stubble rasping against her cheek, the feel of Star's strong and sinewy hand gripping hers.

She swallowed hard. How could she even consider for one instant turning her back on the thing she'd been working toward for so many long years? It was madness.

"This has always been my dream," she said helplessly.

Michel smiled slightly. "But is it still? Dreams can change, ma chère. You must embrace what is in your heart now."

Georgia closed her eyes, hearing the timbre of Star's voice, telling her what it meant to be a Stevens woman, about her gift and her legacy. She thought of the island, of the magic Star claimed was there. Her fingertips tingled as she imagined them running over the ridges of an oyster shell, scooping a bit of honey off the waxy comb. She didn't know if it was magic, but something was drawing her heart back to that place in a way she'd never felt before. It was illogical. It was foolish. And yet it felt so very right.

"I don't know," she admitted reluctantly. She opened her eyes. Michel was watching her with an amused smile.

"Really?" he said. "Are you sure?" The gentle question needled her.

"It's a big decision," she protested.

Michel nodded. "Yes, you are right. One you should consider carefully. I will tell the others that I need a day to make my final decision. I can give you that much time. The restaurant is yours if you want it, Georgia. Let me know as soon as you gain clarity in your heart." He took a sip of water and asked conversationally, "Do you know why I picked you up and gave you a ride that first day I saw you?"

Georgia shook her head. "You felt guilty for running into me with your car?"

"Oh, that was unfortunate, yes," Michel agreed. "But no. It was because when you stood there in the glare of the headlights, bruised from the impact of the hood on your hip, you did not look afraid. You looked impatient, surprised maybe. More than a little fierce. But there was no fear in your eyes. I have never known you to be afraid of anything, not when my driver struck you with his car, and never a day since then. Your courage is extraordinary, my dear. I've never seen you back down from anything you wanted. Don't start now, hmm?" He reached across the table and patted her hand. "Go figure out what it is your heart really wants."

And so for the second time in her life, Georgia packed up her knives and left a kitchen she'd thought she would stay in forever. She headed out into the afternoon sunshine of Paris, hoping to clarify the desires of her heart and figure out if the dream she'd worked toward for so long was still the dream she held most dear.

37

Back in Phoebe's apartment, Georgia slipped off her clogs but kept her chef's whites on. They felt like a second skin to her. She unpacked the contents of the two trolleys, stowing the leftover ingredients in Phoebe's tiny refrigerator. Her stomach growled, and she realized she hadn't eaten all day. She'd been too nervous to eat before the competition. All she'd had was an espresso. Now she was feeling grumpy, confused, and hungry. Confungry . . . was that an adjective?

She grabbed two fresh eggs from the bowl on Phoebe's counter and some of the leftover chèvre she'd used earlier in her dish for Michel, then went hunting for the butter. She found it on the counter in a pretty little patterned dish with a lid. She lifted the lid and stopped short. Sitting on the pat of butter was a single four-leaf clover. Georgia rolled her eyes and picked up the slightly buttery stem.

"Okay," she said aloud. "This is getting ridiculous! What do you want to tell me?" If ever there was a time when she would welcome a secret message, this was it.

Silence.

With a sigh, she set the clover on her plate and turned her attention to her omelet. In her mind, she could hear Julia instructing her step-by-step in the fine art of making the perfect French omelet. No egg dish was simpler or more effortlessly French. It was the first recipe of Julia's she'd really mastered. She put the frying pan over high heat, then cracked the eggs into a little bowl and beat them until they were well mixed.

"Now first you must make sure to use at least a very generous tablespoon of butter," Julia cautioned. Georgia spooned a large dollop of butter into the hot pan. It immediately began to sizzle.

"And then just before the butter begins to turn brown, you quickly add your eggs to the very hot pan."

Georgia poured the egg mixture into the pan and let it bubble for a few seconds, then began to vigorously swirl and shake the pan over the heat.

"Now see how beautifully those eggs are coalescing in the bottom of the pan to make a quintessential French omelet?" Julia observed, looking pleased.

A moment later, Georgia slid her omelet onto her plate and walked outside to Phoebe's tiny terrace. There was a single metal chair wedged beneath a table the size of an envelope. She settled into the hard chair with a sigh, taking a moment to orient herself. Lifting her face to the warm spring sunlight, she listened to the sounds of the city below, drinking in the view stretching out before her. Paris. She'd had so many happy years here. What had changed? The obvious answer was her.

"What are you trying to tell me?" she repeated, picking up the little clover stem from the edge of her plate and twirling it between her fingers. She thought of what Star had told her about her gift, that she brought clarity to people with her cooking. Would it work for her? Could she bring clarity to her own heart?

On impulse, she pulled off the four leaves of the clover and sprinkled them over the omelet. Why not give it a try? Clover was edible, with a slightly lemony flavor. Not a terribly appealing plant to eat, but tolerable in small quantities.

"Today I ask for faith, hope, love, and luck," she whispered, not at all sure this was going to work. "Please show me what I need to see." As she spoke the words, she realized she was not petitioning Julia but speaking to the island, to the Stevens women—Star and Emma and Helen—and to her own heart. She didn't know who or what was sending her these signs in the form of four-leaf clovers. Perhaps it was the island as Star suspected, or the universe, or Emma and Helen. The origin was a mystery, and in a way, the source didn't really matter. She just wanted to know what it all meant. What were the four-leaf clovers trying to reveal to her?

She took her first bite. It was rich and creamy, the eggs just set, with a custard-like texture. The first mouthful was perfect—the flecks of clover a bright and bitter counterpoint to the decadent eggs. She licked her fork and scooped up a second bite. As she did so, she was suddenly struck with an almost overwhelming wave of homesickness. Not for Texas or for Paris, but for the island, the cottage, the few weeks she'd spent there. For Star.

She saw herself sitting at the simple white painted kitchen table—Star and Cole and her and Billy, playing Scrabble. Cole carefully laying out the word "crave," his eyes never leaving hers, and her cheeky response, "kiss." Her face flushed, remembering their heated kisses in the cool dark of the night after the Oyster Shuck. Cole's word on his last turn had been "ache." Georgia had responded with her final word, "gone." But in her mind, she saw herself swap out two of the letters, picking up an "h" and an "m." Instead of "gone," she could have played "home."

There it was. Seeing the word laid out in Scrabble tiles on the table, Georgia felt a stab of longing so intense that for a moment she could not draw a breath. A longing for the gnarled apple trees, for the happy hum of Star's bees, for the brooding but kind man with ice-blue eyes and orange rubber overalls who was wasting his life with regret, for the woman with the gray-green eyes who was holding out her hands to Georgia, for a life that was slipping away with every sunrise she spent here.

She set down her fork with a clatter. What was she still doing in Paris? It all seemed so clear now. Paris was her past, a long-ago dream she'd gotten to live for many years. But Paris was not her future. Her future lay in another direction entirely.

"I want to go back," she said aloud, startling a pigeon on a nearby rooftop. "I want to go back to the island. I want to go home."

It was as simple and as complicated as that.

Georgia looked down at the omelet on her plate. Was this what people experienced when they ate her food? This clarity, almost painful in its intensity? She took another bite and another until she'd cleaned her plate.

As she sat there high above the rooftops of Paris, Georgia gazed out at the city she'd loved and longed for all those years growing up. Paris had always been her dream. How was she ready to leave it now? It felt . . . over. And for the first time, she wondered if Paris had ever really been the thing she sought.

"Was my dream ever really about Paris?" she whispered. "Was it ever even about Julia?" Perhaps Paris and Julia had just been vehicles for the deeper longings of her heart—to be valued, worthy, loved, enough. Things she had desperately desired to hear from her mother, but couldn't until now. Maybe Paris and Julia were simply stand-ins, the best she could do, the closest she could get to finding the acceptance, affirmation, and value she longed for with all of her young heart.

"All these years," she murmured, "I think I might have been chasing the wrong thing, believing it would be the answer." But instead, she had finally found what she desired so deeply, not in Paris, not with the fulfillment of her life's goal, but after her life here had shattered. On the island, she had found the answer she had been looking for. The answer in her lineage of strong women gifted with extraordinary abilities. The answer in Star's calloused hands the first time she cupped Georgia's face with a look of tender wonder in her eyes. The answer in Cole's accepting, admiring gaze as he whirled her around the dance floor at the Oyster Shuck, in his kiss, in his frank admission, *Georgia May Jackson, I have never met someone like you. I think you hung the moon.*

There had been an answer too in the hours she had spent in the Anemone kitchen, regaining her spark, learning to embrace delight again, to use her gift to bring clarity to others. Now that same gift was bringing clarity to her own heart.

She saw it with aching certainty now. It had never been about Paris and Julia. It had been about something so much deeper. On the island, with Star and Cole and Anemone, she had found what she'd been searching for her entire life, the thing that had driven her from Texas to Paris, seeking Julia, seeking to live out her dream. It had been her motivation all these years. She had found belonging, acceptance, a sense of her own worth. She had discovered her true self.

"It took me twenty-some years, but I finally figured it out," she murmured in amazement.

"It's all worth it in the end if things turn out the way they should," Julia said comfortingly, pulling an artichoke from a pot of boiling water with tongs and plunging it into an ice bath.

Georgia nodded. "You're right," she said. "And I know what I need to do now."

She stood, picking up the empty omelet plate speckled with vivid green bits of clover. She was going back to the island. She knew it would be excruciating to watch Star slip away as her illness progressed, but the thought of not being with her mother felt impossible. She had already lost so much time; she didn't want to waste a minute more.

Her revelation did not erase the years of Star's mistakes. Georgia still felt a hard knot of anger and grief low in her belly when she thought of her parents' past actions and how much they had cost her. It did not magically anesthetize the pain she felt over so many years of their bad choices. But she knew one thing clearly: Despite all her hurt and anger, she wanted to be there with Star from here on out, come what may. She wanted to spend the time they had left together, however short it might be. It was worth it. She would untangle the past and her complicated feelings about it later. There was not a moment to lose.

She thought briefly of Cole. They had ended on such strained terms. She cared for him, had been falling in love with him, if she were honest with herself, but would he even want to see her again after their last heated exchange? She had no idea. It scared her a little to think of leaving Paris and returning to the island with no assurances, no idea how things would work out. But how could she do otherwise? She already knew the answer. She pulled out her phone and sent a quick text message to Michel asking if she could meet with him as soon as possible. Despite the risks, despite the unknowns, she knew in her heart what she needed to do.

"*What do you* mean you're not going to take the position?" Phoebe asked in dismay a few hours later. She'd gotten home shortly after Georgia had returned from meeting with Michel, and Georgia had told her the news. "Isn't this what you've wanted for literally your whole life?" She sounded completely baffled.

Georgia poured a glug of chilled rosé into a wineglass and handed it to Phoebe. "It was," she said calmly. "But it isn't anymore."

Phoebe plopped down on the sofa. She was wearing a white leather minidress crisscrossed with chrome zippers and a pair of platform go-go boots in the same white leather. After an intense day at work, her hair was sagging slightly from its high, tight ponytail that cascaded down her back. It was a '60s space-age vibe that she somehow totally managed to pull off. Apparently, the perfect outfit for a photo shoot at Versailles.

"I don't understand," she said, taking a large swallow of wine. "What changed?"

"I don't really know how to explain it," Georgia replied, sinking down on the sofa next to Phoebe with her own glass of wine. She felt strangely calm. "It just . . . didn't feel right anymore. Michel made the offer and I pictured myself in the kitchen of that restaurant and it felt like a prison sentence, like I would be signing my life away. I realized I'd been working toward having my own kitchen my whole life as a way to prove something to myself, to Star, to my dad. To prove that I was good enough, that I was worthy somehow. And after my visit to the island, after connecting with my mom and having her finally tell me what really happened when I was little . . ." She shrugged. "I don't feel like I need to prove myself now. I feel free to do the thing I really want to do, to just be me. And I'm not sure what that is just yet, but I know what it is not. And it's not being head chef at La Lumière Dorée."

Phoebe sat back, still looking stunned. "So what are you going to do now?"

Georgia gave a little laugh. "I don't have any idea. Isn't that crazy? I've always had a plan. Since I was ten years old I've had a plan. And now I think I'm just going to wing it. I know I don't want to stay in Paris." She was clear on that point. "I'm going back to the island."

"Have you told your mom yet?" Phoebe asked cautiously.

Georgia hesitated, then shook her head. "I left in such a mess, I'm not quite sure how to tell her I'm coming back. I think I may just go . . . and figure out what to say when I get there." She paused. "I know I'm not done there. I need to go back. I don't want it to end like this. I want to be with my mom for whatever time she has left."

Phoebe blew out a long, steadying breath. "Wow, this day did not go like I thought it was going to," she commented.

"Tell me about it," Georgia said dryly. Their eyes met and they both burst out laughing.

"So you're leaving Paris . . ." Phoebe began.

"And going to the island," Georgia finished.

Phoebe raised her glass. "Here's to unexpected endings," she said with a grin.

"And new beginnings," Georgia added. They clinked glasses in a toast.

"Paris will miss you," Phoebe said, sobering and giving Georgia a searching look. "I hope you know what you're doing."

Georgia nodded, taking a sip of wine. "So do I."

By the time Georgia stopped to eat dinner a couple of hours later—a takeaway salad and margherita pizza Phoebe brought home—her departure from Paris was all arranged. She had booked a ticket for a flight out of Charles de Gaulle Airport the following afternoon, heading to Seattle. She'd used the last of her earnings from Anemone to pay for the flight. If going back to the island did not work out as she hoped, she had no idea what she would do. She would be broke, homeless, jobless . . . she didn't allow herself to think about that. She was acting on pure instinct.

She could not quite explain it, but that omelet had clarified everything. Paris was still beautiful, but it did not call to her.

What was calling her now was a remote speck of land in the cold Salish Sea, the cottage that finally felt like home for the first time in her life, and Star and Cole—the two people she wanted to be with more than anything else. She was following her instincts and going where her heart was leading her. The thought made her heart flutter with equal parts excitement and apprehension.

She tried to think about the practicalities of her decision. All that she owned was in her two suitcases sitting by the futon. She hadn't even really unpacked. Was there anything else she needed to do before she left Paris?

On her phone, she made a little list of any loose ends she needed to tie up. Pick up a thank-you gift at Ladurée for Phoebe for her hospitality. Order her shuttle from Sea-Tac Airport to the San Juan Island ferry. In the end it was just a few things. Was it really that simple, to leave so many years of her life behind?

She stopped to think for a minute. Was there anything else she needed to do, anything she needed to bring closure to? And then a thought struck her, one that curdled her stomach with dismay.

"Oh no," she murmured. She spent a good twenty minutes trying to talk herself out of the idea, but in the end it was no use. With a sinking heart, she finally acquiesced. There was one place she needed to return to before she left Paris. And it was the last place in the world she wanted to go.

38

The kitchen smelled the same. Sizzling butter, white wine, tarragon and fennel, a whiff of fish, the yeasty odor of fresh bread. Georgia stepped through the back door of La Pomme d'Or during the busy dinner rush and inhaled deeply. It all felt so familiar. Her appearance in the doorway took a minute to register with the staff. There was a ripple of surprised murmurs, and then the bustle of the kitchen fell silent, every head turning in her direction.

"Bonsoir," Georgia said hesitantly, trying to muster her courage. It felt like stepping into a lion's den. She looked around. Celine was staring at her in shock, a bunch of fresh herbs in one hand and a large chef's knife in the other. Cyril was deboning fillets of fish. He stopped when he saw her and glared, then uttered a string of very colorful profanities in French. Ismael was stirring a large pot of the soup du jour. He startled, his mouth hanging open, when he saw her. The soup smelled like the recipe she'd invented in this very kitchen—spring peas, shallots, and cream. She felt a touch of nostalgia as she took in the orderly buzz of activity and the familiar smells of the kitchen. She had enjoyed many good years in this kitchen, up until the very end.

"We have a full house tonight," Damien called as he pushed through the door from the dining room, then faltered at the sight of her. "Georgia? You returned?" He looked thunderstruck.

"It's me," she said, giving a little wave. She felt awkward and self-conscious. She hesitated, glancing around at the familiar faces. They had spent hundreds of hours side by side, working shoulder to shoulder. The thought that she had harmed their reputations or demeaned their efforts in any way filled her with a deep sense of regret.

"Where have you been?" asked Celine softly. "We were worried about you." She laid the herbs on the cutting board and came around the counter toward Georgia, wiping her hands on her apron.

"I had a family emergency in America," Georgia said truthfully. No need to get into the details. "I'm actually headed back there first thing tomorrow morning."

"You are leaving Paris?" Ismael seemed shocked. He glanced down at the soup and gave it a quick stir.

"Good riddance," Cyril muttered.

"I'm leaving Paris," Georgia said, ignoring Cyril's ugly tone. She took a deep breath. "But I had to come see you before I went. I couldn't leave without saying something to you." She looked at each of them, her Paris kitchen family, the people she'd worked side by side with for so many late nights, so many meals. "I'm sorry," she said. "The night Antoine Dupont came here, I chose revenge. I was angry, and I wanted to make Etienne pay for cheating on me with Manon, but what I did was unfair to all of you who have worked so hard for this restaurant. I've regretted it ever since it happened. It was wrong and I'm sorry. I hope you can forgive me."

No one said anything for a long moment. Ismael shifted uncomfortably from foot to foot. Damien cleared his throat and looked sideways at the others.

But then Celine stepped forward and embraced Georgia like a sister. She was still holding the huge chef's knife. "If it was me

I would have cut off his balls," she whispered fiercely in Georgia's ear. "I should have told you when I saw him with Manon. I regret this."

"Thank you." Georgia returned the hug. "I forgive you. I hope you can forgive me." Over Celine's shoulder, she saw Ismael duck his head and shoot her a shy smile.

"You created so much drama." Damien wagged his finger in her direction, chastising.

"I know and I'm sorry," Georgia said regretfully.

"Good thing I love drama," he announced airily, then blew her two kisses from across the room and disappeared back into the dining room. Only Cyril ignored her, keeping his face turned away as though she had not spoken. *Well, you can't win them all*, Georgia thought. At least she had tried to do the right thing and admit her mistake and apologize. It was Cyril's choice if he would accept her apology or not. She stepped back from Celine and looked around the kitchen with a twinge of sadness.

"I'll miss you," she told Celine and Ismael honestly. "Come see me wherever I end up." Then she asked the question she didn't really want to know the answer to. "Is Etienne here?"

"He went to get something in the back." Celine jerked her thumb toward the back hallway.

Stomach tightening with apprehension, Georgia walked down the hallway where only a handful of weeks before, her life had completely unraveled. It felt like a lifetime ago. So much had changed since then. Her life was different. She was different.

The refrigerator door was open, and she had an unpleasant sense of déjà vu. She straightened her shoulders and mustered her courage. She could hear rustling and muttering from the refrigerator. Etienne's voice. She almost turned away, but the muttering was him swearing in French, sounding irritated. It was highly unlikely anything amorous was happening in there. She rapped lightly on the refrigerator door so as not to startle him.

"Entrez." That voice. So urbane and annoyed. She pulled the door open, and there was Etienne, trying to wrestle a Serrano ham from a hook on the ceiling. At the sight of her, he looked dumbstruck.

"Georgia?" His hands dropped to his sides. The ham swung on its hook, clearly stuck and quite heavy. He was perspiring slightly. Warily, he sized her up.

"Hello, Etienne." She sounded calmer than she felt. Through her mind flashed the image of the last time she'd seen him, pants unzipped, his eyes frantic as she slammed this very door. His eyes cut to the door, and he looked a trifle uneasy. She suspected the same thought had just crossed his mind. She felt the sting of humiliation afresh, looking at him now. How could he have done that to her, to their relationship? Had she really mattered so little to him?

He gave up on the ham and crossed his arms, his eyes darting around her, not meeting her eyes. She had caught him off guard, she realized. *He's trying to figure out why I'm here.*

"I heard you left Paris," he said flatly.

And whose fault is that? she wanted to retort, but she bit back the words. It had been for the best. If she had not left Paris, she never would have found Star or learned about the gift she carried.

"I went to see my mom," she said mildly. "Do you need some help with the ham?"

He waved away her offer. He looked tired. He was starting to show his age—the lack of sleep and stress and excessive drinking.

"I'm leaving Paris," she added. "Going back to the States, actually."

He nodded. They faced each other then, neither speaking. He gave her a stony look. She returned his coolly.

"What are you doing here, Georgia?" he asked finally, his tone reproachful. He stepped out of the refrigerator. "You got your pound of flesh. Monsieur Dupont ripped us apart in his review thanks to you. The restaurant has suffered as a result. You got what you wanted. Why come back?" He looked petulant.

Georgia gazed at him, trying to reconcile all the faces of Etienne. His sweet, boyish smile waking up in the morning sunlight. The wicked tilt of his mouth as he'd whispered in her ear in public, telling her how gorgeous she looked, how lucky he was to be with her. That earnest, intent gaze as he carefully selected choice ingredients at the market, how he monitored each plate as it left the kitchen, and the way his brow furrowed as he pored over the accounts. He loved this restaurant and he worked hard. She had done them all a disservice when she set the ruined plate of fish in front of Antoine Dupont. Etienne had the morals of a snake in the grass, but her sabotage of his restaurant had targeted the wrong thing. He had been wrong to cheat on her with Manon, but she had been wrong in her response to his betrayal. She cleared her throat. The words stuck there like crumbs of dry bread.

"I came to apologize," she said, forcing them out at last. She knew it was the right thing to do, to take responsibility for her own wrong action, but it felt hard. He had wronged her first. She felt the sting of that humiliation still.

Etienne raised his eyebrows in surprise. "Apologize," he repeated. He stepped out of the refrigerator and shut the door behind him.

"What I did that night when I served Antoine Dupont was wrong. I'm sorry." Georgia wanted to say more, to justify and demand his apology, to tell him that he'd hurt her deeply, to show him her humiliation and sense of betrayal. But she did none of it. She simply owned her part of what had happened. Etienne was responsible for his own actions.

For a beat, then two, she waited. Etienne said nothing. She saw the hesitation on his face, and for a moment, he almost looked ashamed. But then he tossed his hair back and gave her a cool look.

"You should be sorry," he said. "You caused us a lot of trouble."

She waited a moment more, but he said nothing else. Instead, he met her eyes, his own a touch defiant. Etienne had never been good at admitting wrongdoing, she recalled. It was always someone else's fault. She wasn't sure she'd ever heard him apologize for anything. She looked at her former boyfriend, the sexiest chef in Paris, and felt only pity for whatever woman came into his life next. Etienne cared about many things, but none so much as himself. His restaurant came second, and any woman would be a solid third.

For some reason, Georgia thought of Cole, of his generosity and loyalty, of the way he'd sacrificed his time to help Georgia regain her spark, how he'd cared for Justine until she passed away, how he was helping Star now. She looked at Etienne and saw the difference in the two men. Cole cared deeply for others. He sacrificed for the good of those around him. He was a man who had traveled a hard road but who knew how to love others so well. Etienne knew only how to love himself.

As Georgia stood there in front of Etienne, her thoughts raced backward through their years together. The birthdays and anniversaries, the family dinners, the late nights in bars and cafés around Paris after closing, vacations in Provence and Portugal. She expected to feel longing or loss, outrage or humiliation . . . *something*. Instead, she felt . . . nothing. Perhaps just a tiny bit of relief.

"Au revoir, Etienne," she said at last, turning toward the kitchen. She did not wait for his response. She did not look back, just left him with his excuses and his pride and his enormous, unwieldy ham. She had come to do what she needed to do—to apologize and make things as right as she could before she left. Now she could go.

As she stepped out onto the streets of the Latin Quarter from the kitchen of La Pomme d'Or, Georgia felt giddy with relief. She had just closed this chapter of her life for good. She walked the narrow, winding streets, barely registering the crowded sidewalk cafés or the passersby. She had spent over a decade in Paris and now she was leaving with no idea what the next chapter of her life would hold, and yet as crazy as it seemed, she had the most beautiful sensation of liberation, of anticipation, of hope. It swelled and billowed around her in the soft night air, as light and ebullient as meringue. She was ready for whatever came next.

39

"Star?" *Georgia rapped* firmly on the front door to the cottage, expecting to hear Pollen's deep woof of greeting, but she was met with only silence. She peered through the picture window into the living room. Everything was dark inside. Star's car was not in front of the house. She was not home.

Georgia sighed, her anticipation slowly deflating into disappointment. She had endured a long and turbulent flight across the Atlantic, a flight delay at O'Hare, and a snarl of traffic from the airport to the ferry terminal, all the while buzzing on a combination of anxiety and anticipation at the thought of seeing Star again. Now standing alone on the porch in the gathering twilight, she felt her energy wilt into a profound sense of exhaustion. All she wanted to do was crawl into Star's guest bed and sleep forever.

She hesitated, glancing around, then cautiously opened the front door (Star never locked it), and went in. She wandered room to room, but the house was quiet and empty feeling. No Pollen, no Star, and no hint about when Star might return. Georgia wrestled her suitcases up the narrow steps and stowed them temporarily in the guest room. Star had told her she was welcome anytime, but Georgia didn't want to assume the invitation was still open until she talked with Star. She wondered how long she'd need to wait. She yawned hugely, her jaw cracking with the effort, then caught a glimpse of herself in the mirror over the dresser and frowned. Her hair looked like a clown wig, and there were dark circles under her eyes. Perhaps she should take a shower and freshen up while she waited for Star to return home. That sounded like a sensible plan.

Looking out the bedroom window that faced the bay, she noticed a light on in the cabin. Her stomach flipped over. Cole. For a moment, she considered crossing the lawn and knocking on Cole's door, asking if he knew where Star was and when she'd be home, but it was growing dark and she could barely keep her eyes open. Besides, she looked positively bedraggled after her transatlantic flight. She sniffed her blouse and wrinkled her nose. No way she was facing Cole looking, and smelling, like this. Better to face him in the morning when she'd talked to Star, had a solid night of sleep, and could find her mascara and deodorant.

Her stomach fluttered at the thought of seeing him again. How would he feel about her return? Right now her life consisted of so many variables and unknowns. She decided to get clean and worry about the rest tomorrow.

On impulse Georgia ran a hot bath instead of a shower, adding a generous splash of lavender bubble bath she found sitting on the side of the deep cast-iron claw-foot tub. She slid into the hot water with a muffled cry of relief, letting it soothe her tired body as a soft rain pattered gently on the roof. She sank deeper into the water, her curls splaying out on the surface like duckweed, only her nose and mouth above the mounds of lavender-scented bubbles. It was so peaceful she almost drifted off to sleep as she waited for Star's return.

COLE

Cole was halfway through Søren Kierkegaard's *Fear and Trembling* when he glanced out the window and noticed a light on in the upstairs of Star's cottage. That was strange. Star wasn't due back from Lopez Island for another two days. He frowned. Had she come back early and not told him? Unlikely. She would have texted him. He sat up. It could be island teenagers up to no good. They always seemed to know which houses were not occupied and were known to occasionally amuse themselves with light breaking and entering, looking for a party spot and a liquor cabinet they could raid. Well, they were going to be sorely disappointed on both counts tonight.

Growling at the inconvenience, he pulled on his boots and threw on a wool jacket, grabbing his splitting axe on the way out the door. He didn't have any intention of using it, but wanted it more for the impressive effect in case he needed to intimidate some wayward youth. Probably, it was just Star returning from Lopez Island earlier than expected, but just in case . . .

Feeling irritable, he prowled across the soggy lawn and let himself in the back door quietly, moving like a cat burglar. Nothing was amiss in the darkened downstairs. He peered out the living room window. Star's Subaru was not parked out front. He frowned. It wasn't Star in the house then. The hair on the back of his neck prickled. Who in the world was upstairs?

Axe in hand, he crept up the stairs, avoiding the few that squeaked. There was a light seeping under the closed bathroom door. That was odd. He knocked on the door lightly. No answer. No sound from inside either. Puzzled and growing concerned, he twisted the knob and flung open the door.

There was a mermaid floating in the bathtub. For a brief instant, he caught a glimpse of creamy skin and a nimbus of flame-colored curls amid a mound of bubbles before the naked woman in the bath shrieked loud enough to raise the dead and leaped from the water, sloshing bubbles over the side onto the floor. She grabbed the shower curtain and wrapped it around herself, then stood there shivering and swearing loudly and creatively in French.

"Georgia?" Cole stared at her in bewilderment. He lowered the axe slowly. She was watching him wide-eyed and sopping, clutching the shower curtain as though it were her salvation.

"You're here," he observed stupidly. It felt like his insides were heating up like the coils of a toaster at the sight of her. She had come back. She was standing in front of him, dripping puddles on the floor.

"Hello, Cole," she said, struggling to look as composed as a person reasonably could while hiding naked behind a shower curtain.

His mouth twitched, and he turned his eyes up toward the ceiling, trying not to laugh. He had a feeling she would not appreciate it.

"Sorry, I saw a light on in here. Thought maybe it was island kids getting into trouble. I knocked, but you didn't answer." He studied a crack in the plaster of the ceiling as though it was the most fascinating thing he'd ever seen. He tried not to think about her standing naked five feet from him. The shower curtain was probably more sheer than she realized.

"I had my ears underwater. I didn't hear you." She lifted her chin and stared at him reproachfully. She was starting to shiver in the chill of the bathroom.

He cleared his throat. "Uh, right. Sorry. I'll just leave you to it then." He slowly backed out of the room and closed the door, still holding the axe. He was gobsmacked. What in the world was she doing standing there on the other side of the door, in the flesh? The very attractive flesh. He backed up a step or two, trying to regain his bearings. Through the wood panel of the door, he heard the slosh of water as Georgia got back in the tub and a second later the unexpected sound of her muffled, hysterical laughter.

"Cole?" she called out.

"Yes?" He cautiously approached the door.

"Thank you for not bludgeoning me to death in the bath with an axe," she said a touch tartly. "We would have ended up on one of those true crime podcasts, and that is not how I want to go."

"Happy to oblige," he said with a relieved grin. For a moment, he stood there on the landing, allowing the reality of her sudden appearance and the sound of her laughter to seep through him, sweet as golden honey. She was not a continent away in Paris. She was here. He let out a breath he hadn't realized he'd been holding since the moment she'd walked out his door. It had only been two weeks, but it had felt like an eternity. He had missed her more than he cared to admit.

He paused, struck by a thought. "Georgia, does Star know you're here?" he asked carefully.

Another long pause. "Not yet." Her tone was light, but he heard the uncertainty in it. "Actually, I was wondering if you knew when she'd be home."

He let out a breath and leaned his forehead against the door. She didn't know.

"Georgia?"

Silence, then a cautious, "Yes?"

He took a deep breath. Better not to tell her about Star yet, not until he understood her intentions in coming back. "Why *are* you here?"

A long pause. "I won the competition for La Lumière Dorée," she said at last through the door. "I won. Everything I ever wanted."

"Congratulations," he said flatly. He was wrong, then. She was not back for good. He felt his stomach drop with disappointment.

He heard water sloshing in the tub, then a moment later, the door opened. Cole stepped back, staring at Georgia clutching a skimpy silky robe closed around her, hair dripping on the floor.

"I turned it down," she confessed.

"You what?" He stared at her quizzically, caught off guard.

"I turned it down," she repeated. "I realized I didn't want to win. I don't want to spend my life in the kitchen of a restaurant in Paris. Something changed while I was here on the island. This island changed me; it helped awaken something in me. Star helped me too," she admitted. "And you." She paused, uncertainty flickering in her eyes, then raised her chin. "Going back . . . I thought Paris would feel like home, but somehow it just felt . . . wrong. That isn't the place where my heart is anymore." She stopped, swallowing hard. "So I told Michel no, and I turned down the position as head chef at La Lumière Dorée."

Cole was silent for a long moment, his eyes locked on her. "What are you going to do now?" he asked.

"I don't know," Georgia blurted out. "But I want to stay here on the island. I want to be with Star through her illness and help her stay here at home as long as she can. I know she loves the cottage so much, and now it feels like home to me too. I'm not sure how it will all work, but I know I don't want to miss whatever time Star has left."

She looked at him, dripping and pink and and hopeful. It broke his heart. He had to tell her.

"Georgia," Cole said gently. "Star's gone."

Georgia's eyes widened with alarm. "What?" she gasped. "What do you mean, 'gone'?"

"Not dead," Cole clarified quickly. "She's fine. She's just not here."

"Oh, you scared me." Georgia put a hand to her heart, looking relieved, then puzzled. "But where is she?"

Cole hesitated. "She was gutted when you left," he explained. "I've never seen her like that, not even when Justine died. As soon as you were gone, she sped up her plans to move to Lopez Island. Then about a week ago, a couple here on vacation from California stopped to buy some honey from her stand. Star was outside. They started talking, and she mentioned she was planning on selling the cottage. The wife fell in love with the house at first sight. They had already decided to relocate to the island from California and were looking for a property to buy, so Star let her walk through the place. They made her a very generous offer right then and there, and Star accepted."

The color drained from Georgia's face. "Star sold this house?" she whispered in disbelief. "Can she change her mind?"

"I tried to get to her slow down, but her mind was made up," Cole said, resigned. "After you left, I think she didn't see any reason to delay. Two days ago she signed the sales agreement, then came home and packed up a few personal things. I helped her move over to her new place on Lopez. The new buyers are paying cash and want a quick sale, so Star decided to get herself settled on Lopez as soon as possible and then she's planning to pack up the house in the next couple of weeks."

"Oh no," Georgia breathed. She looked stunned. Water was puddling on the tile floor at her feet.

"I'm sorry," Cole said. He could see how shaken she was by the news. "Georgia." He paused. "For what it's worth, I'm sure Star would still welcome you back, even if things look different than you thought they would."

"Okay." Georgia's voice was just a whisper. "I think . . ." She ran her hands through her wet curls. "I think I just need a minute to process this. It's . . . a lot."

"Why don't you stay here for the night and then I can drive you to the ferry to Lopez tomorrow?" Cole offered. "You can talk to Star and then figure out what you want to do."

Georgia nodded. "Okay," she said in a small, pained voice.

Cole waffled for a moment, fighting the urge to step forward and gather her in his arms, to reassure her that it would somehow be okay, but she had asked for space, and he wanted to respect her request. He stepped back and turned to go.

"Cole." Georgia cleared her throat. "Could you not tell Star I'm here? I want to see her first, to tell her myself."

"Sure," Cole agreed gently. He picked up the axe. "Good night, Georgia."

"Good night," she said. She looked so uncertain. He made himself turn away.

Star was gone? The reality hit Georgia in the chest with a blunt force that left her breathless. After Cole left, she wandered into the guest bedroom and riffled through her suitcases, looking for her warmer pajamas. The news changed everything. She was too late. She had been imagining time with Star in the cottage on the bay, time to get to know each other, time to explore what it meant to be mother and daughter. She had thought she could convince Star not to sell, that she could rebuild what she'd destroyed with her hasty departure. But she was too late.

Where would she live? What would she do? Would Star even want to see her or have anything to do with her? What if Georgia had destroyed their fragile relationship by her return to Paris? Suddenly, the step she'd taken to come back, full of faith and expectation, seemed foolish and doomed. She was homeless, almost penniless, and she'd hopped a plane to a remote island where it now appeared she could not even hope to have a roof over her head. It was a frightening prospect. The future she had dreamed of for herself and Star could never happen now. The house was gone. Star was settled on Lopez Island, and who knows how she'd feel about Georgia coming back. Had Georgia just given up everything for nothing?

And what about you? Georgia had wanted to ask Cole as he stood there in the doorway clutching that axe with a stunned expression on his face. *How do you feel now that I'm back?* But she hadn't. She was afraid to know the answer.

She pulled her phone out, suddenly tempted to text Michel and tell him she had changed her mind, that she wanted the chef position after all, but something stopped her. No, she could not go backward. Even though she had no idea what would happen now, somewhere deep in her heart there was a quiet, steady assurance that she was making the right choice. Not necessarily easy, and certainly so far it was not going at all as she'd imagined it would. But still . . .

"Julia, am I supposed to be here on the island?" she whispered. "Is this the right thing to do?" But Julia was silent. Georgia sighed. This was no one's decision but hers, she understood.

She bit her lip, thinking hard. It was daunting to consider making a life here in Friday Harbor with no job and nowhere to stay. More daunting than when she'd arrived in Paris so long ago, following her dream. Only this time, it was not a dream she was following. Her mother was here on neighboring Lopez Island. And Cole was here too, whatever that meant.

"I want to stay," Georgia whispered. If she did not, she knew she would regret it for the rest of her life. Star had so little time left before her illness took her mind. Georgia would never forgive herself if she left Star now. She reached up and rubbed the four-leaf clover charm, saying a quick prayer for faith, hope, love, and luck. Faith that everything would turn out, hope that what was lost could be restored, gratitude that she had found the love of the woman who had born her, and at the end she tacked on a heartfelt request for a little bit of luck to smooth out these next uncertain, scary steps.

COLE

Georgia was back. Sitting in Martha with the engine running the morning after the surprise bathtub incident, Cole watched her disappear down the passenger walkway onto the ferry bound for Lopez Island. She was going to see Star. He had driven her to the ferry as soon as she'd knocked on the door of his cabin at a surprisingly early hour. She'd been pale and resolute, sitting beside him all the way to Friday Harbor in uncharacteristic silence.

He watched her bright flame-colored curls disappear into the ferry, then reversed Martha and headed toward home, his thoughts churning. The two weeks she had been gone had felt like an eternity. He genuinely feared she was gone forever, and that thought had gutted him. When she'd accosted him in his cabin the day she left for Paris, she'd dropped a nuclear truth bomb on him and then stormed out, leaving him with his thoughts and the best rice pudding he'd ever tasted. As he sat there nursing his wounds and spooning the creamy goodness into his mouth, her words had burrowed into his subconscious. She'd gotten him thinking, and he finally faced some hard truths. As it turned out, that pudding had been a catalyst for things he should have done long ago. He didn't even like rice pudding. But he liked Georgia May Jackson. He liked every single thing about her. No, that was a lie, he thought ruefully as he wound his way slowly through the heart of Friday Harbor. A lot of things about her drove him completely nuts. Like her stubbornness. And her ability to vivisect his wounded heart with her scalpel eye, so casually, and so accurately. It was extraordinarily irritating. But she drew him and motivated him in a way no one had ever done before.

As he passed Kings Market and the movie theater and headed out of town, he pictured her last night, breathlessly telling him she'd turned down winning the competition. What would it mean if she really was back on the island for good? What would that do to his plans? He thought of the fat job offer packet that had arrived a few days ago in the mail, of the plane ticket to San Francisco waiting with his name on it. His real name. The timing could not be worse. And yet, he couldn't keep waiting around, doing penance, hiding away. Georgia had been right. He had to start living. It was time for Dr. Cabot Cole Montgomery to come back to the world. But now she was back . . .

He swore fiercely under his breath and braked for a doe who sprang across the road in front of him. He gripped the steering wheel. What *would* it mean if she was back for good? The thought was incendiary; it set his heart alight. But at the same time it absolutely terrified him. A part of him wanted to run as fast and as far as he could away from her, to protect his battered heart, to keep hiding away so he didn't get hurt again. The other part, the part that made his pulse speed up every time he heard her name, knew he was a goner. He was so in love with her. He was so afraid.

He punched the gas, burning rubber and barreling down the road.

"Don't get your hopes up. She may not stay, now that Star's

moved away," he muttered aloud to himself. He had seen the anxiety and uncertainty in her face when he'd told her about Star's move and the sale of the cottage. It had upended all her plans. Maybe she'd decide it was a safer bet to go back to Paris after all. He savagely spun the wheel and turned right into the driveway for the shellfish farm in a spray of gravel. Whatever the outcome, one thing was clear. Georgia's return was throwing his heart, and his life, into chaos and confusion once more.

40

Georgia arrived on Lopez Island in a light morning drizzle. She disembarked from the ferry and stood for a moment, trying to get her bearings. It had been dry and clear in Friday Harbor with a pale, weak sun, and she was not prepared for rain. She looked around, wishing for an umbrella. The few other foot passengers quickly dispersed, and she was left alone at the ferry dock with not a taxi in sight. She checked her phone. No cell service. Great. She'd saved a copy of the GPS directions to Star's new residence on her phone before she'd gotten on the ferry. It looked like it was about three miles away. Gazing around her once more in the hopes that a taxi would miraculously appear, Georgia mustered her resolve and started walking.

Over an hour later, she was soaked, shivering, and deeply regretting not having had the forethought to call ahead for a ride or at the very least use the bathroom at the ferry terminal. It was a gray, wet, miserable walk on quiet country roads that wound through forests of towering evergreens. No cars passed her. She was utterly alone. She trudged on.

Finally Georgia rounded the last curve and breathed a sigh of relief when she saw the number post. This was it. A long lane led away from the road down toward the sea. In the distance, she counted eight or nine small cottages painted a cheery yellow and a large farmhouse in the same hue. Wincing, she gingerly started down the muddy lane. She'd spent the last two miles fantasizing about throwing her shoes into the roadside shrubbery and going barefoot. She had a blister on her left heel the size and shape of a nickel.

Suddenly a blur of yellow shot toward her from the direction of the cottages like a bolt of lightning, knocking her off-balance. She yelped as Pollen put her front paws on Georgia's chest and licked her chin, happily barking a welcome.

"Pollen, down, girl. Come here!" Star ran out the front door of one of the cabins, chasing down her dog. She stopped short a dozen yards away when she caught sight of Georgia, her expression turning to pure astonishment.

"Georgia May?"

"In the flesh," Georgia said weakly and pushed Pollen off of her. There were two giant muddy paw prints on the front of her blouse, which was so completely soaked that she could see her lace bra clear as day.

"What on earth are you doing here?" Star asked, looking thunderstruck. Through the drizzle, Georgia noted that Star did not seem very pleased to see her.

For a moment, Georgia faltered. "I came back," she said. "I said no to the chef position in Paris and I came back."

"Why in the world would you do that?" Star asked, staring at her in evident dismay.

"I thought you'd be happy . . ." Georgia trailed off uncertainly. This was not going at all how she'd hoped or imagined it might.

"Come in out of the rain," Star sighed. "I'll make tea and then you can tell me all about it."

Pollen pranced happily around Georgia, barking with joy as they made their way back toward the cottages. Georgia winced. The blister made every step agonizing. Her white Esplar leather sneakers were now coated in mud and made strange squishing sounds with every step. Most likely ruined. She sighed in discouragement.

In the kitchen of one of the tidy yellow cottages, Georgia sat barefoot while Star steeped two mugs of tea, feeling like a bedraggled stray kitten. Everything was wet. There were droplets of water dripping off the ends of her curls. She was steaming in the warmth of the kitchen. Star handed her a towel.

"Why don't you get out of those wet clothes," she suggested. "You'll catch a chill. I'll find some dry clothes you can borrow."

Georgia gratefully accepted the stretchy broom skirt and warm sweatshirt Star had found for her. It was not at all her style, and didn't match all that well, but it was warm and dry. She hastily changed and toweled off her hair in the tiny bathroom. The cottage was no more than four hundred square feet, she guessed. She'd glimpsed a small bedroom nestled next to the bathroom and passed through a snug sitting room on her way from the kitchen. It almost looked like a holiday cottage, cute but cramped. The perfect size for one person. She didn't recognize any of the furnishings. It looked like it had come fully furnished. There were a few small items she recognized from the cottage, photos and mementos of Star's.

When Georgia came back into the kitchen, Star set a steaming mug of tea down in front of her and sat down across the table. For a moment, she just looked at Georgia, then heaved a deep sigh. "So you gave up the chef position you were hoping for?"

"I did," Georgia confirmed.

Star frowned. "This wasn't how it was supposed to go," she said, almost as though she were talking to herself.

"How was it supposed to go?" Georgia asked a touch testily. She was bone-tired from the past few days of travel and the regrettable walk through the mud. And now her mother seemed less than enthusiastic about her unexpected reappearance. She took a sip of tea. Mint for wisdom, fennel for strength, and a touch of chamomile for patience. She needed all of it and more.

"You were supposed to be safely in Paris, living your own life. I wanted to see you happy and secure before . . ." Star stopped, staring down at her tea.

"Before what?" Georgia asked.

Star gave her an inscrutable look. "Before my mind fails," she said bluntly. "But surely, you can go back to Paris. It's not too late to do what you want to do."

"I am doing what I want to do," Georgia said firmly. "I left Paris for good. I'm here with you now. This is what I want."

This entire reunion was taking a very uncomfortable turn.

Star shook her head. "You were only supposed to be here for a little while," she insisted. "I wanted to see you again and then I wanted to know you were safely living the life you'd always dreamed of. That's what I wanted for you. Not this." She looked exasperated. "There's nothing here for you, Georgia."

Georgia was hurt and more than a little annoyed. "You don't get to make that decision for me," she snapped. "You blame Daddy for keeping us apart when I was little, but you're trying to do the same thing now. I'm not a child anymore. And I don't want to be safely ensconced in a Paris kitchen while you're here fighting this disease." She took a deep breath to calm herself and said the words that were in her heart. "I want to be here . . . with you. No matter what. For all of it. You're my mother, and we've lost too much time already. Let's enjoy the time we have left. Please."

Star's face fell. "Georgia, no," she protested. "I'm doing okay now, but this is a fast-acting neurological disease. Pretty soon I'm going to start forgetting a lot of important things. Eventually, I won't even know my own name. I won't know you. I don't want you to see me like that. I'll be nothing but a burden to you."

She looked so vulnerable it broke Georgia's heart. Her mother had been trying to protect her for her entire life. She'd left when Georgia was little and kept away all these years in the mistaken belief that her absence was the gift she could give to her daughter, that she had nothing good to offer. Now she was trying to do it again.

"But what if I want to take care of you?" Georgia challenged. "What if I choose to stay?"

"Georgia." Star looked helpless. "Please, I want you to live your life, not waste it here with me while my mind fades away."

"It's not a waste," Georgia said. "For years I've felt like my heart had an empty place in it, ever since you left, a hole right in the center. And for years, I thought Paris would fill it, that achieving my dream would fill it, but it turns out Paris and winning the chef position at La Lumière Dorée didn't fit the shape of that hole after all. Do you know what did?"

Mutely Star shook her head.

"Knowing who I really am, seeing that you love me, being here with you."

Star's eyes filled with tears. She hesitated. "I'm afraid you'll regret it," she said softly. "You think it will be fine now, but I know what it is like to care for someone. At the end, with Justine, it was grueling. It was so hard. I don't want you to see me like that. I can't ask that of you."

"You're not asking," Georgia said gently. "I'm offering." She reached out and grabbed Star's hand, holding on tight. "I'm sorry I left so abruptly last time. I was hurt and angry. I felt like you were leaving me all over again and I had no say in it. It felt too painful to stay. I left you before you could leave me again."

"I'm not leaving by choice," Star interjected softly, her fingers gripping Georgia's. "I'd give anything to change the past, to not make those mistakes all those years ago that hurt you. And I'd give anything to stop what's happening to me now."

"I know," Georgia sighed. She released her mother's hand

and wrapped her fingers around the warmth of her mug. "But you can't. We can't change the past or the future, I know that. But here's the thing I've been thinking about. When we love, we always face loss, don't we? Love and loss go hand in hand. Someday, each of us will have to say goodbye to the ones we love, or they will say goodbye to us. It's inevitable." She toyed with the handle of her mug. "I grew up in Baptist Sunday school. I know that death is not the end of the story. It's just a doorway we all pass through at some point. When we die, our souls live on, and even when death separates us, we'll someday get to be together again. Death is just a 'see you later.' But even 'see you later' is hard. It hurts. I already lost you once. I don't want to lose you just when I found you again." Georgia glanced up at Star earnestly. "I wish I could heal you of this disease. I wish we could have so many more years together here. But if that wish can't come true, then I want to spend as many days as I can with you. And when you close your eyes for the final time, when we have to say that last 'see you later,' I want to be there holding your hand."

Star sniffed and blinked hard. "I don't deserve that," she said bluntly. "I failed you so badly as a mother. I don't deserve your love and your care now." She looked down at her hands twisted in her lap.

Georgia considered her words. "You did fail me," she admitted. "If I'm honest, I'm still really angry with you and Daddy. I'm trying to come to grips with what you did and how much it cost me. I've been wrestling with it since I left. The confusing thing is that I don't know how I can be so angry at you and still love you and want to be with you at the same time. It's a paradox. But I've realized something over the past few weeks."

She thought of her father standing almost larger than life in the bedroom of Star's cottage, his Stetson in his hand, explaining his decision to forgive Star. *As the years pass, you either soften or you calcify,* he'd told her. *It's time to lighten the load.* Words of wisdom about forgiveness from a man she was still struggling to forgive.

"You both failed me in different ways," Georgia explained. "but that's not the entire story. You also shaped me by all the ways you two loved me and cared for me. You gave me the Stevens legacy, and the gift of delight. You gave me Julia and the dream of Paris. And after you left, Daddy gave me a stable and safe home. Those things are not small things. There was a lot of good mixed in with the bad in my childhood, in what you did as parents. It was a mixed bag."

"It always is," Star interjected with a sigh. "Life is a mixed bag."

"I'm learning that family is a mixed bag," Georgia added with a dry smile. "A complicated, pain-in-the-ass-at-times, loving, frustrating, yet worthwhile mixed bag."

Star nodded. "Isn't that the truth."

"I don't want to hold on to this hurt and anger until it turns to resentment," Georgia said firmly. "I don't want to calcify. You hurt me. You and Daddy made a mess of our family. Your failures cost me a lot, but I'm choosing to forgive, to continue to grow in relationship with you because you're my mother. A relationship with you is worth it. You are worth it. I don't love you just because you're convenient or easy all the time. That's not how love works. That's not what it means to be family. I choose you, Mama, including and despite the mess and the pain of the past." She looked at her mother earnestly, pleading for understanding.

Star was quiet for a moment. "Is this what you really want?" she asked, a note of vulnerability in her voice. "Are you sure?"

Georgia nodded. "As sure as I can be."

"It won't be easy," Star warned. She looked hopeful and humble.

"Nothing worth doing ever is," Georgia quoted, echoing one of Buck's favorite sayings.

Star smiled. "For once, your father and I agree," she said dryly. She looked at Georgia and sighed, all her protests seeming to melt away. Georgia beamed, sensing she had won.

"You want some honey toast?" Star asked. "Everything in life is better with honey toast."

Georgia hesitated. "Is it your homemade bread?" she asked.

Star shook her head. "Store-bought, I'm afraid."

Georgia grinned. "That sounds perfect."

Georgia knew that the road ahead would be hard. She had nowhere to live, no income, and Star was facing a long, difficult decline in her health. But for now, they were together. For one brief, warm, shiny moment, everything felt right in the world.

41

The next morning, bright and early, Georgia walked across the lawn to Cole's little cabin holding a plate of fresh blueberry muffins. She'd been awake since four a.m. because of jet lag and had decided to make herself useful, so she'd scrounged up ingredients in the kitchen and busied herself with baking until the clock read a reasonable hour. She didn't know how Cole would feel about her sudden appearance this early, but in her experience, there was seldom a situation on earth that was not improved by the addition of fresh muffins.

Georgia had stayed with Star until evening and then caught the last ferry back to Friday Harbor late the night before. Star had explained that she was not allowed to have overnight guests in her new home, but insisted Georgia stay in the guest room in the cottage in Friday Harbor until the sale was finalized in a few weeks. They had agreed that Star would take the ferry to Friday Harbor the next afternoon so they could start brainstorming about the future. Now Georgia had a few hours until Star was scheduled to arrive, so she decided to go see Cole, peace offering in hand.

It was misting, the rain falling softly over the grass, beading on her hair and eyelashes. Georgia knocked firmly. The door opened, and Cole stood there in the cool gray early morning light, shirtless (as usual) and wearing a worn pair of gray pajama pants. He had a pancake turner in one hand, and the air was thick with the smell of frying bacon.

"You're up," she observed.

"You again," he said, looking ever so slightly amused. She brushed past him, so close she could feel the warmth of his skin. Did the man ever wear a shirt inside? It was distracting. She set the muffins on the counter and perched on the edge of the bed. They eyed each other for a moment, neither quite sure how to break the silence. Just how much had he seen that first night in those few seconds she'd been in the tub? She had a feeling the answer was plenty. Her cheeks pinked at the thought.

"Your bacon's burning," she observed. He whirled and with a few muttered words scooped the strips of bacon onto a plate. She kept her eyes on him the whole time, drinking him in. She thought of Etienne, of their last interaction, and how she'd realized then what she really felt for Cole. It scared her a little. Against Etienne's selfishness she'd measured Cole's quiet, steady care and thoughtfulness. He was easy on the eyes, but he was far more than that. He was a truly good man—intelligent and loyal, and although he could be a little grumpy on the surface, she was seeing more and more of his tender heart.

Now here they were. Together. What she had told herself was impossible when she headed off to Paris was suddenly within reach. But she had no idea what he was thinking. They had exchanged strong words the last time she'd been in this cabin. She wondered how he felt now. She was hoping . . . she had no idea what she was hoping for, but she couldn't seem to keep away from him.

"Bacon?" He turned and offered her the plate. The bacon glistened invitingly from a bed of paper towels soaking up the grease.

"Thank you." She took the least crispy strip and crunched it, aware that he was watching her intently.

"How did it go with Star?" he asked, setting the plate of bacon on the table.

She nibbled the strip of bacon, thinking of his mouth on hers at the Oyster Shuck. It was distracting.

"I told her I intend to stay," Georgia replied. "I want to care for her through her illness."

Cole nodded. "For how long?" he asked.

"For as long as she has left."

"Do you have any idea what you're signing up for?" Cole asked cautiously, eyes narrowing as he looked at her. "How hard that will be?"

Georgia straightened her shoulders and set her chin. "No," she replied honestly. "But I know I don't want to lose another minute with her. I'm not afraid of hard things."

Cole raised an eyebrow. "I believe you. But how are you going to make it work?" He pulled a wooden chair over from the table and straddled it, facing her.

At that question, Georgia faltered. "I don't know," she confessed, shoulders slumping. "I was hoping you'd have some bright ideas. I'll need a place for us to live, and I'll need to get a job." Georgia bit her lip. It was daunting. She glanced out the window at the cottage. "I just wish I'd gotten here before Star agreed to sell," she said regretfully. "I know how much this place means to her. I'll miss it too. It started to feel like home."

Cole chose the most burnt piece of bacon from the plate. "I know, it's hard to let it go," he admitted. "I volunteered to help her with whatever she needed if she wanted to stay here and not sell, but Star insisted she was going to need a lot more care than just I could give her as her disease progresses. She arranged everything so she'd have what she needed when the time came. But I'm sad to see this place go. It feels like home to me too." He took a bite of the bacon and looked resigned.

Georgia cleared her throat. "I guess I'd better start checking into job opportunities and available housing then. Have any hot leads?"

"The seafood shack in town always has an opening on the fry line," Cole deadpanned, his mouth twitching slightly.

She leaned forward and slapped his arm lightly. "That will be the day." She reached around him and took another strip of bacon, noticing as she did so a duffel bag open on the table, a stack of neatly folded clothes beside it. "Are you going somewhere?"

"Ah, yes, actually." He rubbed the back of his neck and looked a little chagrined. "I'm heading down to San Francisco this week to . . . see about a job offer."

She stared at him in shock. "You're leaving the island?" Her heart plummeted straight down to the rough pine floor.

He looked uncomfortable. "After our last conversation, I had some time to think," he admitted. "And I realized that you were right. I was letting shame over what I did to Amy stop me from moving on in my life. And that seemed like a waste. I figured it was better to put my efforts toward trying to make amends, trying to make the world a better place, than just hiding out here farming mollusks. I enjoy shellfish farming. It's a sustainable and ecologically sound business, but I always aimed to do something on a larger scale, with global ecology and tech, the things I was pursuing before. So I poked around, made some calls, and an old buddy of mine knew about a research project that was just starting up. It's right up my alley. Seaweed, actually."

Georgia gazed at him in astonishment. "Cole, that's incredible," she exclaimed at last. "I'm so happy for you." But the thought of his absence filled her with a cold, sick feeling of loss. She had not envisioned a future on the island without him here too. Suddenly, life here felt a lot more lonely.

RECIPE FOR A CHARMED LIFE

"So is it time to start calling you Dr. Cabot Montgomery again?" she asked, covering her dismay with a touch of flirtation.

"Sort of." He looked a little sheepish. "I'm Dr. Cabot Montgomery in professional circles, but personally, here on the island, I still prefer Cole."

"Well, Cole, I'm glad you found your way," she said, cocking her head and gazing at him. "But I can't believe you're leaving the island," she said softly.

"After Star moved to Lopez, I didn't think there was anything to keep me here," he said frankly. His eyes on her were searching.

"Were you hoping for something to keep you here?" she asked. It was a bold question. She wasn't even quite sure what she was asking, and she had no idea what he was thinking. So they had shared a kiss. More than one. A dozen kisses then. Each had been glorious—an earth wobbling on its axis kind of kiss—but a lot had changed since then. Had it meant anything to him too or had it just been an enjoyable evening, a little footnote in the story of his life?

"I guess that would depend on what that something was," he said, his gaze boring steadily into hers. It felt like a question.

For a minute, she considered blurting out the truth. That she liked him . . . so very much. That she thought about him constantly. That when she pictured the future with her and Star, somehow he was always in it. That she didn't want him to go. She wanted him to stay. She wanted *him*. Period.

But when she thought of him pursuing his dream, not living like a penitent monk out here in this little cabin . . . she swallowed all those words. It was the right next step for him. She couldn't keep him here just because she was falling in love with him. Maybe they could have had something special if circumstances were different, but she could not ask him to stay, not at the expense of this opportunity. She had to let him find his purpose in life again. She had to let him go.

"You should go," she said lightly, looking away. "This is your second chance. You can't let anything or anyone get in the way of that, no matter what."

She felt him rise swiftly from the chair. A second later, he sat down beside her on the bed, the springs groaning under his weight as his shoulder brushed hers.

"There's just one problem," he said, his tone serious. Caught off guard, she glanced up and met his eyes. They were surprisingly warm for such an icy blue. "Someone's already gotten in my way," he murmured. "Quite a lot, actually."

"Oh, who?" She was having trouble remembering how to breathe normally.

"Georgia, when I saw you the other night . . ." Cole stopped, his mouth tugging up in a reluctant grin. "You wear a shower curtain surprisingly well, by the way."

She swallowed hard, trying to maintain her composure. "Thank you."

Where was this going? And why was he sitting so close to her? She was tipping toward him as his weight pulled down the mattress. She felt a little light-headed.

"Seeing you again made me realize something," he said.

"What's that?" she asked faintly.

"That I want to be wherever you are."

She stared up at him in astonishment. "Really?"

He smiled and nodded. In an instant, her heart ballooned inside her chest. She felt like she might float straight up off the mattress with joy.

"But what about the job in San Francisco?" she asked.

He paused. "I admit that's a problem," he murmured, his

voice husky. "Now that I've got you back, I don't want to let you go. Have any good ideas?"

She turned to face him, so close the tips of their noses were almost touching. "You need to do what you love, and I need to be here for Star," she said, trying to be firm. But it was hard when he smelled so very tantalizing. She sniffed surreptitiously. Bacon. Difficult to resist a man who smelled like freshly ground coffee, salt, and bacon. "They say absence makes the heart grow fonder." She cleared her throat, feeling flushed and disoriented. "Maybe we should see if it's true?"

"I already tested that theory," he told her, his tone mock serious. "And it's true. I missed you more than I ever thought I could miss anyone ever again." His eyes were locked on her, the glacial depths darkened with longing. "And if you hadn't come back, I was seriously considering following you to Paris."

"Really?" She was finding it hard to keep breathing. Was it suddenly very warm in the cabin?

Cole pulled back a little and looked at her. "From the moment I saw you in Paris, stuffing my tuxedo pocket full of barbecued pork, I thought you were the most gorgeous, infuriating woman I'd ever laid eyes on." He paused, one side of his mouth quirking up just a little. "Je suis amoureux de toi," he said in passable French.

I'm in love with you.

Georgia's eyes widened. "Well, I think you're the most obscenely handsome, stubborn, grumpy, yet secretly tenderhearted genius scientist turned oyster farmer I've ever laid eyes on," she blurted out.

Cole laughed. "No one has ever described me like that."

"You drive me crazy but I can't seem to stop thinking about you," Georgia continued. "Also, your French has definitely gotten better."

He glanced down at her lips. "After the tuxedo debacle, I worked hard to improve so I didn't end up with more pockets full of pork." His eyes flashed with amusement. "I speak German too, and quite a bit of Japanese." He seemed to be having trouble looking at anything but her mouth.

She leaned closer. "Tell me, is your kissing as good as your French?" she asked playfully. "I can't quite remember." He reached out and cupped his hand around the back of her neck, pulling her toward him.

"Better," he said, "definitely better," and then he closed the gap and kissed her.

For the second time in as many weeks, Georgia felt the world shift around her. She could taste bacon and coffee and Cole. She gave a little squeak of surprise as he wrapped his other arm around her waist, pressing her closer, the springs squeaking under their weight. Nothing existed except the delicious, firm pressure of his mouth on hers. She twined her arms around his neck. He groaned, kissing her like it was his only purpose in life. She kissed him back. Georgia lost all track of time. It could have been a few seconds or a half hour when Cole broke the kiss.

"By the way, I meant to tell you," he said, pulling back and breathing like he'd been sprinting the hundred-yard dash. "Anemone is looking for a new head chef again. Apparently, the chef they had, the one who cut her finger, was wanted in a string of burglaries in Florida. The police arrested her over the weekend. Myra texted me yesterday, wondered if I knew anyone."

"Hmm . . ." Georgia traced her fingers down the side of his face, memorizing that chiseled jaw that looked cut from the pages of a magazine, those ice chip blue eyes that could warm her heart so readily. How was this real? she wondered briefly. How was it that only a short time ago she was on the ferry to this island brokenhearted, her life in ruins, and now she was here again, reunited with her mother and snug in the arms of this genuine, intelligent, gorgeous man who turned her knees to jelly? It felt too good to be true. She was reveling in every unexpected minute. She cocked her head. "Cooking at Anemone could be a good way to keep me occupied while you're off in San Francisco," she said, her tone tentative. She wondered if he'd pick up on the offer she was making.

He grinned, brushing a curl from her cheek. "Will it keep you out of trouble?"

"I'm not sure that's possible," she countered with a laugh. "Trouble seems to find me."

"Just as long as I can find you too," he murmured, pressing a kiss against her neck. "I can fly up here on the weekends. It's not that far, right?"

"We'll figure it out together," Georgia promised, her heart soaring.

"That's all I need to hear," Cole said, then tilted her chin up and lowered his mouth to hers once more.

42

"*What are the* odds we'll need two sets of salt and pepper shakers wherever we end up living?" Georgia knelt on the kitchen counter in Star's old cottage and fished another set of salt and pepper shakers from the top shelf of the upper cabinets. She held up a set that looked like ceramic mushrooms and an expensive-looking cut-glass set with tarnished silver tops. "Which ones do you want to keep?"

Across the kitchen, Star looked up from the box of kitchen supplies she was taping closed and narrowed her eyes, considering. "Keep the mushrooms. Donate the glass ones. I got those mushrooms in Northern California when Justine and I were heading up the coast from Arizona. They remind me of our trip out here, searching for a place to call home." She sat back on her heels and sighed, looking around the kitchen with a resigned air. "I thought I'd be ready to let this place go, but it hurts my heart to think of leaving it."

Beside Star, Pollen lay sprawled on the laminate floor, dozing. At Star's mournful tone, she raised her head and woofed gently, nudging Star's knee with her wet black nose. On the radio, Joan Baez was warbling softly "The Wild Mountain Thyme." Georgia frowned and carefully wrapped the mushrooms in a cloth napkin. If only she had come back sooner. If only she'd never left at all. Now they were left scrambling to find a place to rent as soon as the new owners took possession, but they hadn't found anywhere yet. She'd been back on the island a week, and they'd been looking every day with no luck. The pool of rental properties on the island was tiny and expensive, but they had no choice. Star had already signed the purchase agreement before Georgia arrived, and now the real estate agent was bringing the final paperwork for the sale over today for Star to sign. It was truly too late to save the cottage.

"I'm sorry I didn't come back sooner," Georgia said softly, her voice filled with regret.

Star pulled a stack of assorted baking dishes out of a lower cupboard and shook her head. "I was planning to move before you arrived. There was just no way I was going to be able to keep this old place after my diagnosis. And yes, it is hard to let it go, harder than I expected, but that's life. We'll find another place and make new memories there. The most important part is that we're together." Still, she looked a little wistful as she nestled a stack of loaf pans into a big cardboard box.

Georgia carefully set the glass salt and pepper shakers in the donate box and checked her phone. It was just her and Star around this afternoon. Cole was in San Francisco exploring the job opportunity he'd been offered. She was proud of him taking this big step to restart his life again, but she missed him fiercely and it had only been a few days. How were they going to survive being apart for much longer if he accepted the job? She checked her phone again. He had texted, Having sushi. Wish you were here.

Miss you too. Enjoy some uni for me, Georgia texted back, adding a string of heart emojis. She slipped her phone back in her pocket and grabbed a glass jar. Joan had moved on to "A Hard Rain's A-Gonna Fall." This was a depressing soundtrack for packing.

A knock at the front door startled them. Pollen raised her head and woofed a belated warning, then scrambled up and headed down the hall.

"Come on in. We're in the back," Star yelled. A moment later, Star's real estate agent, Ken, poked his head through the kitchen doorway, Pollen at his heels. "Afternoon, ladies." He came into the room with a folder in his hands and stood surveying the clutter. "Packing up, I see?" He chuckled nervously.

"Thought we'd get a head start on it." Star rose with a groan, her back popping, hands on her knees. "That the final paperwork I need to sign?"

The agent looked uneasy. "Well now, that's what I came to talk to you about." He licked his lips and darted a glance around the room. "There's, uh, a slight problem."

"What sort of problem?" Star looked surprised. "I thought you told me the septic report came back clear."

"Oh yes, clean as a whistle," Ken assured her. "Ah, no, the problem is a little bigger than that. Star, there's no easy way to say this. The sellers are backing out of the agreement."

"What?" Star and Georgia gasped in unison, staring at the agent in astonishment.

"What do you mean backing out? Why?" Star asked.

The agent spread his hands. "I'm as baffled as you are. It seems that the sellers received a concerning environmental report packet this morning about this property from an anonymous source. Their agent emailed me a copy of what they got in the mail. I've never seen anything like it. It's chock-full of seismic event predictions, rainfall calculations, soil sample assessments. They don't know what half of it means, but it's got them completely spooked. They called their agent worried about acidic sandy soil, and lack of nutrients and something about the island being in a tsunami earthquake zone. I'm not a scientist, I have no idea what half the stuff is either, but the upshot is that they're pulling out of the sale. I told them they'll lose their earnest money, but they were adamant. They've decided to move to Arizona instead. Their agent and I both tried to talk sense into them, but they're not budging." Ken looked bewildered. "In all my years as an agent, I've never seen this happen before. I'm sorry to tell you, Star, but the deal is off."

Star and Georgia looked at each other and then they both whooped in glee. "That is some of the best news I've ever had," Star announced. Pollen danced in a circle, barking excitedly and wagging her tail at Star's happy tone.

Star turned to Georgia. There were tears in her eyes. "I guess we can unpack those salt and pepper shakers," she said with a little laugh. "Looks like we're staying put."

When Star and Pollen left to usher a still apologizing and bewildered Ken out the door, Georgia looked around. She was surrounded by half-filled cardboard boxes and piles of bakeware. She gazed out the window to the bay, feeling a sweet rush of relief and gratitude. She had a pretty good guess who had sent that ominous environmental report packet. It was a brilliantly strategic move.

"Just proves you really are a genius scientist," she murmured. Now it was possible for Star to keep her home and for Georgia to at last have one. It meant the world to her.

She pulled out her phone and texted Cole.

The craziest thing just happened. The buyers backed out. Something about an anonymous source mailing them an ominous environmental report about soil and tsunamis?

A moment later he responded.

Sounds like the work of Captain Planet.

She smiled and texted back. Newsflash: I think I'm in love with Captain Planet. And then she added a heart emoji. It was undeniable. She was head over heels in love with Dr. Cabot Cole Montgomery.

Star came back into the kitchen, Pollen right behind her. "Huh," she said, looking around at the boxes and packing supplies and kitchenware in piles. She put her hands on her hips. "Well, I guess we can start putting the kitchen back together."

Georgia nodded. "I guess so." They looked at each other for a long moment, then both broke into relieved grins.

"It feels like a miracle," Star said softly. "And I'm guessing we both know who's to thank for it?"

Georgia nodded. "There's only one person I know who could create an ominous environmental report packet," she said with a touch of irony.

"And make magnesium in soil sound scary," Star laughed. "Tell Cole I owe him a debt of gratitude."

"We both do," Georgia said. She could think of several delightful ways to show her thanks to Cole, but they'd have to wait until his return.

"We need some happier music for unpacking," Georgia announced. She switched off the radio, cutting off Joan mid-warble, and put her own choice on her phone. As Édith Piaf began to triumphantly crow the stirring "Non, je ne regrette rien," Georgia took the stack of loaf pans out of the box and slid them back into the cupboard. Now everything could go back where it belonged. Including Star.

"I didn't think it would end like this." Star's voice was a little hoarse with emotion.

Georgia glanced up, surprised. "Me neither."

Star dashed away a tear and smiled at her daughter. Pollen circled the kitchen, sniffing everything and wagging her tail, thumping it against boxes and cabinet doors.

"I didn't want to let this place go," Star said softly.

"I know," Georgia agreed. She met her mother's eyes, feeling her heart lighten and lift. She was still stunned by this turn of events. It all finally felt so right. She touched the charm at her throat. Faith, hope, love, and luck. Her prayer before she left Paris came back to her. She uttered another now, one of gratitude for how things seemed to be turning out for good.

"It still won't be easy, what's coming," Star warned, placing her hand on Georgia's and squeezing gently. "This doesn't fix everything."

"You're right," Georgia agreed, covering her mother's strong hand with her own. Together, they looked out at the bay, at the silver bright water rippling against the rocky shore. Through the open window, Georgia could faintly hear the happy buzz of Star's bees far away against the dark branches of the evergreens, the sound wafting through the open window on a cool, salty breeze. "It won't always be easy, but we'll face it together," Georgia said firmly, "right here where we belong."

Epilogue

THREE YEARS LATER

"River, I've got two orders of mussels with fennel ready," Georgia called out, inspecting the bowls before handing them off to the server. She paused to brush a damp curl from her forehead with the back of her hand. It was a gray midday in May, and the kitchen door at Anemone was propped open, letting in gusts of salty, cool air. The breeze provided a welcome relief from the heat of the gas cooktop. Her sous-chef Fatima was busily assembling rounds of roasted apple and celery root liberally smeared with a chèvre and toasted walnut spread and topped by strips of candied salmon. It was the same dish she had served Michel in Paris and it had become a signature appetizer at Anemone since Georgia took over the kitchen almost three years ago.

She grabbed the pitcher of crème anglaise spiked with local brandy and a touch of Star's honey and started assembling three orders of floating islands. Like all of the food served at Anemone, it was a thoroughly French recipe updated with a San Juan Island twist. She worked with swift precision. It was the beginning of tourist season, and every table was packed for lunch. Georgia liked a full house. It was security for Anemone, but it was also just plain fun. It never got old, the thrill of working in this kitchen, serving guests delicious meals until long after dark, and then walking out into the starry, briny night and heading back to the cottage. There she would tiptoe up the stairs, pause to listen for a moment outside the room where Star and Pollen snored peacefully, then cross the tiny landing to the yellow bedroom. Quietly she would slide exhausted into bed, cuddling up to the sleepy warmth of the genius scientist turned oysterman turned scientist again.

Speaking of which . . .

"Cole's here," Fatima told her, handing off two seaweed salad starters to a server.

Georgia spooned two poached meringues into each bowl of sweet milky custard for the floating islands.

"Hey, Captain Planet," she greeted Cole as he tromped in the back door. He was wearing his field gear—tall olive green rubber boots, waterproof canvas pants, and a quilted waterproof jacket with lots of pockets. Regardless of what he wore, he somehow always managed to look like a walking ad for Filson. She loved it.

"How's my favorite chef?" he greeted her.

"Fine and dandy. How'd collecting samples go today?" She offered her cheek, and he pressed a sound kiss on her cheekbone, his dark stubble rasping her skin. He smelled of seaweed and salt, a little fishy. He looked invigorated. He was never happier than when he was getting wet and muddy outside saving the world one kelp bed at a time.

"Great. We got some good samples." He scanned the counters, looking for something he could pilfer for a snack. He was always ravenous after a morning spent out on the water.

"Wash your hands before you touch anything in my kitchen," she ordered sternly, then broke into a smile. "You know you look like a sexy scientist in those rubber boots." She eyed him appreciatively.

He grinned and good-naturedly scrubbed clean, then snagged

a smoked salmon gougère and popped it in his mouth. "You do have a thing for rubber." He winked at her. "Careful or I'll pull out the orange overalls." He reached for another gougère. "We got a lot of good data to send down to the research center. The San Francisco guys told me we've got the best research set right now." He looked satisfied by this information. After his trip to San Francisco three years before, Cole had accepted the job offer, but with the caveat that the company allow him to set up a research outpost on San Juan Island. Thankfully, there was a lot of seaweed around the island, which made it an appealing location for their project. He traveled down to California about once a month, but otherwise, he was based on the island. He was happy as a clam scouring the shorelines and coastal waters, monitoring and measuring and working hard to protect the island's delicate ecosystem. He was finding great satisfaction in helping to develop ecological innovations and technology that could potentially make a difference on a global scale.

"Rumor has it that the J pod of orcas has been spotted headed this way with a new calf. It's a good year for salmon, so it's going to be a good year for orcas," he informed her.

"And that means a good year for us," Georgia commented happily.

A year after Georgia started work as head chef at Anemone, she and Cole had purchased the restaurant from Myra, who wanted to sell. Now Myra focused all her time and attention on her low-impact organic farm, which supplied Anemone with the bulk of its produce, mostly grown but some foraged. It was a happy pairing for all concerned. Georgia and Cole had continued to run Anemone as an ecologically friendly restaurant, closely tied to and operating in harmony with the islands. Pods of orcas meant lots of tourists, and many would eat at Anemone and then sign up for the ecological impact tours Cole ran each weekend as Dr. Cabot Montgomery, esteemed local ecologist.

"Floating islands are ready," Georgia called out, sprinkling a teaspoon of honeycomb crumbles on top of the dessert. River swooped in and carried the desserts into the dining room.

Cole followed him. "I'll make the rounds this afternoon," he said, heading into the packed dining room. Several days a week, Cole would drop by the restaurant and spend an hour or so chatting with customers in the dining room, spreading the word about the ethos of Anemone and the natural beauty and unique ecology of the islands they were trying so hard to protect. He loved getting to share about the islands and the orcas, and he was—no surprise—always a customer favorite. Those chats were at least partly why Anemone was currently the highest rated restaurant on San Juan Island on Yelp. Georgia's superb local cuisine was the rest of the reason.

Georgia pulled down a medium-sized pot from a shelf against the back wall, then stopped and switched it for a larger size.

"Always begin with a bigger pot than you think you're going to need to use," she whispered, hearing Julia Child's trilling voice offering this bit of sage advice in the back of her head. Georgia talked with Julia far less often now. She didn't need to. She had a pretty good idea of what Julia would say about all of this. Mostly, she just felt her patron saint's presence beaming beatifically over the happy hubbub of Anemone's kitchen.

A knock sounded at the back door, and Star stuck her head inside the kitchen.

"Georgia May? I've got a produce delivery."

She was wearing a wool tunic, a pair of rubber boots, and a green canvas apron with the name of Myra's farm embroidered on it—Bayview Farm. Her hair was curling wildly in a silver cloud around her face, held back by what looked like a piece of twine. She was tan and sinewy and smiling.

"Hi, Mama," Georgia greeted her. "Bring it all in. We've got room in the fridge for it."

From behind Star, Pollen's head appeared as she tried to worm her way around Star into the kitchen. Star blocked the dog with her knee. "Pollen, cut that out. No dogs in the kitchen, you know that," she scolded, then announced, "Myra drove me over with the arugula and asparagus you wanted. Also, we've got some nice wild strawberries we found today. I thought you'd like them."

Georgia blotted her wet hands on her chef's whites. "Thanks, Mama. I'll take everything you've got, especially the strawberries."

"Okay, I'll bring it all in," Star said. She disappeared, whistling a '60s protest tune under her breath, Pollen at her heels.

When Myra had offered Star a job as her assistant gardener at the farm, it had been a boon for everyone. As her health declined, Star had not been able to continue her work with her long-time clients around the island, but she found joy and purpose in her work at Bayview. Myra was a kind and patient boss when Star had memory lapses or got confused, and Myra unwittingly benefitted from Star's gift. She didn't seem to fully understand the ins and outs of Star's almost miraculous way with plants, but she told Georgia more than once with wonder in her voice that since Star had started working for her, her greens had never been more lush, her peaches more juicy, or her golden beets more sweet. She swore Star had magic fingers, and Georgia just smiled and agreed. After all, it was true. For her part, knowing that her mother was happy, productive, and cared for enabled Georgia to concentrate on running the restaurant. In the three years since her diagnosis, Star's symptoms had gradually worsened. She had grown increasingly forgetful, and the tremors in her hands increased as each month passed. It had proven challenging to navigate Star's declining health, but Georgia still considered every day with her mother a gift. They faced each challenge together, making the most of the time they had left.

"We've got your goodies!" Myra called as she and Star lugged a few wooden crates of vegetables through the back door and put them in the walk-in refrigerator. On the way out to her truck for more produce, Myra set a little crate of wild strawberries nestled carefully in straw on the counter beside Georgia.

"Your mom found them in the woods this morning and picked them just for you," she said with a smile before heading back out the door for the rest of the produce delivery.

From the dining room, Georgia could hear Cole's deep voice and the laughter from a table of customers he was charming. Pollen whined, sitting obediently outside but poking her head around the back door and wagging her tail hopefully until Georgia caved and threw her a smoked salmon gougère that had gotten a little too browned in the oven. Pollen trotted happily away, crunching her treat.

In the hustle and bustle of the kitchen, Georgia paused for a moment. She put her hand in the pocket of her chef's jacket, half expecting to find it filled with little green four-leaf clovers, but her pockets were smooth and empty. She did not need the clover anymore. It had pointed her where she needed to go. She was home, living out her dream day by day. Now she shared her own special spark for the joy of it, because she wanted to share the goodness she'd been given. In just the past few days, a couple had spontaneously gotten engaged, a woman had announced to her philandering husband in front of the entire restaurant that she wanted a divorce, and a young man studying for the MCATs had blurted out to his parents over the blancmange with a rosemary reduction (inspired by Michel's recipe) that he was planning to move to Hawaii and open a dive shop instead. It was never dull at Anemone. Every day brought new highs and lows, joys and challenges. Georgia adored it. Even on the hard days, she still looked around her with a sense of wonder that this could be her life. Every day still filled her with delight.

Georgia's fingers drifted to the charm at her throat, the four worn little clover leaves. She rubbed the metal edges, sending a prayer of gratitude heavenward. Faith, hope, love, and luck—the recipe for a charmed life. Once Georgia had thought she could make it happen on her own by planning and striving, by attaining concrete measures of success. Now she saw how wrong she had been. The real recipe for a charmed life was simple. Not easy, but simple. To do the work that filled her with wonder and delight. To walk lightly through the world, giving generously to those around her. To love all in her care as best she could. That's what she had been seeking all along. And Georgia found that now her life, which had once seemed so bitter, tasted so very sweet indeed.

Recipes

Georgia's Easy and Delicious French Omelet

This creamy, luxurious version of a classic French omelet is easy to whip up in a few minutes!

1 tablespoon butter

2 large eggs

Salt and pepper to taste

1 tablespoon chopped fresh parsley

Optional toppings: chèvre, smoked salmon, ham, Brie, sautéed mushrooms, or anything else tasty on eggs!

1. Put a 12-inch nonstick skillet over medium-high heat and heat the pan for a minute or two. Add the butter to the skillet and melt until the butter is bubbling but not browning yet. This takes around 1 minute or so depending on your stove. (It is important that the skillet is hot or the omelet will stick to the pan, but if the butter turns brown it will lend an unpleasant flavor to the omelet.)

2. As the butter melts, crack 2 eggs into a small bowl and mix with a fork until yolks and whites are completely blended. Add salt and pepper.

3. Tilt the skillet to coat the bottom and up the sides a bit with melting butter, then add the beaten eggs to the skillet and swirl the skillet slightly to allow all the liquid eggs to coat the bottom of the skillet evenly.

4. Wait for about 5 seconds until the eggs begin to bubble, then grasp the handle of the skillet and shake the skillet back and forth toward you and away from you over the burner vigorously for about 10 seconds. This dislodges the omelet easily and causes it to fold up and cook just the right amount.

5. At this point, the omelet will be done on one side and delightfully custardy on the other. You can either slide the omelet onto a plate OR if you prefer your omelet more well done, flip it over carefully in the skillet with a spatula and allow it to cook for a few more seconds before plating it.

6. Garnish with fresh parsley. You can also add chèvre or your choice of toppings. Enjoy!

Georgia's Favorite (Not Salty) Mousse Au Citron

Sweet, lemony, and light as a cloud, this deceptively simple lemon mousse is the perfect airy yet decadent dessert. You'll savor every spoonful! (Just be careful not to mix up the salt and sugar! ☺)

8 eggs (4 whole eggs and 4 eggs separated into whites and yolks)

1¼ cups sugar

¼ teaspoon sea salt

Zest and juice of 4 good-sized lemons

1 cup heavy whipping cream

1 teaspoon vanilla extract

1. First, make a bain-marie (French for water bath) by setting a saucepan or heat-safe glass bowl in a larger pot or pan with a few inches of water on the stovetop. You are going to gently cook the lemon mixture in the glass bowl nestled in the hot water. Don't worry, it's easy!

2. Whisk together the following ingredients in the saucepan or bowl: 1 cup sugar, 4 eggs, and 4 egg yolks (set aside the 4 remaining egg whites for later).

3. Add salt, lemon juice, and lemon zest to the eggs and sugar mixture in the saucepan or bowl and stir until combined.

4. Place the saucepan or bowl in the water bath over medium heat and cook for about 10 minutes, constantly stirring, until the lemony mixture thickens and reaches the consistency of loose pudding.

5. Pour through a fine strainer into a large bowl (this strains out the lemon pulp and zest so the mousse will be silky smooth) and chill in the refrigerator for at least an hour.

6. Combine the remaining 4 egg whites and ¼ cup sugar in a bowl. With an electric mixer, whisk until stiff glossy peaks form.

7. Using a spatula, fold the egg whites gently into the chilled lemony mixture. Set aside.

8. Whisk the whipping cream and vanilla in a bowl with an electric mixer until stiff peaks form. Gently fold into the lemony mixture until combined. Hurray, you've made mousse!

9. Spoon the lemon mousse into a larger decorative dish or into individual serving cups and chill for at least an hour or two before serving. Garnish with berries, a dollop of lemon curd, or more sweetened whipped cream. Enjoy!

Acknowledgments

First, thank you to my amazing readers for choosing to read Georgia's story! I am deeply honored. This story is very personal to me. It's a love story and a mother and daughter story, but also a story about identity, failure, and forgiveness. At its heart, it explores the complexities of family and what we do when someone we love hurts us or when we hurt someone we love (and really, isn't that all of us at some point?). How do we forgive others or ourselves for those painful mistakes? How do we move forward in these relationships with honesty and empathy? This story is for anyone who is desiring to move past hurt or shame and do the hard but essential work of forgiveness, to keep going forward toward wholeness in healthy, gracious, and compassionate ways. If this is you, keep up the good work. I'm cheering for you, and I'm doing this work alongside you! If you want to connect further, visit my website at rachellinden.com to sign up for my occasional updates (I'll send you a free cookbook of my favorite recipes!) or to contact me. You can also find me on Facebook at facebook.com/authorrachellinden and Instagram @rachellinden_writer. Come on, let's be friends!

And now . . . *un grand merci* to the following wonderful humans for helping to bring this story to life and getting it into readers' hands! My super-duper agent, Kevan Lyon, who is simply amazing. My delightful and insightful editor, Kate Seaver, who makes every story stronger and brighter and does it all with a smile. Amanda Maurer and the rest of the wonderful team at Berkley—true professionals and lovely humans to boot. Ashley Hayes and Meagan Briggs, the brilliant minds behind Uplit Reads. Bestselling authors Marie Bostwick and Katherine Reay, my always-supportive and smart cohosts of the super-fun author interview show we created together, @The10minutebooktalk (check us out on Instagram, Facebook, and YouTube). My generous and talented author community including the lovely ladies of Tea & Empathy, the PNW author lunch crew, and the wonderfully supportive Debbie Macomber and Adele Macomber LaCombe, Kristy Woodson Harvey, Susan Meissner, and Patti Callahan Henry among many others. My fellow authors are an amazingly creative and gracious group of humans, and I'm still astonished that I get to be friends with them! The entire Bookstagram community—true book lovers with such fabulous style. All my incredible independent bookstore crew including but not limited to Watermark Book Co., Invitation Bookshop, Island Books, Magnolia's Bookstore, Queen Anne Book Company, Griffin Bay Bookstore (yes, it's real and in adorable Friday Harbor), Edmonds Bookshop, and Brick & Mortar Books—you all are simply the best! Special thanks to the following: Katherine Walsh for her extensive knowledge of Paris and Victoria Greenstreet for her first-hand knowledge of professional chefs and restaurant kitchens. Also thanks to Westcott Bay Shellfish Company and Taylor Shellfish Farms for letting me do tasty hands-on oyster research and the patient employees for answering my questions about oysters! Any errors are all mine. Also thank you, Ladurée Paris, for deciding at some point in history to make an orange blossom macaron that I'm pretty sure makes angels sing. A and B, it's a joy and privilege to be your mama. And Y, my big bacon, thank you for fifteen wonderful years of love and support.

Recipe for a Charmed Life

Rachel Linden

READERS GUIDE

Questions for Discussion

1. How does Georgia's dream of running her own restaurant in Paris gradually transform over the course of the story? What is truly the desire of her heart?

2. A major theme of the story is forgiveness of self and others. How is this woven throughout the story? Do you think the main characters make good choices about forgiveness and taking responsibility?

3. How does Star revealing the truth about Georgia's gift and heritage as a Stevens woman transform Georgia's life?

4. In what ways does Georgia's gift bring clarity to those around her? How does it bring clarity to Star and Buck, Cole, and Georgia herself?

5. How do the themes of wonder and delight play out for Georgia over the arc of the story?

6. What do the four-leaf clovers that Georgia keeps finding symbolize?

7. Paris and San Juan Island are both important places for Georgia. How does her relationship to these places and her perception of home change throughout the story?

8. What role does Julia Child play in Georgia's life? How does Julia's role change as the story progresses?

9. By the end of the story, how are the main characters living out their true purposes in life?

10. What do *you* believe is the true recipe for a charmed life?

Rachel Linden is a novelist and international aid worker whose adventures in more than fifty countries around the world provide excellent grist for her writing. She is the author of *The Magic of Lemon Drop Pie, Ascension of Larks, Becoming the Talbot Sisters*, and *The Enlightenment of Bees*. Currently, Rachel lives with her family on a sweet little island in the Pacific Northwest where she enjoys creating stories about hope, courage, and connection with a hint of romance and a touch of whimsy.